Darkness First

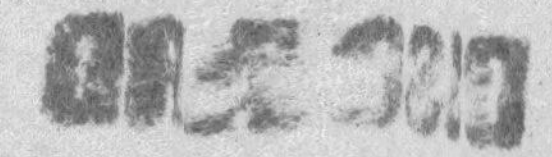

Also by James Hayman

The Chill of Night

The Cutting

Darkness First

A McCabe and Savage Thriller

JAMES HAYMAN

WITNESS
IMPULSE
An Imprint of HarperCollins*Publishers*

Copyright

This book was originally published in 2013 by Penguin UK.

EPub Edition OCTOBER 2013 ISBN: 9780062301697

Print Edition ISBN: 9780062301703

10 9 8 7 6 5 4 3

Dedication

To Sonia and Jock for their
constant friendship and support

Acknowledgments

I'D LIKE TO thank the many people who gave freely of their time educating me about life in Washington County, Maine and the drug problems that are rampant there. These include, in no particular order: Washington County Sheriff Donnie Smith, who never tired of answering my endless questions; Detective Sergeant Tom Joyce, formerly of the Portland Police Department; Sergeant John Cote of the Maine State Police; Sergeant Richard Rolfe, Washington County liaison with the Maine Drug Enforcement Agency; Dr Julia Arnold, a family practitioner in Whiting, Maine; my friend Curtis Rindlaub, a skilled mariner and co-author and publisher of *A Cruising Guide to the Maine Coast*; Natalie Brown of the Eastport, Maine Port Authority; Dr Bud Higgins and Dr Anne Skelton of Maine Medical Center; Pathologist Dr Erin Presnell of the Medical University of South Carolina and veterinarian Dr Jeff Robbins, a fellow islander, who went out of his way to educate me on the effects of animal tranquilizing drugs. Finally, I should mention that, while many of the details described in this book about Washington County and the towns of Machias and Eastport are accurate, I have changed others to suit the tale I am telling. This is, after all, a work of fiction.

Darkness First

Prologue

3:15 A.M., Wednesday, January 7, 2009
The Bay of Fundy

THE VOLUME OF water flowing into and out of the Bay of Fundy on every tide is more than double the combined flow of all the rivers emptying into all the oceans of the world. However, the man standing in the stern of the old fishing boat, peering out through night-vision binoculars, gave no thought to Fundy's legendary tides or, for that matter, any other natural phenomena. He was intent on finding the boys.

For the fourth time in thirty minutes, he raised the glasses to his eyes and scanned the dark expanse of water for any sign of the inflatable kayak. He saw nothing. Just a low blackness broken only by the reflected twinkle of lights from the city of Saint John to his right and from the more scattered buildings beyond the beach at Sandy Cove, a mile and a half dead ahead.

Not one to give up easily, the man divided the sea before him into quadrants and looked with painstaking thoroughness once again. Quadrant by quadrant. Inch by inch. Still he saw nothing. There was no sign of them.

It was already 3:15 on a freezing cold January morning. The two should have been back an hour earlier. The operation had been rehearsed and their instructions were clear. If anything went wrong, anything at all, they were to call. He'd given them disposable cell phones, one each, for just that purpose. Cell reception had been checked and found acceptable. Still he hadn't heard from them. Maybe that's what you got for working with idiots.

Perhaps the kayak had capsized on the way back, dumping the boys, their cell phones and their precious cargo into the icy waters of the bay. If that was the case, the game was over and he might as well crank up the engine and head back to Eastport. Still, it seemed unlikely. Back in the beginning, before he had trained them, it might have happened that way. But both were now experienced paddlers and the sea tonight was a flat calm. No way should they have capsized in seas like this.

Another twenty minutes passed before he felt a vibration in his pocket.

Finally.

'You're late,' he said.

'Yeah. Sorry about that, Conor,' said Rory, at twenty the older of the brothers.

'Problems?'

'No. No problems. Getting to the beach without being seen just took longer than we thought.' The kid spoke in a breathless whisper. 'But we've got the shit and we're heading back.'

'I'll be waiting.'

'I'll tell you, man, everything went smooth as ...'

'Not now.' He cut off the eager voice on the other end. 'Tell me when you get here. Then we can celebrate.'

He broke the connection without waiting for an answer, stuffed the phone back in his pocket.

It took the boys twenty-two minutes to paddle the mile and a half to the boat. He watched them pull alongside. Rory in the stern. His younger brother Scott, who was eighteen, up front. Both looked as excited as little kids on Christmas morning.

The man extended a boat hook and Rory slipped the strap of a waterproof bag on to the end. The man hauled it in. Lighter than he expected. Amazing, he thought, how little five million dollars could weigh. Rory and Scott clambered up the boat ladder and over the gunwale. He told them to haul the kayak on board.

While they worked at that, the man unzipped the bag and checked the contents. It looked to be all there. What he'd been working on for months. Forty white plastic bottles, each labeled with Barham Pharmaceutical's big red B logo. Each with 1,000 80 mg tablets inside. Forty thousand tabs in all. He did the math for the hundredth time. Not because he was uncertain of the answer but simply because he enjoyed thinking about it.

Street value in Maine for Oxycontin was currently 120 bucks per 80 mg time-release tablet. Times 40,000 it came to exactly 4.8 million dollars. At least it did as long as he stayed disciplined, stuck to plan and didn't push too many tablets on to the market too fast. Like anything else, street price was a matter of supply and demand. Maine and Washington County in particular had one hell of a demand. And now, with American pharmaceutical companies changing their manufacturing process to make it more difficult for addicts to crush or melt the tablets for an instant hit, he was in charge of the biggest and best supply.

He opened a bottle, picked out a tablet and examined the small greenish disk. The number '80' was stamped on one side, the abbreviation 'CDN' for Canadian stamped on the other. He dropped the tab back in, screwed on the lid and returned the bottle to the bag. He stowed it in a small cubby in the wheelhouse.

When the kayak was safely on board, the man popped the tops off two bottles of Bud, handed one each to Rory and Scott and told them to go down to the cabin, change out of their wetsuits and warm up. Then they could tell him all about their triumph.

DRESSED IN JEANS and heavy woolen jackets, the two boys sat side by side on the lone bunk and sucked at the beer. 'Nothing to it,' Rory said, grinning like this was the biggest day of his short, meaningless life. 'Security was pathetic, just like you said. Just one old fat guy. He starts asking

Scott some questions, I come up behind, stick the gun in his neck and tell him not to be a hero. He wasn't about to be. Practically pissing his pants. Took us right to the stuff. Right where you said it would be. Scott loaded the bag. We moved fast. In, out and gone in less than three minutes. Two blocks away before we heard the first sirens.'

'Where's the security guy now?'

Rory didn't answer immediately.

'Where's the security guy now?'

'Dead. I shot him. Twice.'

'Twice?'

'Yeah. I wasn't sure he was dead the first time. So I shot him again.'

'No question the second time?'

'No. Half his head was gone.'

The man nodded. 'Good.'

He hadn't been sure Rory could handle killing the guard. Maybe the kid was tougher than he thought.

'I don't know why we had to kill him,' said Scott. 'He wasn't causing any problems.'

'Because, my friend, he was the only one who could link any of us to any of this. He saw your faces. You've both got records. It had to be done.'

'Yeah. Maybe. I guess. Still, it didn't feel right.'

'Cheer up. You did what you had to do,' he said. 'You did good.'

Both smiled at that. Praise from the master.

'You didn't wear your wetsuits inside the building, did you?'

'No. We left them in the kayak like you said. Wore what we're wearing now. But it wouldn't have mattered. Nobody saw us except the guard,' said Scott.

'And he's not gonna be talking any time soon,' Rory added with an imbecilic grin.

The man smiled back. No point ruining their moment of triumph by letting them know the guard wasn't the only one who'd seen them. That the pharmaceutical distribution facility they'd just broken into was under constant video surveillance. Or that, by now, the entire Saint John police force was checking their faces against a computerized database of drug offenders. Probably every cop in the province of New Brunswick had printouts of their images taped to their dashboards. No. There was no point telling the boys any of that. It would just upset them and make finishing the job that much harder.

'Where's the gun?' he asked Rory.

'The gun?'

'Yes, the gun. You know, the one you shot the guard with.'

'It's in there,' said Rory, gesturing at the kayak. 'In my bag.'

'Still loaded?'

'Yeah. Minus two.'

'Did you wipe your fingerprints off ?'

'Not yet. You want me to do that now?'

'No hurry. Finish your beer first. Anybody see you on the way back to the beach?'

'Nope. Nobody. A few cars passed, including one cop car tear-assing to the building. Staying out of sight is why it took longer than we thought getting back.'

'Nobody saw you at the beach?'

'No. Nobody. It was late. It's January. The place was empty.'

'Okay. Good.' Everything was going according to plan. Time to tie up the last of the loose ends. The man didn't like loose ends.

He went up to the wheelhouse and pulled on a pair of latex gloves. Then he removed a Heckler & Koch 9 mm USP compact tactical pistol from his sea-bag and screwed on an 8 inch suppressor he'd crafted for the purpose. He didn't plan on shooting anyone tonight, didn't want the boys' blood on the boat, but he was a careful man, and if it turned out he had to, well, sound carried too far at sea to risk anyone hearing the unmuffled crack of a shot. He slid a fifteen-round magazine into the gun and chambered a round.

He went back to the cabin and pointed the gun at them.

Both boys stopped sucking their beers.

They stared at him wide-eyed.

'The fuck you doin'?' asked Rory.

'Oh this?' the man said in a casual voice indicating the gun he was holding. 'Don't worry about this. I'm not going to shoot you. Not if you do exactly what I tell you. Now put your beers down, stand up, put your hands behind your heads and go on deck.'

Neither of them moved. Just kept looking at him like a pair of deer in the headlights.

'C'mon, now,' the man said, his tone harsher, more threatening. 'Up and out. Or I will shoot you, and I really don't want your blood all over my nice clean boat.'

The boys looked at each other and clambered up the three steps to the deck.

'Good. Now move to the stern, turn around and face the water.'

'Hey, man, c'mon,' said Scott, his voice quavery, uncertain. 'What are you doing this for?'

'I said turn around.'

They did as they were told.

'What is this?' asked Rory.

'Give me your wallets.'

'The fuck you want our wallets for?'

'Just drop them on the deck.'

Both boys reached into their pockets and extracted small leather wallets and let them fall. They were already shivering with cold. Or perhaps it was fear.

The man checked each wallet to make sure photo IDs were still inside.

'Okay,' he said, 'now I'm going to count to three and you're going to jump in the water. Otherwise, I'm going to blow your brains out and throw you in.'

'What? Are you crazy? That water's fucking freezing.'

'Yes it is, Rory. And you'll both probably drown. Or maybe die of hypothermia. But who knows? You're both young and strong and good swimmers. And look at the lights over there.' He pointed at Saint John. 'It's not so far. Maybe you'll make it. And if you do, yes, I'll have the drugs, but you'll have your lives.'

'We'll tell the cops who you are,' said Scott, 'what you done.'

'Unfortunately for you, Scott, you don't know who I am. Conor Riordan doesn't exist. I'm just a guy with no name and a boat. Now jump, or I'll shoot. And trust me, I'm a crack shot.'

'You fucker …'

'It's your choice. Jump, swim hard and maybe make it to shore. Stay here on board and die for sure. Now, I'm going to start counting.'

Rory jumped first. Scott didn't follow until he heard the man start to say three.

The man looked down and smiled as Rory and Scott started swimming toward the lights. He knew there was no way in hell either of them was going to make it. Not that far. Not without wetsuits. Not in forty-degree water. And especially not in the Bay of Fundy with the tide on its way out.

He watched through the binoculars until he couldn't see them thrashing around any more. Emptied the beer bottles and carefully wiped off their fingerprints. Washed and dried them to remove any trace of DNA and tossed them into his recycling bin. Next he pulled out the small bag they'd stowed in the kayak. He checked the Glock 17 Rory had used to kill the guard. Confirmed two rounds had been fired, put it back in the bag, fingerprints intact. Then he put their wallets with their New Brunswick drivers' licenses in the bag as well. If the bodies weren't found or if eventually they washed up bloated or half-eaten, a ballistics check, the surveillance video, the prints on the gun and the IDs in the wallets would all tie them to the theft and the killing of the guard. There was nothing at all that would tie them to him.

He zipped the bag and put it back in the front of the inflatable. That done, he pushed the kayak over the side and threw the paddles in after it. He didn't know if the cops'd find the bodies or the capsized kayak first. Didn't much matter. Either way, they'd never find the tablets. Sunk, they'd assume, to the bottom of the sea. Where the fishes, no doubt, would be enjoying one hell of a high.

Finally the man removed the latex gloves, started the ancient diesel engine, shifted into gear and headed down the coast. He took a cold bottle of Stoli and a plastic glass from the cooler. Poured himself three ounces over ice and raised a silent toast to the memory of his two young helpers and to the very first day of the rest of his life.

Chapter One

7:47 P.M., Friday, August 21, 2009
Machiasport, Maine

AT 7:47 ON a Friday evening in August, Dr Emily Kaplan's office was still open, as it was every Friday night, for the convenience of those who found it difficult to come in at any other time.

She was finishing with her last patient of the day and, for that matter, of the week, a lobsterman named Daniel Cauley who was seated on the other side of the battered antique farm table that had served as Emily's desk ever since she had opened her solo practice, Machiasport Family Medicine, four years earlier come September.

As she handed Cauley a prescription for the cholesterol-lowering drug she wanted him to take, she glanced out the window and caught sight of a young woman standing in the shadows at the end of the driveway staring at the house. Who, she wondered, could be standing and watching so intently at this hour? A late patient waiting for Em to finish with the one she was with now? Or perhaps someone waiting for Cauley. A daughter? Possibly a granddaughter?

'Think these'll help?' Cauley's question brought her back to the moment.

'They will,' she said. 'Even more if you follow the diet I gave you last year. And maybe try getting a little more exercise.'

Cauley nodded. Said he'd try. She doubted he would.

It was five after eight and the office was technically closed by the time Cauley left. Emily walked out to the porch with him, curious to see if the woman was still there. Still watching the house. She was.

She made no move to join Dan when he climbed in his truck. As he put the vehicle in gear and executed a tight three-point turn, the beams of his headlights briefly illuminated her. She looked young with a slender figure and shoulder-length dark hair tied back in a ponytail. She also had what looked to Emily like a black eye and other bruises on her face. The truck pulled out. The headlights disappeared. The woman became, once again, more shadow than shape.

As the sound of the truck faded in the distance, she emerged from the edge of the woods, walked a dozen or so steps toward the office and then stopped as if she couldn't make up her mind. Was she trying to summon up the courage to approach? Or had she seen the tall doctor peering at her from the porch and been put off ? She gave no sign of either. Just stood in the driveway studying the century-old two-story colonial with its peeling yellow paint and black shutters as if trying to memorize its form and structure.

The house Emily grew up in had served as her office ever since she'd come back to Washington County four years earlier with her husband Sam to set up her solo practice. A year later she and Sam divorced and the house once again became her home. A small but pretty colonial farmhouse set at the end of a country road on the outermost edges of the village of Machiasport. A good quarter mile from its nearest neighbor, the property was surrounded on one side by dense evergreen woods and on the other by a blueberry field. It was, she liked telling the few friends from med school who bothered to visit, the global headquarters of Machiasport Family Medicine. They would smile at her small joke and tell her how much they admired her decision to work here, among the people of the poorest and most underserved county in a poor and underserved state. A few told her they were sometimes tempted to do the same sort of thing. But, as far as she knew, none ever had. Her classmates had richer fields to till.

Deciding there was no point in waiting for the young woman to start moving, Emily descended the porch steps and approached her visitor to see how badly she was injured. As she drew closer, Emily guessed she was no more than twenty-one or twenty-two with what, under the bruises, seemed a strikingly pretty face. It might even have been called beautiful if it wasn't so messed up. But, at the moment, her left eye was black and swollen shut. She had a bent and possibly broken nose. A scab had formed over a cut in her upper lip. Emily wondered what other damage she'd find in the examination room. 'Hi,' she said. 'I'm Doctor Kaplan. Who're you?'

The girl didn't respond. Just shook her head.

Emily needed to know who she was dealing with, but it seemed more important to check out her injuries first. She could always ask questions later. She put one hand on the woman's shoulder and began steering her toward the office. 'Okay, come in and let's have a look at you. By the way, how'd you get here?' she asked. 'Somebody drop you off?'

'No. I drove.'

'Really? Where'd you leave your car?'

'Down by the state park. I walked back up.'

Emily wondered why she'd done that. The park was over a mile away. As the two women climbed the porch steps in the fading light of a late-summer evening, a pair of headlights lit them up. Both of them turned and looked. A car had pulled into the driveway but was now backing out again as if it had just been using the driveway as a convenient turn-around. Nothing unusual. Cars did that all the time once the drivers realized there was nothing down this road other than this small medical office.

Her new patient watched the car go, then stood staring into the darkness at the now empty space. Emily realized that, in spite of the warmth of the evening, the young woman was trembling. Either she was in shock or something was scaring the hell out of her.

'Come on in,' Emily urged. 'Let's have a look at your face.'

She held the door open. The woman went inside. Emily followed. The wooden screen door banged shut.

Em led her still nameless patient into the lone examination room and flicked on the fluorescents. Under the harsh lights her face looked even more battered than it had outside. Definitely in her early twenties, Emily decided. Around five-foot-four with a trim figure, and pale skin. She wore designer jeans, tapered at the ankle, and white sandals with silver studs adorning the cross-straps. Around her neck Em noticed a slender gold chain with a starfish pendant that had a diamond, or perhaps zirconium, stud in the center. A black t-shirt with the words *The Killers* emblazoned across the front completed her outfit. Below the words were red silhouetted images of four musicians holding instruments. Emily wasn't sure who The Killers were. Some obscure rock band she supposed. Or maybe not so obscure. Em wouldn't know one way or the other. She mostly listened to Mozart and Beethoven.

The girl carried a small green backpack. Emily told her to toss the pack on to a chair and hop up on the table.

'Was there an accident?' Em asked as she began probing the girl's face, gently feeling for possible fractures. 'Is anyone else hurt? Anyone else who needs help?'

The bony areas around the eye, cheek and forehead all seemed intact. So did the jaw. To be sure, she'd order an x-ray.

'No,' the girl said in a quiet, but firm voice. 'It wasn't an accident. And no one's hurt. At least not in the way you mean.'

The girl winced as Emily opened her swollen left eyelid and peered in with an opthalmoscope. There was some bleeding on both the white of the eye and the inner areas of the lid but there didn't appear to be any serious damage. Emily daubed her split and swollen upper lip with antiseptic and then looked in her mouth.

'All right then, what happened? Who did this to you?'

'It doesn't matter.'

Emily frowned. 'Of course it matters.' She wiggled a front tooth that was loose. 'You'd better have a dentist look at this. It'll be coming out any time now. Do you know a dentist?'

'No.'

'I'll give you some names and numbers before you leave. Now I need you to tell me who beat you up.'

'I told you it doesn't matter. It's not why I'm here.'

Emily frowned. 'Really? Then why *are* you here?'

The girl took a deep breath. 'Because I'm pregnant and I need to get rid of the baby as soon as I can.'

Emily looked at her curiously. 'I don't do abortions, if that's what you're after.'

'I know that. What I was told ... what my ...' The girl paused as if deciding on an appropriate descriptor. '... my *friend* told me was ... you could give me some pills that would cause, I don't know, a spontaneous miscarriage.'

Emily cocked her head. 'Really? And who exactly was the *friend* who told you that?'

'Just a friend.'

Emily sighed. This was going nowhere. 'Okay. What makes you think you're pregnant?'

'I'm late. I've never been late before. Usually, I'm regular as hell.'

'Did you take a home pregnancy test?'

'Yes. It came up positive.'

Emily glanced at the young woman's tummy. If she was pregnant it had to be early. Maybe that's why she'd been beaten up. A boyfriend unhappy learning he was about to become a father.

'What's your name?' Emily asked. 'Where do you live?'

'I told you. It doesn't matter.'

'And I told you it does. You're in my office. You want me to treat you. I need to know your name and where you're from.'

'If it's getting paid you're worried about, I can give you money.'

The girl reached over and grabbed her backpack. She unzipped it, rummaged around inside and pulled out a wad of bills nearly an inch thick. She thrust the bills at Emily. 'Take it,' she said. 'It's a lot of money. I can get more if that's not enough.'

The top bill was a fifty. If the rest were all fifties there had to be at least three or four thousand dollars in the wad. Where in hell did a twenty-something kid in Washington County get that kind of loot?

'Put your money away,' Emily said.

The girl sighed. 'Okay. Then what *do* you want?'

'Your name for starters. Where you live. Who told you to come to me. I'd also like to know who beat you up.'

'I'm sorry. I can't tell you any of that.'

'Can't or won't?'

'Both. Either.'

'But you still want my help?'

'Yes. I need to get rid of this baby. As soon as I can. It's important.'

As she spoke, Emily ran her fingers along either side of the girl's nose. A fairly minor break. 'Hold on,' she said. 'This is going to hurt a little.'

Without waiting for a response she inserted an instrument called a Boies elevator into one nostril. There was a slight tensing of the girl's body as Emily pushed with her thumb against the break and popped the nose back into alignment. A painful procedure she'd experienced more than once when she was still boxing competitively. Still, there was no crying out.

'You're a pretty tough kid, aren't you?' said Emily.

The girl smiled bitterly. 'Not tough enough.'

'How old are you?'

'Twenty-two.'

Emily checked the girl's temperature. 98.5°. She wrapped a blood pressure cuff around the girl's arm and pumped it up. One twenty over eighty. Temp and BP both normal and healthy.

'Who's the guy?' she asked as she drew three small vials of blood.

'What do you mean?'

'You know. The guy whose child you're carrying.'

'Trust me, you don't want to know.'

'As a matter of fact, I do.' Emily labeled and dated the vials and put them in a tray. She'd write in a name later if she ever got the girl to give her one. 'Is he the one who likes beating you up?'

'Look, doc. No more questions, all right? I'm a big girl. I wasn't a virgin. I wasn't raped. I just need to get rid of this fucker's baby so I can get the hell out of town.'

Emily sighed. 'If you want my help, I'm going to need some answers. I'm going to need the truth.'

'The truth? Look, Doctor Kaplan,' the girl said in quietly angry tones, 'I'm sure you're a nice woman and I'm sure you mean well. But I really can't tell you anything more about this than I already have.'

'Why not?'

The young woman slid off the table and looked straight at Emily with her one uninjured brown eye. 'Because if I told you or anyone else what you call the truth, the guy who did this,' she said pointing at her face, 'would do a hell of a lot more than just beat me up. He'd probably kill me. No. I take that back. Not probably. Definitely. And get his rocks off doing it. And if he found out I told you anything about him, he'd kill you as well.'

'Kill?'

'Yes, kill. First me. Then you.'

Chapter Two

IN SPITE OF a natural streak of Yankee skepticism, Emily found herself believing what she heard. One crime and possibly two had already been committed. Assault for sure. Maybe rape. A third crime, murder, seemed to have been threatened. And where had all that money come from? These were things Emily was obligated to report. Aside from anything else, she could lose her license if she failed to do so. But what could she report if the girl wouldn't tell her who she was or where she'd come from or who the guy was who'd beaten her up? If Emily refused to treat her she'd simply disappear into the night.

'All right,' Emily finally said, deciding on a course of action, 'I'll help you with the pregnancy if I can.'

'Thank you.'

'When did you have your last period?'

'Beginning of July. Started around the fifth. Stopped five days later.'

'No period in August?'

'Not yet.'

August was almost over.

While Emily had never performed an abortion, she had on a few occasions prescribed Mifepristone and Misoprostol, drugs that when used sequentially cause spontaneous miscarriages in pregnancies of less than eight weeks. If the girl was pregnant and if she was right about the dates of her last period she was just within the window where the drugs would work.

'All right, first let's make sure you really are pregnant. Then we'll figure out what we can do about it.' She pointed at the bathroom. 'Go in there and pee into one of the little bottles. When you're finished, take off all your clothes and put this on.' She tossed the girl a johnny. 'Then come back in here, lie down on the table and wait for me. I may be a few minutes so you'll need to be patient. I have to get some things I need to check you out.'

'What sort of things?'

'Some instruments that'll help me figure out if I can safely give you these drugs,' Emily lied, 'and if they'll do the job.'

The girl threw Emily a hard, mistrustful stare, slid off the table and went into the bathroom. It was only when the bathroom door was firmly closed and she was about to leave the room that Emily noticed the backpack, still on the chair.

Looking inside a patient's belongings was a serious breach of professional ethics. If she was caught and if the kid complained it could cost her her license. Her career.

On the other hand, this girl had been threatened with death. Emily unzipped the bag.

Under the wad of bills she found a fancy-looking cell phone and under that a wallet. Inside, a Maine driver's license issued to Tiffany Stoddard. An Eastport address. Date of birth April 26, 1987. She memorized the information. Glanced at a photo of a smiling Tiffany Stoddard standing behind a chubby little girl with glasses who looked to be about ten years old. Returning the wallet, she noticed a clear ziplock bag lying at the bottom of the pack. Inside were small greenish tablets. At least a hundred. Maybe more. Emily looked closer and recognized them. Oxycontin 80s. Canadian manufacture. Sometimes it seemed like half the population of the county was addicted to the damned things. But this kid couldn't be just an addict. She had to be a dealer. Judging by the number of pills, a fairly major one.

Emily re-zipped the bag, put it back where she found it and hurried to the outer office. She closed the door and picked up the phone. Because at 8:30 on a Friday night the Washington County Sheriff's office would already be closed, she tapped in Sheriff John Savage's home number. No need to look it up. John's daughter Maggie was Emily's closest friend and Em had spent a significant portion of her childhood hanging out at the Savage household. Even now, with Maggie down in Portland working as a detective with the Portland PD, her mother dead and John remarried, Emily occasionally dropped by to share a glass of wine and sometimes have dinner and listen to the gossip. John and Maggie had even given her shelter on the awful night three years earlier when Emily finally walked out on her abusive and unfaithful ex-husband Sam.

Em turned and faced the window to minimize any chance of being overheard. The phone rang once. Twice. Three times.

'C'mon, John, pick up,' she muttered to herself.

But it was the voice of John's second wife, Anya, that came on. 'You've reached the Savages, please leave a message.'

Shit. 'John, this is Emily. Please call me back. ASAP. It's urgent. I'll try your cell.'

'Who's John?'

Emily turned.

'Who are you calling?'

The girl stood in the open door of the examination room still dressed in her jeans and t-shirt. She was holding the backpack by its straps in one hand. She held a urine-filled sample bottle in the other. She walked across the room to the farmhouse table where Emily stood, holding the phone.

'Who's John?' the girl asked, her voice tight and angry. 'Who are you calling? It was the cops, wasn't it? You've been poking around in my bag too. Don't lie. I looked. Stuff wasn't how I left it.'

Emily sighed and nodded. 'Yes, Tiffany, I looked in your bag. I saw the drugs. I know your name. I was calling someone who can help you,' she said in an even voice.

'You stupid bitch,' the girl said, her voice barely more than an angry whisper. 'You really are going to get me killed.'

Emily didn't respond.

'Is John one of the locals?' she asked. 'Or maybe a pal of yours with the state police? Hell, half the troopers in the county are probably on their way here right now, aren't they? All hot to catch the druggie with her stash before she gets away. Lady, you have no fucking idea what you just did.' She put the urine sample on the table. 'Here. I think you wanted this.'

The girl left. The screen door banged shut. Emily's first irrational thought was that she had to fix the door to stop it banging like that. She went out on to the porch. The door banged again. She watched her now former patient half-walk, half-jog down the darkened driveway to the road. She turned left toward the state park.

Emily heard a series of electronic beeps and realized she was still holding the cordless phone. 'If you'd like to make a call please hang up and try again,' said a computer voice. She hit the off button. Hit talk and punched in Savage's cell number. Five rings and another message request kicked in. 'John, Emily. Get here as soon as you can. It's urgent.'

As a last resort Emily thought about calling 911. But on a summer night in Washington County it could take forever for a cop to arrive. She figured the hell with it. She'd have to handle Tiffany Stoddard herself. Em left the phone on the porch and jogged out to the road. She peered in the direction the girl had gone.

At first she saw nothing. Just black tarmac stretching out before her in the growing darkness. No cars. No Stoddard. Nothing moving at all. Weird. The kid had only left a couple of minutes earlier. Even a world-class miler couldn't be out of sight yet. So where was she?

Seconds later the girl emerged from an opening in the woods a few hundred yards ahead, hoisted the pack on to her back and started walking again toward the park. Then she broke into a jog.

Emily started down the road after her. When she reached the opening in the woods, she stopped and wondered if the girl might have hidden the pills in there. They were the only proof Em had of what had happened tonight. She decided she needed to find them and give them to Savage before the girl came back and got them herself.

As Emily pushed into the darkness of the woods, a little more than a mile away in Machias State Park, hidden behind Tiff Stoddard's rusty green Taurus, a man waited, patiently picking his nails with the tip of a long, thin-bladed knife.

Chapter Three

Portland, Maine

At 7:47 on that same Friday evening in August, the air outside police headquarters at 109 Middle Street was heavy with a kind of heat and humidity more natural to the bayous of Louisiana than to the streets of Maine's largest city.

Inside the building it was even worse.

The antiquated air conditioning system, held together with spit and baling wire for at least a decade beyond its useful life span, had been grinding and wheezing most of the day in a valiant but vain attempt to bring conditions down to a more tolerable level. Two hours back it had stopped working altogether. Any of the cops still on duty who could find the slightest excuse to work outside the building did so. Others simply snuck out, some saying the hell with it and heading home early and more than a few slipping into one or another of the Old Port's bars and pubs to enjoy the cold blast of AC that worked and an even colder pint of Geary's or Shipyard.

On 109's fourth and top floor, where the detectives of the Crimes Against People unit were housed, temperatures had risen almost to triple digits. It was even hotter in the small windowless interview room where Detective Margaret Savage had been confronting a suspect for over an hour and a half. Yet, in spite of the oppressive heat, in spite of the stink of sweat and body odor rising in waves off a 300 pound bozo named Kyle Carnes and in spite of the rivulets of perspiration trickling down under her own arms, Maggie wasn't unhappy. She figured if she could keep Carnes from lawyering up, sooner or later the wretched conditions might just help drill a confession out of him. She was sure she could take the heat longer than he could.

As the senior detective in Crimes Against People, Maggie spent her days and often her nights chasing murderers, rapists and other assorted lowlifes. She didn't like any of them but the creeps she liked least were the ones who got their jollies beating the shit out of the women they supposedly loved.

The guy in front of her was a habitual abuser. The first two times he beat up his current girlfriend, a woman named Mary Farrier, there'd been no witnesses and Farrier had been unwilling to press charges. Same old story Maggie had lived through a hundred times before. A woman too frightened to testify. Too terrified of what Carnes might do when and if he got his hands on her again. Too convinced that in some weird way it was all her own fault.

But this time Kyle wasn't going to get away with using Farrier's face as a punching bag because this time Maggie had a witness. A neighbor willing to swear she heard Kyle screaming through the door at Mary that *he was gonna fuckin' kill her.* Then some grunts and thuds. Then Carnes opening the door and rushing from the apartment in a rage. The neighbor went in, found Farrier on the floor and called 911. The victim happened to hit her head against the sharp stainless steel corner of a coffee table on her way down and was now in a coma in the ICU at Cumberland Medical Center suffering acute cerebral edema. If she died, and the docs thought that was a definite possibility, the aggravated assault charge Carnes was facing would be elevated to murder.

'You're in a deep pile of shit, Kyle,' Maggie told him, her easy smile and friendly tone belying the words as well as the intensity she felt inside. 'Best thing you could do for yourself is stop stonewalling and tell us what went down in the apartment. If you do, well maybe we could talk to the DA.'

Kyle lifted his head, a glimmer of hope in his eyes, and looked at her 'You mean like a deal?'

Maggie raised both hands and offered a noncommittal shrug, one that seemed to say *hey, you never know.* 'I mean like maybe you really didn't mean to hurt her. Not so badly, anyway. I mean maybe you didn't. Or did you?'

Kyle shook his head almost imperceptibly.

'Say it in words, Kyle. Shaking your head doesn't count.'

'I didn't mean to hurt her. Not so bad.'

'You told us you loved her, isn't that right, Kyle?'

This time Kyle nodded, sweat beading on his shiny bald head and dripping down his fat face.

'Words, Kyle, words.'

'I loved her.'

'And she loved you?'

'She loved me.'

'So you think it was you hitting her that did the real damage? Or was it just that stupid table she cracked her head on?'

'It was the table.'

''Cause you didn't hit her that hard?'

'No.'

'No, what?'

'I didn't hit her that hard.'

'How hard did you hit her?'

'Not hard.'

'But you did hit her?'

'Yeah, I hit her. But not hard.'

'Hard enough so she fell down and cracked her head on the table?'

'Yeah, but the table's what hurt her. Not me hittin' her.'

'Even though you were heard shouting, "I'm gonna fucking kill you, you fucking bitch"?'

'I never said that.'

'Oh yeah? Anybody else in the room who might have said it?'

'Just her.'

'No other guys?'

'No.'

'Well that's kind of a problem for you, Kyle, because we've got a witness who says she heard a guy's voice saying those words and since you were the only guy in the room I guess it must've been you.'

'Fuckin' bitch doesn't know what she's talking about.'

'That's for a jury to decide.'

Maggie felt her cell phone vibrate, glanced down, saw the name *Savage, John* appear in caller ID. She hadn't spoken to her father in a while but there was no way she could talk to him now. He'd have to wait.

'The witness also says she saw you pull open the door and rush out of the apartment. She went in and found Mary Farrier unconscious on the floor.'

'I told you, she hit her head on the table.'

'Yes, you did. You also told me you hit her.'

'Yeah, I hit her but not hard enough to crack her head open.'

'So it wasn't your punches that fractured her cheekbone, broke her jaw and knocked out three of her teeth? It was her hitting the table?'

'Yeah, that's right. The table did it.'

'Funny.'

'What's funny?'

'According to the docs over at the Med the table only struck the back of Mary's head. It couldn't possibly have done all that other stuff. You did.'

There was a knock on the door before he could respond.

'Come!' Maggie shouted.

'Sorry to interrupt,' Detective Brian Cleary said. 'This just came in from Cumberland Med.' He handed Maggie a note. Maggie unfolded the sheet. Sighed. Shook her head. Muttered the word 'Shit.'

'What? What is it?' asked Carnes.

'Kyle Carnes,' she said, 'I'm arresting you for the murder of Mary Farrier.'

'Murder?'

'She died ten minutes ago. Brian, will you read Mr Carnes his rights and then get him out of my sight?'

'I didn't hit her that hard,' Carnes said as Cleary was cuffing him.

Maggie, resisting a strong urge to smack the prisoner right then and there, just shook her head and left the room.

She went to her desk, grabbed her bag and weapon from her locked bottom drawer and headed down Middle Street toward Starbucks for an iced mocha and a little air. Too damned hot to call her father back from here. Passing Sebago Brewpub, she changed her mind and opted for a cold beer instead.

A couple of cops hanging at the bar invited her to join them. She waved them off and took a solo stool down at the end, where the blow from a big-ass AC unit hit her right in the face. The cold air felt heavenly.

The bartender, a mid-forties dishwater-blonde wearing a halter-top and too much makeup came over. 'Hate to say it, hon, but you look a little bedraggled.'

'Hate to say it, hon, but I feel a little bedraggled.'

'What can I get you?'

Maggie checked the list of available drafts and ordered a Frye's Leap IPA.

Then she called her father.

'Well, hello, my darling daughter. And how the hell are you?'

'Hot. Very, very hot. What's going on?'

'Well, if you aren't working this weekend, I'd like you to come up and visit. Aside from the fact that it's been way too long there are a few things we need to discuss.'

He was right about it being way too long. She hadn't been home since Christmas and before that only once since John and Anya's wedding, which had been over a year earlier. 'What sorts of things?' she asked.

'Important things.'

'Like what?'

'Nothing I care to discuss over the phone.'

'Is anything wrong? Is anyone sick?'

'Margaret,' he said, his voice taking on a lighter, teasing tone. 'As an experienced police officer, you know perfectly well I have the right to remain silent and I'm damned well going to.'

She shook her head in frustration. 'Listen, I've just spent the last two hours locked in a hotbox with a foul-smelling killer so, please, stop with the humor.'

'Maggie. This is important.'

Maggie had rarely known her father to be this evasive and that alone was enough to worry her. She did have plans for tonight. But there was no reason she couldn't go up in the morning. She was off-duty till Tuesday so she could spend at least a couple of nights in Machias.

'What's the temperature up there?'

'About ten degrees cooler than it is in Portland. They're predicting thunderstorms for later tonight so tomorrow should be even better.'

'Good. Sounds wonderful. I'll leave first thing in the morning. Ought to be there by noon.'

She checked her watch: 8:20. The Sea Dogs game should be going into the seventh or eighth inning. Just enough time to run home, take a quick shower and change before meeting her date at nine.

Chapter Four

8:44 P.M., Friday, August 21, 2009
Machiasport, Maine

'HELLO, TIFF. NOT feeling well?'

Tiffany Stoddard froze at the sound of the familiar voice coming from the darkness behind her car. On the other side of the small lot she could see a second car parked in the shadows.

'You've been to see the doctor, I believe. Dr Emily Kaplan?'

How in hell had he found her? How had he known where she'd gone? She'd been so careful about not being followed. All the way down the back road from Machias, she'd constantly checked the mirror for cars traveling behind her. Only one appeared and she'd pulled over and waited for it to pass her by, its red taillights disappearing in the distance before she drove on. Then, instead of leaving her car in the driveway at the doctor's office, she'd hidden it here at the state park, where she was sure no one would see it.

Yet somehow he did. Somehow he knew. She remembered the car turning around in the driveway at Kaplan's office. It had to have been him.

The man walked out from the shadows and began closing the twenty or so feet between them. He was in no hurry. He never was.

'Betrayal, Tiff,' he said shaking his head. 'It's an ugly word. But that's what you've done. I trusted you and you betrayed me. And now … ?'

Seeing a smile appear at the corners of his lips, Tiff felt a knot form, then tighten, in the pit of her stomach. Her heart began to beat faster. Pounding against the walls of her chest. Pounding so hard she thought it must surely break through.

'I swear I didn't do anything, Conor. I swear I didn't.'

He pulled a pair of white latex gloves from his pocket and slid them on. Flexed his fingers to assure a tight fit.

'Exactly what didn't you do, Tiff ?'

Tiff turned and looked back at the dark road that led to the doctor's office. All her nerve endings were screaming for her to run. But she knew she'd never make it. Her body was already tired and even if she was fresh there was no way in hell she could outrun him. Not for more than a hundred yards or so. Not even if she was wearing her Nikes instead of these stupid sandals.

She turned back and watched with a kind of fascinated horror as he reached back and drew a folding knife from his rear pocket.

He snapped it open.

The blade glinted in the moonlight and for the first time in her life Tiff Stoddard was sure she was going to die. Her death would probably be slow. It would certainly be painful. And, as she watched the man come closer, she couldn't think of a single damned thing she could do to prevent it.

Still she had to try.

'Now,' the man said, 'I need you to tell me what you told the doctor.' An ugly smile crossed his face as he brushed the blade of the knife against hers. 'About me. About us. About what we do, you and I.'

Tiff tried to answer his question, tried to say *I didn't tell her anything* but the only sound she could make was a small, strangled cry.

'What did you tell her, Tiff?'

The man rested the blade against the side of Tiff's face. She closed her one good eye to shut out the image of the thing, so she didn't see, but only felt, the tip of the blade slip inside her left nostril. The man pushed it up just far enough for blood to start dripping. She held her breath to keep from crying out.

'You also need to tell me, Tiff, what you've done with my pills.'

'What pills?'

'This is no time to play games, Tiff,' he said. 'Not with me. By exact count, you've helped yourself to 5,127 Ox

80s. That means you owe me, at today's prices, 615, 240 dollars. I'll be generous. We can skip the sales tax. And no, I don't take American Express.'

'If you kill me they'll find you, Conor.'

He looked at her curiously.

'I've written it all down. The whole story. The police are gonna find it. Everything I know. Who you are. What we've done. All of it.'

'You're lying, Tiff. I always know when you're lying. And even if you're not …' He smiled. Maybe the most frightening smile she'd ever seen in her life. '… it doesn't really matter. You don't know who I am. Or where I live. Or really anything about me. Conor Riordan doesn't exist. Like you once said yourself, I'm the man who never was.'

He pulled the blade, still inside Tiff's nose, through the soft skin of her nostril. Blood flowed down in a steady stream.

She gasped but refused to give him the satisfaction of crying out.

'Now, where are they?'

She said nothing. He whipped the knife across her face. From ear to chin. A shallow cut. But deep enough to leave a scar. But only if she lived long enough for scar tissue to form.

If Tiff thought there was any chance he'd let her live, she'd gladly give him back the pills. But by now she knew he wouldn't. The only question was whether he'd kill her fast or kill her slowly. And while she'd rather go fast, for the sake of Tabitha, she knew she had to hold out as long as she could.

'Where are they, Tiff?'

Tiff stood, as if rooted to the spot, desperately trying to think of a way to escape what now seemed inevitable. She wondered, without much hope, if she could make it to her car. Lock him out. Drive away. Leave this place of death far behind. Her hand slid to her back pocket. Found her keys. Slipped them out. Keeping her hand behind her back she searched for the button on the key fob that would unlock the car door.

'What did you tell the doctor?'

'I … I … didn't tell her anything. Swear to God, Conor …'

Tiff was still talking when she broke in a rush for the car, the driver's side door only ten feet away, her right thumb clicking the unlock button over and over as she ran. Her left hand reaching for the latch that would let her in and lock him out.

Before she was halfway, she felt his hand grab her ponytail. He yanked her backwards on to her ass. She tried getting up. Crawling for the car. He pulled her down again.

He picked up the keys from where they'd fallen and pocketed them. Pulled the green pack from her back, unzipped it and looked inside. Pulled out the wad of bills and her cell phone and stuffed both in his pocket with the keys. He looked again to be sure there was nothing else then tossed the pack aside.

'Okay,' he sighed, 'where did you hide my fucking tablets?'

Without waiting for an answer, he kicked her hard in the gut right where she supposed the baby must be. Her baby. Maybe his. Maybe not his. She wasn't sure. Vomit rose in her throat. Dripped from her mouth. He kicked her again, this time higher up, knocking the wind out of her. She fought for breath. Curled herself into a fetal position, knees up, head down, arms covering her face, hoping he wouldn't kick her again. Hoping he wouldn't kick the baby again. The baby hadn't done anything. The baby was innocent. Eyes closed, Tiff Stoddard prayed to a god she didn't believe in that, when death came, it would come quickly.

She felt hands slip under both her arms. Felt them hoisting her to her feet. Two hands. One under each of her arms. She tried to think clearly. How could he be lifting with two hands and still be holding the knife? Maybe he wasn't. Maybe he'd put it down. Put it away. If she could get the knife, wherever it was, maybe she had a chance.

He pushed her back against the car. She forced herself to open her good eye to look for the knife. But his face, only inches from hers, blocked her view. The smell of food from his mouth made her want to vomit again.

Tiff tried desperately to see beyond his face. She had to find the knife. She couldn't see it on the ground. Had he put it in one of his pockets when she was on the ground?

'Where the fuck are my pills?'

She felt the spray of his spit on her face.

'I hid them,' she said, playing for time, knowing there was no way she could tell him the truth. No way she could betray Tabitha. Her only chance was to keep him talking long enough to let her go for the knife.

'Where?' He squeezed her cheeks together distorting her face. The pain was excruciating. 'Where are they? Huh?'

He pressed his body against hers, jamming one forearm under her chin, forcing her head back against the car. She realized with a kind of shock he had an erection. She could feel it pushing, probing against her leg. Killing her, it seemed, was turning him on.

She slid her left hand to his pants. Found the zipper tab. Pulled it down. His hard cock poked out. She began stroking it softly. In and out. Tickling his balls with the tips of her fingers. His breath came faster.

She pushed her tongue deep into his mouth. He didn't stop her though the flow of her blood was staining his face. She pulled her tongue back, a silent invitation for his to enter her mouth. She edged her right hand around to his ass. Felt the shape of the knife in the back pocket. She rubbed his cock faster with her left hand. 'You know I love you, Conor,' she said, trying as best she could to make it sound seductive, 'I've always loved you.'

She slipped her right hand into the pocket. Found the handle of the knife. Grasped it firmly and bit down hard on his tongue. At the same time she grabbed his balls and squeezed them with all the force she could muster.

'Fucking bitch!' he hissed, leaping back, bending double with the pain of it. Her hand was free of his pocket. She had the knife. She wasted a second searching for the button that would release the blade. Found it.

Snapped it open. Drew back her arm. Drove it forward in a kind of uppercut, wanting desperately to shove the blade in as far as it would go. Draw it upwards. Open him up. Gut the fucker like her father had taught her, years earlier, to gut a fish.

But it wasn't to be. The man grabbed Tiff's wrist before the blade could reach him. Twisted it hard, back against itself. She felt an explosion of pain as the bone snapped. The knife fell to the ground.

Pushing back against the pain, she went for the knife again, this time with her left hand. But again he was too quick. In one swift motion he swept it up and pushed her back again against the car.

'You're already dead, you cunt, you just don't know it yet.'

He was wrong about that. She definitely knew it.

'Where are the pills?' he snarled.

'Fuck you,' she hissed back.

'Cunt.' He slipped the tip of the blade under her lip, its point pressing against the top of her gum. 'Where are they?'

She closed her eyes, her broken wrist pulsing with pain. 'Fuck you,' she said again, hoping to goad him into finishing it fast.

He pulled the blade smoothly through the soft flesh of her lip.

Tiff's mouth filled with blood. She spat it into his face.

He smacked her in punishment. Then he cut open her shirt and sliced through the front of her bra, so that it fell away and hung from her shoulders by its straps. He pulled down her jeans and her thong till they bunched up at her ankles. He took the knife and cut her breasts.

This time she screamed.

'Where are they?'

Her screams diminished to a whimper. She wept. 'I'm carrying your baby,' she gasped, hoping desperately he would care. 'I'm pregnant.'

'Bullshit. Where are they?'

'The doctor's got them. I left them with the doctor.'

'Why?' he snarled.

'She called the cops.' One last desperate attempt she hoped might save her life. 'They're on their way here now.'

For an instant she saw uncertainty in his eyes.

Then it was gone and he pushed the knife in. This time lower. This time deeper. Much much deeper. Again and again.

Dying, Tiff was only dimly aware of a piercing sound that came from the road.

Another woman's scream. The single word, 'Stop!' shouted over and over again.

The man turned and saw a tall figure in white sprinting toward them screaming like a bloody banshee for the killer to stop what he was doing.

The man pulled the knife from between Tiff's legs. Pushed back her head and exposed her neck. He yanked off the gold chain and pendant she wore and slashed a single deep stroke across the whiteness of her throat.

He raced for his car. Started the engine. Pulled out of the lot.

The doctor's got them. I left them with the doctor. Had Tiff been telling the truth?

In the distance, the man could hear the urgent cry of a police siren growing louder by the second. He didn't have much time. He had to get out of here.

Less than twenty yards away, the doctor stood in the middle of the road, waving her arms back and forth, in a desperate effort to get him to stop.

The man stomped on the accelerator and headed straight for her.

Chapter Five

2:22 A.M., Saturday, August 22, 2009
Portland, Maine

IT WAS TOO damned hot to sleep. After a couple of hours tossing and turning, Maggie Savage found herself wide awake, sheets kicked off, body soaked in sweat. Like most Mainers, she'd never considered installing AC and the air in her apartment on Vesper Street felt as dank and steamy as it had in the interview room at 109. But it wasn't just the heat that was keeping her awake. It was the evening she'd just spent with Billy Webb. At least the last part of it.

I really like you, Maggie. I'd really like this to go somewhere.

She'd met Billy back in early June when he arrived in town to take up duties as the replacement pitching coach for the Portland Sea Dogs, his predecessor in the job having keeled over with a massive and subsequently fatal coronary in a bar in Altoona, Pennsylvania, home of the Altoona Curve. Billy had been pursuing Maggie enthusiastically, if unsuccessfully, ever since. The pursuit was, of necessity, intermittent since he was 'a travelin' man', as he put it, available for dates and other social engagements only when the Sea Dogs were playing at home and not off visiting one Eastern League competitor or another. The Binghamton Mets. The Trenton Thunder. The Akron Aeros. All towns and teams Maggie had never been to and had no desire to see.

The two of them had spent the early part of the evening drinking margaritas and eating a steak they'd grilled over a charcoal fire out on Ferry Beach in Scarborough, where the air was marginally less oppressive than it was here in town. Afterward, he'd driven her home and for the fifth time in five dates she turned down his earnest and ardent pleas to allow him into her bed.

I really like you, Maggie. I'd really like this to go somewhere.

Thinking she ought to level with him, she told Billy she didn't think things were going to work out between them. That they probably shouldn't see each other again. He didn't argue. Or even want to talk about why. Just told her he'd call her in two weeks after he got back from the next road trip and drove off into the night.

And now she was lying here by herself. Feeling more than a little lonely and more than a little depressed about the prospect of starting all over again.

Still, she was sure Billy wasn't right for her. Yes, he was a nice guy. Certainly attractive enough. He had a decent sense of humor. But he wasn't what she was looking for. Billy had been married and divorced twice. He was the father of a twenty-year-old son he hadn't seen or spoken to in eight years. And next season he could just as easily be coaching pitchers in Greenville, South Carolina as in Portland, Maine. Maggie was thirty-six. She wanted to get married and have at least one or maybe even a couple of kids before it was too late. A guy who bounced from city to city year after year wasn't a good prospect either as a husband or a dad. However, all of these considerations paled against what was, by far, the single most important entry on the negative side of Billy's ledger. The simple fact that he wasn't the man she wanted to spend her life with and she knew he never would be. Hanging on now, letting it go any further, would be too much like an admission she was getting desperate. Grasping at straws. And she was damned if she was ready to admit that. Not to herself. Not to anyone else either. At least not yet. Maggie was mulling the implications of that when the first four notes of Beethoven's Fifth Symphony rang out. Da-da-da-dum!

She grabbed her phone from the nightstand. Caller ID said 'Savage, John'. Why was her father calling in the middle of the night?

'Okay, what's going on?' Maggie asked. She walked into the living room, turned on a single lamp and sat down on the couch. There was a lot of noise and interference on the other end of the line. 'Where are you?'

'Machiasport,' her father shouted into the phone. 'In the parking area by the state park. We're in the middle of a thunderstorm so if we get cut off I'll call you back.'

Maggie's mind cleared instantly. The phone line crackled. There was a sound like thunder exploding in the background.

'Can you hear me?' her father shouted.

'Yes, I can hear you.'

'You may want to get up here a little earlier than planned.'

'Really? Why's that?'

'We've got ourselves kind of a mess. A double mess actually.'

'What kind of mess?'

'A murder mess. A young woman had her throat cut just a few hours ago. The killer damn near took her head off. Among other things. She must've bled out in minutes.'

'I'm sorry to hear that but what's it got to do with me? Call the staties. It's their jurisdiction.'

'I'm calling you because Emily was nearly killed at the same time.'

Maggie felt her gut tighten. *Nearly killed* he'd said. That meant Em was still alive. 'How bad?'

'Bad.'

'Is she going to die?' Maggie held her breath and waited for the answer. Emily Kaplan had been Maggie's best friend since pre-school. Her fellow star and alter-ego on the Machias Memorial High School state championship basketball team. Em was the closest thing Maggie had to a sister. A twin sister, except Em was three inches taller and a much better athlete. If Emily died a big part of Maggie would die along with her.

'I don't know,' John Savage told her.

Maggie exhaled long and slow. 'What happened?'

'Best we can tell, Em was hit by a car near where the murder victim was found. Cracked her head pretty hard going down. My theory is after the killer sliced up the victim he jumped in his car and literally ran into Emily on the way out. She's been lying in a ditch by the side of the road ever since. Three or four hours at least. Getting rained on for the last hour or so. If a pair of teenagers hadn't pulled into the parking area for a little late-night kiss and giggle, both of them could've been lying there all night. A Life-Flight chopper's on its way now. They'll fly her down to Eastern Maine.'

'Staties there yet?' asked Maggie. The Maine State Police, the MSP, were responsible for investigating all murders in the state of Maine outside the cities of Portland or Bangor. Sometimes they enlisted the support of the county Sheriff's Department and/or local police. Sometimes not.

'Detective named Emmett Ganzer and an evidence team got here about ten minutes ago. Before that it was just me, one of my deputies and a couple of troopers. Now that he's here, Ganzer's marching around like some oversized drill sergeant telling everybody what to do.'

Maggie knew Ganzer from the Academy and didn't much like him. He was a good detective. Smart but overly aggressive and difficult to get along with, especially for the female students.

'Two other things you might want to know.'

'Go ahead.'

'About quarter to nine this evening, Emily called both my phones from her office. Left one message to call her back. Another to get down to her place. Said it was urgent.'

'Where were you?'

'I was taking a shower and Anya was out of the house. I called her back but she didn't answer. So I jumped in the car and headed for her house, lights and siren. By the time I got there she was gone. I was still looking for her when we got the call from the kids.'

'She didn't call 911?'

'There's no record of that.'

'What else can you tell me?'

Savage sighed before answering. 'I'm 100 percent certain the hit and run was no accident. Guy was going at least fifty and from tire marks on the road it's pretty clear he swerved to make sure he hit her.'

'Taking out a witness?'

'That's my reading.'

'What else?'

'Em must've been working. Had on a white lab coat with a stethoscope stuffed in one pocket and a ziplock bag in the other. Bag had over 150 Oxycontin tablets in it. Maybe more. Eighty megs. Canadian manufacture.'

'What the hell was she doing with them?'

'Don't know yet. We'll talk about that when you get here.'

'All right.' Maggie's mind was racing. 'I'll get there as soon as I can. But I'm gonna stop at the hospital on the way up.'

Maggie took a one-minute shower, towel-dried her hair and threw on some clothes. She strapped on her Glock 17, and slipped into a lightweight jacket long enough to conceal the weapon. She shoved her laptop into her canvas computer case and stuffed a duffle with enough clothes for a week. Nothing fancy. Just jeans, t-shirts and underwear. A couple of sweaters in case it got cold. As an afterthought, she threw in two spare magazines for the Glock. As a second afterthought, she added her backup weapon. A lightweight Kimber Solo 9 mm automatic, an ankle holster and a six-round magazine for that. She sincerely hoped she wouldn't need body armor.

Chapter Six

MAGGIE HEADED NORTH on the 295/95 combination out of Portland. It was not only the fastest way to get to Machiasport, it also took her past Bangor and Eastern Maine Medical Center.

At three in the morning the interstate was nearly empty and Maggie pushed her TrailBlazer's big V-8 engine to the max, hoping a brand-new murder investigation and her Portland PD creds would convince any trailing troopers to forget about issuing speeding tickets. Happily, no troopers materialized.

Her father called before she hit the tolls at Augusta.

'Got a call from the hospital. CAT scan showed some bleeding on the brain. But they said it wasn't too bad. She ought to be in post-op by the time you get there.'

'Post-op?'

'Yeah, surgeon drilled a hole in her head to relieve the pressure.'

A hole in her head? Jesus.

Maggie hit the entrance to Eastern Maine on State Street in Bangor less than an hour and a half after leaving Vesper Street. She pulled into a no-parking zone near the emergency entrance, tossed an *Official Police Business* sign on the dashboard and ran in. Typical Friday-night, Saturday-morning crowd in the ER but at least someone was manning the desk.

'Are you a relative?' the woman asked.

Maggie hesitated, unsure if being a relative or a cop would get her information faster. 'Actually, I'm a police officer,' she said, producing her gold shield. 'Detective Margaret Savage. Dr Kaplan was the victim of a crime. I need to talk to her doctor.'

The woman at the desk hit some keys on her computer, muttering to herself, 'Kaplan, let's see, Kaplan. Here she is.' She picked up a phone and asked some questions. 'Uh, huh. Okay. I have a police officer here. A detective.' Pause. 'Okay, I'll send her up.' She hung up. 'Dr Kaplan's just out of surgery but Dr Collins said he can talk to you. Take that elevator over there to the second floor ICU. He'll meet you there.'

A middle-aged man wearing surgical scrubs and a distracted look was standing by the elevator doors talking to a nurse when Maggie stepped out.

'You the detective?' he asked.

'Yes. Margaret Savage,' she said, showing her badge and ID. 'I'm also a close personal friend of the victim.'

'I see. I'm Dr Collins. Stanley Collins. I'm a neurosurgeon here at the hospital.'

Collins pointed Maggie toward some plastic chairs in a waiting area and they sat.

'Is she going to make it?' Maggie asked thinking about what happened to Mary Farrier.

'Yes. I'm very optimistic she'll soon make a full recovery.'

'How soon?'

'Hard to say exactly. She's had a bad blow to the head and is currently comatose. There was some fairly minor blood leakage. We've inserted a catheter through her skull to relieve and monitor any pressure on the brain. We've also got her intubated to help her breathing. Impact with the car also cracked a couple of ribs. Otherwise, except for some scrapes and bruises, she's fine. Overall, considering what she's been through, I'd say she's doing surprisingly well. She's a very strong woman.'

Surprisingly well? Attagirl, Em. You surprise the bastards.

He spun some further medical bullshit Maggie didn't understand but which sounded generally positive. But then he finished with: 'Unfortunately we can't be sure she's 100 percent out of the woods. Soon. But not just yet.'

Just covering his ass, Maggie thought.

'How long will she be unconscious?'

'Hard to say. Could be just a few hours. Maybe a day. Possibly longer. We'll know more after twelve hours.'

'Can I see her?'

'She won't know you're there.'

'I'd just like to have a look.'

The doctor shrugged. 'No reason you shouldn't. You can hold her hand. Talk to her. It all helps. I just suggest you don't stay too long.'

Maggie nodded. She didn't intend to stay long anyway.

Chapter Seven

OUT OF BANGOR Maggie picked up Route 9. The Airline as it was called. Sixty-five miles due east over a string of mountains on a well-maintained two-laner. Her only company the whole way half a dozen pick-ups and a pair of eighteen-wheelers hauling heavy loads of fresh-cut timber. All were easily passed. Best of all, the thunderstorms Savage warned her about had already gone through, leaving drying roads and cooler air. Maggie gazed into a clear eastern sky as it morphed from delicate pink to a full red to a glorious orange. As the shimmering disk of the sun poked up over the horizon, Maggie slipped on a pair of Oakley Inmates she'd splurged on after she started dating Billy. She figured they'd make it harder for friends to spot her sitting in the wives and girlfriends section at Hadlock Field during Sea Dogs games. Then she called her father.

'I stopped by the hospital,' she said.

'They let you in?'

'Just showed my badge.'

'How is she?'

'Still in a coma.' She told him what the doctor told her. 'She's going to be fine. It could have been much worse.'

'Where are you now?' he asked.

'At the moment? Passing through Clifton by Parks Pond.'

Savage started to say something, then his voice cut out. Maggie looked at her phone. A little *no service* message appeared in place of the bars. She put it away.

At Wesley, Maggie turned south on to 192 and descended toward Machias and the coast, passing Northfield and the familiar dock and landing at Bog Lake where John Savage had taught all three of his children, one-on-one, each in their turn, the fine art of fishing for, and occasionally catching, the landlocked salmon that once abounded in the lake and the brown trout that still did.

She wondered if Emmett Ganzer would be running the show and, if so, what his reaction would be when she told him she wanted to join the investigation team. There wasn't an agency in the state that couldn't use an extra pair of experienced hands, and working with the staties would give her access to a lot of resources she wouldn't have working on her own. Still, she didn't know Ganzer all that well, hadn't seen him since they attended the Maine Criminal Justice Academy together. She remembered Emmett as someone who hated it when anyone – but especially a female student and double-especially one named Savage – came up with the answers in class before he did.

She drove through Machias and continued south on Port Road through the small village of Machiasport and on toward the state park. In the early light of a cool summer morning she could see the flashing light bars of a bunch of cruisers from half a mile away. As she drew closer she counted three from the MSP, two more from the Washington County Sheriff's Department plus a couple of unmarked state police cars and her father's white Subaru Outback.

A young trooper signaled her to pull over in front of some yellow crime-scene tape that was cordoning off the entire area from the state park to the spot where she guessed Emily had been hit. 'Sorry, ma'am,' he said, 'I'm afraid you can't stop here. You'll either have to turn around or continue through on that far shoulder.'

The trooper's plastic name badge identified him as J. W. Willett. 'Trooper Willett?'

'That's right.'

Maggie held out her badge wallet and opened it for the trooper. 'Detective Margaret Savage, Portland PD.'

'You're a little far from home, aren't you?'

'See that tall guy down there? I'm with him.'

'Sheriff Savage?' He glanced at her name again. 'You his daughter?'

'Last time I checked.'

'Yeah,' the trooper nodded, 'I can see the resemblance.' He spoke into his shoulder mike. Somebody on the other end told him to let her through.

Maggie parked the Blazer, slipped under the tape and started toward the park. She stopped where the evidence techs had marked the precise point of impact where Emily had been struck by the fleeing car. Had she been trying to stop the killer when he ran into her? Or help the dying girl? Maggie knew Em's first instinct would have been to save a life.

There was nothing much to be seen here except some skid marks that showed where the car had swerved. Other than that, nothing. No paint chips. No blood or broken glass. By now the techs would've collected whatever could be found and tucked it away for analysis.

She continued toward the park. John Savage broke away from the group he was with and came to meet her. A lean six-four, with a gray mustache and a weathered face, Savage looked more like a sheriff in a John Ford western than one in a rural county in Maine. He was even armed like Wyatt Earp with his pride and joy, an original 1873 long-barreled Colt.45 Peacemaker, strapped to his waist. All he needed was a horse and a Stetson hat to complete the image. And somewhere at home Maggie was pretty sure he had the hat. Polly Four, a blond Lab who was John's constant companion, jumped from the open back of the Subaru and trotted alongside. People tended to ask John the significance of the 'Four' in Polly Four's name. Nothing real complicated. Her father always named his dogs Polly ('Keeps things simple,' he'd explain) and this one was his fourth. Polly Four, in dog years, was about the same age John was in people years. Just like Pollys one through three, she had a deputy sheriff's badge clipped to her collar.

Polly Four wagged furiously and butted her nose against Maggie's leg. John opened his arms. Maggie stepped into them, rejoicing in the familiar scent of the only man she'd loved forever. A pot pourri of unfiltered Camels, J. W. Dant Straight Kentucky Bourbon and wet gun dog.

Then she pulled back and examined him closely. He looked thinner than she remembered, but then he'd always been lean. There were a few new furrows on his always furrowed face. A little less hair on his head. None of this, at his age, was much of a surprise. She saw nothing more than worry reflected in the dark-brown eyes everyone said looked exactly like hers. Still, at seventy-four, it was way past time for John Savage to admit he was getting older and stop working so hard at a job he should have retired from years earlier. Except he loved the job. Lived for it. Probably kill him if he quit. Kill him if he didn't. Damned if you do. Damned if you don't.

'How you doing, Mag?' he asked as they broke the hug.

'Hanging in,' she told him. 'How about you?'

'Aching all over. Should have been in bed hours ago.'

As they started back, John reached into his shirt pocket for his pack of Camels, the short unfiltered kind he'd been smoking forever. She waited while he tapped one out and lit up. He took a deep drag and blew a steady stream of smoke into the crisp morning air, the blue smoke tinted bluer by the flashing light bars of the cruisers.

'Thought you promised me you'd give those up,' Maggie said.

'Yup. I did. Promised you. Promised Em. Promised Anya. But the truth of the matter is I don't really want to give them up. I enjoy smoking. I enjoy bourbon too. And sex when I can manage it.'

'The bourbon and sex probably won't kill you.'

'No, but I'm turning seventy-five next month. At this point it seems more'n likely something else'll kill me first.'

Maggie wondered if he had anything specific in mind. But that conversation would have to wait. In the meantime she knew enough not to argue. John was at least as stubborn as she was.

Chapter Eight

'WELL, IF IT isn't Margaret Savage,' Emmett Ganzer said when they joined a small group of cops clustered a little way from the murder site. Ganzer didn't look happy to see her. 'What brings you up here from the big bad city?'

'Keeping the old man company, Emmett,' Maggie said. 'How are you?'

'Me? I'm fine. I'm always fine.'

'Margaret Savage?' The question came from a good-looking man she hadn't met before. 'Are you Detective Margaret Savage? Portland PD?'

'Yup. That's me. Who're you?'

'Sean Carroll. CID out of Ellsworth. I'm the lead on this investigation.'

Sergeant Sean Carroll. Maggie had heard the name before. Seen it in the paper too. Carroll had a reputation as one of the best investigators in the state. Only thirty-three and already rumored to be on the fast track to succeed Tom Mayhew as next lieutenant of the State Police Northern Division CID. He held out his hand. She shook it.

'Nice to meet you too,' she smiled. 'Most people call me Maggie.'

'Okay, Maggie. This is Detective Scott Renzo and Bill Heinrich,' said Carroll. 'Bill is head of our ER team.' ER stood for Evidence Retrieval. 'Y'know, I've heard a lot of good things about you,' he added.

'Really? I'm flattered.'

'Don't be. You've got a damned good reputation as a homicide investigator. You and McCabe both. From what I understand, it's deserved.' McCabe was Detective Sergeant Michael McCabe, head of the Portland Police Department's Crimes Against People unit. Technically, Maggie's boss. More accurately, more importantly, her partner and friend. They'd worked together for nearly five years.

Maggie nodded her thanks and studied Carroll as he turned his attention back to Heinrich for a moment. Six-one or maybe six-two with a trim, muscular build and dark, curly hair cut a little longer than most cops would wear it. She found herself checking his left hand and noting the absence of a wedding band.

'Mind if I take a look at the vic?' she asked.

'It's not a pretty sight.'

'I can handle it.'

'I'm sure you can, but why?' Carroll looked at her through narrowed eyes. 'Are you here for something other than just visiting your father?'

Maggie figured what the hell. Might as well leap in with both feet. 'Yes. I'd like to work with your people on this investigation.'

'Really?' Carroll sounded surprised. 'What's your interest?'

'Emily Kaplan, the woman hit by the getaway car, is my oldest and closest friend.'

'Ahh. So you want to catch the guy who tried to kill her?'

'I do. I also think I can add value to your investigation.'

'Such as?'

Maggie shrugged. 'I grew up in Machias. Still have a lot of contacts here. Plus Emily trusts me. She'll talk to me more freely than to any of your other detectives. Also, if you're coordinating your investigation with the Sheriff's Department, I'm obviously well connected there as well.'

Carroll nodded. Maggie felt his eyes, an almost startling gray-blue, study her as if there were no one else in the small circle of cops or for that matter anywhere else in the world. Just her. She felt them drawing her in.

'Let's talk about this in my car,' he said, 'I think it merits a private conversation.'

Carroll led Maggie to an unmarked gray Impala with state police plates. She got in the passenger side. He slid behind the wheel. They sat side by side in the dark.

'You seem very intent on this,' he said.

'I am.'

Carroll nodded, his eyes still on her. 'You know normally if a detective with your experience and reputation volunteered to help in what could be a very difficult investigation, I'd jump at the chance to bring you in.'

'But ... ?'

'But I have concerns.'

'Such as?'

'Such as whether your relationship with Kaplan will affect your ability to weigh the evidence objectively.'

'I can promise you it won't.'

'I'm not sure that's a promise you can keep. You do know we found a stash of illegal drugs, over a 150 Oxycontin tablets, in your friend's pocket?'

'Yes, my father told me. I don't know why those pills were there,' Maggie said, choosing her words carefully. 'But I'm sure Emily has nothing to do with buying or selling Oxycontin. Or with the murder of that young woman.'

'Tell me something,' Carroll said. 'If I say thanks for your generous offer, but no thanks, I have plenty of good people assigned, what would you do? Go home quietly? Or nose around on your own anyway?'

'I'd have to think about that.'

'But you might decide to play private eye? Work it on your own?'

'I might.'

'I need a more definitive answer than that.'

'All right. The definitive answer is yes. I'd work it on my own. I'm not going to sit quietly by while some scumball takes a second shot at my friend.'

'Even if I told you, warned you, that if you did that I might feel obliged to issue a formal complaint up the line, maybe as far as the Attorney General's office.'

'I'd go ahead anyway.'

Carroll exhaled loudly. He turned away and stared out the window. Maggie hoped he wouldn't decide to punt.

'How long are you here for?' he asked after what seemed like a long time.

'I'm due back in Portland Tuesday morning. But since I just cleared the only case I was working on I'm sure I can stay longer if necessary.'

'If I say yes, will you agree to report directly to me? Play by my rules and not go off freelancing on your own?'

Though she knew she wasn't being completely honest, she gave Carroll the affirmative answer she knew he required. If he stuck her out in left field just to get her out of the way, all bets were off.

'Okay. Tell you what,' Carroll said, 'we'll give it a shot. See how it goes until Tuesday, when you're due back in Portland anyway.'

'That's not a lot of time.'

'Consider it a free trial offer.' Carroll smiled and Maggie was struck again by the blueness of his eyes. They were quite intoxicating. 'A chance to see how we get on together,' he continued. 'If it works we'll take it from there. If not, no further involvement. No harm done. Fair enough?'

Maggie knew she wasn't going to get a better offer so she decided to play by Carroll's rules. At least until Tuesday.

'Fair enough?' he asked again.

'Okay. Fair enough,' she said.

They headed back and joined the assembled group. Maggie slipped a pair of paper booties over her shoes and continued down to where Tiffany Stoddard's body lay a few feet away from a rusty green Taurus.

Chapter Nine

VIOLENT DEATH HAD been Maggie Savage's stock in trade for a long time. Six years in uniform and eight more working homicide had brought her face to face with more of the dead than she cared to count or remember. Human beings stabbed to death, shot to death, bludgeoned to death and burned to death. Bodies torn apart in accidents. Bodies fished out of the bay, bloated and rotting from weeks in the water. Bodies lying naked and exposed on stainless steel tables awaiting the final indignity of the pathologist's blade.

Fourteen years of living with death and yet the first encounter with a victim as brutalized as Tiff Stoddard wasn't easy. One of the hardest parts was not letting her genuine feelings show through. As a woman she had to seem tougher than that to the guys she worked with, most of whom would see any honest display of emotion as further proof of female weakness. But the simple truth was she still took each death hard. Especially when the victims had their damned eyes open and were staring at her, or, as in the case of Tiffany Stoddard, one eye open.

The viciousness of Stoddard's killing seemed incongruous in the sweet cool air of an August morning. She was lying where she fell, in the middle of a pool of drying blood, bra hanging loose, pants pulled down, one eye battered shut, the other mirroring the horror of her last moments. Tiff's hands still clutched her nearly severed neck, her final futile attempt to keep her life from bleeding out.

Maggie squatted down and studied Tiff Stoddard's bruised and beaten face. Noted the cuts through her nostril and her lip. The cuts on her breasts. The shallow vertical cut down her middle. The bloody mess the killer's knife had made between her legs. Lips, breasts, vagina. A sexual sadist's work. Assuming his fun and games had been interrupted by Emily's appearance, had he been forced to finish fast by going for the jugular? Coitus interruptus? Sort of. She was sure Emily's unexpected arrival must have frustrated his sadistic desire, stoked his rage, his need to cause pain.

'She probably wasn't his first.'

Maggie turned at the sound of Carroll's voice. She hadn't heard him approach.

'Really? You've found others?' she asked, rising from her squatting position. 'Cut up like this?'

'Just one. Woman named Laura Blakemore. Body turned up third week in February.'

'Who was she?'

'Part-time waitress. Part-time drug dealer. Twenty-three years old. Attractive. At least she was before she was cut into pieces and stuffed into four heavyweight garbage bags, the kind they use on construction sites. The killer tossed all four into a dumpster behind a Wal-Mart in Brewer. It was only by accident she didn't end up as landfill.'

'Who found her?'

'Homeless guy rooting around in the dumpster for throw-away food. He opened one of the bags and saw Blakemore's severed head staring back at him through a layer of Saran Wrap. Poor bastard almost had a coronary. Anyway, he had enough sense to flag down a Brewer patrol car and we took it from there.'

'Your case?'

'Yes. One of the privileges of rank. I get to pick and choose what I work on.'

'But you haven't found the killer.'

'No. The investigation's still open.'

'You attend the autopsy?'

'Such as it was. More of a reconstruction project than an autopsy.'

'Did she have cuts like these?'

Carroll shook his head. 'Blakemore was in twenty pieces. There were cuts everywhere.'

'Any other connection to Stoddard?'

'Yes. Oxycontin. Blakemore was wholesaling Canadian 80s all over Penobscot County, mostly to small-time pushers. Maine DEA had her in their sights and was using her to connect the dots to her source of supply.

Unfortunately, someone learned she was about to turn snitch and she ended up in the dumpster before providing any significant information. What I'm wondering is if Blakemore's supplier might not have been Stoddard. Or, admittedly less likely, Kaplan.'

'It wasn't Emily.'

Carroll sighed. 'Y'know, that's the kind of assumption that made me hesitate bringing you into this case. There *are* doctors who break the law. Sometimes easy money can be very tempting.'

Maggie decided not to argue the point.

'Anyway, we know the origin of the Canadian product. You ever hear of Saint John?'

'I assume you mean the city and not the apostle?'

'That's right. The city. Saint John, New Brunswick. Up until this winter selling Ox in Maine was mostly a mom and pop business. Phony prescriptions for thirty tabs. People with legit prescriptions making a few bucks selling their leftover pills. Very occasionally somebody would bring in a few hundred tabs from out of state. Until this year almost all Oxycontin sold in Maine was manufactured by Purdue Pharmaceuticals in the US.'

'Then what?'

'Last January that all changed. Forty thousand tablets with a street value of nearly five million dollars were stolen from a big pharmaceutical distribution center in Saint John. Within weeks, Canadian tabs, CDN stamped right on them, started showing up all over the state. Our DEA guys say they've got to be from

Saint John. Our neighbors to the north claim we're just blaming them for our drug problems.'

'Even though the pills are obviously Canadian?'

'Even though. They say the thieves in Saint John were two local kids arrested previously for dealing. They tried to get away by water and capsized their kayak. Their bodies washed up down the coast a couple of days later. Both were positively identified from surveillance videos which show them killing a security guard and taking off with the goods in a small duffle bag.'

'The drugs didn't wash up with them?'

'Never found.'

'How about the kayak?'

'That turned up a couple of days after the bodies. A bag was still in the storage compartment containing their wallets and a Glock 17 with one of the kids' prints on it. Two shots fired. Definitely the same gun that killed the security guy.'

'A little neat, isn't it?'

'I agree. But the Canadian cops insist the drugs sank to the bottom of the Bay of Fundy. Or maybe washed out with the tides. DEA says that's nonsense. Far too many "CDN" tabs turning up in Maine for it to be anything else.'

'So somebody else brought the drugs back to Maine. A third man?'

'Yeah. Except what if the third man happened to be a woman?'

'Stoddard?'

'Possibly. She's roughly the same age as the kids who killed the guard. Maybe they were in on it together. Let's say she's on a boat.'

'A getaway boat?'

'Why not? The boys kayak out, toss the drugs on board and she takes off. They try to paddle back to shore. But it's the Bay of Fundy and they're fighting an outgoing tide. Eventually they capsize. She comes home and opens her candy store. Hires Blakemore as a helper.'

'Only one problem with that theory.'

'Yeah? What?'

'Tiffany Stoddard didn't commit suicide and she sure as hell didn't sexually mutilate her own body. And Emily Kaplan didn't drive a car into herself. So who did?'

Carroll shrugged. 'I don't know. My guess is a would-be competitor who decided to take over her business. What you might call a hostile takeover.'

'Very hostile,' agreed Maggie. 'Same guy who killed Blakemore?'

'I think so. Same guy. Same motive. Blakemore was the first step on the distribution ladder. Let's say he uses her to work his way up to Stoddard. He kills her. Then he tortures and kills Stoddard. Forces her to tell him where the rest of the goods are. Kaplan's just collateral damage.'

Maggie nodded more to herself than Carroll, uncertain if his takeover theory made sense. What she was sure of was that whoever killed Stoddard didn't do it just for the drugs. Or the money. Maybe as a male, Carroll didn't feel the sexual nature of the attack as sharply or deeply as she did. Or maybe he thought hunting down a sexual deviant complicated his otherwise straightforward drug investigation. 'Can you get me copies of the case files on Saint John?' she said. 'Both ours and the Canadians? Also the file on Blakemore?'

'I'll have somebody deliver a set to your father's office later this morning. We're setting up temporary headquarters there. Saves driving back and forth to Ellsworth.'

'Also can you put a trooper on Emily's room at Eastern, Maine. Once the bad guy figures out she isn't dead …'

'Yup. Got it. I'll take care of it,' Carroll said before Maggie finished the sentence.

'Okay. Good. In the meantime what do you want me to do?'

'First thing? Go to Eastport and inform Stoddard's next of kin. While you're there find out whatever you can about her, including where she was in January. Specifically the sixth through the eighth.'

Chapter Ten

MAGGIE FOUND HER father leaning against his Subaru, sipping coffee from a thermos and smoking another Camel. Polly Four was sleeping at his feet.

'That coffee?'

'Yup.'

'Mind if I take a sip?'

'Nah. Take as much as you like.'

The coffee was hot, strong and black, the way Maggie liked it. She hoped the caffeine would help. She hadn't had any real sleep in more than twenty-four hours and it'd been a rough twenty-four.

'Heard you signed on to be Sean Carroll's sidekick.'

'For the time being. What do you know about him?'

'Not a lot. Except he's supposed to be smart. Ambitious too from what I hear. I gather Tom Mayhew thinks he walks on water. Lets him pick and choose his assignments.

Which means he only hangs out in Washington County when something like this hits the fan.'

She took another sip of her father's coffee. 'You know anybody in Eastport?'

'Sure. Lots of people. What do you need?'

'I'm going up to inform Stoddard's next of kin. Be good to have a little background before I knock on the door.'

'Go see Frank Boucher. He's chief of the Eastport PD. Frank and I go way back. I'll let him know you're coming.'

IT WAS EASY for Maggie to spot the grey Impala hanging on her tail. Would have been easy even if Route 1 had been clogged with a full complement of summer-weekend traffic. But at this hour on a Saturday morning it was very nearly empty and whoever was following was making no effort to hide his presence. He could have passed her a half a dozen times but didn't. When she went faster, he went faster. When she eased up on the accelerator, so did he. Growing bored with the game, Maggie unsnapped her holster, laid her Glock on the seat next to her, flipped on her directional to give her pursuer fair warning and made an unscheduled left on to a small road called Dinsmore Lane.

She slowed to a stop on the grassy shoulder about a hundred yards in. The Impala pulled up behind. It had state police plates. She rolled down her window and waited. The driver's-side door opened and Emmett

J. Ganzer stepped out. He walked the twenty feet between the two cars.

She slipped her gun back in its holster. Ganzer went around to the other side and climbed into the seat next to her. He was a big guy. At least six-two. Broad shoulders. Hard body. Thick neck like an NFL linebacker. He wore his hair in a closely cropped military-style crew-cut, sides shaved, the short hair in the middle standing straight up from his head. His bright little eyes darted this way and that. Checking out the car. Checking out Maggie.

'Why are you following me, Emmett?'

'Because I didn't want to have this conversation in front of a crowd. It's between you and me.'

'All right. What do you want?'

'Y'know, Savage, this is a big-money case. Five million dollars big. Major media big. The kind that makes or breaks careers. Mine. Yours. Carroll's. If I clear this one I'm a cinch to get my sergeant's stripes just as soon as Carroll moves into Mayhew's shoes. Only problem is you just pushed me out of the way. Tough to be a hero when you're playing second fiddle to a good-looking babe. Media loves good-looking babes. So does Carroll.' She felt Ganzer's eyes examining her, mentally undressing her.

'I'm not trying to push you anywhere, Emmett.'

'Y'know, Savage, we don't get many cases like this up here in the boonies. I know that's why Carroll came prancing in on his white horse at four in the morning. And isn't it interesting? You show up all the way from Portland just a couple of hours later.'

'If you think I'm looking for publicity, you're out of your mind.'

'I'm a good cop, Savage. Got a good record. This is my case and I want it. I can't do much about the boy genius horning in. He's my boss and I do whatever he tells me. But you? You're a whole different story.'

'I don't care who catches this guy, Emmett. If it's you, I'll cheer loudest. But I plan on doing what I can because whoever killed Tiffany Stoddard also damn near killed my best friend.'

'Is that the story you told Carroll? You know something? I don't believe you. I think maybe you talked about me instead. Told him you weren't sure I had what it took to do this job. Or maybe you just batted those big brown eyes at him? Or wiggled your cute little ass? Carroll never could resist a cute little ass.' He waited a beat. 'But you know, since you're here, why don't you and I work together on this thing. You know? As partners. Might work for both of us.' As he spoke he slid his hand on to her knee.

'All right, that's it, Ganzer. Get your hands off me and get the hell out of my car. I've got work to do.'

Ganzer didn't move. 'Don't decide so quick, Savage. I've got a feeling the two of us might just get along pretty well.'

Maggie pushed his hand from her leg. 'Get out of this car and get out now.'

Finally he opened the door and climbed out. 'Okay. I know you're here through Monday, and there's nothing I can do about that. But come Tuesday I want to see you on the road heading south. If you're not, I'll do whatever I need to do to make sure you regret it. And enjoy every minute. That, Detective Savage, is a promise you can take to the bank.'

AN HOUR LATER, still irritated by Ganzer's bullshit, Maggie crossed the causeway on State Route 190 that connected the center of Eastport on Moose Island to the rest of Maine. The town was once home to more than a dozen sardine canneries but both the fish and the canneries had been gone for decades. Other businesses had closed more recently and the city's population, once considerably larger, now hovered around 1,500. In spite of a picturesque waterfront and a reputation as something of an art colony, Eastport shared the general poverty of Washington County and depended primarily on lobsters, scallops and summer tourism for income.

Maggie hadn't been here in a couple of years. She did a quick circuit of the historic waterfront, which looked just as pretty as ever. Noted license plates on the diagonally parked cars from Wisconsin, Michigan, Florida and Illinois. She parked in front of the building just off Water Street that housed the town's six-man police department.

Chapter Eleven

8:27 A.M., Saturday, August 22, 2009
Eastport, Maine

CHIEF FRANK BOUCHER stood up from behind his desk in his small, paneled office. Photos of former Eastport chiefs going back to the early 1900s lined the walls with dates of their years of service.

'So you're the big man's daughter, are you?'

Maggie smiled and nodded. 'Maggie Savage. Nice to meet you, Chief.' She held out her hand and he shook it.

Boucher looked to be in his early sixties. A receding hairline accentuated the roundness of his face which kind of matched the roundness of his belly, which extended well out beyond his belt.

'You had breakfast yet?' he asked.

'Not yet,' she said. Truth be told, Maggie was starving. She and Billy had done more drinking than eating last night and she hadn't had anything since.

'Good. Let's walk up the street to the WaCo. They keep a table on the deck permanently reserved for me.'

The WaCo Diner, pronounced whacko, which kind of fit the décor, was an Eastport institution, having been established, according to the blue awning over the front door, in 1924. Some natives claimed the original WaCo opened even earlier than that. As Boucher promised, their table on the deck had a glorious view of the water. Campobello Island on the Canadian side was just a stone's throw away. At least it was if you happened to have a good throwing arm.

The Chief ordered blueberry pancakes. Maggie opted for scrambled eggs with bacon and home fries. When the food arrived, they both tucked in.

'Tall like your father, aren't you?'

'Five-eleven. Some days six feet. Depends on my mood.'

'Y'know, I remember you from when you played basketball at Machias Memorial. You and that Kaplan girl. The two of you were something else.'

'She was a lot better than I was.'

'You were pretty damn good yourself. Our daughter Lizzie played for Shead at the time and the two of you were not only way taller than anybody we had, you were way better. Jackie Comer, the old Shead coach, used to call you the "Twin Towers" – course, that was before 9/11. Anyway, my wife and I would go to the games and, man, you guys kicked our butts three years in a row. State champs as I recall.'

'Three years in a row,' Maggie smiled.

'Anyway, you didn't come here to talk basketball. John told me about the Stoddards' daughter. Anyone know who did it?'

'Not yet. We only discovered the body a few hours ago. I'll be going over to the Stoddards as soon as I leave here.'

'Tough job informing next of kin. 'Specially parents. Done it a few times myself and it's never fun. How can I help?'

'Any background you can give me about the family would be helpful.'

Boucher leaned back, patted maple syrup from his mouth and chin and sipped his coffee. 'Pike and Donelda Stoddard. That's a whole other song,' he said. 'They're both in their late forties. He's from here. Eastport going back forever. She's from away. LA, I think. She wandered into town back in the eighties and hooked up with Pike. Been with him ever since. Donelda still comes off like some sort of overage hippie. Flouncy skirts. Long grey hair down to her butt. That sort of thing.'

'Children?'

'Three daughters. Teresa was the oldest. Three years older than Tiff in the middle. Youngest is named Tabitha. Guess they had a thing for names starting with T. Anyway, Tabbie was the afterthought kid. She just turned eleven. More than ten years younger than Tiff. Going into sixth grade next month. She's the only one left now.'

'You mean they already lost one child?' Maggie hadn't known.

'Yeah. Teresa. Terri. Their first-born. Beautiful girl. Even prettier 'n Tiff. Always a hell-raiser like her old man. Tiff had some of that in her too. Like the old song goes, "Born to Be Wild". Now they're both dead.'

Jesus. Two out of three kids gone. This was going to be even harder than she thought. 'What happened to Terri?'

Boucher looked away and exhaled long and slow. It was obviously a story he didn't like telling. 'Motorcycle accident that was her father's fault. Pike used to tear-ass around here on this big black Harley he brought back from the marines. Always tinkering with it. Bike was his first love. Anyway, he's out riding one summer night, June I think it was, three years ago. Terri's on the back, arms around her old man. Neither one of 'em's wearing a helmet. Pike takes a blind curve way too fast. Meets a truck coming the other way. Trying to avoid a collision, he skids out and just misses slamming into a tree. Terri flies off and hits the tree head-first. Killed her instantly. I was the first responder that night and I've got to tell you seeing that beautiful girl lying there with her brains splattered all over the road and knowing there was not a goddamn thing me or anyone else could do about it, well, that was one of the worst sights I've ever seen. Later, going around to the house and having to tell Donelda her daughter was dead and her husband, who was on a helicopter heading down to Bangor, was responsible for it, well, that was one of the hardest.'

'What happened to Pike?'

'For better or worse, he didn't hit the tree. Just the stone wall behind it. Ended up with a severe spinal injury. Paralyzed from the waist down. Gonna be confined to a wheelchair the rest of his life. Donelda's been angry at Pike and Pike's been angry at the world ever since. Blames the truck driver for what happened. Blames the doctors. Even blames the tree and the stone wall. Blames everybody but himself. But the truth of the matter is the whole damn thing was his fault and Donelda won't ever let him forget it. I figure somewhere deep down inside he gotta know she's right. He was way over the limit ...'

'Speed or alcohol?'

'Both. He never should have been riding that night. Especially not with his first-born on the back. I can't imagine how much guilt that man must be carrying around.'

'He do any hard time for that?'

Boucher shook his head. 'No, but he should have. Judge let him off with a suspended sentence. I guess because of the paralysis and maybe because he figured the man suffered enough killing his own daughter. I'll tell you it's a terrible thing to lose even one child, let alone two, even for a natural born sonofabitch like Pike Stoddard. All I can say is you've got one nasty day ahead of you.'

'What do they do for a living?'

'Pike used to be a fisherman. Mostly scallops and lobster, which is pretty much all that's left around here. Few fish when he can find them. Still owns a thirty-five-footer named the *Katie Louise* after his mother. Used to captain her himself but since the accident he's had to hire crew. Pays 'em like most owners do with a split of the catch. But there's not many that like to work for him. Pike's an angry man. Angry and suspicious. Always accusing his crews of trying to under-report. Cheat him out of money. As a result he usually ends up with the bottom of the barrel. Guys nobody else wants to hire. Barely makes enough to cover his loans. Donelda makes a few bucks digging for winkles and bloodworms. Paints watercolors to sell to the tourists. Picks up winter work where she can. Mostly making Christmas wreaths. It's a hard living.'

'Tiff know how to handle the boat?'

Boucher shrugged. 'Grew up on it. I'd be surprised if she didn't.'

'Pike ever had any other trouble with the law? Before the accident, I mean.'

'Sporadic. I personally hauled his ass out of bars a few times back in the day. Mostly for being drunk and obnoxious and for beating people up. From what I hear, he still drinks a lot but mostly at home and mostly alone. Now he's stuck in the wheelchair Donnie's got him where she wants him. Poor sonofabitch can't even take a crap without her helping him. My guess is she makes what's left of Pike's life a whole lot more miserable than any jail cell would have.'

'How about the kids? Any history of drug use?'

'Tabbie's a little young. Tiff? I don't know. You can usually tell the addicts. Look undernourished 'cause they'd rather snort or shoot up than eat. Have that haunted look in their eyes. Tiff never looked that way. Anyway,

I always thought Tiff was too smart to get involved with Ox. Wild, yes, but smart too. Street smarts, anyway.'

'How about Tabitha? You know anything about her?'

A big sigh from Boucher. 'Yes, I do. My wife Alma's taught all three of the Stoddard girls each in their turn. According to her, Tabbie's a totally different story from the other two. Terms of looks she got the short end of the stick. Kind of nerdy looking. Wears these big round glasses. Quiet. Not many friends. Always felt sorry for Tabitha marching through life behind a pair of drop-dead beauties like Terri and Tiff, knowing she was never gonna measure up to either one of them.'

'Maybe it's a blessing,' said Maggie.

Boucher nodded. 'I take your point. Long as what happened to her sisters doesn't screw her up too much.'

Chapter Twelve

9:36 A.M., Saturday, August 22, 2009
Eastport, Maine

MAGGIE HAD NO trouble finding Pike and Donelda Stoddard's house at 190 Perry Road. A plain, grey-shingled Cape with a red front door set off by itself on a quiet road. Blinds on the windows either side of the door were drawn. One had a couple of broken slats. Flowerbeds looked weedy and uncared for. A 'For sale by owner' sign on the front lawn looked like it had been there a while, a phone number magic-markered underneath. Were the Stoddards trying to sell because they needed money? Or because they wanted to get out of town?

On the left side of a patchy lawn an American flag hung limply from a white pole. Below the stars and stripes, a bright red flag, its Marine Corps globe and anchor hidden in the folds of the fabric. A ten-year-old Jeep Cherokee Sport sat in the dirt-and-gravel driveway.

The car had a handicap symbol on its plates and a bumper sticker Maggie had seen often enough before stuck on the rear hatch. It read 'National Marine Fisheries Service: Destroying Fishermen and their Communities since 1976.' A bitter but in some ways true sentiment that was shared by just about every Maine fishing family she knew.

Before going in to face the Stoddards, Maggie called McCabe. There was bound to be press coverage, her name might be mentioned, and she didn't want him blindsided by events. He picked up on the second ring. 'Hiya, Mag. What's up?'

Maggie could hear a chatter of voices and some music playing in the background. 'Where are you?' she asked.

'Down at Lou's place, having brunch.'

Lou's place was Tallulah's, McCabe's favorite Portland watering hole. A big comfortable bar and restaurant halfway down Munjoy Hill with oversized booths separated by tall dividers, great steaks, good burgers and a big enough selection of single malts for McCabe to sample a different one every day for a month, which is exactly what he did when he first started going there. McCabe always said walking into Lou's place after arriving in Portland and seeing all those bottles was one of the first things that convinced him that he, a born and bred New Yorker, could be happy making a new life in a small city in Maine.

'A little early for you to be out and about, isn't it?' asked Maggie. At 9:30 on a Saturday morning, when he wasn't working, she half expected that McCabe would be still in bed. Probably, with his girlfriend Kyra.

'Too damn hot to sleep last night,' he said. 'Too hot this morning. Kyra's away so Casey and I came down here for some cheese omelets and a little cool air.' Casey was McCabe's drop-dead gorgeous sixteen-year-old daughter. Wanting someplace more kid-friendly than the mean streets of Manhattan to bring her up was a big part of why he'd moved to Maine in the first place. 'Why don't you come on down and join us?' he asked. 'Your apartment's got to be even hotter than mine.'

'I'd love to. Unfortunately, I'm working. I also happen to be about four hours away.'

'Really? Where? Working on what?'

Maggie told him about the middle-of-the-night call from her father. About Stoddard's murder and Blakemore's. She also told him about the injury to Emily. McCabe had met Em a number of times and liked her a lot.

He listened without comment as she described the details of what had gone down in the parking area of Machias State Park and about her conversation with Sergeant Sean Carroll of the Maine State Police.

'What's Carroll like?'

'Don't really know. Aside from being way too handsome for his own good.'

'I see. And Sergeant Handsome agreed to let you help?'

'He agreed. But just through Monday. After that it's on a let's see what happens basis. I may want to put in for some vacation days next week, assuming you'll approve them.'

McCabe didn't answer immediately. Seemed to be considering what she'd told him about the killings.

'Okay,' he finally said. 'I'll let the higher-ups know what you're doing. Not that much going on at the moment so they should be okay with it.' He told her he and Cleary could handle the arraignment of Kyle Carnes. If anything else came up, he'd do his best to cover for her. Or, if necessary, let her know it was time to come back to Portland.

'One last thing,' he said. 'Did Carroll assign you a partner or you gonna be working up there on your own?'

'Supposedly directly with and for Carroll. Whether he's going to hang back and play supervisor or get down in the weeds and work with me is still unclear.'

McCabe waited a beat. She could tell he wasn't happy with her answer. 'I see,' he finally said. 'In that case I want you to give me a call if things start getting hairy.'

'Not necessary, McCabe.'

'Necessary. I'm not crazy about you being the new kid on the block working alone in what sounds like it could be a dangerous situation.'

'I'll be fine,' Maggie insisted. 'I have no intention of dragging you into this.'

'No dragging required. Just let me know and I'll be there in a heartbeat. You'd do the same for me.'

She didn't argue. He was right. She would.

No cop ever volunteers for next of kin notification. There's never an easy way to tell someone their husband or wife or especially their child is dead. All the standard phrases – 'I'm sorry for your loss', 'She didn't suffer very much', 'She's probably in a better place' – no matter how sincere, always come out sounding wooden and rehearsed. Given the tragedies the Stoddard family had already suffered, this NOK promised to be one of the worst.

The only response to Maggie's knocking on the Stoddards' door was a series of deep-throated barks. She knocked again. The barking got louder. She was debating going around back when the door opened a crack. The black and tan muzzle of a big Rottweiler pushed into the crack, its barking replaced by a low, threatening growl. Above the dog's head, at wheelchair height, a pair of dark, suspicious eyes and a gaunt, white face.

'Pike Stoddard?'

'Who wants to know?'

Maggie held up her Portland shield and ID. 'Detective Margaret Savage,' she said.

'Portland?'

'I'm on special assignment with the state police.'

'Savage, huh? You related to the Sheriff?'

'I'm his daughter.'

'Jesus,' Stoddard snorted. 'Another Savage. How many damn Savages they got down there in Machias? All right, Sheriff's daughter, what do you want?'

'May I come in?'

'No. Not unless you tell me what the hell you want.'

Stoddard was making this tougher than it had to be.

'Is your wife home?'

'What do you want her for?'

'I'd like to talk to you both at the same time.'

Pike Stoddard's eyes narrowed suspiciously. He ordered the dog to lie down and shut up. The animal obeyed and Stoddard opened the door an inch or so wider.

'What's all this about?'

'Please. May I come in? It's something I'd rather not discuss on the steps.'

He peered at her for a few seconds more, then reversed his motorized chair, pulled the door open and waved her in.

Boucher had told her Stoddard was in his late forties. That'd make him about the same age as Billy Webb. A few years older than her brother Trev. He looked ten years older than either. Grey stubble added to the impression of age.

'Come in, if you're coming.'

'He's okay with that?' Maggie cocked her head toward the dog, which hadn't taken its eyes off her.

'He's a she, name's Electra and she does what she's told. You don't want to mess with her but she won't go for you unless I tell her to.'

Maggie walked into a room furnished with the kind of living-room set you saw advertised on cable TV. *All five pieces just $999!* Only this set was old, dirty and beat up. Tightly closed blinds covered every window. Dozens of cheaply framed watercolors, mostly seascapes, many showing the red and white striped lighthouse at Quoddy Head State Park, leaned two and three deep against the walls. Half a dozen more hung on display. Donelda Stoddard's stock in trade, she supposed.

'All right, lady detective, what's this all about?'

'It's about your daughter Tiffany.'

'What about Tiff?'

'Is your wife here?'

'Hasn't been in an accident has she? She done something wrong?'

'I need to talk to both of you.'

'Oh, for chrissake.' He rolled to the bottom of the stairs. A chair elevator was installed on the banister. Stoddard's wife probably had to lift him on to it every time he went up or down. 'Hey, Donnie,' he shouted. No answer.

'Jesus Christ, damn woman's deaf as a post. Donnie,' he shouted again, this time louder.

'What?' An irritated female voice from upstairs.

'Get the hell down here. Some cop's here. From Portland. Needs to talk to us about Tiff.'

'Aw, shit, what now? All right, give me a minute. Just got out of the shower. I gotta get dressed.'

Pike Stoddard turned to Maggie. 'Look, why don't you just tell me what you've gotta tell me?'

'I'd rather talk to you both at the same time,' said Maggie, wondering if she was going to be able to do what she came to do. Not only inform the Stoddards of the death of their daughter but, since Pike Stoddard owned a boat more than capable of making the run to Saint John, also probe for their possible involvement in it.

Stoddard rolled back into the living room. Sat silently looking at Maggie, who busied herself looking at a few old family photos hanging on the wall. One shot was of Stoddard's three daughters, aged maybe eighteen, fifteen and five. They were standing on the deck of a red-hulled lobster boat. Terri and Tiff on either side, wearing waterproofs, and the youngest, Tabitha, the afterthought kid, standing in the middle, wearing thick glasses, short shorts and a t-shirt. A pre-accident Pike stood behind them, a hand on his two older daughters' shoulders.

'Girls ever work on the boat?'

'Time to time when I was active. Not scalloping. Summers mostly when they were out of school, I'd take 'em out lobstering.'

'Know how to handle her?'

'They could handle her well enough. Taught all three of them the basics. Terri was never all that interested. Tabitha's still a little young. Tiff is the knowledgeable one. Knows her way around a boat damn near as well as I do. Knows her way around an engine too.'

Another photo showed a much younger Pike Stoddard, perched on a shiny black Harley. A pretty young woman with long, dark hair was holding on from behind, arms wrapped around Pike's middle. Pike looked happier, at least less angry, and much, much younger.

'Who are you and what do you want?' A woman's voice behind her.

Maggie turned to see an older, painfully thin version of Tiffany Stoddard standing on the bottom step, eyeing her. Donelda's mostly grey hair, still wet from her shower, hung limply below her waist. She was dressed in loose jeans and an oversized men's shirt spattered with paint stains.

'Can we sit down?' Maggie asked.

'You're a police officer?'

'That's right. Detective Margaret Savage. I'm on assignment with the state police.'

The suspicion in Donelda's eyes morphed into fear. Strange, Maggie thought. Somehow people always knew. Maybe not the specifics. But they always knew when you came to tell them something terrible had happened. 'I'm afraid I have some bad news.'

Donelda put a hand out and steadied herself on the banister. 'Is she dead? Is that what you're here to tell me? Another one of my babies is dead?'

Maggie took a deep breath. Nodded. 'Yes. I'm very sorry.'

Tiff Stoddard's mother closed her eyes, breathed in and out slowly a couple of times, then opened them again. She nodded almost imperceptibly. 'What happened?' she asked in a small voice. 'Tell me what happened.'

'Please sit down. Mrs Stoddard?'

'I don't damn well want to sit down,' she said, her voice suddenly harsh and angry. 'Just tell me what happened to my daughter!'

Maggie had to wait a couple of beats before she could get the words out. 'She was murdered.'

The thread that was barely holding Donelda Stoddard together broke. Her face crumpled in on itself. She slid to a sitting position on the bottom stair and covered it with her hands.

'Her body was found early this morning lying next to her car in the parking area of Machias State Park,' said Maggie. 'She was stabbed to death sometime earlier. Probably late last night.'

She heard Pike's voice behind her. Quiet. Trying to hold in any emotion he felt. 'You're sure the person you found was Tiff?'

'We're sure. We found her backpack and wallet with photo ID next to the body. Her car was parked a few feet away.'

A harsh primal sound, something between a sob and a guttural wail, heaved from the depths of Donelda's body. She wrapped her arms around herself and began rocking back and forth.

Maggie started toward her, the urge to comfort nearly overwhelming.

Donelda sensed the approach without looking up. She held up one shaky hand. A signal for this stranger, this messenger of death, to come no further. 'You stay away from me.'

Pike sat motionless as if any verbal or physical expression of emotion was beyond him. Just sat in his chair staring first at Maggie, then at Donelda. Grief? Anger? Fear? Maggie wasn't sure what she saw in his eyes. Neither husband nor wife looked at each other. Neither made any attempt to comfort the other. Maggie could see no sign of affection here. No relationship. Pike and Donelda seemed to be nothing more than two strangers cohabiting a common space. Fellow passengers completing the wretched journey of their lives alone.

'Where is she now?' asked Donelda. 'Where's Tiff ? Where have you got her?'

'Her body was taken to the medical examiner's lab in Augusta early this morning. An autopsy is required by law. When the autopsy's complete, Tiff's remains will be returned to you for whatever service you and your husband plan.'

'All cut up like a gutted fish?'

'They'll do what they can to restore her for burial but an open coffin's probably not a good idea.'

'I see. Okay,' said Donelda.

A minute or two passed. No one spoke.

'I'm so sorry for your loss,' Maggie finally said. Stupid inadequate words that tumbled out only because Maggie felt a need to break the suffocating thickness of silence. *I'm so sorry for your loss.* Just words. But somehow words seemed better than silence. 'I'm so very sorry.'

Pike rolled his chair over to a sideboard. Found a glass. Poured some whiskey and drank it down fast. Offered none to his wife. 'Who did it?' he asked. 'Who killed her?'

Donelda looked up, her face red and twisted with crying. She shook her head. The look she gave her husband was one of pure hatred.

Pike poured himself another whiskey.

Chapter Thirteen

'HAVE YOU CAUGHT him?' Pike Stoddard asked again. 'Have you caught the bastard who killed my daughter?' He swallowed the remains of his second whiskey of the morning.

'No, not yet,' said Maggie. 'It would help if I could ask you two some questions.'

'Now?' asked Donelda, looking up, her eyes red and tearful. 'You march in here and tell us our daughter's been murdered and you want to ask us questions? Interrogate us? Now?'

'Now would be the best time.'

'Look, lady, why don't you just ask your questions some other time,' said Pike.

'I'm sorry, Mr Stoddard. Pike. I understand how you feel. But trust me when I say we have a much better chance of finding Tiff's killer if we don't wait until "some other time".'

Pike started to protest again but Donelda held up a hand to silence him and nodded her assent.

Since both Stoddards were possible suspects in the drug-smuggling scheme, standard police procedure would have been to first interview them separately, then maybe bring them together. Under the circumstances, Maggie didn't think that was an option. She turned on a small digital recording device and started with some general questions. 'Tell me about Tiff,' she said. 'What kind of person was she? What did she want out of life?'

'The first thing to know about her is she wanted to get the hell out of Eastport,' said Donelda. 'What you've got to understand about this town is there just isn't much here any more for a young person. It's real pretty. Real picturesque. But there are no jobs. No future. We've got summer people buying up some of the houses on the water but they mostly take off after Labor Day and that's about it.'

'Okay, Tiff wanted out, I get that. But what was she looking for?'

'What she called the good life. First one in this family to even think about going to college. She talked sometimes about becoming a TV news reporter. Or maybe selling pharmaceuticals. Said a smart, good-looking female could make a lot of money doing either of those things.'

Selling pharmaceuticals? It was kind of hard letting that go by without comment but Maggie did.

'Mr Stoddard, Pike, you told me earlier Tiff handled your boat, I think your phrase was "pretty damn near as well as I did".'

'Yeah, so?'

'Did Tiff ever ask to borrow the boat? Use it when maybe you weren't?'

Pike eyed Maggie warily. 'Use it herself? Nah, not really. Why?'

'Not really? Or not ever?'

'Not ever. Why?'

Maggie ignored the question. 'Can you tell me where your boat was last January? Let's say from the sixth to the eighth?'

Pike eyed Maggie suspiciously before answering. 'Where it should have been in the middle of scallop season,' said Pike. 'Out scalloping.'

'You got a regular captain?'

'Old mate of mine. Guy named Luke Haskell. Luke picks up whatever crew he needs.'

'And Haskell had your boat in January?'

'That's right.'

'It's a pretty quick run from here to Saint John, isn't it?'

'What are you getting at, detective?' asked Donelda.

'We have reason to believe Tiff or maybe someone Tiff knew took a boat to Saint John and back in the first half of January. I wondered if maybe it was your boat. And if it wasn't Tiff who took it, I wondered if maybe you rented the *Katie Louise* to someone else.'

'No,' Pike said. 'I wouldn't rent my boat out. Certainly not to someone I didn't know.'

'How about to someone you did know? Or Tiff knew?' asked Maggie.

'No. Not to anyone. Lot of insurance and licensing issues. Get in a heap of trouble that way.'

'So you're sure it was Luke Haskell who took your boat out in January to go scalloping?'

'Yeah, I'm sure. Go ask him yourself. He'll tell you.'

'You have Haskell's number?'

He gave it to her. She wrote it down.

'Luke'll be out on the water now. Hauling lobster. Ought to be in this afternoon. Three, four o'clock. When he's done unloading he usually heads straight for a dive called Dirty Annie's.'

'Where's he sleep?'

Pike shrugged. 'Sometimes with Annie if she happens to be in the mood. Otherwise on the *Katie Louise*. Specially in summer.'

'Let me ask you something, Pike,' said Maggie. 'What if somebody offered you money, let's say a whole lot of money, to rent – or maybe *borrow* would be a better word – to borrow your boat? Then maybe offered you more money to keep your mouth shut about it. What would you say to that? Hell, I'd understand if you said okay. Times are tough, money's hard to come by. Why not take a little easy cash?'

'I don't rent out the *Katie Louise*. Or let anyone borrow her either.'

'You're sure of that?'

'I'm sure.'

'Y'know, I'm sorry to hear you say that, Mr Stoddard,' said Maggie, wondering if she could bluff another story out of him.

'Yeah? Why's that?'

'Because just this morning somebody who seemed to know what they were talking about told us that you *did* rent out your boat. Now if that somebody was right ...' Maggie put her hands on either side of Pike's wheelchair, leaned down so she was only inches away and looked straight into his frightened face, 'and if you'd be willing to tell me who it was you rented it to, well, we just might have the key to finding out who the sonofabitch was who beat the shit out of your beautiful daughter and then picked up a great big knife and slashed open her neck like a hog in a slaughterhouse.'

'You get out of my house.'

The dog looked up, alerted by the anger in Stoddard's voice. Maggie's hand slid to her Glock but otherwise she ignored the animal. 'What do you say, Pike? Are you going to tell me the truth? Or not?'

'I already told you. I didn't rent the boat. I don't rent the boat. I would never even consider renting out the goddamned boat.'

'You lying bastard,' Donelda Stoddard said, staring across at her husband. 'You did it, didn't you? You went ahead and did it. First you killed Terri. And now you've killed Tiff as well.'

'You shut the fuck up,' Stoddard snarled at his wife. 'You don't know what you're talking about. And you,' he said to Maggie, 'you get the fuck out of my house.'

Maggie looked at the two of them: first Pike, then Donelda. Then she looked over to the staircase and saw a child, Tabitha Stoddard, peeking down and, no doubt, listening to every word. Maggie wondered how much she'd heard.

'What about it, Donelda? Pike says you don't know what you're talking about. But you do, don't you?'

'I know now,' said Donelda. 'And if he doesn't have the balls to tell you, I will.'

'I'm listening.'

Donelda spoke in a voice choked by the effort to hold back tears. A voice Maggie had to strain to hear.

'It was December twenty-first. Four days before Christmas. I was working late over at Wiley's. Packing and shipping the last of the wreaths for this year. I remember the date because the twenty-first, long as it's not a Sunday, is the last day we can ship wreaths if people want them in time for the holiday, and we're always in a rush to get them packed before the UPS guy makes his last run.

'Anyway, I got home about ten o'clock and Tiff's car was in the driveway. I was pleased because I figured she'd come home early for the holiday and maybe we'd get to spend some time together. Tiff's always making out like she's got something more important to do.

'I walk in and they're both sitting here. Pike where he is now and Tiff on the couch next to him. As usual, he's drinking whiskey. She's drinking something else. Coffee brandy, I think. They both stop talking soon as I walk through the door.

'"What's going on?" I ask Pike.

'"Nothing," he says. "We're just talking about what to get you for Christmas."

'Well, a three-year-old would've known that was bullshit, 'specially the way he said it, so I ask them again what's going on.

'"Go ahead, tell her," says Tiff. "The boat's half hers."

'So Pike looks me square in the eye and says Tiff wants him, us, to lend the *Katie Louise* to somebody for a week or so.

'"*Lend* the *Katie Louise*?" I say. "In the middle of scallop season?"

'"Yeah."

'"To *somebody*?"

'"Yeah."

'"Somebody who?"

'"This guy she knows. Conor something," says Pike.

'"Conor being his first name or last name?" I ask.

'"His first name," Tiff tells me. "Last name's Riordan. Conor Riordan. He's a friend of mine," she says. "Somebody we can trust."

'"And what's this Conor Riordan want our boat for?" I ask. "Scalloping?"

'She laughs at that. "No," she says. "He's not interested in scalloping. He just needs a boat. But you can't say anything about it to anybody. Can't breathe a word."

'"Oh yeah?" I say. "Some guy named Conor Riordan needs a boat. Our boat. What for? Pleasure cruising off the coast of Maine in the middle of January? Jesus, Tiff, you must think we're nuts. Or maybe stupid. Why in hell would we lend an 80,000 dollar boat to some guy we've never met and is probably up to no good?"

'"Because," says Pike. "He's willing to pay us 10,000 dollars cash for one lousy week. No crew split. No taxes. No nothing."

'"Ten thousand up front?"

'"Up front. And another 2,000 a day every day he needs her beyond the week. Plus another 10,000 cash security deposit we only give back to him when he brings the boat back undamaged. Shit, Donelda, we can live for six fucking months on 10,000 cash. How many fucking bloodworms you have to pull for that kind of money? How many lighthouses you have to paint? Jesus woman, use your fucking head."

'"Ten thousand dollars? Twenty with the deposit? Boat's worth four times that," I tell them. "What if he just takes off with it? Never comes back?"

'"He's not gonna do that. I told you. He's a friend of mine," says Tiff.

'"Yeah. Fine. He's a friend of yours. What if this *friend* never comes back?"

'"Boat's insured," says Pike. "We just report her stolen. Get the insured value on top of the twenty and blow the hell out of here. Go down to the Keys, sit in the sunshine and forget about the whole damn thing."

'"You got it all planned out, don't you, Pike?" I say.

'"Yeah. Something like that."

'"But you weren't planning to tell me?"

'"No. Because I knew you'd fuck it up. Just like you fuck up everything else."

'"And if the boat disappears you think the insurance company's just gonna hand you a check for 80,000 dollars without conducting an investigation? You think they're that stupid? Are you that stupid?"

'"Nothing's gonna happen, Ma," says Tiff. "Conor's a good guy and he knows what he's doing."

'"And how would you know that?"

'"Because I took him out on her today and, trust me, he knows what he's doing."

'"I suppose you're sleeping with this Conor guy. Screwing him?"

'"No. No, of course not," she says. Tiff tells me this all wide-eyed and innocent like I'm supposed to think she's some kind of virgin.

"Bullshit," I said.

'"Okay," she says. "Fine. You're right. I'm screwing him up one side of the bed and down the other. Just like you were screwing Pa five minutes after you rode into town. But you know something else? This deal has nothing to do with sex. It's strictly a business deal. Ten thousand cash for you guys, maybe more. And you don't have to do a thing to get it except not ask any more questions. Take it or leave it, 'cause there are other boats in Maine and this conversation's going nowhere." '

'What did you do?' asked Maggie.

'Well,' said Donelda, 'I've got to admit it was tempting. Ten thousand may not be a lot of money to some people. Maybe some of the tourists down in Bar Harbor spend that much for a two-week vacation. But it'd mean a hell of a lot to us. But it was too damned obvious this Conor guy was up to no good. He wanted the boat for something illegal. My guess was smuggling drugs 'cause that's what everybody around here who wants to make money's into these days. It's about the only big-money business left in Washington County. Drugs and blueberries, and everyone knows drugs are a whole lot more profitable. I didn't want anything to do with it. It struck me as stupider than shit to get involved in something illegal with some guy we never even met and who, for all we knew, was working some kind of sting for the DEA. Boat's half mine. So I said no.'

'You said no?' asked Maggie.

'Yeah. Pike argued with me for a while. Tiff bitched and moaned. But I said no and Pike finally said okay, just forget it. Forget the whole fucking thing. Told me I was right anyway. Said he hadn't considered the possibility of a sting.'

'So, that was that?'

'Or so I thought. I thought Pike was gonna tell the guy to get lost. But you know what? I was wrong. I just figured it out. My asshole husband's got 10,000 bucks salted away somewhere and I've got nothing. Not even my second daughter. 'Cause now he's gone and killed the two of them.'

Donelda started weeping again. Great heaving sobs. Then she rose and walked to Pike's chair and smacked him as hard as she could across the face. He sat there and took it. 'This, you fucker, is for lying to me.'

She smacked him again. 'This is for killing Terri.'

Smacked him a third time. 'And this one is for Tiff.'

Donelda turned and went up the stairs.

'Anything you'd like to add to that?' Maggie asked Pike.

'Only that what you just heard is pure bullshit. Yes, Tiff came here with this offer and yes I was tempted. But when Donnie said no that was that. And that's all I've got to say to you. Now unless you want to arrest me for the fantasies my wife just dreamed up, I want you out of my house.'

'Listen, Pike. I don't care about the boat. Or the drugs. All I'm interested in is finding the guy who killed your daughter. And if you want to help me do that, just tell me what this Riordan guy looked like. And maybe where I can find him.'

'Never laid eyes on him. Never called him on the phone. Never asked Tiff about it.' Pike Stoddard wheeled to the door and opened it, 'Now get your ass out of my house before I sic the dog on you.'

Maggie pulled out a card. Wrote her cell number on it and left it on a table near the door.

'You or Donelda have a cell number?'

'Yeah, like that's all we need. An extra expense.'

'I want you to search your memory, Pike, and your conscience. Search them very hard and make sure you're telling me the truth because, whoever Conor Riordan is, I'm willing to bet he's the guy who killed your daughter. The number I wrote on that card is my private number. Any information you provide will be just between us. Nobody else need ever know.'

'Lady, I think I just told you to get out of my house.'

'One more thing before I leave,' said Maggie. 'Don't you ever threaten a police officer with that animal again or you'll find yourself behind bars before you know what hit you.'

Maggie glanced up and saw Tabitha sitting motionless on the stairs, staring at her through thick, round lenses. She looked at the child and felt a quiet sorrow for what her life must be like. What it would be like from now on. Then she left.

Chapter Fourteen

1:16 P.M., Saturday, August 22, 2009
Bangor, Maine

'WHAT ARE YOU doing here?' Emily asked without opening her eyes.

'Holding your hand.' Maggie squeezed. Em squeezed back. 'How'd you know it was me?'

'I always know when you're around.'

'I came to visit you. See how you're doing.'

'How long have you been here?'

'This visit?'

'Yeah.'

'About five minutes. Hospital called late this morning. Told me you'd woken up. You were sleeping when I arrived but they said it was just sleep.'

'You were here before?'

'Yes. Last night after they brought you in. You look great compared to how you looked then.' Maggie was only lying a little.

'Well, I feel pretty shitty, I can tell you that.' Emily's voice was little more than a raspy whisper. 'Collins tells me I'm doing remarkably well. No fractured skull and my intracranial pressure's back to normal. The fact I still understand what intracranial pressure is is a pretty good sign there's no brain damage. As for the rest of it, two cracked ribs and about 900 scrapes and bruises. Still, I don't think I've ever taken such a shellacking in my life. Remember that time when we were twelve and Danny LaBouisse tripped me and I fell down a whole flight of stairs at school?'

'Of course I remember,' said Maggie. 'I punched the little bastard out. Probably the most embarrassing moment in his life. Being beaten up by a girl. In front of all his friends no less.'

Em tried to smile but smiling hurt. 'Well, the pain from that wasn't even close to how much this one hurts.'

'Can't they give you something?'

'Anything strong enough to be effective will make my brain fuzzy. I'd rather be clear-headed and put up with the pain. The worst thing right now is, hard as I try, I can't remember the thirty seconds or so before I went down. I remember the girl screaming. Then the screaming stopped and someone was running for the car. Then it all goes blank.'

'He hit you. Drove the car right at you. He wanted to kill you. Guess he thought he did.'

'It's weird but I have no recollection of that at all. I'm familiar with the syndrome. It's called retrograde amnesia and its common enough among people who've suffered traumatic concussion. Still it's weird when it happens to you. It's like there's this black hole in your mind.'

'Will your memory come back?'

'Sometimes it does. Not always, but sometimes. What happened to the girl? Did he kill her?'

Maggie looked down at her friend a long minute before answering. 'Yeah. He killed her all right.'

'How?'

'With a knife.' Maggie left it at that. Em didn't need the gruesome details. At least not yet.

'Killed her.' Emily repeated the words and shook her head as if analyzing their meaning. After that she just lay there for a couple of minutes studying the ceiling. 'I could have saved her, you know. Should have.'

'Don't be stupid. How could you have saved her?'

'Dozen different ways. I could've grabbed her and tied her up and kept her from leaving the office.'

'That's called kidnapping.'

'Better than having her murdered.'

'You didn't know that was going to happen.'

'Even after she left, if I hadn't wasted time looking for the pills and had just run a little faster. Or if I hadn't alerted the guy by yelling and screaming for him to stop. Just run up silently and whacked him one instead.'

'Then he might have killed you as well. He had a knife.'

'Maybe. He tried to kill me anyway.'

'Yes, he did. But you can't blame yourself for what he did to Stoddard. It wasn't your fault.'

'I could have saved her.'

Maggie shook her head. It was just like Emily to think she could fix anything. That it was her job to save the world and everyone in it.

'You know,' said Emily. 'The girl, Tiffany Stoddard, told me he was going to kill her. At first I didn't believe her. But then, when I saw how scared she was, I did. I just didn't think it would happen so soon.'

'Did she tell you who the guy was? The one who was going to kill her?'

'No, nothing. Not her name. Not his. Not where she lived. The only reason I know those things is I broke every rule in the book and looked in her backpack. Checked the ID in her wallet and saw the pills. Did they find the pills?'

'Yeah. In your pocket.'

'Great. If any of this stuff gets out I could be looking for a job. And not as a doctor.'

'Let's just say there were extenuating circumstances.'

'Where are the pills now?' asked Emily.

'In an evidence locker in Machias. Maybe you better tell me how they ended up in your pocket. In fact, maybe you better tell me the whole story.'

'Are you asking as a friend or as a cop?'

'Does it matter?'

'Not really. I just wondered.'

'The answer is both. The state police have jurisdiction. I'm helping out on a semi-official basis.'

'Okay. What are your questions?'

'How often do you prescribe Oxycontin?'

Emily shook her head. 'Hardly ever. I can check my records, but I'll bet it hasn't been over half a dozen times over the last four years. And I don't give refills. Not in Washington County. Too easy for people to abuse.'

'Okay, good.'

'What else?'

Remembering Carroll's words, *you know there are doctors who break the law,* Maggie said, 'I need you to remember where you were on the night of January sixth. Other cops might be asking you that.'

'January sixth? What happened January sixth?'

Maggie ignored the question. 'It was the Wednesday after the New Year's weekend.'

Emily gave it a few seconds thought but no more. 'That's easy then. First Wednesday every month I go to a book group at the Porter Library. The book was *Cutting for Stone* by a writer named Abraham Verghese. Since I suggested it, I led the discussion.'

'How many people saw you there?'

'Probably seven or eight.'

Maggie asked for the names and wrote them down. 'Okay, now why don't you tell me what happened last night? Everything you remember.'

'Where do you want me to start?'

'The beginning.'

Emily pointed to a pitcher on her side table. 'There's some ice chips over there. Can you get me a cupful of them?'

Maggie handed Em the plastic cup. She put a few of the bigger chips in her mouth and began to suck. After she'd swallowed a few, she began. 'Okay. It started when I first saw Tiffany Stoddard.'

'When was that?'

'Around eight o'clock last night.' For the next twenty minutes Emily took Maggie through the whole story. How the young woman had come in to the office, her face beaten and battered. What she looked like. What she was wearing. How Em checked her bruises and reset her broken nose. How she wouldn't tell Em her name or where she had come from or who had beaten her up.

'Did you ask her why she wouldn't give you any of that information?'

'She said if she told me any of it, the guy who beat her up would probably kill her. Then she corrected herself. Said there was no probably about it. He would definitely kill her. And he would kill me too.'

'She used those words? Kill her? Kill you?'

'Yeah. At first I thought she was exaggerating. But she said it with such intensity I figured maybe it was true and somebody really had threatened to kill her.'

'What happened then?'

'She told me she was pregnant.'

'Wait a minute,' Maggie interrupted. 'Tiffany Stoddard was pregnant?'

'Said she was. I never had a chance to check but she said she missed her period and a home pregnancy test turned up positive. Told me the real reason she came to see me wasn't because of the beating but because she wanted me to terminate the pregnancy.'

'As far as I know you don't do abortions.'

'No, but very occasionally, I have prescribed drugs that terminate early-stage pregnancies. Somehow Stoddard knew about it.'

'How?'

'She said a friend told her. Told her to come see me.'

'What friend?'

'I asked. She wouldn't tell me that either.'

Maggie held up one hand. 'Hold on a second would you?' she said. She found her phone and speed dialed Terri Mirabito's cell. Mirabito was one of the Assistant Medical Examiners for the state of Maine. She was also a good friend.

'Hi, Mag, what's up?'

'You doing the autopsy on the kid they brought in this morning? Tiffany Stoddard?'

'Yup. That'd be me. Heard you were working with the staties on that one.'

'Yeah? Heard it from who?'

'Emmett Ganzer. He didn't sound real pleased.'

'Well, that's his problem,' she said. 'When are you cutting?'

'Early tomorrow morning. First thing. How can I help you?'

'I just found out Stoddard may have been pregnant.'

'Couldn't be very pregnant.'

'It's early stage. Maybe six weeks.'

'Interesting. You think it's the daddy-to-be who offed her?'

'Yeah, maybe. Listen, if there's a fetus in there, can you get the DNA reads as fast as possible?'

'All I can do is alert Joe Pines. Try to light a fire under him.' Pines was the DNA guy at the state lab in Augusta. 'You have any suspect matches for Joe to check them against? Any idea who she was having sex with?'

'Not yet, but I'm working on it. Plus we may get a hit out of CODIS. I think the guy may be a sex offender.'

CODIS, or the Combined DNA Index System, was an FBI-controlled database that kept DNA profiles of all sexual offenders in the United States as well as most other criminals convicted of a felony.

'Sex offender? Jesus, Maggie, based on what he did to this kid I'd love to personally cut his balls off. And I don't mean after he's dead.' Maggie had never heard Terri sound so angry about wounds inflicted on a victim. 'This creep used his knife like a substitute penis. Must have gone in and out of her twenty times. I'm just wondering if he actually came.'

'Any signs of ejaculate?'

'Not on her body or clothes. And trust me I looked. But maybe Heinrich ought to double-check the killing zone. Fucker might still have been dripping as he ran to his car.'

Terri took a deep breath to calm down before continuing. 'I'll also have Joe check if the fetal reads match any foreign DNA I find on Stoddard's body. If we get a match with fetal, that'll at least tell us if the killer and the father are the same guy. How's Kaplan doing?'

'Other than looking like she just went fifteen rounds with Mike Tyson, pretty damn well. Awake and alert. She's the one who told me about the pregnancy.'

'Okay. Good. I'll give you a call soon as I know.'

'Thanks, Terri.'

Maggie broke the connection. 'Okay, first order of business. Who knew you prescribed these drugs? Maybe told Stoddard about them?'

'Lord, I don't know. Like I said, I've only prescribed them, let me think, three times. The first time I was still down in Portland. Patient was a thirty-eight-year-old woman who already had three kids, no job and a boyfriend who'd just walked out on her. She was desperate not to have another. I suppose she might have known Tiffany Stoddard and mentioned it but that seems really unlikely. The second time was right after I opened my practice in Machiasport. About four years ago. Patient was a twelve-year-old girl who'd been raped by her father. Mother and daughter have since moved out of the area and the father's doing time. Again unlikely.'

'And the third?'

Emily sighed. 'I guess that's the one. I never told anybody about it before because, frankly, I really didn't want anybody to know. Not even you. It was right before my divorce from Sam, when the marriage was really turning ugly. This young woman, a student over at UMM, tells me she's pregnant and wants to terminate the pregnancy. Unlike Stoddard, she's perfectly willing to give me her name and insurance card and all the other necessary information. I ask her if she knows who the father is and, if she does, do either of them have any interest in getting married and maybe having the baby. Well, she laughs at this. Thinks it's kind of funny. Says yes indeed, she knows who the father is and, no, she doesn't think he's going to want to get married. I ask why. She says, among other reasons, because he's already married.' Emily paused and shook her head. 'I almost hate to ask you but by any chance was Tiffany Stoddard a student at UMM?'

'Yes, and somehow I think I know where you're going with this,' said Maggie.

'Yes, I'm sure you do,' Emily sighed. 'Did Stoddard ever take any English courses? Creative writing perhaps?'

'I guess we'll just have to find out.'

'Maggie?'

'What?'

'Before you talk to Sam, make sure you call Detective Louisa DelCastro on the Philadelphia Police Department. Ask her about what happened about three and a half years ago at the Palomar Hotel in Philadelphia. Sam is more than just the preppy, wiseguy drunk he pretends to be. Be careful.'

Before leaving the hospital, Maggie called Detective DelCastro. She wasn't available. Maggie left a message asking the detective to please call her back as soon as possible. It concerned a murder and was urgent. Her second call was to her father.

Chapter Fifteen

2:03 P.M., Saturday, August 22, 2009
Eastport, Maine

TABITHA STODDARD STARED vacantly out her bedroom window at the irregular patterns of sunlight and shadow that stretched across the yard like witch's fingers pointing toward the toolshed at the back.

She was sitting, knees up, head and back propped against the painted white wooden slats of the headboard Pike had made for her when she was little. Just before the accident that killed Terri.

Back then, when Pike could still use his legs, he did things like that for her. Made headboards and showed her how to handle the *Katie Louise.* He used to keep the boat painted up and in good shape instead of letting her slowly disintegrate into the rotting bucket she'd become.

Sometimes back then, Pike would take all three of his girls out to cruise around the harbor. He'd tell the other captains and anyone else who'd listen how he liked showing off his three beautiful daughters. But Tabbie knew, even then, that it was only Tiff and Terri who were beautiful and not her. No, Tabitha was the ugly duckling. Only this ugly duckling was one who would never grow up to be beautiful or graceful or smart. This ugly duckling would never grow into a swan.

Still, Tabbie loved the headboard. Each of the slats had a carved wooden bird perched on top. Pike drew up the design himself. Cut out each of the bird shapes with his jigsaw so they all were exactly the same size and shape, the only difference being that the ones on the left side of the bed faced right, and the ones on the right side faced left. When he screwed the two sides together and placed them behind the bed, the two birds in the middle ended up looking into each other's faces, beaks about half an inch apart, like they were squaring off to have a fight or something. Over the years Tabitha named all the birds. The two in the middle were Roxie and Dick.

Making the headboard was the last special thing Pike ever did for her. He screwed it together and attached it to the bed frame just days before he crashed his motorcycle into the tree, killing Terri and crippling himself.

Afterwards he never did much of anything except drink whiskey and scream at Donelda and sometimes at Tabbie that he needed one of them to get her ass down here right away to do something for him and what the fuck was taking her so goddamned long anyway.

Tabbie knew Pike wasn't as helpless as he pretended to be. He managed to get stuff for himself – food for lunch, treats for Electra, the TV remote – when she was at school and Donelda was out digging for winkles and bloodworms or sometimes during blueberry season, when the two of them were out together raking berries to make a few extra bucks.

She knew Pike spent a lot of time training Electra. He was good at that. Liked talking about how, if someone tried to sneak into the house, *she'd tear their fucking throats out before they knew what hit them*. Pike also spent a lot of time cleaning his gun. He always kept his gun with him just in case somebody tried to break in. Although why anybody'd want to break into this house she couldn't imagine. Sure as hell wasn't anything worth stealing.

Tabitha was the last of the daughters. The afterthought they called her. The accident. Now with Terri and Tiff both dead she really was the last. Tabitha was quite certain that if Pike and Donelda knew they were only going to have one daughter left, they certainly wouldn't have chosen her. They'd have taken either Terri or Tiff way before her. Trade Tabitha in on one of the others about as fast as they could get the words out.

Tabbie supposed, if she was really going to be super honest about it, she couldn't argue with that. She'd do exactly the same thing in their shoes. It was the only logical choice considering how beautiful and cool Tiff and Terri both were and how semi-fat and funny looking she was.

Tabbie got up, went to the bathroom and pulled a length of toilet paper off the roll. She wiped away the tears that had been rolling down her cheeks most of the day, blew her nose and flushed the paper away.

No, Tabbie wasn't much good at anything and she didn't have any friends except Toby Mahler, who was in her class at school and was clumsy like her and much fatter and no good at sports or much of anything except computers. All Toby ever did was screw around on his computer and talk about stuff she didn't understand. She figured he knew even more about computers than Mr Cory, the science teacher. Still, he was a real dork. But at least he kind of liked her and hung out with her and almost no one else did. Though she was pretty sure she didn't like him back. Leastways not in a *romantic* way.

In fact, the only things Tabitha really liked doing were reading, *Harry Potter and the Chamber of Secrets* being her all-time favorite, and sitting in her room or up in the attic letting her mind wander. Anyway, she told herself, she shouldn't be thinking about herself now. She should be thinking about Tiff being dead and what she was going to do about that.

Tabitha had been sitting here in the same position since about 10:30 this morning, when the cop left. The lady cop who told them about Tiff being dead. What the cop said – and Tabbie remembered her words exactly – was that some sonofabitch had *picked up a great big knife and slashed open Tiff's neck like a hog in a slaughterhouse*. She was pretty sure the cop couldn't have seen her peeking around the side of the stairwell when she said those words. Wouldn't have said them if she knew an eleven-year-old was listening. An impressionable eleven-year-old with a *vivid imagination*. 'Tabitha has such a vivid imagination,' Miss Weigel, her fifth-grade teacher, wrote on all her report cards last year. 'I only wish she would concentrate more on her studies and not let her mind wander in class.'

Miss Weigel was right. Tabitha's mind did wander a lot. But right now it wasn't wandering at all. It kept coming back to the last time she saw Tiff. Yesterday afternoon. Tiff sent her a text in the morning. *Need 2 C U. Alone! Don't tell anyone!!! 3:00 @ school playground.*

Tabitha rode her bike over to the school in plenty of time, locked it in the bike rack and was sitting on one of the swings when she saw Tiff's green Taurus pull into the parking lot. Her sister waved her over.

'Hi, hop in.'

'Jeez, what happened to your face? Somebody hit you?'

'Don't worry about that. Just get in the car.'

Tabitha climbed in and they started driving.

'You didn't tell anyone you were coming to see me?' Tiff asked.

'No. No one.'

'Swear to God?'

'Swear to God. Why? Where are we going?'

'Nowhere.' Tiff handed her a package. It was wrapped in layers of newspapers and taped tight. 'I need you to hide this for me.'

The package weighed next to nothing. Tabbie shook it and thought she heard some stuff rattling around inside but couldn't tell for sure.

'Don't do that,' said Tiff.

'What's in it?'

'A secret. Something I don't want anyone to know about or see. Including you. So don't open it. I'll know if you do because I wrapped it in a special way. When you get home hide it where nobody will find it and don't say anything to anybody. That's very important. You can't tell anyone. Not Mom or Dad. Not any of your friends. Nobody. Ever. Can you promise me that?'

'I guess. How long do you want me to keep it?'

'I'll come and get it from you when I'm sure the coast is clear. Or call you on the iPhone and tell you where to send it.'

'Okay. I won't open it.'

'You promise?' asked Tiff. 'You're the most honest person I know, Tabitha, so if you make a promise I know you'll keep it.'

Tabbie looked at her big sister, a serious expression on her face. She didn't know what all this was about, but it seemed important. 'I promise.'

'Tell me what you're promising.'

'I promise to hide your package where nobody will find it and not open it or anything and not tell anybody anything about it.'

'No matter what they tell you?'

'No matter what they tell me.'

'You promise?'

'I promise.'

And because Tabitha made a promise and because she always kept her promises, when she got home she did exactly what her sister asked. She cut open the back of Harold, her biggest stuffed teddy, who was a hand me down from Terri and Tiff, pulled out Harold's stuffing and pushed the package deep inside. It just about fit. Then she pushed as much of Harold's stuffing back inside him as she could. She sewed the teddy back up so you couldn't see any stitches and put him back on the bookcase between the bunny and the panda. The package kind of pushed Harold out a little bit in one or two weird places so he didn't look quite as much like Harold as he used to but she didn't think anybody else would notice.

'I'll come and get it from you in a few days when I need it.' That's what Tiff had said. 'And honey, when I do I'm going to blow this town. This county. This whole freezing-ass state. And believe me, once I get out of Dodge, I am never, ever coming back.'

'Can you take me with you?'

'I wish I could,' said Tiff. 'But that just won't work. I'm going to be moving fast. I don't even know where I'm going except it's gonna be someplace warm, and the last thing I can deal with is a kid trailing along with me.'

Tabitha said she understood. But she really didn't. She wouldn't be any trouble at all. She was never any trouble to anyone and someplace warm sounded awfully good. But now Tiff was dead and wasn't coming back to get the package or anything else. She wasn't going anyplace warm either except maybe to hell.

Tabbie had a hard time thinking of Tiff as dead. Everything about her big sister had always seemed so alive. Tiff was everything Tabitha always wanted to be but knew she never would. She was beautiful. Smart. Fun and funny. The idea of someone like Tiff being dead seemed crazy. Ridiculous.

Tabbie told herself to stop being stupid. Anybody could be dead and at eleven years old a person really ought to understand what being dead meant. Dead was dead. Just like Terri was dead and had been for three years. Just like Grammy Katherine was dead. And their old dog Lucy. She was dead too. Tabbie'd gone to the vet with her mother when they gave Lucy the shot. The vet put the needle in and just like that Lucy went from being an alive thing to a dead thing. At eleven years old a person obviously knew what dead meant.

What she wasn't all that sure about was what happened after you were dead. Were you just not there any more? Gone. *Poof.* Like you never existed? Just a rotting lump of meat in a box underground being eaten up by bugs and worms? Or was dying more like what they said in church? Tabitha was by no means certain it was, but if it was, well then there was a distinct possibility Tiff was flying around somewhere in either heaven or hell. She was in what Mrs St Pierre who lived up the road called *a better place.* Mrs St Pierre came over with some cupcakes after she heard on television about Tiff being murdered. Tabbie didn't know why she thought cupcakes would help.

'Donnie,' Mrs St Pierre said, 'I know this is hard for you to accept but please believe me when I tell you she's in a better place. They both are. Both Tiff and Terri. Together again. Safe in the arms of Jesus.'

Tabitha thought her mother might throw Mrs St Pierre out of the house along with her cupcakes because she knew her mother not only didn't believe in God but also thought Mrs St Pierre was pretty much full of shit about everything. But to Tabbie's surprise her mother didn't say anything except thank you.

Tabbie tended to think her mother was right on the religion thing. But if it turned out she wasn't and Mrs St Pierre was right, well, Tabbie thought that might make a pretty good argument for killing yourself. Who wouldn't want to be in a better place? Especially if you lived in Eastport. And double especially if your spirit didn't actually have to have a body and thus didn't have to put up with being semi-fat and wholly clumsy.

Killing herself would be easy. She knew where Pike kept his gun. The bullets too. And she knew how to load it and use it. Pike had taught her himself. So maybe she *would* kill herself. Or maybe not. She couldn't make her mind up about that. Tiff might get pretty damned pissed if she showed up unannounced in heaven or hell or wherever Tiff had gone to. She could just hear Tiff saying something like: 'Oh Jesus, what are you doing here? I told you the last thing I can deal with is a kid trailing along with me.'

The house was quiet again. Tabitha hadn't heard her parents screaming at each other for at least an hour so she figured they'd both fallen asleep. Her mother on her bed and Pike downstairs in his chair.

She picked up the old 3G iPhone Tiff had given her last month when she got the brand-new one for herself.

'I can't afford this,' she told her sister when she gave her the phone. 'I don't have any money.'

'Don't worry, Tabs. It's in my name. I'll pay the monthly charges. I just need a private way to call you. You just pay for any apps you download. Deal?'

Tabbie couldn't believe it. Not a single other kid in her whole class had an iPhone. Not a single one. Not even Toby Mahler, whose family had plenty of money. Just her. It had to be about the best present she'd had ever gotten from anybody. Except maybe for the headboard from Pike.

'Deal,' she said.

Tabbie looked again at the text message she got yesterday. *Need 2 C U. Alone! Don't tell anyone!!! 3:00 @ school playground.*

She missed her big sister so much she kept speed dialing Tiff's new cell phone number. Of course she knew there would be no answer but she liked hearing Tiff's voice on the message that kept kicking in even before the phone rang. 'Hi, this is Tiff. You know the drill. Leave your number and I'll call you back.' Must have listened to that about twenty times.

This time, for the first time, she decided to leave a message. 'Hi Tiff. This is Tabitha. I know you can't hear me or call me back but I just want you to know I'm really, really going to miss you. You really, really don't know how much. I'm really, really sorry you couldn't *get the hell out of Dodge* like you said. Then maybe you'd still be alive. But it's okay. I know you tried to make it happen. The one thing I'm wondering, though, is what the heck you want me to do with that package you gave me?'

Chapter Sixteen

3:22 P.M., Saturday, August 22, 2009
Machias, Maine

THE AFTERNOON SUN was throwing golden light on to the porch of the old house on Center Street as Maggie pulled in. A white Victorian with black shutters built in more prosperous days, it was the house she was born in. The old maple in the corner of the front yard was heavy with late-summer leaves and still had a rope swing tied to one of its lower branches. Not the same one Maggie and her brothers played on for years. A new one with a plastic seat instead of wood, yellow nylon cord instead of clothesline. Her father must have hung it for his granddaughters, Ali and Louise. Trevor's girls. Maggie's nieces.

She watched John Savage unwind his long frame from the green wicker rocker on the porch, the one he called his smoking chair, and walk down the steps to greet her.

He slipped his arm around her waist and walked her back toward the house. 'Welcome home,' he said. 'You must be kind of tired.'

'I'll live.'

It had been eight months since Maggie's last visit at Christmas. Four months before that she'd come for a weekend. Before that not since John and Anya's wedding a year ago last June. A few times in between, she'd spent weekends with Em, usually hiking or canoeing the wild waters of the Machias River. On those visits she'd only stopped in for a quick hello.

The gaps *were* too long, she told herself. Although she once loved coming home, these days there always seemed to be some good reason not to. It wasn't that John's new wife made her feel less welcome. Or that Anya was a bad woman. Or even that Maggie's mother would have resented John marrying again. During the last stages of her illness, with the impossibility of recovery too obvious to allow the use of phrases like *when you get better* or *when you're well again*, Joanne Savage told her husband she wanted him to marry again and marry soon. Asked Maggie to help make sure it happened. Once she even said she thought Anya, a neighbor and friend who was herself recently widowed, might make an excellent replacement.

No, there wasn't anything not to like about Anya. It was just that, for Maggie, this house was and always would be Joanne's. Her mother had laid out and planted the flower beds, selected and hung the wallpapers, roasted and served more than thirty Thanksgiving turkeys from its kitchen.

For Maggie, the ghost of her mother would always hover around this place and, fair or not, that made her feel uncomfortable with another woman running the show. Maggie would have preferred it if Anya and Savage had sold the house and found somewhere else to live. She'd told her father twice how she felt about that but he brushed off the suggestion both times. He'd lived here for forty years, he said, paid off the mortgage and didn't want to live anywhere else. 'They'll damn well carry me out of this place,' he said. 'Just like they did your mother.'

Up on the porch John Savage welcomed his only daughter home. The child who looked most like him, the one they both secretly knew he loved the most. He squeezed her hard. She squeezed back. 'It's been too long, Mag. Much too long. It's not such a long trip from Portland that we can't see you more often. And not just when there's a crisis.'

'I know, Pop. I'm sorry. Things have been kind of busy.'

'You're a cop. Cops are always busy. You have to make time.'

'I know. I said I was sorry.' She hoped he wouldn't make a continuing issue of it.

'Speaking of cops, one of Carroll's troopers dropped this off for you a little while ago. He handed her a large orange envelope. The case files. She'd read them in the privacy of her childhood bedroom. Either before or after she got a few hours sleep.

'How's Anya?' she asked.

'She's fine. So are Trevor and Cathy and the girls.'

'How's Harlan?'

'Hard to say. Don't see him all that often.'

All through school Maggie and her two brothers, one older, one younger, earned a reputation as 'independent', meaning wild. So 'independent' they'd been known by just about everyone as 'the little Savages'.

Trevor, four years older than Maggie, was the leader back then. He earned a degree in business from U. Maine Machias and married a girl he met in college. Trev and Cathy lived just a few blocks over on North Street and their two little girls, ten and six, were John's only grandchildren, at least for now. Possibly forever, Maggie thought, the way things seemed to be going with her so-called love life.

Trevor had a good job as plant manager with Clement's Wild Blueberries, one of the largest processors in the country. Like Detroit once produced cars and Silicon Valley makes chips, the hard stony soil of Washington County produced lowbush blueberries. Billions and billions of them every summer.

Harlan, the youngest, also ended up close to home. Never much of a student – *boy's got learning difficulties*, Joanne confided in whispers to her most trusted friends – Harlan joined the marines right out of high school. He served two tours in Iraq, first in special ops and then later as a sniper. He barely survived the battle of Ramadi, when a piece of shrapnel lodged in his brain. But he did survive. Surgeons at the Naval Medical Center in Bethesda managed to take it out and, after months of rehab, Harlan came home.

At thirty-one he was still a wild child who, according to his father, spent 'too damn much time in the wrong kind of bars messing around with the wrong kind of women, 'specially for a cop's kid.'

Aside from a few bucks picked up shooting pool at the Musty Moose on Main Street, no one really knew how Harlan made his living, not at any given time, but most figured that, like a lot of people in Washington County, it was how and where he could. A little lobstering, a little construction work, a little logging. A little of whatever the hell he could find. No one was real sure. Joanne Savage blamed Harlan's seeming lack of ambition on the traumas of war. PTSD she called it and maybe it was but Maggie knew, even before he went off to fight, Harlan was and always would be the wildest of the little Savages.

Maggie followed her father through the house and into the kitchen, where Anya was busy washing some dishes. John's second wife dried her hands and the two women greeted each other with a hug. The room hadn't changed since Anya had taken charge. The same old appliances Maggie had grown up with. The same oak table. The same formica countertops. Maggie thought she caught the scent of her mother in the room. Had to be her imagination. It was four years since Joanne Savage had died and Maggie didn't believe in ghosts.

Savage refilled his coffee cup. 'I'll see you outside when you get what you need.' He headed back to the porch.

'Would you like something to eat?' Anya asked.

'No thanks,' she said, still full from breakfast at the WaCo.

'Anything to drink?' she asked. 'Coffee? Tea?'

'Iced tea might be nice if you have it.'

She watched Anya open the door of the old green GE refrigerator.

Not green, you understand. Avocado. Maggie could still hear Joanne's voice mocking the marketing people at the General Electric Company. Avocado. That's what they called it back in the seventies, when her parents bought the house.

Anya poured the tea and handed it to her. 'It's nice to see you, Maggie,' she said. 'It's been a while.'

'I know. I should come up more often.'

'You should. Your father misses you. And none of us is getting any younger.'

They say men tend to marry the same woman twice and physically this was true. Anya was ten years younger than Joanne would have been, but she had the same tall, thin build. The same fair Scandinavian coloring. The same ramrod-straight stance. But there were differences as well. Anya presented a more serious mien than Joanne Savage. Even when Joanne was dying with pancreatic cancer she could make everyone smile with a self-deprecating quip. Maggie wondered if Anya ever made jokes. She'd never heard one.

'You didn't bring a bag?' asked Anya.

'It's still in the car. I'll get it later.'

Anya pointed at Maggie's holster and sidearm. 'Would you mind terribly putting that away? I don't like people wearing firearms in my house.'

Maggie bridled for an instant. It's not *your* house she thought. Then she pushed the thought away. It *was* Anya's house now and not Maggie's. Not any more. And not Joanne's either. 'If you don't mind,' she said to Anya, 'I'll hold on to the gun. I'm going out later. I'll want to take it with me.'

Anya pursed her lips. 'I'll leave you and John to it. I know you two have a lot to talk about. Terrible thing, this whole business with Emily. And that Stoddard girl.' With that she turned and climbed the stairs.

Chapter Seventeen

OUT ON THE porch, Maggie parked herself next to her father in the second of the two big green wicker rockers, the same ones Mag had helped paint and repaint a dozen times over the years.

As if on cue the two of them, father and daughter, lifted their long legs up on to the railing. Polly Four gave Maggie's leg a peremptory shove with her nose and Maggie responded, stroking the dog's head and ears. John found one of his small Camels and lit up.

'How long you here for?'

'Carroll gave me till Tuesday.'

'What then?'

'He's got an option to renew.'

'If he doesn't?'

Maggie shrugged. 'I'm here however long it takes.'

'Even if Carroll tells you Tuesday morning it's not working out? Tells you to go home?'

'Even if.'

'He won't like it.'

'Nope. Probably howl like a stuck pig. Might even submit a formal complaint to the AG's office.'

'You could lose your job.'

'Maybe. Or maybe just a suspension. Or a demotion. Depends on Chief Shockley and whether or not I catch the bad guy. Shockley'd just love letting the media know how it took one of *his* hotshot Portland detectives to clear a murder case the staties' hotshot couldn't.' Maggie smiled. 'Hell, if it happens that way, Tom might even promote me. On the other hand –' Maggie held up both hands, palms out and shrugged. 'Who knows? There are other jobs. I'll handle it.'

'I can always swear you in as a deputy. I've got three open slots.'

'Forget it.'

'You need anything from me?' Savage asked.

'You get the information I asked for? About what Tiff was studying?'

'Yup. I spoke to Ellie Morse in the registrar's office. Took a bit of doing. Ellie actually made me get a warrant before she faxed over Stoddard's records. Anyway, she had a dual major. English and Business.'

'Ever take creative writing?'

He reached for a stapled fax that was sitting in a pile of papers on the table by his chair. 'Yup. Here it is. Took our friend Sam Harkness's non-fiction course last fall and "Exploring the Short Story" in the spring. A-pluses in both. Gee,' Savage chuckled, 'wonder what Stoddard wrote that deserved an A-plus from Sam.'

Whatever it was it ought to be on her computer. 'You go over to Stoddard's apartment this morning with Ganzer and the evidence guys?'

'I was there.'

'Find anything?'

'Quite a bit. Kid was a slob. She had clothes strewn all over the place. Lot of it new and expensive. Some still had store tags on it. And not from Walmart either. But no cell phone, no computer or peripherals. None of the electronics you'd expect from a twenty-two-year-old college student. No drugs either.'

'Bad guy may have cleaned it out. How about prints or other people's DNA?'

'Plenty of prints and DNA. Mostly Stoddard's but some from other sources.'

'Where's the apartment?'

'Cheap one-bedroom in a little four-unit that caters to students near the river on Water Street. Number forty-one. Apartment three. Second floor right if you're facing the place. Landlady's name is Laverty. Paula Laverty. She's nosy and a gossip. Claimed Tiff brought a lot of guys home. Emmett brought her in and showed her a bunch of pics to see if she could ID any of the guys.'

'Did she?'

'You'll have to ask him. Emmett doesn't fill me in on his discoveries. Aside from that, Carroll's got two teams interviewing anybody and everybody they can find who might have known Stoddard. You need anything else?'

'Yeah.' Maggie decided to press it. 'Number three's the biggie.'

'Oh yeah? What is it?'

'Whatever it was you wouldn't talk about on the phone yesterday.'

Savage nodded. 'As usual, you're saving the best for last. You used to do that with your dinners. Pushed the good stuff off to one side and saved it till you ate the required allotment of string beans or asparagus.' He sipped the last of his coffee, then stared out into the empty street.

A couple of minutes passed in silence.

Chapter Eighteen

MAGGIE STUDIED HER father's face in profile. 'I'm not going anywhere,' she said. 'Not till you tell me what's going on.'

'Lymphoma. Non-Hodgkin's. That's the nasty kind but the docs tell me we caught it early. I started chemo down in Bangor last week. So far they tell me the results are good.'

A chill went through her. A fear that had lain dormant since Joanne's death was now hanging right in front of her. That ugly word. *Cancer.* Once again big, fat, and very, very real. She'd already lost one parent to that bastard of a disease. And now she was facing the prospect of losing another.

'Anya know about this?' she asked in a calm voice, no sign of distress showing through. At least she didn't think there was.

'Of course,' Savage said. 'She's the one who insisted I tell you. I didn't want to. I know the toll it took on you when your mother was ill. Trev knows as well. Didn't want to tell him either. But I don't want either of you telling anyone else. Not even your pal McCabe.'

'Most people will just want to help,' Maggie said, determined to sound reassuring. Not sure she was succeeding.

John Savage shook his head. 'I suppose. But there's nothing much they can do and there's more than a few around here who don't even like the idea of a healthy seventy-four-year-old sheriff. If they found out I was sick they'd use it as a lever to get me the hell out of office. And I'm not ready to go yet. I've got three years left on term number five and if I beat this thing I may run for number six. So let's keep this our business. Family business. As long as it doesn't affect the performance of my duties, we don't tell a soul. You cool with that?'

'I'm cool,' she said, not feeling cool at all. 'You said Trevor knows. What about Harlan?'

'I haven't said anything to Harlan yet. In fact, I haven't seen or heard from him in months. Never even stops by to say hello.'

Maggie's fears for her father morphed into a need to defend her younger brother. 'You don't see much of me either.'

'Yeah, but you live 200 miles away and we talk pretty regular. Harlan lives around the corner and never even bothers returning my calls. If he ever does decide to call, I may or may not tell him about the cancer. Haven't decided yet. He'd probably just react like he did when your mother was dying. I still haven't forgiven him for that.'

Maggie hadn't either. Harlan Savage missed most of the last stages of his mother's illness. Hadn't bothered coming to see Joanne more than a couple of times in spite of his father's entreaties. Once told Maggie he didn't visit because he couldn't bear to see his mother looking so sick. That may or may not have been the truth. Maggie wanted to think it was. But she was pretty sure it wasn't.

After Joanne died, John, not being one to mince words, let Harlan know exactly what he thought about that behavior. Gave it to him straight between the eyes the day of the funeral. Harlan gave it right back. Maggie would never forget the sight of the two big men, both of whom she loved, confronting each other face to face yards away from the freshly dug grave of her mother. John and Harlan had barely spoken since. Maggie knew it hurt her father to practically disown his second son and youngest child. She also knew he was too stubborn to be the first to reach out. She'd have to find Harlan herself and tell him about his father's illness. She hoped he'd care.

'Emily know?' Maggie asked.

'No. Em's not my doctor. Bill Brill is. I'll tell her in good time. When she's out of the hospital and the guy who tried to kill her is locked up or dead and buried.'

'You mind if I tell her? She'll want to know.'

'I guess not. Not as long as she doesn't go blabbing it to all and sundry.'

'Em's not a blab.'

Maggie and Savage spent the next twenty minutes talking about white cell counts and blood platelets and treatment protocols and whether the Cancer Center at Eastern Maine in Bangor was the right place or whether John should go down to Portland or even Boston for treatment. He told her Bangor was as far as he was willing to take it and he was happy with his docs there. 'What we hope for is that the chemo works and this thing goes into remission until I drop dead from something else. Brill says the amount of smoking I do there's a decent chance of that. So does the oncologist. In the meantime, I'm gonna try real hard to keep doing my job.'

'If the chemo doesn't work?'

'The next step is more chemo. Maybe radiation. After that it'll be time for me to be calling on either you or Trev and asking if I can borrow some stem cells from your bone marrow, whichever one of you turns out to be a better match for a transplant. At that point that's the best shot for a cure.'

'What if Harlan's the best match?'

John Savage didn't answer. Just lit up another Camel, took a long drag and again stared out into the street. A few cars went by. A dog walker Maggie didn't recognize waved at the two of them from the sidewalk. 'Beautiful day,' the woman called up. 'That your daughter?'

'Sure is,' Savage called back. 'Maggie, meet Alice Flannery. Alice bought the Carter house after Jake died last year.'

The Carter house was across the street and four doors down.

'Nice to meet you, Maggie,' Alice Flannery said. 'I'd come up and say hello,' the woman said. 'But Rufus needs to finish his business.' As if to emphasize the point the dog, a mix of German Shepherd and something else not clearly discernible, lifted his leg against the white picket fence that surrounded the Savage yard.

Maggie smiled and called out, 'Nice to meet you too, Ms Flannery.'

Maggie watched Alice Flannery and Rufus reenter what she'd always think of as the Carter house. 'You didn't answer my question,' she said.

'Which question?'

'What if Harlan's the best match?'

'Guess I'd just have to go for second best.' Savage blew a long stream of smoke into the air. 'It's hard for a man to reject his own son,' he finally said. 'But I don't think I'd want to ask Harlan for much of anything these days and, if I did, I seriously doubt he'd be willing to give it to me.'

'Don't you think you're being a little hard on him?'

'I don't think so.'

Maggie looked at her father's long, furrowed face, set hard as stone, staring out into the afternoon. 'You can't imagine how sad it makes me to hear you say that.'

Her father got up and went into the house.

Maggie watched him go, then picked up the files Carroll had sent over and followed him in. She climbed up to her old bedroom, lay down on the familiar down comforter and fell, more or less instantly, into a deep sleep. She was awakened three hours later by the sound of her cell phone.

Carroll calling from the road. He was on his way back from briefing his boss, Tom Mayhew, and the head of the Maine State Police, Ed Matthews, in Augusta and wanted an update on what she'd learned in Eastport. Instead of discussing it over the phone he suggested drinks and dinner. 'You know a place called 44° North in Milbridge?'

'I know it.'

'Good. Can you meet there at, say, 7:30?'

Chapter Nineteen

7:36 P.M., Saturday, August 22, 2009
Milbridge, Maine

MAGGIE SPOTTED CARROLL in an end booth when she walked through the doors of 44° North a few minutes late. No question about it, he was a good-looking guy. Dark, curly hair. Chiseled features. Except for the light blue of his eyes, he looked a lot like Dominic West, the actor who played Jimmy McNulty on *The Wire*, which, until it went off the air last year, was about the only cop show Maggie ever watched and that was mostly because she liked watching McNulty.

She headed back to the booth and Carroll rose to greet her. He was neatly dressed in a black cotton pullover and jeans. No jacket. If he was carrying a weapon it was out of sight. Most likely an ankle holster.

A college-age waiter told her his name was Damian and asked if she wanted anything to drink.

'What are you having?' she asked Carroll.

'Scotch.'

She wrinkled her nose. She checked the list of draft beers. 'I'll have a Drop Dead Red.'

'Twelve, sixteen or twenty-two ounces?'

'Well, let's start at twelve and we'll take it from there.'

'Yes, ma'am.'

Ma'am? Jesus, first the trooper and now this guy. When had twenty-somethings started calling her ma'am? She sure as hell didn't feel like a ma'am.

The beer came and she took a long pull of the rich amber brew, licked the foam off her lip. Then leaned back and exhaled.

Carroll watched. And smiled.

'What?'

'Nothing. Just that I'm not sure I've ever seen an attractive woman look happier chugging a large glass of beer.'

'Is that a compliment?'

'Definitely a compliment.'

'Okay, then. Thank you.'

'You're welcome. You've eaten here before?'

'A few times. Usually on my way up or back to visit my parents. Little out of the way otherwise.'

'Food's basic but pretty good. Plus I like it 'cause it's not a cop bar. Hate running into people who work for me when I'm having dinner.'

'Would it matter if you did?' Maggie asked. She wondered if Carroll might be thinking of this dinner more as a first date than as a business meeting. Studying his face, she found herself kind of hoping he did.

Carroll shook his head. 'No, it wouldn't matter. Not really. But if someone like Ganzer saw us eating together, he'd do whatever he could to start the rumor mill going.'

Maggie shrugged and changed the subject. She didn't want to talk about Ganzer. 'How was your meeting with the brass?'

'Filled them in on what we know so far. Which, unfortunately, isn't all that much.'

'You tell them about me working on the case?'

'Yes. I said I was using you as a special investigator because of your local expertise.'

'And?'

'They nodded and said fine. They tend to give me a long leash.' Carroll changed the subject. 'How long since you lived in Machias?'

'Full time? Not since I went away to college. Nineteen ninety-one.'

'College college or the Criminal Justice Academy?'

'College college. I spent four years at Orono getting a BA before going to the Academy. But I always knew I wanted law enforcement. It's kind of the family business.'

'Certainly is. Your father's an institution around here.'

'Yeah, I know. World's longest-serving sheriff.'

'One of the best as well.'

'I agree but then I'm prejudiced. Anyway, my plan was to get my BA first and then maybe join up with the Fibbies.'

'FBI huh? What happened to the plan?'

'I decided I'd rather stay in Maine instead of going off to DC or Quantico or to whatever field office they might decide to send me to. So I applied for a job with the Portland PD.'

'Why Portland? Why not us?'

'Well, for one thing I like Portland. I wanted to live there. For another I wanted to work for the best law enforcement agency in the state.'

Sean cocked his head questioningly and raised one eyebrow. Maggie smiled at the reaction. 'No offense intended, sergeant, but I think we're way better than you guys.'

Carroll smiled back. 'An arguable point but let's not go there.'

He tapped the third finger of her left hand. 'No ring. Never married?'

Okay, she thought, first physical contact. First genuinely personal question. She decided to let it pass. 'Not yet.'

"That's by choice I assume. You're an attractive woman. Must've had lots of guys lining up.'

This guy's good, Maggie thought. 'Guess I just haven't found the right one yet. I assume you're not married either.'

'Not any more.'

'Divorced?'

'No. Widowed. My wife passed away.'

'Oh. I'm sorry. Some kind of illness?'

'Liz died in a fire. Our house burned to the ground in the middle of the night. I was out working a stakeout and she was home alone. Asleep. I like to think she died of smoke inhalation before the flames got to her, but maybe that's too much to hope for.'

This time it was Maggie who did the touching. She reached across the table and put her hand on his. 'Sean, I'm sorry. Really, really sorry. That's a terrible story,' she said before withdrawing it.

'Worst part,' Carroll said softly, 'it wasn't an accident. Forensic guys found signs an accelerant had been used.'

'She was murdered?'

'Yes. It's not something I like talking about.'

'Then don't. It's okay.'

'No. I really have to.'

'Why?'

'Because Liz's death may be related to this investigation. If you're going to be working on it there are some things you ought to know. I take it you haven't read the case files yet.'

'No. Not yet.'

He paused a minute. Maggie waited.

'The theory is the fire was started by someone out to get one or maybe both of us. But there was never much question the primary target was Liz. She was a cop as well. State police. That's where we met. Last couple of years she worked as liaison with Maine DEA. At the time of her murder she was working undercover on the Canadian Oxycontin theft.'

'Are you saying whoever killed Stoddard is the same person who killed your wife?'

'I can't prove it yet, but yes, I'm pretty sure of it. Blakemore as well. Same day as the fire, Liz told me she thought she was closing in on someone involved in the Saint John theft. But she wouldn't tell me who. Or anything else about it. Said the information was too preliminary. There was nothing she could prove. Anyway, I think the bad guy must have known Liz was getting close and decided to take her out before she could screw up his operation.'

'But you never found out who she was targeting?'

'Unfortunately not. The old *need to know* principle. She didn't even tell Mayhew or the people she was directly working with. One of whom was Emmett Ganzer.'

'That's odd. Why not?'

'I don't know. I can only guess she was trying to tie up some loose ends before going public but ...' Carroll shrugged and shook his head. 'I suppose if I'd pressed the point that morning, she might have told me and then maybe we could have gotten the guy. And maybe Liz would be alive today. Blakemore and Tiff Stoddard too.

'Anyway, when Liz was killed I lobbied Mayhew to put me in charge of the case. It was the only time he's ever said no to me. I asked why. "Conflict of interest," he said. "You're too close to the victim to keep your objectivity. Our work has to be about justice. Not vengeance." '

'Pretty much what you said to me this morning.'

'It's the party line. But I thought it was bullshit at the time and I still do. In the interest of full disclosure, I ought to tell you that my marriage wasn't in great shape at the time Liz was killed. We'd discussed divorce and had she lived we probably would have separated. Still, she'd been my wife for five years and it angered me that my boss wouldn't even let me go after the scumbag who burned her alive.'

It occurred to Maggie that one reason Mayhew might not have wanted Carroll on the case was that, as the victim's husband, he had to be considered a suspect. Husbands always are. Unless, of course, he had a solid alibi. Unlikely he'd have been on a stakeout alone, so he probably did.

'My feelings about that,' he continued, 'are the main reason I decided to let you work on this one. You wanted to go after the guy who tried to kill your friend. I understood that.'

'I also told you I'd work the case even if you told me not to.'

'Yes, you did. It shames me I didn't say the same thing to Mayhew. I left the investigation to other people and they never got the guy. Never even got close.'

'Maybe you wouldn't have either.'

'Maybe not. Whoever killed Liz and the others is clever. He covers his tracks well. But I'm a better cop than the guys who investigated it and would have felt a whole lot better if I'd at least tried. Anyway, just a couple of days after Liz's death, Blakemore was killed. Canadian Oxycontin again. And once again, no arrests. Six months go by. Then last night, I heard about Stoddard's murder and the Canadian drugs turning up in Kaplan's pocket. I was convinced it was the same guy. So I called Mayhew in the middle of the night and told him this time, no bullshit. I was assigning myself to run things and that if he didn't like it he could take my badge and, if you'll pardon my French, stick it where the sun don't shine. So, anyway, here I am.'

'Yes. And here *I* am,' said Maggie.

'Between you and me, I'm glad you are.'

Maggie smiled. 'So am I.'

Damian brought the Scotch and asked if they were ready to order.

Maggie hadn't even glanced at the menu. 'You go first if you know what you want. I haven't decided.'

'I'll just have the house salad. Balsamic vinaigrette. And the grilled salmon. No butter.'

'Watching your figure?' Maggie teased.

'Something like that.'

'Well, good for you. As for myself, I'll have half a rack of the barbequed pork ribs. Extra sauce, sweet potato fries and a side of coleslaw.'

She noticed the amused expression on Carroll's face.

'I'm the original junk food junkie,' she explained, handing the menu back to Damian. 'I'll switch to the salmon regime if I ever start putting on weight. So far ...' She held up both hands, palms out in a *go figure* kind of gesture '... not a problem.'

'I'm jealous. Tell you what. Why don't we cancel the salmon, get a whole rack of ribs instead of half and I'll split them with you. That is, if you don't mind.'

'No, that's fine,' she said.

'You got it,' said Damian.

'Okay, now, since this is supposed to be a business meal, let's talk business. Fill me in on your day.'

'Well, for starters, Emily Kaplan's awake and talking.'

'Really?' said Carroll. 'That's good news.'

'Yes, I went down there after leaving Eastport and it looks like she's going to make a full and fast recovery.'

'Trooper watching her room?'

'Yes. Thanks for making that happen.'

'You're welcome.'

'Anyway, Em has no memory at all of the car hitting her. Or of the driver. What they call retrograde amnesia. Her memory may come back. It may not. It probably doesn't matter. Car was coming straight at her in the dark. Traveling fast. Lights shining in her eyes. Maybe she could ID the guy or possibly the car but I doubt it. And even if she could I doubt a prosecutor would be able to sell it in court. I'm afraid the bad guy's got nothing to worry about from Emily.'

'Anything else?'

'Yeah. Tiff Stoddard may have been pregnant.'

'Really?' Carroll's face registered surprise.

'Terri will know as soon as she does the autopsy. She's giving it top priority so if there is a baby in there we ought to have preliminary fetal DNA in a few days.'

Carroll sat pensive for a minute or two. Maggie supposed he was thinking about the implications of a pregnancy on their handling of the case. Finally, he looked back. 'Okay,' he said. 'We'll check the reads with CODIS. See if we can find a match. Now tell me about your trip to Eastport.'

She skipped the run-in with Ganzer and spent twenty minutes taking Carroll through her conversations with Frank Boucher and then with Pike and Donelda Stoddard. He listened attentively. Asked a few questions but not too many.

'I assume Conor Riordan is an alias,' he said.

'I'm sure it is. Though we better check it out. Maybe it's a name he's got some connection with.' They both knew aliases are often variations on a bad guy's real name or other intersections in their lives.

'Anything else?'

'No, except that there were a couple of times, especially toward the end, I thought I might have to shoot the damn dog.'

'Well that certainly would have capped off your next of kin notification nicely,' Carroll laughed. '"Pardon me, sir, your daughter's dead and ... oops, by the way, so's your dog." '

Maggie didn't laugh back. Remembering the size of Stoddard's Rottweiler, especially its teeth, she didn't find it all that funny.

'Anyway, on this whole boat business? You think Pike's lying and Donelda's telling it the way it was?'

'Yes. I'm sure of it.'

'Based on what?' asked Carroll.

'Right now, nothing but instinct. I intend pressing a little harder on it. I'll go back tomorrow. Come down hard on Pike. Ask around down on the pier. If any of the locals saw Tiff or this Conor Riordan guy take the *Katie Louise* out in January, I intend finding out.'

'Okay. Anything else?'

'Soon as I feel we have probable cause, I'll get a search warrant for the house. See if we can find Pike's 10,000 dollars.'

'Think he'd keep it around the house?'

'Doubt he'd put it in a bank.'

Carroll looked thoughtful. 'You know what I don't get? Why would Pike Stoddard lie to protect somebody who might have killed his daughter? Why would any father?'

'You mean aside from the fact that Pike hates cops and his first instinct is to lie?'

'Yeah. Aside from that.'

Maggie shrugged. 'Bunch of possible reasons. Major jail time is the most obvious. Taking money for the boat makes him an accomplice in one of the biggest drug heists in local history. Number two: If he's got the 10,000 dollars, he probably wants to keep it. Losing it to us isn't going to bring Tiff back. Number three: Simple fear. If he talks and Conor Riordan finds out he could end up as dead as Tiff.'

'But he told you he never laid eyes on Riordan.'

'He could be lying about that, too.'

Maggie downed the remains of her beer, caught Damian's eye and pointed at her glass.

A minute later he brought their food and drinks, two extra plates, a big pile of paper napkins and a bunch of wet-naps.

'Okay, you win,' he said, eyeing the ribs. 'Dietary virtue ain't always what it's cracked up to be.'

Maggie pushed the platter into the middle of the table. They each cut off a rib and started gnawing.

Chapter Twenty

9:10 P.M., Saturday, August 22, 2009

AFTER LEAVING THE restaurant Maggie turned north on Route 1. About ten minutes later, the first four notes of Beethoven's Fifth sounded from inside her jacket pocket. Caller ID showed a 215 area code. Philadelphia.

'Detective Savage?'

'Yes?'

'This is Detective Louisa DelCastro returning your call.'

'Thanks for getting back to me.'

'No problem. Just wanted you to know, before I called, I confirmed your bona fides with a Sergeant Michael McCabe at the Portland PD. He told me you were working TDY on a murder case with the Maine State Police. How can I help you?'

'Does the name Samuel Harkness mean anything to you?'

'Is he a suspect?'

'Not yet. I was just wondering if you could fill me in on an incident that took place three and a half years ago in a suite at the Palomar Hotel.'

'Indeed I can,' said Detective DelCastro. 'Indeed I can.'

For the rest of the way into Machias Maggie listened to the details of Sam Harkness's adventures in the City of Brotherly Love, asked a few questions and made her mind up that tonight was as good a time as any to drop in on Emily's ex.

MAGGIE FELT A stab of familiar things forever lost as she turned her Blazer into Sam Harkness's driveway at the end of Schoppee Point Road in Roque Bluffs. Investigating a murder where you grew up, among people you grew up with, might turn out to be tricky.

She squeezed in next to an old Nissan Maxima with a UMM decal on the rear window. Not Sam's car. He wouldn't be caught dead driving anything so plebeian. Sam preferred swanning around in vintage Mercedes convertibles or, when he felt a need to show his macho side, slumming in a rusty old Chevy pick-up.

From outside, the house hadn't changed a bit since Maggie had last been here or, for that matter, since Sam's great-aunt Julia built the place in the early thirties. A plain-Jane, shingled cottage with a wraparound porch set on three acres of oceanfront property between Great

Cove and Englishman Bay. Just behind the house was the barn Julia had converted into an artist's studio. Maggie wondered if Sam still had the paintings Julia left behind when she died. Wondered especially if he had the ones of her.

Maggie's last visit had been a little over three years ago. Just before the break-up. Em invited her for dinner the night before Maggie was due back in Portland. She had some news, she said cryptically. Something she wanted to tell Maggie in person.

It had been an unusually warm night for late April, warm enough to allow them to sit on the porch after dinner and watch the tide come in. Sam for once was on best behavior. Hadn't been too flirty. Hadn't had too much to drink. Just enough to make his accent a little more southern, a little more Louisville than it was when he was totally sober. Perhaps he sensed what Emily had in mind.

After coffee, Maggie and Em walked down to the beach and Em told her the marriage was over. She'd had enough, she said. Couldn't take any more of Sam's drinking and rages and endless womanizing. She'd taken her wedding vows seriously and given the marriage everything she had until now, at long last, there was nothing left to give. 'Nothing at all. I'm running on fumes.'

Maggie knew it was all true.

Did Sam know, she asked?

No, not yet. Not officially. Em planned to tell him in the morning. That was the only time of day she could be reasonably sure he'd be sober enough to discuss it. He'd still blow up, of course. His ego couldn't take rejection.

He'd yell. Scream. Make ugly threats. Remind Emily in a snarky tone of the *till death do us part* line in her vows. Warn her that she wouldn't get a dime. Not now. Not ever. Warn her of that even though he knew perfectly well she didn't give a damn about Julia's money. Whatever might be left of it. Which, given Sam's ceaseless and careless spending, probably wasn't all that much. The only thing Em told Maggie she regretted was they'd never had a baby. She'd always wanted a child and now, given the dearth of eligible bachelors in Washington County, it seemed unlikely she'd ever have one. Though she could, she supposed, go out and find a sperm donor and do it all on her own.

Maggie listened as she'd listened so many times before to the gruesome details of her best friend's marriage. Even so she was surprised it was finally coming to this. That Em was actually calling it quits. Emily, the eternal team captain who, even when they were ten points down with less than a minute to play, would still try to rally the troops, still try to convince them there was a way to win.

It was the first and only time Maggie had ever known Emily to give up on anything she'd committed herself to. To actually admit there was something she couldn't effect through sheer force of will. But no, Emily said, not this time. Not any more. She was finished blaming herself for Sam's ugly behavior. This time, at long last, she was moving out. Filing for divorce.

Maggie supposed Sam must have sensed what was coming. Supposed that was the reason for his subdued demeanor during dinner.

'Where will you go? Back to Portland?' Maggie asked.

'No, I'm not giving up my practice. Just my marriage. I plan on converting the second floor over the office into a small apartment. I'll live there. Back where I began.' Emily gave her a sad smile as they started back toward the house. 'At least it'll be a better commute.'

Maggie forced her mind back to the present and walked across the lawn to where Sam was sitting. He was midway between the cottage and the beach, slouching on an aluminum lawn chair, one of the cheap, old-fashioned ones with green and white plastic webbing. There was a second, similar, chair, empty, next to him.

Sam was dressed as Sam always dressed in summer. A blue-and-white-striped button-down dress shirt, the top three buttons open at the neck, tails pulled out over khaki shorts, beat-up Topsiders on his feet. He held what looked like an icy martini in his left hand. Stoli, she remembered, with less than an eyedropper's worth of vermouth and a pair of baby onions nestled on the bottom. She supposed it was possible Sam's tastes had changed in the years since she'd seen him last. Maybe he'd gone and done something radical like switching from Stoli to Absolut or maybe even gin but somehow she doubted it.

He held an oversized racquet in his right hand and was bouncing a worn tennis ball up and down on the strings, reducing the young and eager Springer Spaniel in front of him to a state of quivering yelps. After the fifth or sixth bounce the former captain of the Exeter tennis team neatly rotated his wrist and managed, without spilling a drop of the martini, to hit a graceful forehand that sent the ball flying, then skipping, thirty or forty yards down the lawn toward the beach. The spaniel followed in hot pursuit.

'Hello, Sam,' said Maggie.

He looked up, acknowledging her presence for the first time. 'Well, if it isn't the beautiful Maggie May.'

An old nickname she hadn't heard in a while. 'Nice to see you,' she said, returning his smile.

'And you.' Sam nodded then turned his attention back to the dog, who'd already raced back from the beach. He put down the martini and pulled the slobbery ball from its mouth.

'To what do I owe the pleasure?' he asked. The soft southern accent and the subtly slurred words suggested he was already well into his cups.

'I was hoping you could spare me a few minutes. Something I need to talk to you about.'

'I don't see why not,' he said. 'Maggie, this is Willie. Willie, Maggie. I don't believe you two have met.'

'No,' Maggie said. 'No, we haven't.' She knelt down and scratched the spaniel behind his long silky ears. 'How old is he?'

'Willie joined me shortly after my former wife – I believe you remember my former wife – after she announced – the phrase she used, if memory serves, was that *she could take no more*. Willie arrived, just in time to fill the aching void Emily's departure left in my heart.'

'Aching void? Jesus, Sam, give me a break.'

'I'm serious, Margaret. I loved Emily and when she left she did leave an aching void in my heart.'

Maggie decided not to tell Sam that, if he loved Em so much, he had strange ways of showing it. There was no need to go down that road.

'Anyway,' Sam continued, 'that'd make Willie, oh let's see, just about three now.'

Sam downed the remains of the martini including the onions, tossed the ball in the air and hit it again. Harder and farther this time. It bounced into the water. Willie followed.

'May I sit?' Maggie asked nodding at the empty chair next to Sam's.

'Of course, how rude of me.' Sam rose, bowed and gestured toward the chair with the formality of an usher showing the mother of the bride her honored place in the front pew. 'Anyway, I was just going to fix myself a refill. May I bring you something?'

'I don't think so, Sam.'

'There are a couple of cold bottles of Piper in the back fridge. I remember how much you enjoy good champagne.'

'No. Really. I just dropped by for a chat. I probably won't be here long enough to justify a drink. Not even champagne.' Maggie bent down and picked up a pair of women's flip-flops that were neatly lined up beneath the chair she was sitting in. 'Besides, it appears you have company. Am I breaking up a party?'

'Hardly a party. Just a student who came by for a critical evaluation of her efforts.'

'Her writing efforts?' Maggie asked.

'Why, of course, Margaret. I teach writing.' Sam's brows went up in a display of injured innocence. 'Whatever else would I be talking about?'

'Of course. Whatever else? How were they? Her efforts, I mean.'

'Not very good, I'm afraid. She's inside resting now.'

'Recovering from your criticism?'

'No, actually. From three of my martinis. The poor thing usually only drinks beer. Bud Lite, may the Lord forgive her.'

Unlike the fine wines he so enjoyed blathering about, Sam wasn't improving with age. His Exeter/Harvard snobbery, barely noticeable in the young man she first met as a teenager, now seemed both obvious and obnoxious. Perhaps it was simply his growing bitterness that he'd never become the celebrated novelist he'd so carefully created his persona around. Of course, Maggie thought, it wouldn't have hurt if Sam spent more of his time writing and less of it drinking. Or evaluating his female students' efforts.

She took off her light summer jacket, revealing the 9 mm Glock 17 strapped to her hip and the gold detective's shield clipped next to it. She hung the jacket on the chair behind her.

Sam glanced at the weapon. 'I see you've come armed.'

'Yes. You remember, I'm a police officer.'

'Of course I remember. Always amazed me. Female cops aren't supposed to be attractive. Except, of course, on TV. There they're always beautiful.' Sam threw her another smile. 'Like you.'

Maggie supposed Emily's leaving and the divorce that followed made her a more legitimate target of Sam's attentions. Though, to be honest, he'd made a clumsy pass or two back in the day.

'Well, thank you, Sam,' she said with only a hint of sarcasm. 'By the way, speaking as a cop, I do hope your inebriated guest is over twenty-one. I'd hate to think you were serving alcohol to a minor.'

Sam shook his head. 'For once in your life, dear Margaret, you leave me utterly speechless.' He turned and headed for the house, walking what some might have considered a straight line, though to Maggie's eye he did seem to be listing a bit to starboard. 'I shall return,' he called out, waving the racquet over his head.

Willie trotted back, wet and sandy from his swim, and dropped the slobbery yellow ball by Maggie's feet. When she showed no interest in picking it up, he retrieved his prize and followed his master into the house.

Maggie sat, watching slivers of moonlight reflect off the still water that lay beyond the narrow stone beach and thought about Emily and Sam. Where, she wondered, had that beautiful boy gone, the one they both met the summer after high school graduation and had both fallen in love with, though, of course, it was Emily he'd chosen.

Images from that summer of 1991 flooded back into Maggie's mind. Sam, three years older than Maggie and Em, was spending the summer between his junior and senior years at Harvard here at Julia's house. Julia had offered him the house as an escape hatch, hoping it would give the young and talented writer time and space to finish his first novel away from the dismissive attitudes of his more immediate family, who all summered along the coast in the more fashionable environs of Northeast Harbor. Without exception they considered Sam's dream of living what he called *the writing life* little more than foolishness.

And so Sam came to Machias that summer. To great-aunt Julia's in Roque Bluffs, to finish his first novel. He probably would have too if he hadn't wandered into Ed Kaplan's hardware store on the Friday before the Fourth of July weekend looking for a surf-casting rod and had run, instead, into the store owner's tall, beautiful eighteen-year-old daughter. Sam's chances of doing much writing after that quickly dissolved from slim to none.

Most of his days were spent daydreaming about Emily instead of concentrating on the book. Most nights, Em would head out to Roque Bluffs as soon as she finished work. More often than not Maggie tagged along and the three of them would sit around a fire on the beach, smoking Julia's pot or drinking her expensive French champagne. Julia, at eighty-one, was still living in the house and seemed to have an unlimited supply of both.

When Em and Sam wanted to be alone, which at some point in the evening they always did, Maggie'd wander up to the barn that served as Julia's studio. Julia would break out some more pot or more champagne and, while she worked at her easel, tell Maggie tales from her life as an artist and an outcast.

'I built this cottage in 1934,' she said, 'as a summer place for myself and my friend Zanie Theobold. Zanie and I weren't welcome in Northeast Harbor, where my brother, who was Sam's grandfather, and our various cousins spent summers in what they like to call *the family compound*. Actually, I don't think they started calling it that until after Jack Kennedy was elected president. If the Kennedys had a compound, then the Harknesses damn well wanted one too. Anyway, Zanie and I escaped up here to Washington County, where we figured no Harkness would ever deign to tread.'

'Why weren't you welcome down there?'

'Well, for one thing I was a painter and Zanie was a poet. My family looks upon anything remotely artistic with great suspicion. For another Zanie and I enjoyed what in those days was called "a Boston marriage".'

'You were lesbians?'

'Were. Are. Always will be. Of course, Zanie's dead now so I guess she's not technically a lesbian any more. I don't think dead people can be said to have sexual feelings one way or another. Most of the figure studies both at the house and here in the barn are of Zanie at various stages of our life together. As you can see, she was built like you. Wonderful body right up until the end. Of course, she died far too young.'

'How old?'

'Fifty-seven. Just keeled over from a heart attack one day walking up to the house from her morning swim. Never knew what hit her.'

Maggie studied the paintings. A dozen hanging on the wall. Dozens more propped up around the studio or stacked in a loft overhead. Impressionistic nudes of a tall, angular woman with slim hips and smallish breasts. She told Julia she'd wondered who the model was. Told her how wonderful she thought they were. Julia was pleased that Maggie liked her work. It pleased Maggie, in turn, that she was able to please the old woman. That seemed, somehow, an important thing to do.

In the end, she supposed that was why she agreed to pose for Julia. That and the twenty dollars an hour Julia paid her, more than three times what she was earning as a cashier at the CVS store in Machias.

After that, for the last week in July and for all of August, three afternoons a week, while Em was working at the hardware store and Sam was in the house supposedly working on his novel, Maggie came to the studio and Julia painted or, more often, sketched her. Usually quick gestural sketches of athletic, dancelike poses. No more than five minutes each.

During one of these sessions she noticed Sam standing at the open window gazing in at her naked body. He didn't turn away when she caught his eye. Just smiled a mischievous smile and continued to look for a minute or two longer, his expression betraying desire. Maggie stood there, returning Sam's gaze, holding her pose, feeling a small trill of guilty pleasure from the almost certain knowledge that if she really wanted Sam, on this day or any other, she could have him. At least until someone newer and more interesting came along.

'Stop staring at Maggie, Sam,' Julia said when she noticed him at the window. 'It's rude. Go back to your writing.'

Maggie never told Emily anything about the encounter. How could she? Nothing happened. Nothing at all. Just a look, a smile, a silent invitation. Still she wondered now, as she had wondered so often in the past, how much their lives might have changed had she had the courage back then, when they were both eighteen, to tell her best friend that the man she blindly loved from that summer on should never have been blindly trusted.

Julia died two years later. She left the house, several hundred paintings, including a dozen or so of Maggie, and a chunk of her considerable fortune to Sam. She said, in her will, that she hoped he would use the house as she had, as a place to create art and to share his life with someone he loved.

Chapter Twenty-One

10:17 P.M., Saturday, August 22, 2009
Eastport, Maine

DIRTY ANNIE'S WAS well named. It was without question the darkest, dirtiest, dingiest bar anywhere in Eastport or, for that matter, anywhere in Washington County. In fact, had anyone been foolish enough to hold a competition for the least-appealing watering hole anywhere in Maine, Annie's would have been an odds-on favorite to walk away with the prize.

Even so, the place had been in business a long time and most locals expected it would remain in business a long time going forward. Annie sold cheap liquor at cheap prices and didn't care too much about what you did on the premises as long as you didn't break anything doing it or, if you did, as long as you were willing to pay for it. Annie's drew a pretty good crew of hard-drinking regulars, most of whom either couldn't afford or didn't want to go anywhere else.

Luke Haskell was one of Annie's best customers. Had been for years. Came in every afternoon after docking the *Katie Louise*. Had a couple of drinks. Appetizers he called them. Then something to eat. A bowl of chili or fish chowder. After his stomach was full, the serious drinking began and Luke would spend the rest of the night consuming as much liquor as his skinny body could hold. Most nights Annie poured him out of the place one drink short of passing out, pointed him up Water Street in the direction of the breakwater and reminded him to set an alarm before he went to bed as he had to get up early in the morning to go chasing lobsters for Pike Stoddard.

On this Saturday night, as on most other nights, Luke nodded at Annie's instructions and started weaving his way toward home, home being another night spent alone in the cramped dark cabin of the *Katie Louise*.

Being in no condition to notice anything beyond the necessity of putting one foot in front of the other, Luke failed to notice the man who slipped out of the alleyway next to Dirty Annie's and fell into step twenty or so feet behind him.

Luke's progress was of necessity slow. Every now and again, to avoid falling backward on to his ass or, more painfully, forward on to his face, he was forced to stop and balance himself against the side of a building with his left hand or, if he happened to be closer to the curb, against a parked car with his right. On these occasions the man behind him would also stop and wait patiently in the shadows for Luke to get started again.

Proceeding in this manner, it took the two of them nearly twenty minutes to walk the quarter mile to the deserted breakwater. Seeing no one else in the vicinity, the man closed the gap between himself and Luke and followed close behind as the old fisherman staggered down the steep and narrow ramp, holding both rails tightly in his two hands. At the bottom they continued in tandem to the end of the dock, where the *Katie Louise* was tied up. When they finally got to the boat, Luke, perhaps sensing a presence behind him, turned and for the first time noticed he was not alone. Someone was standing right behind him, holding a small brown paper bag.

Luke peered at the man's face, trying to figure out if he'd ever seen it before. The face did look familiar. He was sure he'd met him but couldn't recall where.

Conor Riordan pulled a pair of white latex gloves from his pocket and smiled. 'Nice evening, Luke. Don't you think so?'

'Who are ya? Whatcha want?'

'Luke, I'm hurt. You don't even recognize an old shipmate? From scalloping? From last winter?' The man pulled an unopened pint of Jack Daniel's, Luke's favorite, from the paper bag. Held the bottle up for Luke to see.

The old fisherman squinted more closely at the man's face. Then at the bottle in his hand. He literally licked his lips, first the upper, then the lower, at the sight of the familiar label. 'Oh, yeah, sure, scalloping. Last winter.'

'Thought it might be nice for us to catch up. Maybe have a nightcap while we talk. You know? One for the road.'

'Okay,' Luke nodded. 'Guess one for the road wouldn't hurt.'

Luke climbed aboard the boat. The man followed. Once on board, the two men eased themselves down into sitting position on the deck. The man handed Luke the bottle of whiskey. 'Old friends first. Help yourself,' he said.

Luke unscrewed the top, took a long pull at the bottle and handed it back. 'What's it you wanna talk about?' he asked.

Riordan took the bottle carefully in his gloved hands so as not to disturb any of Luke's fingerprints.

'Here's to you, Luke. It's been a pleasure knowing you.' He raised the bottle but didn't drink so as not to add his own saliva to Luke's on the rim.

Luke didn't notice. Just took the bottle eagerly when the man handed it back.

'Yeah. To you too, whoever you are.' Luke took another long pull.

By the time the bottle was mostly empty, Luke was sound asleep. Riordan got up and kicked him lightly in the butt just to make sure he was really out. Then he tied a line around one of Luke's boots, hoisted him over the side and lowered him head first into the bay.

The frigid Maine water shocked Luke into a kind of drunken consciousness but it took only a minute or two of flailing and flopping for the old sailor to suck up enough salt water to fill his lungs and sink. Even so the man waited a couple of minutes longer. Just to be sure.

Then he pulled Luke in like a big dead fish, unwound the line from around Luke's ankle and let the body slip into the darkness below.

That done, he poured the meager remains of the whiskey into the water and placed the empty bottle, still bearing Luke's fingerprints and saliva, on to the deck where the police would no doubt conclude Luke had knocked off one too many and, in so doing, had inadvertently tumbled overboard to his death.

As Conor Riordan climbed back on to the dock and walked to his car, he wondered if Luke Haskell actually remembered him or not. Didn't much matter. He wouldn't remember him any more.

Chapter Twenty-Two

10:31 P.M., Saturday, August 22, 2009
Roque Bluffs, Maine

THE SOUND OF the screen door banging against its frame shook Maggie from thoughts of the past. She turned to see Sam and Willie coming back from the house, Sam carrying a bottle of Piper and two delicate champagne flutes, Willie carrying his grungy tennis ball.

'I thought I'd try to convince you to change your mind. Celebrate our reunion.'

Maggie was about to turn him down again and then figured, what the hell, why not? Sam might be more relaxed about telling her what she needed to know if she shared the champagne and came at him more as a friend than as a cop. 'Okay. Just a little.'

The cork exploded from the bottle. Willie galloped after it. Sam poured out two glasses of Piper-Heidsieck. He handed Maggie one.

'To old friends,' he said, raising his flute.

She tapped her glass against his, took a sip of the delicious bubbly stuff. 'Old friends.'

'Now, tell me, Maggie May, what is it you want to talk about?'

'Tiffany Stoddard.'

'Who?'

'Tiffany Stoddard.'

Sam's expression turned blank. 'Sorry. The name doesn't ring a bell.'

'It should. You gave her an A in your non-fiction class last fall. Another A in your short story class this spring. An attractive young woman, at least in her pictures. About five-four. Slim. Dark hair.'

'Tiffany Stoddard?' Sam said as if searching his memory. 'Oh yes, I do remember her.' The hardness in his face faded. The jokiness returned. 'Unfortunate name, Tiffany. I've always felt people shouldn't name their daughters after jewelry stores.'

Maggie ignored the sarcasm. She wasn't about to allow herself to be distracted by Sam's bullshit. 'What was your relationship with her?'

'Relationship?' Sam shrugged. 'She was my student. I was her teacher. As you noted, she took my non-fiction class last fall. Short story this spring.'

'You gave her As in both.'

'She wrote well. Her short story was very good in fact. I gave her an A for it because she deserved an A.'

'Where is her story?'

'No idea. I graded it. Made some comments. Suggested she might try for publication in one of the smaller magazines or perhaps online. Then I gave it back to her.'

'You didn't keep a copy?'

'No. But I'm sure she has one.'

'Was the non-fiction class the first time you met her?'

Sam studied her. Maggie supposed he was trying to decide whether or not to lie. Sam, as Emily had learned so often during their years together, was an accomplished liar.

'No,' he said, 'we initially met on campus the previous spring. She was wandering around Kimball Hall, that's where the English Department's housed, looking for her academic advisor's office. Walked into mine by accident.'

'And?'

'You know me, Maggie,' Sam smiled. 'I took one look at those luscious legs and invited her in. We talked. She told me she was interested in writing. More specifically in journalism. Said she wanted to be a reporter. I suggested she sign up for my non-fiction class for the fall semester. I gave her an A in that class as well.'

'Were you fucking her, Sam?'

Sam said nothing. Just hit the wet tennis ball for Willie and watched the dog race for the beach.

'Were you fucking her?'

'Of course not. It's against the rules for a professor to have sexual relations with one of his students.'

The wooden screen door slammed again and both Maggie and Sam turned to see a naked and obviously very drunk young woman stagger down the porch stairs. She stopped by Maggie's chair to pick up her flip-flops and then continued on her way, apparently heading for the beach. Willie followed, eager for new games.

Maggie watched her go. 'Anyone you know?' she asked. 'In the biblical sense I mean.'

'Don't be sarcastic, Margaret. Sarcasm doesn't suit you.'

'Sam, I really don't care what you do with your personal life. Particularly since you and Emily are no longer married. I just need to know if you were having sex with her. Tiffany Stoddard I mean. Not Lady Godiva down there.'

'It may surprise you, Margaret,' Sam sighed, 'but I don't have sex with all my students.'

'No, Sam, I'm sure you don't. Just the good-looking females you can bully, bribe or otherwise cajole into bed.'

'You know, Maggie, you're beginning to sound more like a cop and less like a friend. You're also beginning to irritate me.'

'Actually, I'm here as a cop, Sam.'

'Really? And why is that? Why are you asking about Tiffany Stoddard?

'She was murdered.'

Sam's face registered shock. 'How did it happen?'

'With a knife. Down by the state park in Machiasport. Somebody stabbed her a number of times, then cut her throat and left her there to die.'

Sam grimaced. 'I'm very sorry to hear that,' he finally said. 'Tiffany was not only pretty, she was also a talented and ambitious young woman. Do they – do you – know who did it?'

Maggie studied Sam before answering. Still unreadable.

'Do you know who did it?' he repeated.

'No, not yet, Sam.'

Maggie considered the possibilities. Could Sam have been Stoddard's accomplice in the drug trade as well as her lover? Perhaps the source of the 10,000 dollars offered to Pike Stoddard in return for the use of his boat. Writing fiction and teaching college English seemed an unlikely apprenticeship for drug dealing but maybe Sam craved excitement. More likely, he needed money. His tastes and lifestyle required large amounts of it. According to Emily, at the time of their divorce he'd already worked his way through much of what Julia left him. If all he had left at this point was the house and his salary at UMM, well, it wasn't nearly enough for his needs. Five million dollars might be very tempting, especially if Tiff did most of the dirty work.

'Any suspects?' he asked.

'Yes, Sam. I need you to tell me where you were last night between eight o'clock and roughly two A.M.'

'You're not suggesting I killed Tiffany Stoddard? You can't be serious.'

'Just answer the question. Where were you?'

'Here. At the house.'

'Alone?'

'Yes. Alone.' The drunken slur was gone. Suddenly Sam seemed very aware of what he was saying. 'I was in the studio working. Writing. I'm trying hard to finish the new novel. Not an easy task. The words don't come as easily as they once did.'

'By the studio you mean Julia's studio?'

'Yes. I've turned it into my office, my writing room.'

'Anyone see you there?'

'No. When I write, I write alone and I don't encourage interruptions.'

'I see. While you were there, writing alone, did you make or receive any phone calls?'

'No. There's no phone in the studio. And cell reception out here is practically non-existent. Why?'

'Just that there'd be a record of a call being made. An indication that you're telling the truth.'

'Just an indication? Not a proof?'

'No, not a proof. Somebody else might have used your phone. When was the last time you worked on the book?'

'Last night. I was at it quite late.'

'I assume you write on a computer?'

'Yes. Of course. Why do you want to know?'

'I'd like you to show me the computer.'

'Not until you tell me why.'

'Computers are precise machines. Yours will have kept a record of when you last modified the manuscript.'

'So it would. All right, come with me.' Sam got up from his chair and led Maggie across the lawn. Willie trotted behind. The old barn had been transformed. Instead of Julia's colorful chaos of paints and canvases and the smell of oils and turpentine, the room was now furnished as a writer's office and filled with books and magazines, some neatly stored in bookcases, others strewn carelessly about. Half a dozen of Julia's paintings hung from the walls. Three seascapes and three nudes. Two of Zanie and one of Maggie herself at eighteen. Half the age she was today. It was a good painting and she decided not to allow herself to be distracted or embarrassed by its presence.

An antique pine desk occupied the middle of the room. On the desk, she saw a slender silver laptop bearing the ubiquitous Apple logo. A light at the front of the case indicated the machine was still turned on, in sleep mode.

She sat. Sam stood behind her. She opened the computer and tapped the space bar, waking the machine from its slumber. Her eyes scanned an on-screen desktop littered with dozens of files and documents. Sam was not a meticulous electronic housekeeper. 'Which one?' she asked.

He pointed to a file.

'*A Slender Thread*?'

'Yes. That's the working title. It's about a murder actually. An older man has an affair with a younger woman. He kills her when she tells him she's dumping him for a younger man.' He smiled mischievously. 'Naturally, the murder is investigated by a beautiful female detective.'

Maggie turned and stared up at him.

'Relax, Margaret. I'm only joking. It is about a murder but there are no beautiful detectives in the book. Or anywhere else I suppose. Present company excepted of course.'

'Not funny, Sam. If you think my investigation or Tiffany Stoddard's death are things you should be joking about, trust me, I have ways of changing your mind very quickly.'

'I'm sorry. That was in bad taste. I apologize.'

Maggie double-clicked the file labeled *A Slender Thread*. In the column labeled 'Date Modified' she read that the last changes had been made to the manuscript just this morning, August 22, 2009 at exactly 1:12 A.M. At 1:12 A.M. both Tiff Stoddard and Emily Kaplan were still lying on Port Road. Still being rained on by passing thunderstorms.

'Satisfied?' asked Sam.

Actually all the 'Date Modified' entry indicated was that someone had made and saved a change, perhaps as simple as a single key-stroke, at 1:12 A.M., more than four hours after Tiffany Stoddard's throat was cut. If Sam was counting on that to establish his innocence, he was mistaken.

'You work late,' Maggie said and closed the computer. She swiveled around in the chair. 'Now it's time for you to answer my original question. What was your relationship with Tiffany Stoddard?'

Sam drank down the last of his champagne, put the flute on a coffee table and sat down in the blue couch across from the desk.

'Okay, I didn't kill her. But I did have sex with her. A number of times.'

'When was the last time?'

'A few months ago. May, I think. At the end of the semester. Having achieved her A-plus she dropped me for someone else. Someone younger I suppose.'

'Where did you do it?'

'Have sex you mean?'

'Yes.'

Sam shrugged. 'Usually here. In what was once my marriage bed. Let me see, where else? We had a lovely time one evening on a blanket down on the beach in front of a fire. Then there were a couple of times in my office in Kimble Hall.'

'Ever go to her apartment?'

'Only once. It was a grubby little place on the other side of the river from campus and, frankly, a little too close for my taste. I didn't want to be seen going in and out of a student's apartment.'

'But your fingerprints might be there?'

'Do they last that long?'

'Yes.'

'Then they might. We also did it a couple of times here in the studio while we were discussing my book.'

'Did you know she was pregnant?'

'Yes. Though I doubt the baby was mine. In any event she wanted to get rid of it.'

'When did she tell you that?'

'Yesterday. Early afternoon. She showed up here. She was a mess. Somebody had beaten her up. Broken her nose. Blackened her eye. I asked her who did it. She told me it was none of my business. Then she asked me if I knew anyone who could abort a pregnancy. I asked her if she was the one who was pregnant. She said yes. I asked if the lucky dad was the same guy who beat her up. She wouldn't say. I told her I didn't know any abortionists but I did tell her about Emily and the drugs she sometimes prescribes. She wrote down Em's name and address and left. The next thing I know is you showing up and telling me she's been murdered. That's it, Maggie. Really.'

'So it wasn't you who beat her up? It wasn't you who killed her?'

'You really think I'm capable of that?'

'Sam, I've seen your rages. I know you threatened Emily with physical violence on more than one occasion. I also know you were arrested three and some years ago for beating up a woman named Kristen Hauser who you picked up in a hotel bar in Philadelphia. You attacked Ms Hauser ostensibly because, when you couldn't get it up after your seventh or eighth martini, she made fun of your sexual prowess. Guests in the next room heard the ruckus and called hotel security. Hauser only dropped assault charges because you wrote her a check with a whole bunch of zeroes on it.'

Sam shook his head. 'Jesus, who told you about that? Emily?'

'No. The arresting officer. Detective Louisa DelCastro of the Philadelphia PD. She and I had a chat just before

I drove out here. Turns out Detective DelCastro feels just about the same way I do about assholes who beat up women.'

Sam refilled his champagne flute, this time with vodka. He started pacing around the studio. He was considerably more wobbly on his feet than before.

'Did Tiff ever mention the name Conor Riordan?'

Sam looked at Maggie curiously. 'Yes. Conor Riordan is the name of one of the characters in my book. The bad guy. The killer. I was looking for an unusual name and Tiff suggested it. It seemed to fit the character perfectly.'

Maggie managed not to visibly react. Just said, 'Oh, really? Did she say where she got it? If maybe it was the name of somebody she knew?'

Sam shrugged. 'No idea. I assume she just dreamed it up.'

'Did she make other suggestions for the book?'

'Yes. Quite a few, actually. As I told you, Tiff was both talented and imaginative.'

'Would you print out a copy for me? I'd like to read it.'

'No. Not till it's finished.'

'Sam, this is not about literature, it's about murder. I promise I won't criticize its literary merit.'

'I don't think so.'

'Think again. I can always get a warrant if I need one. Also, since you were one of Tiff Stoddard's sex partners, I need you to come to the Sheriff's Department first thing tomorrow morning and provide us with a set of fingerprints and a DNA sample.'

Sam sighed. 'Very well. Is that all?'

'No. I thought you might be interested in knowing Emily was injured last night by the same guy who killed Stoddard. But don't worry. She'll be fine.'

Chapter Twenty-Three

11:37 P.M., Saturday, August 22, 2009
Machias, Maine

IT WAS SATURDAY night and even late on a Saturday night in August the Musty Moose was jammed. Maggie waited for a twenty-year-old Ford Bronco to pull out of a close-in parking spot and hustled to beat an equally ancient Corolla to the space. The driver scowled but didn't make an issue. Maggie smiled sweetly and offered a little wave of thanks.

Maggie had wasted more than a few good hours hanging out at the Moose back in the day. Though it had been a while since she'd been there, when she walked through the door it looked as if nothing had changed. The big horseshoe bar in front of her was jammed with drinkers. Three full-sized pool tables in a separate room to the right appeared to be as busy as ever. The booths and tables to the left where dinner could be had before the serious drinking began were pretty much full.

Perhaps the most defining feature of The Moose was the dozens of stuffed heads that stared down from the walls through beady glass eyes. More heads, in Maggie's opinion, than you'd be likely to find in most museums of natural history. She always thought it would be a nice touch if they included among the deer and moose and bears, a few of the heads of local drunks who'd dropped dead in the place over the years. Among them would be Charlie Harbison and Duane Cuyler, both of whom were grossly overweight and both of whom suffered fatal heart attacks, three years apart, falling off the same stool at the bar. Perhaps the most famous Moose incident of them all was the killing of Clarence 'Squidgy' Kelly, who choked to death on a cue ball stuffed down his throat by a 300 pound logger who was irate he'd come in second to Squidgy in a high-stakes game of straight pool. It had taken a much younger Sheriff John Savage and three of his deputies to wrestle the logger to the ground and get the cuffs on him. He ended up doing twenty to life at the old prison in Thomaston for murder.

Maggie scanned the main room but didn't spot any familiar faces. A bluegrass group, Bobbie Rae and the Sunrise Pickers according to the sign propped in front of them, were making some nice sounds in the far corner. Since The Moose was the only real bar in town it drew a wildly eclectic collection of both casual and serious drinkers. Pretty much everybody within a ten-mile radius who had an inclination for booze and the money to pay for it hit the Moose at one time or another. Tonight, as on most Saturdays, especially in summer, the bar was packed three deep with a noisy, laughing mass of ex-hippies, aging rednecks, gray-haired bikers, some with ponytails and one with dreadlocks, a few local business types and a bunch of college kids, most of whom may or may not have been legal but sure as hell didn't look it.

She took a deep breath and plunged into the maelstrom, finally managing to squeeze in close enough so that one of the two bartenders might actually notice her. For a couple of minutes neither did. The one Maggie didn't recognize was a sour-faced young woman in her twenties who couldn't seem to handle the stream of orders being thrown her way. Tiffany Stoddard's replacement, Maggie supposed. C'mon, honey, she silently urged, if you don't get that scowl off your face and prove you can handle the hustle better than this, Tommy'll toss you out on your ear.

The other bartender was, of course, the maestro himself, Tommy Flynn. Tommy could do it all simultaneously. Take orders, mix drinks, throw out a cheerful Irish insult and never miss a beat. Tommy had been a fixture at the Moose as long as Maggie had been old enough to go there. Matter of fact, it was Tommy who mixed and served her her first legal drink. A frozen margarita. Salt on the rim. Tab on the house. A twenty-first birthday present. Seemed exotic as hell at the time.

It only took him a minute to notice her.

'Well, my God, if it isn't the love of my life.' He leaned across the bar and gave her a peck on the cheek. 'Up visiting the old man?'

'You got it, Tommy. Can't believe you're still working here.'

'Darlin', I'm just like your father. Never give up a gig that works. Anyway, I don't just work here any more. I own the place. Half of it anyway. Josh Bender sold me fifty percent for a whole bunch less than it was worth and took off for the sunshine three years ago.'

While he was talking Tommy flipped the caps off three bottles of Pabst Blue Ribbon and handed them to three of the college kids and mixed and poured two icy martinis, which he set down in front of a pair of aging preppies propped up at the other end of the bar. 'Anyway, what can I get you?' asked Tommy. 'Saturday nights, I give away the PBR for two bucks a pop.'

PBR had its fans, but Maggie wasn't one of them. 'No thanks. Have any Geary's Summer?'

'Just in the bottle.'

'That'll do.' Maggie looked around at the crowd. 'Anybody I might know in tonight?'

'Your baby brother got here just a while ago. Last time I looked he was working a couple of suckers in the other room at table three.' Maggie glanced over. You couldn't see the third table from where she was standing. Tommy got the beer and set it down in front of her then grabbed a bottle of Canadian Club and started pouring whiskey over ice. 'How long you in town for?'

'I don't know. Maybe a while. Heard you lost one of your bartenders last night.'

Tommy looked up, instantly getting it that Maggie might be here for more than a beer and a chat.

'Former bartenders. Tiff hadn't worked here in a while. Hell of a way to go, though. Got her head damn near cut off is what I heard.'

'That's close enough.'

'You working this case?'

'Just helping the staties out,' she said. 'Can I pull you into a quiet corner for a couple of minutes?'

Tommy thought about that. 'Sure. I guess I owe Tiff that much. Must be due for a break anyway.' He looked around and called over a young man who'd been waiting tables and told him to take over at the bar.

'Let's go out back,' he said. 'It's quieter there. Less public.'

'Why don't you get yourself a drink?' she asked. 'My treat.'

Tommy smiled. 'Never touch the stuff while I'm working.'

Tommy led her through the kitchen, where the cooks were frying up a storm. Haute cuisine it wasn't. Practically everything on the Moose's menu that wasn't a lobster, a burger or a side-salad was either deep-fried or barbequed. Only place she knew that actually served chicken-fried artichoke hearts. The two of them went out through a back door on to a small deck. The noise behind them, while still audible, was no longer deafening.

'Tell me about Tiffany Stoddard.'

'What do you want to know?'

'You've got a good eye. Let's start with your general impression.'

Tommy shrugged. 'I've got nothing but good to say about her. Pretty girl. More than pretty, actually. Good bartender too. Unlike that sourpuss I've got now, Tiff could bullshit with the customers and handle the drinks at the same time. Smart, too. Like you in that regard. Nothing much got by her. I always figured Tiff Stoddard could go as far as she wanted in this world. Do anything that took her fancy. Never dreamed anything like this would happen to her.'

'Any idea what it was she wanted to do?'

'Talked about being a writer sometimes.'

'Really? You mean like fiction?'

'Nah. More like working for a newspaper. Or maybe a TV station. Y'know, a reporter.'

Same thing both Sam and Donelda had said. Maggie took a swig from the Geary's bottle. 'How long was she working here?'

'A couple of years. Ever since she started at UMM. Washington County kid. Folks live up in Eastport.'

'Was she an addict?'

'Oxycontin?'

'Yeah.'

'No way. Tiff was too smart for that.'

'Think she might have been dealing?'

'Jesus, I wouldn't have thought so. Tiff was a girl who knew where she wanted to go.'

'Why'd she quit?'

'Said she had enough saved up and wanted to concentrate on her studies. But I don't know. Even if she had the savings, I would have thought she would still want to make some money. Sure as hell enjoyed spending it.'

'You know anything about any boyfriends she might have had?'

Tommy shrugged. 'Just about all the unattached guys who came in this place hit on Tiff from time to time. Some of the attached ones too. She was happy chatting them up but far as I know none of them ever scored. None she ever talked about anyway.'

'Was there anybody she saw regularly?'

'I wouldn't know. But, come to think of it, you might want to ask your brother about that.'

'Harlan?'

'Yeah. I saw the two of them leave together more than once. But do me a favor. Don't tell Harlan you got that from me. Sonofabitch has an unpredictable temper and I don't want to get on the wrong side of him.'

Chapter Twenty-Four

11:45 P.M., *Saturday, August 22, 2009*
Eastport, Maine

THAT NIGHT, TABITHA Stoddard dreamed she saw the December Man again.

In her dream it wasn't summer any more but every bit as dark and icy as it had been just before Christmas, when Tiff brought him to the house to give Pike the money for the boat.

Tabitha dreamed she was outside by the breakwater. Snow was falling. Millions of small, hard flakes swirling in circles all around her. She was walking down a long wooden dock that seemed to stretch forever out into the cold, black sea. She was carrying Harold in both arms. He still had Tiff's package inside him, still wrapped in layers of newspaper and packing tape exactly as it was when she'd gone to meet Tiff in the playground. Having the package scared her and she wanted to give it back to Tiff.

She walked past fishing boats that were tied up, one after the other in parallel lines on either side of the dock. The *Katie Louise* was at the end, the very last boat in a very long line. In spite of the darkness Tabitha could see her father's boat clear as day, its silhouette outlined in tiny white Christmas lights, its diesel engine idling, churning up the water behind. In the dream, the *Katie Louise* wasn't dirty and beat up any more, but freshly painted bright red and white. She was brand new all over again.

She saw Tiff standing in the stern dressed, in spite of the cold, in a gauzy white summer dress. Her high school graduation dress. Her hair was down and she was smiling and waving. Tabitha had never seen her look more beautiful.

'C'mon, slowpoke,' Tiff called to her. 'We'll never get out of here if you don't hurry.'

'Where are we going?'

'It doesn't matter. You just have to hurry.'

But Tabitha didn't want to hurry because the December Man was standing behind Tiff, staring at her with icy eyes and holding a big knife.

The December Man wasn't smiling.

Tiff called out to her again. 'Come on, goose. A promise is a promise.'

She wanted desperately to warn Tiff the December Man was there. Warn Tiff the December Man was going to kill her.

But, try as she might, she couldn't get the words out, and so she just watched as the December Man reached around Tiff's head with the knife and drew the blade across her neck. Tiff screamed. Blood poured from the wound. Waves of blood. Oceans of blood that just kept coming and coming until it turned Tiff's white dress and the deck of the *Katie Louise* and even the black ocean itself a bright, blood-soaked red.

'See, just like I told your father,' said the lady cop who for some reason was standing beside Tabitha, one hand on her shoulder. 'Cut her open like a hog in a slaughterhouse.'

Tabitha turned and ran. The December Man jumped down from the deck and ran after her, still holding the knife, wanting to cut Tabitha's neck open as well.

Tabbie ran as fast as she could but she was just a fat little kid and her fastest wasn't even close to fast enough. Before she was halfway up the dock, she felt a hand grab her by the wrist. The December Man turned her around and grabbed Harold from her arms. Then he pulled her toward him. Lifted the knife. Tabitha closed her eyes and screamed and screamed waiting for the knife to cut her throat. But instead, all she felt was a pair of strong hands lifting her and holding her, a familiar voice telling her it was all right. It was just a bad dream. Nothing but a bad dream. She opened her eyes. The December Man was gone and her mother was there.

Donelda pulled Tabitha toward her, held Tabbie's rigid body tight against her bony chest, rocked her back and forth and told the last of her three daughters that it had only been a bad dream. A nightmare. Told her that everything was all right and she mustn't be frightened. But Tabitha couldn't stop sobbing because she knew very well her mother was wrong. Everything was not all right. Nothing would ever be all right again.

Chapter Twenty-Five

11:45 P.M., Saturday, August 22, 2009
Machias, Maine

THE POOL TABLES in the side room at the Moose were crowded with the usual assortment of players and hangers-on. She spotted Harlan in a game at table three and leaned in against the wall under the head of a long-dead bear some taxidermist had stuffed with its mouth open and fangs exposed, in full roar. The creature looked like it was seconds away from leaping off the wall and gobbling up the nearest player.

She watched her kid brother sweep the table till all that was left was the eight ball pressed against the far rail about a foot from the pocket. He had a good eye, that was for sure. Probably why they'd made him a sniper in the Corps.

Harlan sized up the table. The cue ball lay all the way down on the other side at only a slight angle to the eight. A tricky shot. He walked the table, checked the angles then leaned down and drew back his stick. As he glanced up at the eight he spotted Maggie standing in the corner and smiled a smile that was uniquely his. She smiled back. He nodded. She nodded back. Raised her bottle in silent salute.

'Hey, Harlan, you shootin' pool or pickin' up pussy?' hollered some goofball who was leaning on a cue stick and wearing a t-shirt with a slogan that made even Maggie smile. 'Save a tree. Wipe your ass with an owl.'

'Watch your mouth, asshole, there's a lady in the room,' said Harlan, then added in a softer voice, 'Far corner right.' He gently tapped the cue ball and watched it roll, laying it in exactly where the eight ball met the rail. The eight slithered right, sticking to the rail, rolling so slowly Maggie thought it would surely stop before it arrived. But it had just enough behind it and fell gently into the pocket.

'A lady who happens to be my sister.' Harlan picked up a small pile of bills from the side of the table, handed his cue to the guy with the t-shirt. 'Your game.'

He stuffed the money in his pocket, retrieved his beer and walked to where Maggie stood.

'Hello, Magpie. Didn't know you were coming to town.'

'I didn't either. Not until about two o'clock this morning.'

He wrapped his muscular arms around her and gave her a hug, still hanging on to his beer bottle. She hugged him back, still hanging on to hers.

'Good to see you, Harlan.'

'Yeah, you too. What brings you to God's country?'

'Partly the old man. Partly murder.'

'Tiff Stoddard?'

'Yeah. Heard you used to hang out with her.'

'Oh really?' Harlan leaned in close, eyes narrowed. 'Now who exactly did you hear that from? Tommy been shootin' off his mouth again?'

'Don't take it out on Tommy. I'm a certified expert in getting people to say more than they intend. Including Tommy.'

'Buy you a drink?' asked Harlan.

She held up the mostly full bottle of Geary's. 'Haven't finished the one I've got. Listen, why don't we grab that booth over there. Those people are leaving.'

They waited while a waitress cleaned off the dirty dishes and gave the table a quick swipe with a rag. They slid in. Harlan ordered a burger and fries and another beer. Maggie declined food.

'You did hang out with her, didn't you? Tiff Stoddard I mean.' The place was crowded and noisy enough so Maggie could speak in a normal voice and be confident no one outside the booth could hear them.

Harlan looked as if he was weighing his response. Then he shrugged. 'Tiff? Yeah. We saw each other. Mostly back when she was working here. Not so much lately.'

'What was your relationship?'

'We messed around from time to time.'

'Messed around?'

'I'm not really sure it's any of your business. But, yeah, you know, messed around. We liked each other. We had, what do you call it? Good chemistry. I'd come in. Sit at the end of the bar. On slow nights we'd start bullshitting about this or that. Some nights, by the time most of the customers were gone and Tommy was getting ready to close, we'd still be yacking away. I'd wait while she finished cleaning up. Then we'd go over to her place. Sometimes sit around and talk some more. Sometimes more than that. Really we were more friends than anything else.'

'Friends with benefits?'

'Like they say.'

'Always her place? Not yours?'

'Hers was closer.'

'Where are you living these days?'

'Out in hell and gone. Single-wide in Whiting. Kind of a dump. Nowhere you'd want to visit.'

'When did you find out about the murder?'

'Heard the radio reports this morning coming in on the truck. Got some construction work helping renovate a summer place in Bucks Harbor.'

'Did you know Em was nearly killed by the same guy who killed Tiff?'

'No.' Harlan blinked across the table at his sister. 'No, I hadn't heard that.' Em and Harlan were close. She'd taught him most of his best moves on the basketball court. 'She gonna be okay?'

'Yes, thank God, it looks like she will.'

Harlan nodded. 'Good.'

'You don't sound very shocked by Tiff's death.'

'I'm not. I feel bad about it. Real bad. But I'm not shocked.'

'Why not?'

'Partly because Tiff was into stuff she shouldn't have been. Partly, I guess, because death hasn't shocked me for a very long time,' said Harlan. 'Seen too much of it.'

Harlan waited for Maggie to say something. When she didn't he started explaining, 'That's what war does to you, Magpie. What it did to me anyway. It saddens me to lose friends. And to be honest Tiff was way more than a friend. But I'm no longer shocked by it.'

'Not even by the death of a woman you made love to?'

'No, not even by that.'

Maggie realized Harlan was staring blankly over her shoulder as he spoke. She turned to see who or what he was looking at but there was nothing there.

'Sometimes after a roadside bomb there was nothing left of your buddies but an arm or a leg and it was tough to figure out who the hell it belonged to. One time all they could find was an ear. I always wondered if the guys who collected body parts ever sent that ear home to the guy's family for burial. What the fuck do you do with an ear? Stick it in a six-foot box in a six-foot hole and play taps? Requiem for an ear? But sometimes that was all that was left to send.'

'You killed people there as well.'

'Yes, I did,' he said, his voice flat, without affect, still gazing over her shoulder. 'Twenty-three insurgents. Three of them women. One not much more than a kid. Twelve in Fallujah. Eight in Ramadi. Most through a scope from a distance but a couple pretty close up.' He spoke as if reciting statistics that had nothing to do with him, as if he was watching himself perform these acts of violence, narrating a documentary film that ran only in his mind. 'I killed one guy close up with a knife. I remember him standing right up against me. Smelling food on his breath.'

'Harlan,' Maggie said, trying to break into wherever his mind was and failing.

'Guy's trying to get me and I'm trying to get him. We're holding on to each other like a slow dance on prom night.'

'Harlan,' she said louder this time, putting both her hands over his right fist that was clenched tightly on the table.

He heard her this time. Shook his head as if waking from a dream. His eyes darted around the room checking for anyone watching. Or listening. No one was. His smile returned. A thin smile.

'Where were you just now?'

'Right here with you, Magpie. I never left.'

'Don't lie.'

He shrugged. 'I'm a liar.'

'This happen a lot?'

'It happens. They're called flashbacks. Shrink in the hospital in Bethesda said a lot of combat guys get 'em.

Usually, I flashback to Fallujah or Ramadi. They were the worst. Sometimes some other place.'

'It's not like you're just remembering it?'

'No. It's not like remembering. It's like being there. In Fallujah where I killed that guy with the knife, I was back there just now. I could smell the fear on the guy. Feel the warmth of his blood pouring out over my hand. Anyway,' he said, shaking it off, 'tell me what happened with Tiff. Somebody got her with a knife's what I heard.' There was still no emotion in his voice.

'Yeah, he got her all right. Most of the gory details have been on TV all day.'

He sat quietly for a few seconds, thinking, she supposed, about Tiff's death. 'Hey, want another beer or anything?'

'Harlan, was there something more between you and Tiff Stoddard than you're telling me?' Maggie looked straight into the soft, brown eyes everyone said were nearly identical to her own.

'Like what?'

'Like, oh, I don't know, like maybe you were in love with her?'

He sighed. Looked at her. Nodded, finally engaged. 'Yeah, I guess. Tiff and I could have had something special. Been something special. But she wouldn't let it happen. It had to be her way or no way. We were good together. Good chemistry. Great sex. So yeah, I guess I loved her. But as for her getting hung up with the likes of me? No way. Never happen.'

'Why not?'

'It would have screwed up all her plans for the future. Tiff always said she was *never* gonna let what happened to her mother happen to her. At least her old man owned a fishing boat. I couldn't even offer her that.'

'When was the last time you saw her?'

'About a week ago. When we broke up. When she dumped me.'

'Why'd she quit the Moose?'

'Like I said before, Tiff was into stuff she shouldn't have been. It was taking more and more of her time.'

'Dealing?'

Harlan looked around to see if anyone was listening. No one was. Even so he lowered his voice so Maggie had to move closer to hear him. 'Big time. Tiff wanted to get rich quick, and Ox seemed to her the fastest way to go about it. I told her more than once she was messing around with the wrong kind of people and sooner or later she was gonna get hurt by it. But whenever I said anything like that she'd just laugh it off. Thought she was tough enough to handle it. Hell, Tiff thought she was tough enough to handle anything.'

'I need to know if you have an alibi for last night, Harlan.'

'Wait a minute. You're asking *me* if I have an alibi?'

'Yeah. I'm asking you.'

'You're telling me you think I killed Tiff?'

'No. But because you had a sexual relationship with her some people might. So I'm asking you where you were when it happened. It's my job, Harlan.'

'You working on this or something?'

'Yeah. Or something. TDY. With the state police. So where were you last night?'

'I was here. Shooting pool. Probably twenty people'd swear they seen me.'

'What time did you get here?'

He shrugged. 'Ten. Ten-thirty. Thereabouts. Left when Tommy closed up. Round one-thirty.'

'Then what?'

'Spent the rest of the night at the Bluebird Motel.'

Maggie's eyes narrowed. 'Who with?'

'See that little blonde up there banging away on the tambourine?' He nodded toward the band. 'Name's Francie something or other.'

Francie something or other saw Harlan looking at her and smiled.

'A replacement for Tiff?'

'Not even close. More like a one night stand. The lady may or may not want to confirm my presence in her bed since she was wearing a wedding ring at the time.'

'How about before you got here? Say between eight and ten?'

'Home. Alone.'

'Tiff ever mention the name Conor Riordan?'

Harlan spent longer than he should thinking about how to answer that. 'Look, Magpie, you're my sister but you're also a cop. So's my old man. There are people around here who hold that against me. Try not to put me in a difficult position.'

'Who's Conor Riordan, Harlan?'

'Where'd you get the name from?'

'Let's just say from an unnamed source. Tiff ever mention it?'

There was an almost imperceptible hesitation. 'Yeah, she mentioned it,' Harlan said in a low voice barely audible in the noisy bar. 'Once or twice.'

'Who is he?'

'The man that never was. The man nobody is willing to admit they knew. Tiff knew. But now she's dead. And that, big sister, is all I'm going to say on the subject.'

'What do you know about Conor Riordan?'

'Stop asking about Conor Riordan.'

'I can't.'

Harlan shook his head and blew out a long sigh. He took both his sister's hands in his and looked her straight in the eye. 'Do us both a favor, Magpie. Forget Conor Riordan. Don't go looking for trouble you don't need. Have a nice visit with the old man and then go back to Portland and forget you ever heard the name. I don't care how good a cop you are or how many pals you've got on the state police. You're my sister and I love you and I don't want to see you get hurt. Or worse, killed.'

Chapter Twenty-Six

12:51 A.M., Sunday, August 23, 2009
Machias, Maine

LIGHT FROM A solitary lamp and the flickering images of what looked like a Red Sox game shone through the living-room window as Maggie climbed the porch steps. Since it was nearly one in the morning, the game either had to be a rebroadcast or the Sox were playing on the coast. She peered in. The only sign of life was a pair of size 13B, stockinged feet hanging over the arm of the sofa. Her father must have dozed off in front of the box.

She checked for the key under the geranium pot to the left of the front door. Still there. Anya hadn't changed that. Least not yet. Maggie let herself in.

Her father was stretched out fully clothed, a baby-blue afghan that Joanne Savage had crocheted decades ago covering the lower half of his long frame. Maggie turned off the TV and studied her father's face in repose. Dark shadows from the single lamp accented circles under his eyes. She saw no point in waking him just so he could go upstairs to sleep in a bed.

She thought about a framed photo, still upstairs she supposed, on the bureau in her parents' bedroom. It showed a much younger John Savage, waist deep in the bone-numbingly cold Maine water, hoisting a three-year-old Maggie over his head, expressions of unutterable joy lighting both their faces. The idea of this impossibly strong man, this force of nature, his big, bony hands forever holding her high in the air, forever holding her tight, the idea of this man, her first true love though she hoped not her last, the idea of John Savage ever succumbing to the frailties of age or disease, of somehow needing her more than she needed him, seemed ludicrous. The inevitability of losing him was something to be fought to the bitter end. Never give up. Never give in.

She made a silent vow to visit more often while she still could and then bent down and kissed him on the forehead. Gently so as not to wake him.

She hauled her bag up to her old room. Nothing had changed here except for the clean set of towels neatly laid out for her on the wooden chair in the corner. Feeling a need to wash off the accumulated grubbiness of the last twenty-four hours, she pulled off her clothes, wrapped herself in a big, fluffy towel and tiptoed down the hall, hoping the sound of the shower wouldn't wake Anya. She had no idea whether or not her father's second wife was a light sleeper.

She let hot water course over her tired and aching body and resolved not to think about the case. The resolution lasted less than a minute. So many strands of what had happened to Tiff Stoddard seemed woven around the most intimate relationships of her own past. Emily. Savage. Sam Harkness. And now Harlan. She worried most about Harlan. He seemed the most vulnerable. Her mind was whizzing around in circles. She told herself to slow it down. She washed her hair.

LATER, DRESSED IN her standard summer sleep outfit, a pair of men's boxers, size small, and a Sea Dogs t-shirt, size XL, she sat down at her old desk, the one she'd used through high school, and opened her laptop. Went to Google first. Feeling a slight sense of betrayal, she typed the words 'Iraq War Veterans Murder PTSD' into the search box. She was stunned. Six-hundred and twenty-seven thousand hits. Probably two years' worth of reading. She read the first couple of pages, articles one through thirty, the most interesting being a series by the *New York Times* about soldiers coming home from Iraq who'd committed murder, suicide and/or sexual assault. Sometimes raping or killing total strangers. Sometimes loved ones. Wives, children, girlfriends. Often members of their own families.

The numbers cited in the articles were large, though Maggie wondered how much larger they were than the numbers you might find in any random sample of unhappy or angry young men who'd experienced violence and were comfortable with the use of firearms.

Still, it seemed logical that service in the random chaos and brutality of the war in Iraq could lead a veteran to a greater propensity to violence when he got back home. Harlan told her he'd killed twenty-three people, one with a knife. Killing was nothing new to him. Death no longer shocked him. Even the violent death of someone he loved.

Harlan, even more than Sam, had to be considered a suspect. He had no alibi for the hours between eight to ten, when Stoddard was killed. And only an unreliable alibi for the hours after leaving the Moose. If Francie the tambourine player was indeed married, it was unlikely she'd publicly testify that a man she met only hours before had spent the night in her bed. It sure as hell wouldn't do her marriage any good.

On the other hand, there was no evidence at all that Harlan had had anything to do with the murder. At least none she was aware of. Also she was sure the vicious sexual aggression visited on Stoddard's body was something Harlan wouldn't do. Couldn't do. Certainly not the Harlan she'd grown up with. Though how well she knew the Harlan who'd come home from Iraq, she wasn't certain.

Moreover, even if her brother was innocent, if he was accused of the crime and it somehow went to trial, any prosecutor worth his salt would try to use his war record and the possibility of PTSD as levers to prove his guilt. At this point, she wasn't even sure his own father would rush to his defense.

Maggie went back to the Google search bar and typed in 'Liz Carroll', 'Murder', 'Arson', 'Maine'. Far fewer hits here. The most interesting was a series of articles by a

Portland Press Herald crime reporter named Tracy Carlin on the death of Sean Carroll's wife and the subsequent investigation. Carlin, Maggie knew, was an old pal of McCabe's. Maybe her partner could help after all. She'd call him in the morning.

She read through the articles twice. The murder of an undercover cop in a high-profile drug investigation is a big deal in any law enforcement agency, and the state Drug Enforcement Agency and the Maine State Police CID Division threw both manpower and resources into the effort to find the killer. Scores of small-time Oxycontin dealers were dragged in and grilled for hours. Known informants were pressed hard for information. Those who admitted any contact with Liz Carroll or any knowledge of the Canadian drug theft were bullied, cajoled and in some cases offered confidential deals to reveal their contacts' distribution sources. Only one useful lead was mentioned. A local distributor admitted she had negotiated a deal with Liz Carroll to reveal her sources in return for protection as a confidential informant and immunity from prosecution. Unfortunately the anonymous informant disappeared and her dismembered body turned up a few days later stuffed into a dumpster behind a WalMart in Brewer.

Maggie closed her computer, flipped off the light and climbed into bed. As she drifted off to sleep she found herself thinking about her dinner with Sean Carroll and wondering if maybe, just maybe, there might be something there.

Chapter Twenty-Seven

MAGGIE CALLED MCCABE as soon as she woke at seven A.M. There were three rings then the single word 'What?' His voice sounded groggy with sleep. 'What's up?'

'You're still asleep,' she said.

'Yeah. I'm still asleep. What's going on?'

'Who's on the phone?' Maggie could hear the sleepy voice of Kyra Erikson, McCabe's girlfriend, in the background.

'Hold on a sec,' said McCabe. 'Let me go in the other room.'

She held on.

'Okay, now talk to me.'

'Listen, McCabe, I'm sorry,' she said. 'I shouldn't have called so early. But it turns out I really could use some help.'

'What do you need?' he said, sounding suddenly alert.

'Let me give you a little background first.' She filled him in on everything she'd learned yesterday. Her conversations with the Stoddards and Emily. Her visit to Sam Harkness's house in Roque Bluffs and to the Musty Moose. She told him about her conversation with Harlan, his relationship with Tiff Stoddard and his reaction to the news of her death. McCabe asked a few questions but mostly listened.

Finally she told him about her dinner with Sean Carroll and what Carroll had said about his wife's death, Laura Blakemore's death and the Canadian drug connection.

'Okay. What do you need me to do?' he asked.

'First off, please read Tracy Carlin's articles about the Liz Carroll murder. Then talk to Carlin. See if maybe she knows anything more about the killing than what she wrote in the paper.'

He said he would.

As soon as Maggie broke the connection, Terri Mirabito called.

'Was she pregnant?' Maggie asked.

'Yup. Only about six weeks but definitely pregnant.'

Cause of death, Terri said, was exsanguination. Manner of death, cutting of the carotid arteries on both sides of Tiff Stoddard's neck.

'She must have bled out in seconds. If the killer was facing her when he cut he would have ended up covered in blood.'

'Any defensive wounds?'

'Nothing under her nails. But she did have a scaphoid fracture of the right wrist. My guess is he grabbed the wrist while she was trying to hit back. Snapped it back and broke it.'

'Murder weapon?'

'A sharp, thin-bladed knife, double edged, the blade less than two centimeters wide.'

Maggie wondered if Harlan owned such a weapon. Or, if he did, whether he'd gotten rid of it.

'I already sent fetal DNA to the lab. Pines ought to have preliminary reads in a couple of days. In the meantime you should send him any potential matching material you might have. Joe will send his reads down to the FBI to see if we can pick up a match with any of their databases.'

'Good. Let Joe know I'll be sending him two saliva samples,' said Maggie. 'One from a man we know had sex with Stoddard. One from me.'

'Why you?' asked Terri. 'I'm reasonably certain you're not the father of Stoddard's baby.'

'No, but my brother may be. If I'm not mistaken my saliva will work as well as his in establishing a match.'

'Yes, it will,' said Terri. 'Maggie, I'm sorry to hear about that.'

'Yeah. Me too. Ask Joe to put it on the front burner. Call me soon as he's got preliminary reads.'

The call ended and Maggie went down to the kitchen and poured herself a mug of coffee. Savage was sitting at the table, leafing through a pile of Sunday papers, ignoring Emmett Ganzer's image three feet away on the tiny kitchen TV. The sound was muted.

She clicked the mute button and Ganzer's voice filled the room: '... comment on that yet. As I said before the investigation is just getting under way.'

'What's this?' Maggie asked, tilting her head at the screen.

'Initial press briefing,' Savage said without looking up. 'Yesterday afternoon. Carroll's got a gag order going so Emmett didn't get to say a whole lot. Just a basic description of the victims and the crime scene followed by a bunch of *no comments*, *no suspects at this time* and *anyone with information please contact blah, blah, blah*.'

Maggie clicked the mute back on. She dropped a couple of pieces of bread into the toaster.

'How come Ganzer's out there and not Carroll? Everybody says he loves being the center of attention.'

'Carroll wants to be the star of the show, not the warm-up act. He won't take his turn until he can leap up on the stage and announce, ta-da! An arrest! All the preliminary crap goes to understudies like Ganzer.'

Maggie buttered her toast and Savage went back to reading the papers. Maggie slid the ones he wasn't looking at out from under him. Tiff Stoddard's murder was the lead story in both the *Press Herald* and the *Bangor Daily News*. It even made the front page, albeit below the fold, in the *Boston Globe*: 'Co-ed Brutally Slain in Downeast Maine. Drug Connection Suspected.' Not much in the way of details. Her father was quoted twice saying the

Washington County Sheriff's Department was offering logistical and manpower support to the state police and was already helping in any way they could. Jena Sculley, one of the kids who found the body, described the scene in some detail. Emily wasn't mentioned till paragraph four:

> In a related incident a local physician, Dr Emily Kaplan, was struck and injured by a car driven by the alleged killer as he fled the scene. At this time, it is uncertain what Dr Kaplan was doing there. She is currently in stable condition at Eastern Maine Medical Center in Bangor. A hospital spokeswoman described her injuries as serious but not life-threatening.
>
> When asked about the possible connection between the murder and the theft of a large amount of Oxycontin in Canada last winter, Detective Ganzer would only say that, while a connection had not yet been firmly established, it could not, at this time, be ruled out.

A photo of Tiffany Stoddard, a kind of formal shot probably taken from her high school yearbook, accompanied the article.

Savage looked up from the paper he was reading. 'What time did you get in last night?'

'Around one or so. You sleep on the couch a lot?'

'Occasionally. Once I fall asleep there, Anya's learned there's no point trying to wake me. I just get cranky. I have an old man's prostate so I wake up at least once during the night. At that point, I go upstairs and climb into bed. Last night it was about three A.M. Make any progress?'

'I talked to Harlan.'

'You tell him about the cancer?'

'No. Not yet. Time wasn't right.'

'Then what did you talk about?'

'The murder. Turns out Harlan had something going with Tiff Stoddard.'

Maggie knew Savage wouldn't be happy hearing that. His expression confirmed it.

'You tell Carroll yet?'

'No.'

'But you're going to?'

'Of course. No choice in the matter. Sleeping with the victim automatically makes Harlan a suspect. Makes me a suspect's sister. Carroll'll have to bring him in for an interview and you can bet it won't be me doing the interviewing.'

'Goddamnit,' Savage said, slamming a folded newspaper loudly against the table. 'That's just effing great. The reporters are gonna eat this shit up. Can't you just see the headlines now? "Sheriff's younger son and key detective's brother named as possible suspect in drug-related killing".'

He sighed deeply. Stared blankly out the back window then turned back to Maggie and asked the obvious question. 'You think there's any chance he might actually have done it?'

'No, I don't.'

'You just being loyal?'

'I don't know. Maybe. The Harlan we knew growing up? There's no way he could have done something like this. He was a hell-raiser for sure but no way a pervert or a sadist. Whoever butchered Tiff Stoddard was both.'

'They say war changes people,' said Savage. 'Traumatizes the mind. I never experienced it personally. Too young for Korea. Too old for Vietnam. Your mother sure as hell thought the war changed Harlan. The newspapers and Internet are chockablock full of stories about Iraqi vets coming home and committing murder and/or suicide.'

'Yeah, I read a bunch last night. Harlan told me he killed twenty-three people over there. One close-up with a knife. That's got to do something bad to your head. So does shrapnel lodged in your brain. Still, there's no hard evidence he had anything to do with this murder.'

'Does he have an alibi for the critical hours?'

'Yes and no.' She told Savage what Harlan had told her about his whereabouts.

'This is going to make it tougher for Carroll to keep you on the case.'

'I know.'

Chapter Twenty-Eight

9:30 A.M., Sunday, August 23, 2009
Portland, Maine

THE SEVEN-STORY PILE of tan bricks at the top of Exchange Street had housed the newsroom and offices of the *Portland Press Herald* ever since the building had been erected and opened with great fanfare back in 1923, the glory days of print journalism.

It stood, then as now, amidst the most impressive centers of local power. From windows on one side, the paper's reporters and editors could look out at Portland's century-old beaux arts City Hall. From the opposite side they could admire the neo-classical lines of the Federal Courthouse and its plainer sister, the Cumberland County Court, just beyond. Police headquarters at 109 Middle Street was two blocks away.

At this hour on a Sunday morning, Detective Sergeant Michael McCabe had no trouble finding a parking space directly across the street. He crossed over and entered the building. An attractive blonde in her late thirties stood waiting for him at the bottom of the narrow stairs. They exchanged chaste kisses.

McCabe and Tracy Carlin had dated casually during his first year in Portland. His BK year as he called it. Before Kyra. Their personalities meshed and they formed a fast and easy kinship. Both were into old movies and good Scotch. Both were single parents of young daughters. And both had gone through and survived messy divorces with habitually unfaithful spouses.

Things might have slipped naturally, without much thought or effort, into something more serious had McCabe not wandered into Portland's North Space Gallery during one of the city's First Friday Art Walks and met a gorgeous young artist named Kyra Erikson.

Once Kyra was in the picture, it quickly became apparent to both Carlin and McCabe that friendship was a better option than romance. The friendship lasted and for the past few years, they had gotten together occasionally for drinks or lunch and, when it was in their mutual interest, to exchange useful bits of information. Always discreet. Always off-the-record. Never for attribution. When McCabe had called Carlin to arrange the meeting, he'd let her know today would be one of those days.

'He's with me, Harry,' Tracy called to the elderly man seated at the security window. The man nodded and waved

McCabe through. Carlin led him up the stairs to the newsroom on the second floor. The place was a rabbit warren of small cubicles with a just a few private offices belonging to the paper's senior editors lined up along one wall. He followed Carlin to her cube. She pulled over a second chair.

'How are you doing, Tracy?' McCabe hadn't seen her for a couple of months. 'Like your new assignment?' She'd recently moved from the crime desk to covering the State House.

'I do. Aside from having to haul my backside back and forth to Augusta all the time, it's working out well. Especially now that Ronnie's old enough not to need sitters. Anyway, you didn't come up here on a Sunday morning to make small talk. What do you need?'

McCabe looked around. The large newsroom was nearly, but not quite, deserted. McCabe could see only three other journalists seated at separated desks. Two were hunched over computer terminals and pecking away at what McCabe supposed were stories for Monday morning's edition. The third, Charlie Issacs, who covered Portland's art scene, was leaning back, feet on his desk, phone to his ear, talking animatedly to whoever was on the other end. Issacs noticed McCabe and waved. McCabe waved back.

'Anywhere we can talk privately?' he asked Tracy.

She cocked her head and gave him a questioning look and then nodded. 'Sure.' She got up and led him to the empty office of Joe Fields, the *Press Herald*'s managing editor. She closed the door and perched on the edge of Field's desk. 'Okay, what's this all about?'

McCabe sat down in the visitors' chair. 'Well, for starters a state police detective.'

'Which one?'

'Sean Carroll?'

'Ah, the young princeling.'

'Why do you call him that?'

'That's what he is. The heir apparent. Only thirty-three and already odds-on favorite to take Mayhew's job when Tom retires at the end of the year. Wouldn't be at all surprised to see him running the whole show before he hits forty.'

'Is he that good?'

She considered the question. 'Yes. Sean's smart, charming and ambitious as hell. And way too good-looking on top of it. What's your interest in Carroll?'

'He's running a murder case up in Machias.'

'Yeah, I heard. Tiffany Stoddard. Gruesome enough to knock my piece on Senator Hardesty's fundraising scandal out of the lead position in this morning's paper.'

McCabe smiled. 'People always prefer reading about gruesome murders to gruesome politicians.'

'Definitely. Especially when the victim's a sexy young woman. Anyway, what's your interest in Carroll?'

'A good friend of mine is working with him and I want to make sure she doesn't get screwed.'

'Figuratively or literally?'

'Either. Both.'

Carlin smiled. 'Who's the lucky girl?'

'Maggie Savage.'

'Maggie? Really? Now that is interesting. What's a Portland detective doing working on a Machias murder?'

'She's from there. The doctor who was injured is a close friend. Carroll agreed to take Mag on as a special investigator. What I need to know is: can Carroll be trusted?'

Tracy arched a single eyebrow. 'Interesting word, trust,' she said. 'If you mean is he a good cop? Absolutely. I haven't checked lately but I'll bet he still has one of the highest clearance rates in the history of the state police CID.' Tracy paused.

'Sounds like there's a but.'

'There is. Like a lot of ambitious men, under the charm, Sean can be ruthless. He'll do whatever it takes to get where he wants as fast as he can get there.'

'Running the state police?'

'For starters. After that maybe politics. Or possibly business. I get the feeling money and power are both important to him. I'm not sure which is more important.'

Over the years McCabe had run into a few cops like that. One was currently running the Portland PD. And thinking about running for governor.

'What can you tell me about the murder of Carroll's wife?' asked McCabe.

'You read my stories on it?'

'I read them. I guess what I want to know is if there was anything about the murder that didn't make its way into your stories?'

'First tell me why you – or Maggie – might be interested in that.'

'Apparently, Carroll thinks whoever killed Stoddard may be the same person who killed his wife.'

'What's the connection?'

'Canadian Oxycontin. As you know, Liz Carroll was killed investigating what became of the drugs stolen in Saint John. What you don't know is a bagful of Canadian tabs were found last night at the scene where Stoddard was killed.'

'Really? Now that *is* interesting.' Tracy's reporter instincts were kicking into high gear. She slid off the edge of the desk, rummaged in her handbag and found a pack of Marlboros. She walked over to the window, raised it about a foot, lit up and eased her butt down on the sill. 'Everything I found out at the time was in the articles,' she said, blowing blue smoke out the open window. 'Except for one thing. Something I was told by an anonymous source in the state police who made me promise not to reveal his name. I decided not to write anything about it because I could never get any confirmation he was telling the truth. I think the guy may have had an ax to grind. But even supposing he *was* telling the truth I'm not sure how important that particular truth is. Or why it might be relevant to the Stoddard case.'

McCabe said, 'Can you tell me what he said?'

'You know better than I do when a wife, any wife, is murdered, investigators almost always consider the grieving husband a possible suspect. At least they do unless the grieving husband has an absolutely airtight alibi. Well, it turned out Sean had an airtight alibi.'

'Yes, he was on an all-night stakeout. That's what you wrote.'

'Yes, that was the official story. But you're the guy with the photographic memory so I'm sure you remember my lead-in to that sentence.'

McCabe's mind instantly pictured the words he'd read on his computer screen hours earlier. 'According to state police investigators assigned to the case ...' he said.

'That's right, Michael, *according to state police investigators assigned to the case.*'

'Are you saying the state police investigators assigned to the case may have been lying? That there may have been some kind of cover-up?'

Carlin took a deep drag of her cigarette. 'What I'm saying is that my source in the MSP, admittedly someone who didn't like Sean, was jealous of his success, told me, strictly off the record, that, while Sean did indeed have a rock-solid alibi for that night, he wasn't on any stakeout.'

'How does your source know?'

'Because he was on the same stakeout. And he sat there all night all by himself.'

'Okay, so where was Sean?'

'According to the same source ...'

'Who had an ax to grind and didn't like Sean Carroll?'

'Yes. According to that source Sean spent the night in the bed of a woman who wasn't his wife. My source reported it up the line and investigators interviewed this woman on a strictly confidential basis and, somewhat reluctantly, she confirmed he was there. He didn't leave her apartment until a phone call woke them both up at about five A.M., informing Sean of the fire. He jumped out of bed, got dressed and arrived at the scene, supposedly from his stakeout, about twenty minutes later.'

'Any possibility the woman was lying?'

'I doubt it. She's not the lying type. Besides, she had nothing to gain and quite a bit to lose by coming forward.'

'You ever talk to the woman?'

'She refused to talk to me. Either on or off the record.'

'So you're saying the cops investigating Liz Carroll's murder got behind the stakeout story to protect Sean's career?'

'Yes. To protect Sean's career. And the woman's career as well.'

'Who was the woman? And who was the cop who told you about it?'

Carlin took a deep drag on her cigarette. Blew the smoke out the window. 'I'd rather not say.'

'No one will ever know either name came from you.'

Carlin said nothing.

'As I recall, Tracy,' said McCabe, 'you do owe me a favor or two. If you let me have the name, the tables will be turned and I'll owe you a couple. And you may help catch a murderer.'

Tracy stubbed out her cigarette on one of the yellow bricks just outside the window. Wrapped the dead butt in tissue and tossed it in Joe Fields' wastebasket.

Carlin sighed. 'You know, McCabe, I will tell you. Not because of any favors owed or expected but because, if there is a cover-up here, somebody ought to shine a little light on it. Truth should be served. One of the reasons, back in my idealistic youth, I became a journalist. My source was a state police detective working on the case.'

'Name?'

'Emmett Ganzer.'

McCabe had never heard of him. 'And who was Sean Carroll's bedmate?'

Tracy Carlin put her hand on McCabe's shoulder and quietly whispered a name in McCabe's ear as if she thought the room might be bugged.

'Jesus, really?'

'Jesus, really. So remember, if you do talk to her, please don't say you heard it from me. I don't need that kind of grief.'

Given the identity of the woman, it appeared Carroll's alibi for the night of his wife's murder, even if he wasn't on stakeout with Ganzer, *was* in fact rock-solid.

McCabe thanked Carlin for her time and left. Since it was such a lovely summer day, he thought he might just put the top down on the Bird and take a nice long drive downeast.

Chapter Twenty-Nine

9:45 A.M., Sunday, August 23, 2009
Machias, Maine

SEAN CARROLL HAD scheduled a detectives' meeting to start promptly at ten. Maggie decided to walk. It was only a few blocks from the house to the Sheriff's Department on Court Street and between the reporters, state troopers and tourists in town for the last day of Blueberry Festival, parking would be tough, if not impossible, to find. She managed to slip in the back door without being seen by any of the reporters clustered out front.

She checked with a deputy to make sure Sam Harkness had shown up as scheduled. He had. She was told he'd been fingerprinted and had left a saliva sample but nobody knew anything about a manuscript. Next she looked for Carroll and found him standing in the hall, talking with a couple of MSP detectives she hadn't met before. He made introductions. Maggie smiled, shook hands and told Sean she needed a minute.

'Can it wait till after the meeting?'

'I think it's better if we talk first.'

Carroll nodded and led her into Savage's office, about the only place in the building that afforded any privacy. He sat behind the beat-up oak desk that had been her father's for seventeen years. She settled back in the guest chair.

'What do you have for me?' he asked.

'Couple of things you need to know.'

'Go ahead.'

'It appears that Tiff Stoddard was sexually promiscuous.'

'Why does that not surprise me? You have the names of any partners.'

'Yes. Two. An English professor at UMM named Samuel Harkness.'

'Kaplan's ex-husband?'

'Yeah. My guess is she was screwing Harkness for grades. Or maybe because he's rich. He came in this morning and gave us some prints and DNA.' She didn't mention the manuscript.

'Okay. Who else?'

Maggie sucked in a deep breath. Let it out slowly. 'My younger brother Harlan.'

Two deep frown lines appeared between Carroll's brows. 'Your brother? Is he rich?'

'Anything but.'

'That complicates things,' he said. 'How do you know about it?'

'I stopped by the Musty Moose last night after dinner. Harlan was there. We talked. He told me.'

'He say anything else?'

'Yes. Harlan was aware Tiff was involved in selling Oxycontin. I don't think he was involved himself but he's heard the name Conor Riordan.'

'Really?' The frown lines got deeper. 'In exactly what context did your brother know Conor Riordan?'

'All he would say was that Tiff had mentioned the name once or twice. I had to work hard to get even that much out of him.'

There was a brief silence.

'Are you going to ask me to stop working on the case?' Maggie asked.

Before answering, Carroll held up one finger to signal a time out, picked up John Savage's desk phone and punched in a number. 'Emmett? It's Carroll. Listen, I'm going to be a few minutes late for the meeting. Would you please ask everybody to hang in and I'll be there quick as I can. Thanks.'

'Are you going to ask me to stop working on the case?' Maggie repeated the question.

'What do you think?'

'I think you'd be nuts not to.'

'So do I. You're off the case.'

'Will you complain to the AG's office if I don't leave town?'

'I don't know. Maybe. It's obvious your local contacts make you a valuable resource. I have a feeling you may be able to find out more about this whole affair than Ganzer or any of my other people.'

That much was true. Maggie knew Tommy Flynn never would have tipped off anyone else to Harlan's relationship with Tiff Stoddard.

'So here's what I think,' Carroll went on. 'You keep nosing around. Working your contacts. Asking your questions. Just do it discreetly. Don't flash your badge or tell anyone you're working for us, 'cause you're not. Just keep me posted on anything you find out and I won't tell a soul where it came from. Not the AG's office. Not my boss. Not your boss either.'

'In other words you want me to become your snitch?'

'I prefer the term confidential informant.'

Chapter Thirty

11:55 A.M., Sunday, August 23, 2009
Whiting, Maine

MOST SUNDAYS HARLAN Savage slept late. Especially when he was sleeping alone, as he was on this particular Sunday. According to the electric clock next to his bed it was a few minutes before noon when he rolled over for the third time, intending to snooze a little longer. That's when he was jarred awake by the sound of a vehicle pulling up in front of the ramshackle single-wide that had been his home going on four years now.

Not expecting company, Harlan leapt out of bed and grabbed the loaded M40A3 Marine Corps sniper rifle he always kept within reach. A bolt-action weapon that fired only one round at a time. Harlan had learned long ago that he seldom, if ever, needed more than one round. Not as long as he was shooting at only one target.

He opened the door still in his skivvies and pointed the rifle at a big guy with a square jaw and a crew cut and just the beginnings of a gut. The guy was staring back at Harlan with small piggy eyes and was wearing a tie and jacket. This, in Harlan's view, meant he was either a cop or, since it was Sunday, possibly a bible thumper. From the look of him Harlan opted for cop.

'Who are you and what do you want?' Harlan asked.

'What is it about you Savages?' the man asked, shaking his head and holding his arms wide to show he wasn't reaching for a weapon. 'Do you always get all hostile and defensive when all the other person wants to do is have a pleasant conversation?'

'Who are you and what do you want?' Harlan repeated.

'Name's Ganzer. Detective Emmett J. Ganzer. Maine State Police.'

Detective Emmett Ganzer pulled one flap of his jacket aside and revealed a gold shield clipped to his belt. 'If I'm not mistaken, you're Harlan Savage.'

'And what if I am?'

'Well, Harlan, if you'd kindly put that rifle down, I think you and I ought to have a little chat.'

''Bout what?'

Harlan couldn't see anyone else sitting inside Ganzer's car. He scanned the woods and the dirt road leading out of the place for a second car. Or at least a second cop. He didn't see one. This he considered odd. Having grown up in a cop's household, he was well aware that pretty much the first rule of law enforcement was never to confront a potentially violent suspect without backup.

And Maggie hadn't minced words telling him he was a suspect.

'Only take a few minutes,' said Ganzer. 'I just want to talk to you about somebody I believe you knew.'

'Oh really? Now who would that be?'

'Put the gun away and then we'll talk.'

Seemed reasonable. Also seemed reasonable to get dressed instead of standing out here in the yard talking in his underwear. Harlan went back inside the trailer. Came out a minute later without the rifle and wearing a pair of khaki-colored cargo pants, black boots and a black t-shirt with the logo of a group called The Killers on it.

'You live all the way out here alone?' asked Ganzer.

'Alone suits me. Now what is it you want to talk about?'

'Young lady by the name of Tiffany Stoddard.'

'Never heard of her.'

'Be better if we didn't play games, Harlan.'

'I said I never heard of her.'

'That's not what you told your sister last night.'

'What I told my sister is between her and me. It doesn't concern you.'

'In fact, it does concern me because I happen to be investigating Tiff Stoddard's murder.'

'I don't know anything about that.'

'Funny,' said Ganzer, looking right at Harlan's chest.

'What is?'

'That t-shirt you're wearing? The Killers?'

'What about it?'

'The name of the band for one thing. Considering that you may become a suspect for murder. Also the fact that it's identical to the shirt Stoddard was wearing when we found her body. Except Tiff's shirt was all cut up by the killer's knife. Just like the rest of her. Cuts all over. 'Specially the sexy places. Her boobs and between her legs. That kind of thing turn you on. Harlan?'

Harlan closed his eyes and the image of Tiff's body lying on the ground filled his brain. Not just her shirt but all her clothes cut off. Blood pouring from a dozen different wounds in a dozen different places. And just for an instant she wasn't lying in a state park in Maine but on a dusty street in Ramadi and he couldn't understand how Tiff had gotten there or why. Couldn't understand why they had to kill her. But he knew he wasn't the one who killed her no matter what they thought. He knew that. Or did he? Yes. For an instant he wasn't sure but then he was. He hadn't. At least he didn't think he had.

The sound of Ganzer's voice broke through. 'Funny the two of you,' the cop said, 'wearing the same exact shirt like that, isn't it?'

Harlan opened his eyes and looked hard at Ganzer, trying hard to keep himself in the moment. 'Yeah?' he said in a toneless voice. 'Well. I guess we just liked the same kind of music.'

'Probably go to the same kind of concerts, huh? I heard that band, The Killers, was playing down in Bar Harbor a month or so ago. Tickets going for a hundred bucks a pop. Even more for the good seats. A lot of money for a guy like you, Harlan, doing odd jobs and all like you do.'

'Well, you never know, now do you, how much an odd job might pay.'

'What I also heard was you and Tiff Stoddard were getting it on. Can't say I blame you. Good-looking girl, that one. And you're supposed to be some kind of a stud yourself. Willing to stick it in just about anything that walks.'

Harlan took a deep breath to keep himself from going after the cop. Big as he was, the cop looked slow and Harlan figured he could take him. Especially if Ganzer didn't know what was coming. Still, it wasn't a good idea, he told himself. Not a good idea to beat the crap out of a cop. 'Since what I stick it in sure as hell doesn't include an oversized pile of shit like you, Ganzer, why don't you go back to whatever hole you crawled out of and fuck yourself?'

Ganzer's face turned red with anger. 'All right, Savage, why don't we just cut the shit. We both know you were fucking Tiff Stoddard. Now we can talk about what else you might have done to her right here or we can go into town and talk about it at the Sheriff's office. Makes no damn difference to me.'

'I don't have to talk to you. Not about Tiff Stoddard. Not about anything else. So unless you've got a warrant for my arrest just get the fuck off my property and leave me alone.' Harlan turned and started back toward the trailer.

'All right, Mr Savage, I suggest you hold it right there.'

Harlan stopped, sensing Ganzer had drawn his weapon and was pointing it at him. Harlan had never liked people pointing guns at him. But since Ramadi he really, really didn't like it.

'Now drop flat on the ground and put both hands behind your head.'

'You telling me I'm under arrest?'

'I'm telling you to do exactly what I say. Put your hands on your head.'

Harlan turned around slowly and stared into the little black hole pointing at him from the end of Ganzer's automatic. 'Or what? You'll shoot me?'

Ganzer smiled. A nasty little smile. 'Don't tempt me Savage or I might just do that. Hell, why not? An armed man resisting arrest. Threatening a police officer with a deadly weapon. Feel good to finish this case fast.'

Harlan moved a step closer to Ganzer.

'That's close enough, Savage.'

'An armed man resisting arrest? You're the only one armed.'

'Yeah,' Ganzer said with a mean little grin. 'But nobody knows that except you and me. Now get your ass on the ground.'

Nobody knows that except you and me? Was that why Ganzer had come alone? He didn't want any witnesses, not even another cop, when he shot and killed the suspect he could claim was resisting arrest. A suspect with a loaded rifle lying nearby with the suspect's prints all over it. Maggie was right. They wanted him for Tiff's murder. What she didn't know was the way they wanted him was dead.

Harlan put his hands behind his head. Started telling Ganzer to relax. That he wasn't gonna give him a hard time. But before he finished telling him that,

Harlan's right foot landed, the boot hitting Ganzer's gun a microsecond before the cop pulled the trigger. The kick knocked the barrel wide to the left. But not quite wide enough.

A 9 mm slug tore through the right side of the Killers t-shirt just above Harlan's waist, taking a small chunk of flesh along with it. Before Ganzer could swing the gun back and fire again, Harlan slid his left arm through Ganzer's right. After more than a year as a hand-to-hand combat instructor at Pendleton this part was easy, even with a guy who had to outweigh him by thirty pounds. He snapped the cop's wrist backward and at the same time used his left leg to sweep Ganzer's right leg out from under him. The cop went down hard. His Heckler & Koch automatic skittered beyond reach. Ganzer reached for it, sensing there was no way he could take Harlan without it.

Harlan picked up the weapon first and then, hoping Tiff was looking down from somewhere in heaven cheering him on, he slammed his size twelve steel-toed workboot into Ganzer's face. The cop rolled over on to his knees. Blood poured from his broken nose.

Harlan pulled a hunting knife from his back pocket, and lifted it to strike. To finish it off. For an instant all he saw, all he felt, was the warm red blood of a young Sunni fighter pouring out all over his hand.

He closed his eyes to break the spell. Opened them again, not on the streets of Ramadi but on the verdant Maine landscape. He slid the knife back in its sheath. Instead of killing the cop who'd come to kill him, he settled for kicking him again. This time in the balls. The cop gasped in pain.

Harlan opened the base plate on Ganzer's automatic and emptied the seven hollow-point rounds from the nine-round magazine as well as the one that was lodged in the chamber. He threw them into the woods. Tossed the empty gun after them. He removed Ganzer's back-up weapon from an ankle holster, thought about it for a second and then tucked that in his own waistband.

He started back toward the trailer. Changed his mind and turned back. The dazed cop was now sitting up, blood pouring from his nose, trying to focus his attention, or perhaps just his eyes, on pushing some buttons on his cell phone. Calling for the backup he should have brought with him. Harlan walked over, pulled the phone from the cop's hand, and placed it on a good-sized rock. He picked up a second, smaller rock and slammed it down, crushing the phone between the two. He then took the smaller rock to Ganzer's car and used it to smash the radio, adding, he supposed, destruction of government property to the charge of assaulting a police officer.

Harlan tossed away the rock and pulled his knife from its sheath, debating whether or not to go for the trifecta. At this point cutting Ganzer's throat was a very tempting thing to do.

'You better kill me, soldier boy, while you've got the chance,' the cop said. ''Cause if you don't, I promise you, you're fucking dead meat.' The cop spat out a mouthful of blood, turned over on to all fours and started crawling toward the car. Harlan caught up with him. Kicked him one more time in the side of the head and Ganzer was out.

Harlan looked at the unconscious cop. Looked at his knife. Then walked to Ganzer's car and used it to slash and flatten all four tires.

That done, he went back inside. Pulled off his shirt. Splashed alcohol over the wound. Taped a double layer of cotton gauze over it and changed his shirt. He stuffed all the cash he had, ninety-two dollars and twenty-six cents, into the pocket of his cargo pants. Then he rolled his sleeping bag. Stuffed a backpack with half a dozen high-protein breakfast bars and a few other necessities, including a fleece jacket, a night-vision sniper scope and a spare magazine for the M40A3. He threw in a disposable cell phone that still had a few minutes left on its card. Finally he added a roll of tape and a half dozen more gauze pads and the alcohol. The bleeding from the wound hadn't stopped yet. Last thing he needed was for the damn thing to get infected.

The enemy had declared their intentions. They wanted him dead. Well, they just might get their wish because he had no intention of being taken alive. He turned off the lights. Locked the door.

Outside, he went back to Ganzer. Pulled the wallet from his jacket pocket. Left the credit cards but took the cash. One hundred and twenty-six dollars. That gave him a total of nearly 220 dollars. Enough to get started. He tossed the wallet on the ground, climbed in his truck and set off. At the end of the dirt track, he turned right, heading away from Route 1. A mile further down he turned left on to another dirt track, drove to the end and pulled the truck as far as he could into the woods, got out and threw some loose branches over the back. Satisfied that he'd hidden it about as well as he could, he climbed out, unscrewed the plates and stuck them in his back-pack, locked the truck and set off on foot. If he needed a vehicle, he'd borrow, or if necessary requisition, one later. In the meantime, ATLs, Attempts to Locate, would go out for a '97 dark-green Dodge Ram pick-up which they wouldn't find. Leastways not on the road.

Chapter Thirty-One

5:14 P.M., Sunday, August 23, 2009
Machias, Maine

MAGGIE HAD CALLED Luke Haskell's number half a dozen times, but her calls kept going directly to message. While Haskell might have been on the water, outside of cell range, on a Sunday morning, it didn't seem real likely he'd still be out there at five in the afternoon. Most lobstermen started early. Finished early. Maybe Haskell didn't take calls from 'unknown callers'. Or maybe Pike Stoddard had warned him not to.

She also tried Stoddard's phone a couple of times. But Pike wasn't answering either. She was about to call Frank Boucher to see if he'd be willing to run Haskell down for her when the doorbell rang.

Sean Carroll was on the doorstep, Emmett Ganzer stood behind him, sporting a black eye and a bandaged nose. More bandages around his right wrist. A pair of state police cruisers in front of the house, light bars flashing, made it clear this was an official visit.

'Jesus, Emmett,' she said, 'what the hell happened to you?'

'Where's your brother?' Ganzer asked.

'Which one?'

'Don't play cute with me, Savage. You know damned well which one.'

'If you're talking about Harlan, I have no idea where he is,' she said. 'He the one who beat you up?'

Ganzer pushed his way past her into the small center hall.

'He's not here, Emmett,' said Maggie. 'You can take my word on that.'

'Yeah? Then you won't mind if we look around.' Ganzer was already poking his head left and right into the dining and living rooms.

'As a matter of fact I do. If I tell you Harlan's not here, he's not here. If you don't believe me, find yourself a judge and get a warrant.'

'Do you know where he is, Maggie?' asked Carroll. He spoke softly but he wasn't smiling.

'No, I don't, Sean. If he's not at his place up in Whiting, you might try the Musty Moose. He hangs out there a lot. Though usually not this early.'

'He's not in either place. We also checked room twelve at the Bluebird Motel. But he's not there either and Francie Joplin checked out at eleven this morning.'

'It might help if you told me what's going on.'

Carroll nodded. 'Fair enough. May I come in?'

Maggie led both detectives into the living room. Ganzer chose the couch. Maggie and Carroll sat in the twin wing chairs on either side. Polly Four plopped herself on Maggie's foot.

'We have a warrant for his arrest,' said Ganzer.

'Assaulting an officer?'

'Yes. For one thing.'

'I'm surprised you let him get the drop on you, Emmett. Of course, he is trained in hand-to-hand combat. Pretty good at it, I guess.'

'Unfortunately,' said Carroll, 'that's exactly what happened. After you told me about Harlan's relationship with Tiff Stoddard, I asked Emmett to go out to his place and either interview your brother there or, if Harlan was willing, bring him back to Machias and talk to him at your father's office.'

'So what happened?'

'Harlan didn't want to cooperate. He attacked Emmett instead.'

'Really?' Harlan had a quick temper but she didn't think he'd be that stupid. 'What did you do to provoke him, Emmett? Wave a gun in his face and threaten to shoot him if he didn't come peacefully?'

'It was the other way around,' said Ganzer. 'Soon as I get there your brother charges out of that shithole he's living in. Points a rifle at me, tells me to get off his property. When I tell him I just want to talk to him about Tiff Stoddard, he goes berserk and slams me in the face with the butt of the gun.'

PTSD or no PTSD, Maggie didn't think Harlan would just flip out like that. Not without provocation. Not with a police officer.

'There's been an ATL out for your brother since 2:30 this afternoon. I've got every available unit out looking for his truck now. So does your father. We're also looking for the Joplin woman's car in case they took off together. We've also alerted the Warden Service in case he decides to try to head into the woods and live off the land. Since he took his rifle with him as well as Emmett's back-up piece we've told all units to consider him armed and dangerous.'

'What do you want from me? I already told you I don't know where he is.'

'You're his sister,' said Carroll. 'This morning you said you knew Harlan as well as anybody. I hoped you might have an idea where he'd go if he was running from the law.'

'I don't. I also don't believe Harlan killed Stoddard. Or rammed into Emily.'

'Look, Maggie, I'm sure you love your brother. But please remember, like your father, you're a police officer. It's your sworn duty to uphold the law. You've had a pretty distinguished career up till now. I'd hate to see you blow it. If you have any idea where he is you ought to tell us. You know as well as I do he's just getting himself in deeper by running.'

Maggie sighed. 'Did he take a vehicle?'

'Drove off in his truck. He knows we're after him so he might have ditched it for another vehicle. Or he might have dumped it and fled on foot.'

'Any stolen vehicle reports?'

'Not yet.'

Harlan had plenty of buddies in the area who might lend him a car or truck. And maybe honor a request not to tell the law. On the other hand Harlan didn't need a vehicle. If anyone was capable of disappearing into the wilderness without a trace it was Harlan.

'He could be anywhere,' she said.

Carroll's phone rang. He checked caller ID, got up and walked outside to the porch.

Maggie studied the injuries to Ganzer's face. They were unsightly but none looked in any way life-threatening. 'I take it you think Harlan killed Tiff Stoddard,' she said.

'That's what I think.'

'So, how come he didn't kill you?'

'What do you mean?'

'Well, he beat you up pretty bad.'

Carroll returned from the porch but didn't interrupt. Just stood by the front door, listening to Maggie.

'If Harlan's the killer, I'm wondering why he didn't kill you while you were down. Chop you up into little pieces and toss you into a dumpster like Blakemore. Or cut your throat like you think he did Tiff Stoddard. Or maybe just weighted you down with a bunch of stones and dumped you into the ocean. But he didn't do any of those things. Why not?'

'What's your point?' asked Carroll.

'Just seems like Tiff Stoddard's killer is not some-one who shows a pattern of leaving survivors behind to identify him. If Harlan is Conor Riordan, how come Emmett's still alive?'

'Maybe he was smart enough to know killing a police officer ...' Carroll said.

Maggie interrupted. 'Your wife was a police officer, Sean. I'm sorry to bring up a painful memory, but Conor Riordan, assuming it was Conor Riordan, had no problem killing her.'

'Maybe he was in a hurry to get away,' said Carroll. 'Didn't want to take the time.'

'Bullets travel pretty fast. Wouldn't take hardly any time at all to blow poor Emmett here all to bits.'

Ganzer's big body squirmed in the corner of the couch, not pleased with the direction the conversation was taking.

'And I can assure you, even before he became a marine, when Harlan shot at something he pretty much never missed.'

'Well,' said Carroll, 'it's an interesting question, Maggie. But, at this point, it's a little academic.'

'Really? Why is that?'

'That was Heinrich on the phone. His people found a bunch of interesting things up at your brother's place. He wants to show us what he's got before he sends it down to Augusta for analysis. Since you're so sure Harlan's innocent, why don't you come along and see for yourself?'

Chapter Thirty-Two

On a Sunday afternoon in late August most of the traffic on Route 1 was going the other way. Vacationers and weekenders returning to their real lives in Portland or Boston or New York.

Carroll drove the unmarked MSP Impala. Ganzer rode shotgun. Neither spoke. Not to each other and not to Maggie, who sat silently in the back seat, strumming her fingers against one leg and looking out the window.

After they passed through East Machias and into Whiting, the commercial buildings and eventually the houses became more scattered. The woods on either side of the road denser. Whiting's 450 year-round residents were thinly spread over a mostly empty fifty square miles. Carroll turned left on Camp Road, followed it a mile or two and then turned right on a narrow, unmarked dirt track. He seemed to know where he was going.

They bumped a couple of hundred yards down the track before it opened into a narrow clearing. Harlan's small, dilapidated mobile home sat in the middle. The techs had strung yellow crime-scene tape around the entire place, which seemed kind of superfluous since nobody except a cop was likely to wander this far off the beaten track. A pair of state police cruisers was parked. So was an ERT van.

Heinrich approached Carroll's car as the three detectives exited.

'Looks like this is our guy, Sean,' said Heinrich. 'Took no time at all to find stuff that confirms Savage had an ongoing relationship with Stoddard. Other stuff that ties him to the murder.'

Heinrich handed out latex gloves and everyone put them on. 'May as well look at the good stuff first. Follow me.' They walked around to the back of the mobile home to a couple of green plastic trash bins. 'Found these inside a sealed garbage bag in here.' Heinrich held up a plastic bag containing a pair of latex gloves not unlike the ones they were all wearing. Except these had what looked like blood spatter all over them. He passed the bag to Carroll, who looked closely then passed it to Maggie. She gave it to Ganzer, who peered at the gloves, shined his penlight on the bag to light them up.

'You're sure that's blood on there?' asked Carroll.

'I'm sure. I'll send the gloves down to the lab tonight. I'm willing to bet it'll turn out to be Stoddard's. We found this in the same garbage bag as the gloves.' Heinrich pulled a black, long-sleeved shirt out of another evidence bag and held it up for viewing. It was almost totally covered with dried blood.

'Given the difference in height between Stoddard and Savage,' said Heinrich, 'the blood pumping from Stoddard's severed arteries would likely have concentrated just about here.' Heinrich pointed to a place midway down the shirt where the blood seemed the thickest.

Jesus Christ, thought Maggie, *why couldn't Harlan have gotten rid of this stuff somewhere a little less obvious than his own damned trash can? He was smarter than that, wasn't he?*

'What else?' asked Carroll.

'Follow me.'

They went around to the front of the trailer. 'It's all right to come in. We've finished going over everything. Still, I'd like you to wear these inside.'

He handed them each some booties. The detectives slipped them on and followed Heinrich up three steps into a narrow rectangular space divided railroad style into three small rooms. The front door in the middle brought them directly into the living room. The kitchen was off to the right, a single bedroom to the left. An open door next to the bedroom led into the tiny bathroom with a toilet, sink and a cheap metal stall shower the manufacturer had just managed to cram in. All the walls were covered in fake wood paneling. The furniture seemed mostly to be third-hand Salvation Army junk plus a few decent pieces Maggie recognized from home. She wondered if Joanne had given them to Harlan when he got back from Bethesda or if Savage had made a donation of things Anya didn't want once she moved in.

Maggie paused to look at three framed photos hanging in a row on the wall. She recognized the first. A formal portrait of Harlan, nineteen years old, in marine dress blues. The picture, or one just like it, used to hang in her parents' bedroom at home. The look of earnest expectation Harlan wore on his face pulled at Maggie's heart. This was her handsome younger brother the way she remembered him. Or maybe, she supposed, the way she *wanted* to remember him.

The middle shot was more disturbing. Harlan with four other marines. All dressed in desert camo with body armor and combat gear. All grinning at the camera. One of them, not Harlan, was standing with his right foot planted on the chest of a dead insurgent like an old-time hunter showing off the big game he'd bagged. In the picture black *x* s were magic-markered over two of the marines' faces. Comrades, she supposed, who never made it home. Finally there was a shot of the Savage family, all five of them, with Maggie and her father both dressed in uniform. She couldn't remember who'd taken it. Or when. There was no black *x* over her mother's face.

'Are you with us, Savage?' Ganzer's voice.

Maggie pulled away and joined the others in the kitchen, where Heinrich was showing off two more evidence bags. Each held a folded knife. One had a red handle. The other black. 'We found these in a utility drawer here in the kitchen.'

Ganzer took both bags from Heinrich and peered through the plastic at the knives. A nasty smile made Maggie wish Harlan had broken more than his nose.

'Both knives have blades we think fit the wounds we saw Friday. We'll know better when we get the autopsy report. On this one ...' – he pointed at the knife with the red handle – '... we also found what appears to be a black pubic hair stuck in the cavity the blade folds into.'

Carroll looked even closer. 'Is it still there?'

'Yes. It's hard to see but it's there. The lab'll be able to tell us for sure if the hair is Stoddard's. We think it might have gotten stuck in there when he pulled out the knife and ran.'

Maggie took her turn and studied the knife with the red handle. When she held it up to the light coming through the window, she could just see the strand of hair through the plastic. *If the AG's office accepted all this stuff at face value* ... Maggie didn't bother finishing the thought.

'Did you find his stash of drugs?' asked Carroll. 'Oxycontin 80s? Thousands of them.'

'Yes and no. We didn't find THOUSANDS of them. But we did find this. Sitting under his underwear in a drawer in the bedroom.' Heinrich held up a plastic bag with several hundred small greenish ovals inside. 'You want us to keep looking?'

'Please do. Take this place apart. Though he probably took the main stash with him when he ran.'

'You got it. Meantime there are a couple of smaller things you ought to see.' Heinrich led them back into the living room. Lying on a coffee table was a digital photo wrapped in a plastic sleeve.

'Found this in a bedside table drawer.'

It was a picture of Tiff and Harlan taken at night. The two were standing in what looked like an outdoor concert venue. You could see a crowd of people milling around, some bleachers in the background. Both Tiff and Harlan wore broad smiles and black Killers t-shirts. Harlan had his arm around Tiff's waist. She hadn't seen her brother look that happy since he got back from the war.

'The Killers played a concert in Bar Harbor last month,' said Ganzer. 'It looks like they went down to catch the show.'

'This doesn't prove anything,' said Maggie. 'Except they had a relationship.'

'Yeah. They had a relationship. Until last week, when she dumped him. Gives us what we need, Savage. Motive for murder. You know, the jilted lover? It's classic. Happens all the time.'

Maggie seethed at the smug certainty of Ganzer's words. The snarky little smile that darted across his face. Visions of sergeant's stripes no doubt dancing in his head like sugarplums on Christmas Eve.

'We still don't know for sure it was Harlan who killed her,' she maintained stubbornly.

'Give me a break, Savage. I know this guy's your brother but even you've got to recognize a slam-dunk conviction when you see one.'

'Is that what you think too, Sean? That my brother not only killed Stoddard but also killed your wife? And Laura Blakemore?'

Carroll gave her a hard look before answering. 'We don't know for sure about Liz or Blakemore yet. But if Harlan and Tiff were running the drug trade together it's entirely possible. You never did ask him where he was last January, did you?'

'No.' Maggie answered in a small voice. 'I never did.'

'Maybe you should have. Anyway, as far as Stoddard goes, your brother's starting to look pretty damn solid.'

'We've got more proof of the relationship,' said Heinrich, handing the photo to Carroll along with a magnifying glass. 'Take a close look at the pendant she's got hanging around her neck.' Carroll peered through the glass at the photo then handed it to Ganzer, who did the same before giving it to Maggie. Using the magnifying glass, she could clearly make out the color and shape of the pendant. A gold starfish with what appeared to be a small diamond stud in the middle.

'Okay,' said Carroll. 'A starfish pendant. What about it?'

'We found it in the drawer under the photo.' He held up another plastic bag that contained a piece of jewelry identical to the one Tiff was wearing in the photo.

'If you turn it over you'll see a tiny inscription on the back that reads "To Tiff. We've only just begun. H." '

Maggie's heart sank. H. had to be Harlan. By itself the pendant didn't prove his guilt. Any more than the t-shirts did. But what Maggie hadn't told Carroll or anyone else was something Emily had said in the hospital the day before. That Stoddard had been wearing a gold starfish pendant when she arrived at Em's office. That she still had it on when she left. Since they hadn't found it on her body or anywhere around the crime scene, the only logical conclusion was that the killer pulled it from her neck before cutting her throat. Taken it with him when he fled. And now here it was. The first seeds of doubt about Harlan's innocence began taking root in Maggie's brain. She tried pushing them away, but they refused to go. Maybe Iraq had changed Harlan more than she could ever have imagined.

Chapter Thirty-Three

MAGGIE SAT QUIETLY all the way back from Whiting listening to Ganzer whoop it up in the front seat. A couple of times she caught Sean Carroll glancing back in the rear-view mirror. Once she saw him mouth some words that in the reverse image of the mirror looked like, 'I'm sorry.'

Maggie turned and stared out the window. She was sorry too.

Carroll pulled up in front of the house on Center Street a little before six.

A beautifully restored cherry-red '57 T-Bird convertible was sitting, top down, in the driveway behind Maggie's Blazer and Savage's Subaru. Carroll walked over and looked at the Bird admiringly.

'Man, that is one gorgeous car,' he said. 'Not yours, is it?'

'No, it belongs to a friend,' said Maggie, wondering what McCabe was doing here but, at the same time, with all the evidence piling up implicating Harlan, feeling glad she had at least one certain ally.

'Your boyfriend?' asked Carroll.

'No. Just a friend.'

'Lucky friend,' said Carroll. 'Car like this must have set him back a bundle.'

As he walked around the T-Bird, gazing admiringly both at the body and the interior, he started talking to Maggie in a low voice. Anyone watching would have assumed they were talking about the car.

'I didn't want to say this in front of Emmett and I'm sorry to keep hammering away on it, but Maggie please make sure you let me know if your brother contacts you in any way. Or if you figure out where he's gone. Things will go much better for him if he gives himself up and coöperates than if we have to hunt him down. That's especially true if, somehow in spite of the evidence, it turns out you're right and he didn't do it.'

Maggie folded her arms around herself. The air was feeling decidedly cooler. 'But you don't think that will be the case do you, Sean? You're certain he's guilty.'

'Yes,' he said. 'Given what we've just seen, I am. And so should you be.'

'Don't you wonder, even the tiniest bit, why someone like Harlan, who grew up in a house with two cops who talked constantly about crime and criminals and the rules of evidence, why somebody like that would be so incredibly stupid as to leave all that stuff – the gloves, the murder weapon, the bloody shirt, the pills – just lying around where he had to know the police would find them? Didn't even try to hide anything or burn it or bury it? Left it more than twelve hours after I personally warned him he was going to be considered a suspect? Left it even after Emmett shows up to question him? Doesn't take it with him when he flees? Don't you find that level of carelessness a little bit strange? No, not a little bit strange. Totally nuts? And,' she added with more conviction than she felt, 'as far as I'm concerned, totally unbelievable.'

'Yes, it does sound crazy. But your brother happens to be someone who, maybe because of his experiences in Iraq or maybe because of the brain injury he sustained in the war, may, in fact, be mentally unbalanced.' Maggie wondered how Carroll knew all that stuff about Harlan. Maybe Savage had told him. 'Or maybe,' Carroll continued, 'Harlan left all that stuff because deep down he feels so guilty about what he did that he wants to get caught. Wants to be punished for it. Psychically *needs* to be punished. We've all seen stranger behavior from criminals.'

'I don't buy it, Sean,' she said with more certainty than she felt. 'Even if Harlan is suffering from some form of PTSD or guilt disorder or whatever you want to call it, don't you think the evidence we saw at his house today was just a little too perfect? Everything a prosecutor could possibly ask for all placed exactly where anyone with half a brain would know the cops would look first and have no trouble finding it.'

'You're saying you think someone planted the evidence?'

'Yes.'

'And that someone is ...?'

'Whoever really killed Tiff Stoddard. He's the only one who would have had access to it. The only one who would benefit by having us pin the crime on Harlan. Assuming, of course, it's all genuine and both the blood and the hair match Stoddard's.'

'And this real killer of yours figures the cops will buy it?'

'That's right, Sean. He figures the cops will buy it.' Maggie was starting to tire of the conversation and wanted to be done with it. 'In fact,' she added with more than a little anger, 'it looks like the cops have already bought it. Including the one cop who's so hot for a promotion to lieutenant that maybe he figures a fast conviction on a high-profile case will get him where he wants to go just a little faster than he would have gotten there otherwise.'

'That's what you really think of me?'

'Yes, Sean. That's what I really think. Of you and of that jerkwater buddy of yours over there who's convinced himself the minute you make lieutenant he's getting sergeant's stripes.'

'Jesus Christ. I don't believe this.' Carroll sighed deeply and shook his head. 'If you actually think I would play games like that when there's more than a damn good chance whoever killed Stoddard also killed my wife, well all I can say to you, Maggie, is why don't you just go fuck yourself.'

She closed her eyes and took a deep breath to get control of her anger. 'You're right. I'm sorry. I shouldn't have said what I said. It wasn't fair and I am sorry about what happened to your wife.'

But Sean Carroll didn't hear any of that because by the time she opened her eyes he was already heading for the driver's side of the unmarked Impala. She repressed an urge to call him back. To apologize to his face. To hope he accepted it.

Maggie stood next to McCabe's T-Bird and watched Carroll and Ganzer drive off. She was still gazing into the empty street after the car was long out of sight. As she stood she was aware of tears forming in her eyes. She didn't want anyone to see them because everybody knows cops don't cry. Certainly not the cop Detective Carl Sturgis down in Portland liked to call 'Little Miss Hardass'. She heard a familiar voice behind her. 'C'mon, Mag, let's go inside.' McCabe slipped his arm around her shoulder and walked her back toward the house.

'What are you doing here?' she asked before they went in.

'Like I told your old man, it was a beautiful day for a drive.'

Chapter Thirty-Four

8:12 P.M., Sunday, August 23, 2009
Machias, Maine

ANYA SERVED COMPANY dinner. Roast chicken with pan gravy, mashed potatoes, snap peas from the garden and home-made buttermilk biscuits.

Savage opened a bottle of a good California Cabernet and shared it around.

'How long are you in town for, Mr McCabe?' Anya asked.

'Two or three days. And please call me Michael or Mike or even just McCabe. That's what Maggie and most everybody else in Portland calls me.'

'Okay, McCabe,' she smiled. 'You call me Anya.'

It was obvious to Maggie that Anya had noticed the absence of a wedding band and was sizing McCabe up as potential husband material for Maggie. Anya made no bones about thinking it was wrong that Savage's only daughter was already well into her thirties and still unmarried. On the other hand, she had no idea that a woman named Kyra Erikson even existed. For better or for worse, McCabe was taken.

'Well, I know you've made reservations down at the Inn but it seems kind of silly to pay for a hotel when we've got two perfectly good bedrooms going begging right here.'

'That's very kind of you, but I don't want to impose.'

'Nonsense. I insist.'

'Well, thank you. Let me think about it.'

After that there was nothing but the sound of eating and drinking for a good five minutes.

Finally Maggie figured somebody had to acknowledge the 800 pound gorilla in the room.

'I went up to Harlan's place this afternoon. With Carroll and Ganzer.'

Everybody looked up. Nobody spoke.

'They're going to charge Harlan with Tiff Stoddard's murder. I expect they've already got a full-scale manhunt underway.'

A pained expression appeared on Savage's face. 'They already had one,' he said. 'But it was for assaulting a cop. Not for murder.'

'It's about to be upped to murder,' said Maggie. 'I'm sure they've already issued ATLs. To all their own units plus every local department in Maine and New Hampshire. Probably Canada as well, considering how close we are to the border.'

'Jesus,' said Savage, looking at Maggie from the head of the table. 'That was mighty quick. What makes Carroll so sure Harlan did it?'

'Carroll, Ganzer and I just got back from Harlan's place in Whiting.'

'Wait a minute,' said McCabe. 'Are you talking about a detective named Emmett Ganzer?'

'Yeah,' said Maggie. 'Why? You know him?'

'I've heard his name. Just this morning. In kind of an interesting context.'

'Such as?'

'I'll tell you later. You finish up what you were saying first.'

John Savage listened stony-faced as Maggie went through the evidence Bill Heinrich's techs had found at Harlan's place earlier in the day. 'Sean Carroll's convinced Harlan's the killer,' Maggie concluded.

'And you're not?'

'No. I don't believe Harlan could ever do what I saw done to Tiff Stoddard.'

'My God, Margaret,' Savage shouted. A loud bang reverberated through the room as he slapped the table hard with an open palm, clattering the china and nearly spilling his wine. 'All that solid evidence and you're still not willing to accept it?' There was an angry edge to Savage's voice. 'I swear to Christ you're exactly like your mother. Joanne's beautiful baby boy could do no wrong. Ever. Not even when I caught him in the act. What in hell is it gonna take to convince you that your little brother is no damned good? More than no good. He's a goddamned killer.'

John Savage rose from his chair and stormed out on to the porch, slamming the screen door loudly behind him. Maggie got up and followed. And then McCabe.

Anya sat by herself for a minute, surveying the wreckage of her meal. Then she quietly rose from her seat and began clearing away the remains of the half-eaten dinner.

'CAN'T YOU SEE it, Pop?' Maggie stood close by her father's side. He was leaning against one of the porch columns, not looking at her, instead staring out into the night. 'Or are you so filled with anger and hatred for Harlan that it's blinded you to the truth?'

'And what truth would that be, Margaret?'

'For one thing, if Harlan really killed that girl there's no way he'd be dumb enough to leave all that stuff lying around. About the only thing they didn't find implicating Harlan was a notarized letter of confession.'

'Harlan's always been careless.'

'Careless, maybe, but not stupid. And not looking to be locked up the rest of his life. All that stuff had to be a plant.'

'Not stupid, you say? He was stupid enough to attack a cop, wasn't he?' Savage spat out the words. 'Whacked him in the face with a rifle butt's the way I heard it.'

'Oh, for Christ's sake, that's bullshit too. Big as he is, Harlan wouldn't have needed any rifle butt to take

Emmett Ganzer down.' Maggie was surprised how angry and defensive her own voice sounded. But at this point she didn't give a damn. She was as pissed at her father as she ever had been.

'So you think everybody's making all this stuff up. That the state police are so hot to pin this murder on poor innocent Harlan that they went out and planted fake evidence all over the place just so they could get their man. Is that what you think?'

Maggie took a deep breath, determined to keep her temper in check. 'No. I don't think the evidence was faked. I think it was the real thing, planted by the real killer.'

'And why would this real killer decide to pin the murder on Harlan?'

'Because he found out about Harlan's relationship with Stoddard and decided to take advantage of it.'

'Someone like who?'

'I don't know. Maybe it was Emmett Ganzer. We know he was all by himself on Harlan's property for we don't know how long.'

'You think a cop did this?'

'No,' she shook her head. 'Maybe. I don't know. It wouldn't be the first time a cop turned bad. Or maybe it was Sam Harkness. I know he was having sex with Stoddard and, unlike Harlan, Sam has a record of assaulting women. Most likely I think it's somebody we haven't thought of yet. The investigation's not even forty-eight hours old and I get the feeling Tiff was the kind of girl who was involved with a lot of guys.'

Savage didn't respond. Just tamped out the remains of the butt on the bottom of his boot. Field stripped the paper and tossed the unburned tobacco over the railing and on to the lawn.

'Maggie,' said Savage, 'maybe you're right. I hope you're right. But we're both cops, you and I. It's our job to weigh the evidence as best we can and then act on it. Not twist the evidence to fit some theory concocted to protect someone you love.'

'Or maybe concocted to convict somebody you no longer love.'

Savage stared hard at his daughter, then went inside, ending the conversation. At least he didn't slam the door.

Maggie walked down the porch steps. 'I'm going for a walk.'

'Mind if I come along?' asked McCabe.

'Suit yourself. Just don't talk.'

They walked side by side in silence, heading north up Center Street away from the center of town. Then they circled around and came back south.

Chapter Thirty-Five

10:21 P.M., Sunday, August 23, 2009
Machias, Maine

IN THE LANGUAGE of the Passamaquoddy, the earliest inhabitants of Washington County, the word Machias means *bad run of water* and for most of its seventy-five miles the Machias River lives up to its name, twisting and raging through a forested wilderness before indulging in its final, swirling tantrum, a short whitewater rush down a rocky incline in the center of the city of Machias called Little Bad Falls.

After walking in near-total silence for more than an hour, Maggie and McCabe found themselves standing side by side on the narrow footbridge that spans the river just below the falls. They stopped midstream, leaned against the steel railing and looked down at the rush of water coursing furiously over and around the rocks below. On one side of the bridge was the campus of UMM, where, in the English Department offices in Kimball Hall, Sam Harkness first met Tiff Stoddard. *You know me Maggie, I took one look at those luscious legs and invited her in.* Just a few hundred yards upstream on the other side of the bridge was the small four-unit where Tiff Stoddard had lived.

'Ever go to her apartment?'

'Only once. A grubby little place on the other side of the river from campus and, frankly, a little too close for my taste.'

She thought about Sam committing murder and planting incriminating evidence at Harlan's place. She supposed it was something he might do if he was drunk enough and pissed off enough about Tiff dumping him. But Tiff had dumped Sam way back in May and Sam, always impulsive, always slightly out of control, would have gone after her right away just like he did the woman in the hotel room in Philadelphia. No way would he have waited two minutes let alone two months before striking out. Nor would he have killed Tiff in such a sexually savage way. No, Maggie didn't think Sam was the killer. As far as Sam was concerned, what she was most curious about was what else beside the name Conor Riordan might have found its way into his manuscript.

Maggie and McCabe stared silently at the rushing water below for another five minutes.

It was McCabe who finally spoke. 'Still angry with your old man?'

'Yes. And with Sean Carroll.'

'How about Ganzer?'

'Ganzer's just an oversized jerk with too much testosterone. I wouldn't have expected anything better from him.'

'Aren't you overreacting a little?'

'I don't think so. And if you plan on taking sides on any of this, McCabe, please make sure it's my side.'

McCabe didn't respond.

'I'm sorry. That wasn't fair,' said Maggie.

'Not a problem.'

'I think my father's buying into this bullshit without thinking it through because he's always been ready to think the worst of Harlan.'

'Why?'

'Just the way it's always been. Trevor was the good son. Harlan the bad one.'

'How about you?'

'I'm the only girl and the only one to honor what my father did by following him into law enforcement. But Harlan never had a chance. He never was and never could be the good and dutiful son my father wanted and expected. He's impulsive and uncontrollable. He drinks too much. Gets into fights in bars. Makes his living, such as it is, bouncing from job to job. None of those things are likely to endear him to a father who's a lifelong law enforcement officer. But, more than any of that, my father has never forgiven Harlan for not being around more when our mother was dying of cancer. I haven't forgiven him for that either. But it doesn't make him a murderer. And it doesn't make him somebody I can't or won't love.'

'Mag, I know how difficult this has got to be for you.' McCabe reached out and took one of her hands in his. 'But can you really discount all the evidence against your brother on nothing more than gut instinct?'

'I'm not discounting it. The evidence is real. I don't question that. My problem is only an imbecile would bring all that stuff home and leave it lying around just begging to be found.'

'Maybe not an imbecile, Maggie. Maybe just someone so consumed by guilt, at killing Tiff, or maybe from killing all those people in Iraq, he couldn't live with what he'd done.'

Maggie pulled her hand from his in a sudden surge of anger. 'You too, huh?'

'No, not me too, huh. You told me on the phone this morning Harlan showed no remorse, no emotional reaction at all to Tiff Stoddard's death except to start talking about how many people he'd killed in Iraq. Yet this was a woman he supposedly loved. We both know there's something wrong with that picture. Isn't it at least possible the brain injury made him into someone you no longer know? It does happen.'

'Yes, it does happen and I'm sure he has problems coming out of the war. Displaying emotion may be one of them. *Death hasn't shocked me in a very long time.*'

'What?'

'That's what Harlan said when I asked him how he felt about Tiff's death. Then he started talking about Iraq. Having flashbacks to Ramadi. That's where he was wounded. He said he gets the flashbacks a lot. They're not like remembering, more like he's really there.'

'Isn't it possible he killed her in the middle of one of those flashbacks? Maybe thought she was one of the enemy?'

'I don't know,' Maggie sighed. 'That's pretty much what Sean Carroll said.'

'Carroll may be right. He's supposed to be a smart detective.'

For a moment Maggie felt herself reluctantly accepting McCabe's words. Then she stopped herself. 'No, damnit. I don't think he is right,' she said, punching the railing on the bridge with her fist.

'Why not?'

'You didn't see the cuts on Tiff Stoddard's body. I did. The killer cut her nose and lips and breasts. Mutilated her vagina with multiple stab wounds. He attacked all the places on her body that made her female. This guy's a pervert who on some level hates women. Derives sexual pleasure from torturing them. That's not Harlan. Never was and never could be, no matter what happened to him in Iraq. Even if he thought he was killing an Iraqi woman, an enemy, no way would he have killed her like that. I think the real killer, let's call him Conor Riordan, was involved with Tiff in the drug trade. Probably killed her because of some kind of falling out. But it wasn't a simple execution. One drug dealer bumping off another. This was a sex act. This killer enjoyed what he did. Got off on it. And when he finished his little blood orgy, he went and planted all the incriminating evidence at Harlan's place so he could get away with it and maybe do it again some other place with some other woman. Maybe Emily, if he thinks she can identify him.'

'Okay, I respect your instincts. So let's say the killer's not Harlan. But if he isn't, what made the killer choose him as the fall guy?'

'That one's easy. Harlan and Stoddard were lovers. Maybe the guy learned she was having sex with Harlan and didn't like it. Or maybe he saw their affair as an opportunity to cut the investigation short. Being an Iraq veteran makes Harlan a great choice for a frame-up. Papers are full of stories about vets coming home and doing bad things. People almost expect it.'

'Who knew Harlan and Tiff were lovers?'

'Who knew?' Maggie shrugged her shoulders. She hadn't thought about that. 'I don't know. Probably a lot of people. Me, 'cause Harlan told me. My father, 'cause I told him. Sean Carroll knew, because I told him as well. Most likely everybody who attended Carroll's detectives' meeting, including Ganzer and Heinrich. Tommy Flynn, the guy who owns the Musty Moose. That's where Tiff worked. Emily's ex-husband Sam Harkness may have known, 'cause Tiff dumped Sam to hook-up with, quote, *someone younger.* Sam told me he wasn't pleased about that. And anyone else who might have seen them together, including Tiff's landlady, a woman named Paula Laverty, who according to my father is a big-time gossip who might have mentioned it to anybody and everybody in Machias.'

McCabe frowned. A lot of possibilities. 'But Carroll knew for sure,' said McCabe. 'Emmett Ganzer as well?'

'Yes, Ganzer knew. No way Carroll wouldn't have mentioned it at the meeting.'

'We also know Ganzer went to Harlan's place yesterday. Easy enough to plant the evidence after he was done licking his wounds.'

'So you're saying Ganzer's the killer? That Emmett Ganzer's the real Conor Riordan?'

'I'm thinking about it,' said McCabe.

Maggie pictured Ganzer's leering face as he sat in her car the previous day. His hand sliding on to her leg. His last threatening words before he got out. She had no problem seeing the guy as a psychopath. A sadist.

'I'm thinking,' McCabe continued, 'that maybe Ganzer didn't just go there to plant the evidence. If Ganzer *is* Conor Riordan and he wants Harlan to take the fall he sure as hell wouldn't want the case going to trial, where, planted evidence or not, a tough defense attorney might start asking difficult questions. On the other hand, if the presumed suspect ...'

'Harlan.'

'Yeah, Harlan. If Harlan is dead, hey, guess what? No trial, no defense attorney, no tough questions. And no more Conor Riordan. Everybody's happy.'

'So Ganzer went there intending to kill Harlan?'

'Yes. To plant the evidence and at the same time to kill Harlan and call it self-defense. We both know that song by heart. Words and melody. *Justifiable use of force against an armed suspect resisting arrest.* No witnesses, because Ganzer didn't bring back-up. But when Harlan's body was found, a loaded weapon with his fingerprints on it would no doubt have been found lying next to him. And all the evidence any prosecutor could possibly wish for is right there lying all over the place.'

'Means. Motive. Opportunity,' said Maggie.

'They're all there,' said McCabe. 'Now all we need is some evidence proving Ganzer's the bad guy that's not totally circumstantial.'

They stood silently for a while, watching the falls, enjoying the feel of the soft summer night.

'McCabe?'

He turned and looked at Maggie standing close to him, her dark hair reflecting moonlight, taking in the familiar scent of her shampoo. While he knew it had been much smarter for him not to accept Anya's offer to stay at the house on Center Street, he was kind of sorry he hadn't. On impulse, as if pulled by some magnetic force, he leaned in and kissed Maggie on the lips. She slipped her arms around him and kissed him back. At first softly and then harder.

Finally she pulled back.

'I don't know about you,' he said, avoiding the silent question on her face. 'But right now I could use a drink. And maybe something to eat. Didn't get more than a nibble of that chicken dinner.'

Chapter Thirty-Six

12:40 A.M., Monday, August 24, 2009
Pleasant Point, Maine

STAYING AWAY FROM the roads, traveling cross-country, avoiding contact with the cops or, for that matter, anyone else, Harlan spent most of the day and much of the night getting as far as the Passamaquoddy tribal lands at Pleasant Point. The most dangerous part of the trip lay just ahead. If the troopers were already out in force, as he suspected they were, passing over the narrow causeway on to Moose Island and then into Eastport was where he'd most likely be spotted. Cops didn't take kindly to anyone taking down one of their own. At least he hadn't killed the sonofabitch. Though he'd been sorely tempted.

It hadn't been a conscious decision to head for Eastport to find Tabitha. Harlan's legs just seemed to know where they were supposed to go. He supposed it was destined to come to this. Right from the beginning he'd told Tiff it was a dumb idea to steal the drugs, an even dumber idea to ask an eleven-year-old kid to hide them for her. But Tiff, being Tiff, insisted she knew best. Anyway, he was in the middle of it now. He knew what he had to do.

Harlan's plan was simple in concept, trickier in the details. First find Tabitha Stoddard. Somehow convince her to give him the Oxycontin. Once he had the pills and Tabitha was safe, he'd use them as bait to lure Riordan into the open. Get the fucker to show his face. Then kill him. As slowly and painfully as he had killed Tiff. He owed Tiff that much. Owed himself that much as well.

When Riordan was dead and the drugs destroyed, Harlan didn't much care what happened next. If it turned out to be violent death at the hands of a state police SWAT team, so be it. If he had to turn his own gun on himself, that was okay too. The only thing he wouldn't let them do is lock him up. Not now. Not ever.

As he walked, his mind flashed back to the night that began the final act of his affair with Tiff. He remembered the dancing and the loving and the song that was destined to become the soundtrack for what he guessed would be the last days of his life. *I will follow you into the dark.*

IT HAD BEEN a warm, wet Tuesday near the end of June. Tiff was working the bar at the Moose and Harlan came in late like he usually did. The place was empty except for a couple of regulars shooting pool in the side room. He slid on to the last stool and Tiff came over. They started shooting the shit about nothing in particular. He bought her a drink and she put on some music she liked. A Ray LaMontagne song. Since there was nothing else to do, she told him she felt like dancing. He wasn't much of a dancer but she came out from behind the bar, took his hands and pulled him on to the floor. He put his arms around her and they started slow dancing, though he supposed some people wouldn't have called it dancing at all.

Mostly it was the two of them standing there, holding on to each other and swaying to the soft, sexy sound of LaMontagne's 'All the Wild Horses', which, for some reason, Tiff had set to play over and over. 'All the Wild Horses'. He guessed it was just Tiff's kind of song.

Tommy kicked them out at one in the morning. Told Tiff to take Harlan home if that's what she was planning to do. Told her not to worry about the cleanup. He'd take care of it himself. Wasn't much to do anyway.

They drove in convoy through a summer rain back to her place. Then ran up the wooden stairs on the side of the building, Tiff just ahead of him, his hands on her ass, pushing her up to her place on the second floor. They stopped on the deck and kissed for a while before she had a chance to find the key.

Once inside, there was a hurried tearing at clothes until they both fell naked on to the bed in Tiff's room. Not really a bed. Just a king-sized mattress on the floor. The first time they made love that night it was eager and urgent and they both came quickly.

After they finished, and Harlan was lying there still breathing hard, Tiff got up and put on some more music. Not LaMontagne's 'Wild Horses' this time but Death Cab for Cutie's 'I Will Follow You into the Dark'.

With the music on, Tiff came back to bed and they made love again. Not fast and hungry like the first time but slowly, sweetly and full of promises he knew, even then, they'd never get to keep. When they finished, the two of them lay side by side, a warm breeze from the window playing over their naked bodies, the prophetic lyrics playing in the background. *I will follow you into the dark.*

That night, for the first time since they'd started seeing each other, he told her he loved her. She laughed a wicked laugh and told him to be careful using words like love because one of these days she might make him prove that he meant what he said.

He told her he was ready to prove it any time she wanted.

She tucked her body in close to his, her head resting on his chest, one leg draped over the two of his.

'If I asked you,' she whispered, 'would you go away with me? Just pick up and get away from this place as far as we can go? Never let anybody know where we are and never come back?'

He asked her what she was getting at. What this was all about.

'Just answer the question,' she said. 'Would you do it? Go away with me? Follow me into the dark?' she said, mimicking the song.

He laughed and said he would.

'Even if it was dangerous? Even if somebody might try to kill us if we left?'

He thought at first she was kidding. But there was something in the way she said it that told him she wasn't. So he told her yes, he was ready to risk dying if it was for something as good as her. He meant it, too.

That's when she first told him about Conor Riordan and the drugs. About arranging the boat for him. About Riordan's run to Canada and back. How she was in it up to her ears and, even though she wanted out, she knew he'd kill her if she tried walking away. She said there was only one way anybody ever left a job with Conor Riordan and that was dead.

'Conor Riordan? That his real name?'

'I don't know. I think it's just a name he uses. Nobody knows his real name.'

'But you know he's killed people?'

'I can't prove it but I know it. He likes hurting people. He likes hurting me. It turns him on.'

He didn't ask her what Riordan did to hurt her because he didn't want to know.

She told him about her plan to steal some of Riordan's drugs. 'He goes away sometimes,' she said. 'Two or three days at a time. Sometimes more. I don't know where he goes but it doesn't really matter. What's important is I found out where he keeps the stash,' she said. 'The drugs and the money.'

'He doesn't take the stuff with him?'

'No. Too easy to get caught with it.'

'How'd you find out?'

She smiled a wicked smile and told him she knew how to find out things.

'No, really.'

'It's better you don't know too much. But the next time he leaves, I'm going to take what I figure he owes me. Y'know? For services rendered? No more. No less. He's got so damned much I'm not sure he'll even notice what's missing. We can use what I take for seed money to start a new life together as far away from this fucking town and this fucking county and this fucking state as we can possibly get.'

Harlan lay there thinking about what she said and the more he thought about it the surer he was it wouldn't work.

'Tiff, listen to me. Forget the drugs. Forget the money. Wherever we go we can make out on our own. We can work. We can get jobs.'

'The money's mine, Harlan. I earned it. I want it.'

He shook his head. 'If you take the drugs, what do you think this guy Riordan's going to do? Just shrug his shoulders and say, "Oh well, I guess I owed Tiff that much"? Baby, he won't. We'll be looking over our shoulders the rest of our lives. Every time somebody looks at us a little funny we'll be thinking the next sound we hear is gonna be the bullet that blows our brains out. Only we won't hear it, 'cause by the time the sound gets to us, we'll already be dead.'

'Not if you kill him first,' she said.

'I'm not killing anyone,' he said. 'At least not so I can start selling drugs to a bunch of fucking addicts. I don't want you selling them either.'

She got pissed when he said that. Jumped out of bed and started pacing around the floor. Insisted she wasn't going to go away poor. With him or anyone else. Wasn't going to go without her share of Riordan's nearly five million dollars. She'd worked too hard for it, taken too many risks. She'd earned her share and she wanted it.

'Harlan, I know you killed people in the war and maybe you've had enough of killing. But you say you love me and I'm telling you I've had enough of living poor. Last thing I want is to end up living like my parents. I'd kill myself first. Or take the chance that Riordan'd do it for me. If you won't help me, I'll handle it myself.'

Harlan didn't agree to it. But he didn't tell her no right away either. That didn't come till later. When he finally knew he wanted no part of it. And he never agreed with her idea of hiding the drugs with Tabitha. Which he always thought was nuts.

That night after Tiff calmed down and came back to bed, they lay together for a while listening to the sound flowing from the expensive speakers she'd bought with money earned from selling drugs. Then they made love for a third time listening to the words. *I'll follow you into the dark.*

AFTER CROSSING OVER on to Moose Island, Harlan found himself a hidey-hole. A shallow depression in the earth surrounded by thick vegetation where he couldn't be seen by anybody unless they practically tripped over him. Since he figured he couldn't go knocking on Pike Stoddard's door till morning, he might as well get a few hours' sleep. He spread his ground cloth on the cool earth and lay down. But sleep wouldn't come. His mind kept going back to the cop who'd wanted to kill him. Detective Emmett Ganzer. He was sure Ganzer had intended to shoot him. What he couldn't figure out was why.

Last night at the Moose, Maggie told him, because he and Tiff were lovers, he'd automatically be considered a suspect. Okay, fair enough. But there had to be more than a little wiggle room between being a suspect and getting yourself shot for no good reason at all.

Unless, of course, the cop, Ganzer, had something to gain from shooting him.

Harlan could only think of two possibilities.

One ugly. The other uglier.

Ugly was Ganzer killing him, then planting evidence 'proving' that Harlan had killed Tiff. Ganzer gets credit for clearing the case. Gets a raise or a promotion or whatever the hell they give you in the state police for being a good cop.

Uglier was Harlan's growing suspicion that maybe Ganzer *was* Conor Riordan. He'd never considered the possibility that Riordan might be a cop. But why not? Wouldn't be the first cop in history who turned bad. And with what Tiff'd told him was a nearly five million dollar payoff Ganzer/Riordan had a whole lot more to gain from killing Harlan than just a promotion or a pat on the back.

The more Harlan thought about this scenario the more likely it seemed.

Which is when a definite 'oh shit' thought struck him for the first time. What if Ganzer/Riordan knew Tabitha had the drugs? What if he'd tortured the information out of Tiff before he'd killed her? Harlan got to his feet and got his shit together. He had to get to Stoddard's house long before morning. If he wasn't already too late.

Chapter Thirty-Seven

Eastport, Maine

At a little after two A.M. on a Monday morning, even in the tourist month of August, the city of Eastport was asleep. Its streets lay deserted. Few lights shone from either stores or houses. Even the small police department on Water Street appeared locked up for the night. The only movement Conor Riordan could see as he cruised the streets was a feral cat darting into an alleyway. Another solitary hunter in pursuit of what it no doubt hoped would be easy prey.

He doused his lights before pulling up in front of the house on Perry Street. He sat for a while in the darkness, watching for visible signs of life from within. There were none.

He studied the place. The peeling paint. The rotting clapboards. The *For Sale by Owner* sign. The flags hanging limply atop the aluminum pole. He supposed lowering the flag on this summer night hadn't been a high priority for the homeowners. Understandable, just hours after learning their second daughter had been murdered. Just minutes before they would decide their own lives were no longer worth living.

Riordan replayed the last words on the last voicemail on Tiff Stoddard's cell phone: 'The one thing I'm wondering about, though, is what the heck you want me to do with the package you gave me.' He remembered the girl peering through the upstairs window that freezing night back in December. Tabitha. *What the heck do you want me to do with the package you gave me?* Once he had the package he'd have to kill her. He'd never killed a child before. He wasn't sure if it would bother him or not. Didn't see why it should. Children die every day. Why not this one?

He slipped the car into gear. Drove far enough down the road that no one passing an unattended parked car would connect it with the house or what was about to happen there. He slipped on a pair of surgical gloves. Unzipped a small canvas gym bag and made sure that everything he needed was there. Paper booties and cap. A pair of needle nose pliers and a screwdriver. A single sheet of plain white paper, a note written on one side in clumsy block letters. A penlight. A canvas wallet containing a set of lock picks. And, finally, the Pneu-Dart breech-loading CO2 powered pistol acquired just for this purpose and a 3 cc tranquilizer dart. The vet he'd consulted in Bangor had recommended (and supplied for an exorbitant fee) a drug called Etorphine. Brand name M99. To knock out an eighty-pound Rottweiler the vet warned him to use a minute amount of the stuff. It was 10,000 times more potent than morphine and the 3 cc the dart was capable of delivering was more than enough to take down an elephant. It would take only one one-hundredth of that to knock out the dog in just seconds. It sounded perfect.

Riordan walked back to the house and cut across the yard to the back. His first stop was the gray box on the rear corner where the phone company connected its line.

THE SOUND THAT woke Tabitha Stoddard was neither particularly loud nor particularly menacing. Just the snap of a twig on the grass below. Yet she sat up with a start. Peered out her window, a hollow feeling in the pit of her stomach. Tabbie thought she saw something move in the darkness below but couldn't tell what it was. Maybe nothing more ominous than a raccoon checking the garbage bins. But she didn't think so. She looked and listened hard. Neither saw nor heard anything more. Yet somehow she sensed an alien presence. In her heart she was sure the December Man was back.

THE MAN MOVED silently to the back door, climbed the three steps to the landing. Knelt on one knee and checked the lock with the penlight. A cheap Kwikset pin and tumbler deadbolt. Easily breached. He removed the lock-pick set from his bag and selected a slender tension wrench and the thinnest of three stainless steel picks.

TABITHA CLIMBED OUT of bed. Not seeing anything more from the window, she stared at the bedroom door. Had the December Man brought the long knife she remembered from her dream? If she opened the door and ran to her mother's room would he catch her by the wrist, turn her around as he had in the dream and *cut her open like a hog in a slaughterhouse*? A tiny whimper escaped Tabbie's lips. She wished Tiff was here. Oh please God, she prayed, why can't you let Tiff come back? But she knew even Tiff couldn't save her now. Not from the darkness. Not from the December Man. Tiff hadn't even been able to save herself.

THE MAN PROBED the lock with the slender pick. One by one he found each of the pins and eased them up on to the narrow ledge of the cylinder. When all five were clear, he gently turned the wrench. The lock slid open. He turned the knob with a gloved hand and pushed the door open. Just enough to poke the muzzle of the dart gun through to the inside.

Electra lifted her head at the scent of a stranger. Rose from the pile of old blankets that served as her bed. Curled her upper lip, baring her fangs. A low rumbling rose from the depths of her broad chest. Her nails clicked on the linoleum floor as she trotted back to investigate the invader she could smell just on the other side of the kitchen door.

TABITHA PULLED THE blanket off her bed, grabbed Harold from his shelf, took her iPhone and the lady cop's card from her drawer and scrambled inside her closet. She closed the door, lowered herself to the floor, pulled the blanket over her head. Tried to arrange a pile of dirty laundry over the blanket so anyone looking in the closet might mistake her for nothing more than that. A pile of dirty laundry. Inside this makeshift hideout she wrapped her arms tightly around Harold and bit down hard on his ear to keep the sound of her crying too soft for anyone to hear. Even if Mrs St Pierre was right about heaven being a better place and Tiff and Terri being safe in the hands of Jesus, Tabitha knew now she really, really didn't want to go there. She wanted to stay right here. Even if Eastport was, as Tiff so often said, a real shithole.

THE SNARLING ROTTWEILER flung herself at the narrow opening in the door. When she was a few inches away, the man fired. The dart struck home, burying itself in the middle of her muscular chest. Electra barked once, then looked down, puzzled by the alien thing sticking out of her. She wanted to pull it out, but couldn't reach it with either her mouth or paws. She staggered once and then again, trying to maintain her balance, and then toppled over on to her side. Her legs jerked spasmodically. She lay still.

DONELDA STODDARD HAD always been a light sleeper. But tonight her sleep was especially troubled, both by the death of her second daughter and the terrible nightmares of her third. Startled into alertness by Electra's single bark, Donelda looked across to the other side of the bed. No sign of Pike. No doubt the so-called man of the house was still downstairs, still dead to the world, the gun he kept by his side as useless as his alcohol-soaked brain. She picked up the phone to call 911. The phone was dead. She closed her eyes. Had Tiff's killer come to kill the rest of them? She wished they'd gotten themselves a cell phone but it was yet another expense they couldn't afford.

THE MAN PULLED the spent dart from the Rottweiler's chest. He kicked the dog once to make sure it was really out. He kicked it a second time, harder, just for the hell of it.

UPSTAIRS, TABITHA SQUEEZED herself further into the corner of her small closet.

DRESSED ONLY IN a long cotton sleepshirt, Donelda opened the bedroom door and went out into the hall. She stood and listened again. She heard nothing but her husband snoring. Perhaps Electra's bark, the dog's appearance at the door, had frightened the intruder away. Please God, she prayed, let it be so. She went to the hall window and looked down into the yard. She saw nothing. No cars. No movement. No one running from the house. She hoped against hope that, for the moment at least, what was left of her little family was safe. But then she heard it. An almost imperceptible sound between Pike's snores. The whisper of a foot moving gently on the floor below. And then another. Whoever this enemy was, whatever he wanted, he was in the house. And she was on her own.

THE MAN LISTENED to the wet snores coming from the silhouetted figure in the wheelchair. He flicked on the penlight and saw Pike Stoddard sitting slumped on the other end of the room, his legs covered by a lightweight summer blanket. An empty whiskey bottle lay on the floor next to him. Another, half empty, was on his lap. The man started forward, then stopped and listened when he heard a floorboard creak overhead.

FROM INSIDE HER cocoon of blanket and laundry, Tabitha pressed a button on her iPhone, creating enough light for her to read the number the lady cop had written on the card. She pressed the numbers on her keypad.

DOWN IN MACHIAS the first four notes of Beethoven's Fifth Symphony sounded in a darkened bedroom. Once. Twice. And then a third time. Maggie Savage, still half asleep, reached an arm across, patted the bedside table with her hand until she found her phone.

FROM INSIDE HER closet, Tabitha heard her bedroom door open, then softly close again. She poked her head outside the blanket. Saw no band of light at the bottom of the door. Whoever was in her room wasn't turning on the lights. She pursed her lips tight. Retreated back into her cocoon. Tried not to breathe, knowing she couldn't make a sound.

Through the phone she heard the lady cop say, 'Hello.'

Tabbie dared not answer. If she spoke, the December Man would hear where she was. The December Man would kill her.

'Hello?' Tabitha heard the lady cop's voice again from the phone. 'Is anyone there?'

Tabitha heard footsteps walking to her bed. Terrified the December Man would hear the lady cop's voice, Tabbie broke the connection. She turned off the phone and bit down hard again on Harold's ear. Her body shivered uncontrollably. Warm pee streamed out from between her legs.

Hearing no more steps overhead, the man walked to the wheelchair. He shone the penlight on Pike's face. His head lolled to one side. His mouth hung open. A string of spittle hung suspended from his lower lip in seeming defiance of the laws of gravity. A raspy snore punctuated the rise and fall of his chest.

The man pressed Pike's thumb and fingers against a white sheet of paper and then slipped it between two bottles on the shelf where Pike kept his booze. That done, he went behind Pike's wheelchair. Tiff told him her old man always kept a loaded pistol tucked in the chair where he could reach it fast. He slid one hand under Pike's blanket on the right. No gun there. He did the same on the left and felt a small-caliber automatic. Pike was a lefty. Good to know. The man checked the load. Chambered a round. Working carefully, he wrapped Pike's left hand around the grip, placing each of the fingers in the correct position, easing the index finger inside the trigger guard. He painstakingly bent Pike's left arm up to what seemed a natural position, the barrel of the automatic less than an inch away and pointing directly at Pike's temple.

Pike snored on. It looked like the poor sonofabitch was going to sleep through his own suicide.

MAGGIE SAVAGE TURNED on the light: 2:35. Who the hell was calling at 2:35? Whoever it was had hung up. Maggie rubbed the sleep from her eyes and returned the last call received. The phone rang once and went immediately to message. A child's voice. 'Hello,' the child said, 'you have reached Tabitha Stoddard's iPhone. If you'd like me to call you back, please leave your number and I will do so as soon as I can.' Maggie hung up without leaving a message. It would take her the better part of an hour to get from Machias to Eastport, but Frank Boucher was right there. She punched in his home number.

TABITHA HEARD FOOTSTEPS approach the closet. On the other side of the door the intruder paused. Tabbie closed her eyes tighter. Bit down on Harold even harder. She felt the blanket rustle in a sudden stirring of air. The door swung open. Tabitha supressed a violent urge to scream.

'Tabitha?' a familiar voice whispered.

Tabbie dropped the blanket and peered up at her mother.

'Sssshhh. Be quiet,' Donelda whispered. 'Get dressed. Quickly.'

'HELLO,' BOUCHER'S VOICE at the other end of the phone.

'Chief, this is Margaret Savage. Get some people over to Pike Stoddard's place right away.'

She must have woken Boucher from a deep sleep, because he sounded barely compos mentis.

'Huh? What? Why? What's going on?'

'I don't know. But something's seriously wrong there. Get whatever assets you have to Stoddard's now.'

DONELDA HELPED HER youngest daughter strip off her pajamas. Handed her some underwear. Then jeans and a sweatshirt. While Tabitha dressed, Donelda pulled the two sheets off the bed and tied them tightly together. Using one end to form a makeshift sling, she slipped it under her daughter's arms. This is how they always did it in the movies. She hoped to hell it worked in real life. She pulled the screen from the window. Laid it on the floor.

'Get over here,' Donelda ordered in a loud whisper.

Tabitha didn't move.

She tried to pull the frightened child toward the window.

'Wait,' Tabitha said. She ran back to the closet. Emerged with her iPhone and Harold.

They both froze at the sound of the shot from downstairs.

Her mother pulled her toward the open window. Tabitha threw Harold out and climbed up on to the sill.

'I'll lower you down. When you get to the ground, pull the sheet off and run.'

'Where?'

'Just run. And don't come back!'

Tabbie hesitated. Tears poured from her eyes. Donelda lifted her youngest child, hugged her tightly, kissed her hard.

'Just remember,' she whispered, her words barely audible. 'I love you. More than anyone or anything in the world. And I always will. No matter what.'

'I love you too.'

She helped Tabitha out the window and lowered her slowly, hand over hand, foot by foot, down to the ground. She watched her daughter pull the sling from over her head, grab the stuffed bear, look up once at her mother, who was leaning out the window.

'Run!' Donelda called in the loudest whisper she dared.

Tabitha threw her mother a tentative wave. Then ran.

Donelda pulled up the sheets, threw them in a heap on the floor, and slipped as quietly as she could out of Tabbie's room, shutting the door behind her.

A MAN STOOD at the bottom of the stairs. Donelda went out to the landing, determined to give her daughter as much time as she could.

'Where's the child?' the man asked, pointing Pike's gun up at Donelda's chest.

Donelda said nothing. To the man's surprise she started silently down the stairs toward him. She came slowly. Step by step.

'Where's the child?' the man repeated.

'What do you want with her?' asked Donelda, surprised how calm her voice sounded, at least to her, in spite of the fact that her heart was pounding so hard she could almost hear it. The longer she could keep the man talking, she told herself, the better. She descended a few more steps. The man backed off a little. He didn't want her too close.

'She's only a child. She can't hurt you in any way,' Donelda said. 'Leave her be.'

'She has something that's mine,' the man said. 'Where is she? Tell me now or I'll shoot you where you stand.'

'You'll shoot me anyway. Just like you shot Pike.' She glanced over at the figure slumped in the chair. 'Is he dead?'

'Yes. He's dead. Killed himself. Suicide.'

Donelda snorted. 'You did him a favor. He was killing himself anyway. The bullet was just a lot faster than the booze.'

Curiously, she felt no fear. Just hatred for this man standing in front of her.

'One more chance,' the man said. 'Where's the child? If she gives me what I want I won't hurt her. Or you.'

Liar, thought Donelda. She looked the killer in the eye. 'She's not here,' Donelda said. 'We sent her away.'

'Sent her where?'

'A sleepover,' said Donelda. 'At a friend's house. To take her mind off what you did to her sister.'

'What friend?'

What friend? Donelda searched her mind desperately for a name to give him.

'She's at the Bouchers',' she finally said. 'Frank and Alva Boucher. They live by the airport.' Boucher's house, if he dared to go there, was more than three miles away. It would put more distance between Tabitha and almost certain death. 'She's staying with them. Frank's the police chief here in Eastport.'

She saw a flicker of doubt flash across Conor Riordan's eyes.

Donelda started toward him.

He backed away, into the living room. She followed. He positioned himself directly behind Pike's chair.

When Donelda was only four feet away, he pointed the gun at the middle of her face. She took another step forward. He pulled the trigger.

Chapter Thirty-Eight

MAGGIE HUNG UP before the chief could ask any more questions, threw on some clothes and ran downstairs to her car. She had no idea why Tabitha Stoddard had called. But, whatever the reason, she was sure it couldn't be good. She backed out of the driveway and stomped on the gas.

CONOR RIORDAN CHECKED the room and smiled to himself. It was as close to perfect as anyone could have made it. Gunshot residue on Pike's hand and temple. The angle of the shot that killed Donelda came from where Pike was sitting. The position of her body, the spray pattern of blood on the floor and wall seemed exactly right. The only thing he hadn't counted on was the missing kid.

MAGGIE TRIED SEAN Carroll's cell number from the road. His phone went directly to message. She tried again. Same result. She left a message telling him to call her as soon as he could and then slipped the phone back in her pocket. There was no way in hell she was going to call Emmett Ganzer.

STEPPING CAREFULLY AROUND the woman's blood, Riordan went upstairs. He found Tabitha's room, opened the door, turned on the lights and quietly seethed. The tied-together sheets, the open window, the screen discarded on the floor. The story told itself. The mother had lowered the child to safety before coming downstairs to give her daughter time to get away. Probably sent her to a neighbor's to call for help. Which meant the cops would likely be here in minutes. Which meant the entire plan was totally fucked up. Trying to calm the rage boiling up inside him, he untied the sheets, tossed them on the bed. Then he pushed the screen back in place, hurried downstairs and went out the way he came in. Locking the door behind him, he ran back to the gray box and reconnected the telephone.

TABITHA WAS LESS than a hundred yards from the house when she heard the sound of the second shot. The one she was sure was intended for her mother. *Run, Tabitha, run!* her mother's voice pleaded. But how could she run? She had to go back. Her mother might be hurt. Her mother might be dying. She might need someone to call for help. To call for an ambulance. *Run, Tabitha, run!* No! She couldn't just run and leave her mother to die. Clutching Harold by a single leg, she started back. That's when she saw the silhouette of a man coming toward her. She froze.

THE SOUND HAD come from the woods that bordered the back of the property. Riordan was sure of that. Someone or some thing crashing through the underbrush not far from the house. Maybe the kid hadn't run to a neighbor's after all. Maybe she'd been hiding back there all along. Maybe things weren't as fucked up as he thought. Still, he didn't have much time.

He scanned the wood line for any sign of movement. Saw none. Stuffed everything but the penlight back in the gym bag and hurried in the direction he thought the sound had come from.

TABITHA SET HAROLD on the ground. It was too hard carrying the oversized bear and trying to get away at the same time. She heard her mother's voice pleading with her once again. *Run, Tabitha, run!* She ran.

HEARING THE SOUND, the man crashed into the woods. He figured the kid couldn't be more than thirty or forty yards ahead of him. He called out, 'Tabitha, leave me Tiff's package and I'll leave you alone. I promise I won't hurt you. I want Tiff's package. Not you.'

There was no answer.

Holding his arms in front of his face to keep from being scratched by hanging branches, Conor Riordan charged ahead, unconcerned whether the child heard him coming or not. It was time for this to be over.

He pulled to a stop, squinted into the darkness at something he didn't recognize. The blackened silhouette of what seemed to be a small animal perched behind some brush maybe twenty yards ahead and slightly to the left. Was that what he'd heard crashing around? Some animal and not the kid? Whatever the creature was, it wasn't moving. Just sitting and staring in his direction. He flicked on the penlight. The beam was too weak to offer more information. From the shape of its ears the thing looked like a small bear. A young cub. But wherever there was a cub, a mother bear was certain to be close by. He pulled out his weapon and advanced slowly, listening for the approach of an angry mother bear, irritated by the fact that the child, if she was here, was getting further ahead of him.

The cub, if that's what it was, didn't move. The man knelt on one knee, aimed carefully and fired. The bullet struck its mark. The creature dropped and lay motionless on its back. A child's voice cried out in anguish from the depth of the woods: 'Harold!' Riordan looked toward the sound. He saw the child running toward the dead bear cub. Lifting it up in her hands. 'Oh, Harold,' she cried.

Riordan heard sirens screaming their urgent message and closing fast. Two police cars screeched to a halt in front of the house. He had no time.

Tabitha felt a large hand grab her wrist. Another clamped itself over her mouth, making it impossible for her to scream again. Or to make any sound at all. She felt herself being lifted off the ground. The December Man was carrying her deeper into the blackness of the woods.

She tried to struggle free but couldn't. He was far too strong. *He's going to cut me open*, she thought, *like a hog in a slaughterhouse.*

Chapter Thirty-Nine

IT WAS 3:15 before Maggie Savage pulled in behind Chief Frank Boucher's car in front of 190 Perry Road. A second Eastport cruiser and a MedCu unit were there as well, their flashing lights lending an eerie glow to the quiet night scene. An Eastport cop was stringing yellow crime-scene tape round the perimeter of the property.

Frank Boucher leaned in through the open window of Maggie's Blazer. 'Two dead. Looks like Pike shot Donelda from his chair and then put the gun to his own head. Piece is still dangling from his finger. Empty whiskey bottle on the floor. Half-empty one on his lap. And a suicide note on the table next to him.'

'You read it?'

'Yeah. Looks to me like the guilt finally got to him.'

'Where's the child?' she asked.

'No sign of Tabbie.'

'You looked?'

'I looked and didn't find her. Called her name. Didn't get an answer. But she might still be hiding somewhere in the house. I didn't want to do any kind of thorough search till the evidence folks have been through. State police run murder cases and the last thing I need is Emmett fucking Ganzer accusing me of messing up his crime scene. In any case I figure Tabitha was so terrified by what was going on she just ran away.'

'Get me some gloves, Frank. Also a Maglite. I'm going in.'

Boucher looked like he was about to say something.

'Frank, don't argue,' Maggie said softly but firmly. 'Just move. If there's any chance that kid is in there, maybe wounded, maybe bleeding to death, we've got to find her.'

Boucher ran to his car. He met Maggie at the front door. She had on a telephone headset. Told Boucher she wanted him to stay on the line while she went through the place. Just in case. Maggie went in through the front door. Closed it behind her.

'Tabitha,' she shouted. 'Are you here?' Pause. 'This is Detective Margaret Savage.' Pause. 'You called me earlier tonight.' Pause. 'Please let me know if you're here.'

The only answer was silence.

She swung the Maglite around the living room. The scene was as Boucher had described. An obvious murder-suicide. She'd check the bodies later. Finding Tabitha had to take priority.

She opened a small coat closet near the front door. Coats and hats and boots plus a few more of Donelda's paintings inside. No small bodies. No one bleeding.

She moved to the kitchen and frowned. The black and tan Rottweiler was lying listlessly on the kitchen floor. It glanced up at Maggie but made no effort to rise. Not a bit like the Electra she met on Saturday.

'Frank,' she said into her headset.

'What?'

'The guys on the MedCu unit still here?'

'Of course.'

'I want the dog on the kitchen floor muzzled and chained. And then I want one of the EMTs to draw a blood sample for me. Two blood samples.'

'Why?'

'I'll explain later. But it's important. Just do it.'

Boucher grunted. Maggie drew her gun and left the kitchen. The downstairs bathroom was empty. So was a closet under the stairs.

The only other room on the ground floor was an eight-by-ten bedroom in the back that had been converted into a small art studio. Empty except for an easel and some brushes and paints. And more paintings of lighthouses. Tabitha wasn't here. Nor was the killer.

The door at the top of the stairs opened into a small bedroom with a queen-sized bed. Only one side had been slept in. Donelda's clothes, the same ones Maggie saw her wearing on Saturday, were piled on a chair. Okay. So Donelda had gotten up from her bed and gone downstairs. Why?

'Tabitha?' Maggie called again. 'Can you hear me?'

No answer.

There was a small armoire pushed against one wall. Big enough, Maggie gauged, to contain a child's body. She pulled it open. Nothing but Donelda and Pike's meager wardrobes hanging limply from the crossbar. Some shoes on the floor.

In the bathroom Maggie pulled the shower curtain aside. Again nothing.

She opened the door to a second bedroom. Two beds neatly made. Photos of Tiff and Terri hung from the walls. Other shots of what Maggie figured were high-school friends. The small closet lay nearly empty. No one had used this room for quite a while. No one had dusted it either.

'Any luck?' Boucher's voice boomed through the headset.

'No. Not yet. You have people outside looking for her?'

'Yes. We already checked with the nearest neighbors. Tabbie didn't go banging on any of their doors. I've got a couple of guys searching the woods behind the house now. One of my guys is waking up some folks in town as we speak. Should have a good-sized search party fanning out from here inside of an hour.'

While Boucher was talking, Maggie entered the bedroom at the end of the hall. Tabitha's room. A single bed with a headboard made of fence pickets with identical birds perched atop each picket. A bookcase full of books. Other books lay on the floor. On the top shelf, a couple of stuffed animals, a bunny and a panda. An empty space between the two.

The sheets had been ripped off the bed and tossed in a pile on the floor. Why? Maggie wasn't sure. Next to the sheets a pair of little girl pajamas lay discarded. Had Tabitha gotten dressed before she left?

'Find anything?' the unexpected sound of Boucher's voice coming through the earpiece made her jump.

'Not yet.'

'Gone through the whole place?'

'Not yet. I'll let you know.'

The closet door hung open. Inside Maggie could see some kid's clothes on the floor. Looked like a pile of laundry. Under them, a lightweight blanket. Had the closet been Tabbie's hiding place while the murders were going on? If it was, maybe someone had found her. But if he had why didn't he kill her as well? Why wasn't her body lying on the closet floor?

Maggie pulled off her headset and called out. 'Tabitha, if you can hear me, please answer! This is Detective Margaret Savage. I'm here to help.'

Maggie stood stock still, hardly daring to breathe, listening for the slightest response, the slightest sound from anywhere in the house. There was none.

Was there anywhere in the house she hadn't looked?

She went to the hall. Pointed the light at the ceiling. A thin cord hung down, connected to a set of pull-down attic stairs. Could Tabitha have gone up to the attic to hide? Had Donelda closed the door after her? Maggie reached up and pulled the steps down. Climbed halfway up. Poked her head through. She swung the light around a small attic space with sharply angled ceilings.

'Tabitha?' she called out. Again, no answer. No sign of the child either alive or dead. She climbed the rest of the way up and then out on to the plywood floor. The ceiling too low to stand upright, she crouched as she searched the place, shining the light this way and that, hoping that if she did find the child she would still be alive.

One end of the small attic was filled with cardboard boxes. Too small to contain a child's body. Too small for Tabitha to hide behind.

At the other end Maggie could see the detritus of three children's lives. A disassembled crib. An ancient high chair. A car seat. A homemade rocking horse. Beyond them what appeared to be a child's play area. Crouching down to avoid hitting her head, Maggie duck-walked to the end. She saw a child-sized chair and desk. A bunch of cushions and half a dozen young adult books scattered on the floor. Tabitha must have come up here to read. Maggie saw a standing lamp and turned it on. A newsprint sketchbook lay open on the floor. Some Crayola crayons and a mostly empty box in the familiar green and yellow colors were scattered across the page. Maggie picked up the sketchbook. An image showing the back of a fishing boat. The *Katie Louise*. The kid wasn't a bad artist. Maybe she got that from her mother. On the deck a dark-haired woman stood arms flung out to the side. Behind her a man, much bigger than the woman, was holding her by the hair with one hand. In his other hand he held what looked like a sword against her throat. The woman's mouth was drawn into a wide-open oval reminding Maggie of the scream in Edvard Munch's famous painting.

A splash of red poured from the woman's neck. At the bottom of the drawing Tabitha had written the words *Like a Hog in a Slaughterhouse* three times, stacked in three neat rows.

The words, Maggie's own, leaped off the page. She remembered the eleven-year-old Tabitha, round owlish glasses peering down at her from the corner of the stairs. She hadn't noticed the child till after she'd said them. But Tabitha must have heard. Maggie looked at the picture again and heaved a sigh of regret at the carelessness of what she'd said and how she said it. She tore the sheet of newsprint from the pad, folded it and slipped it into the rear pocket of her jeans. She headed back toward the attic stairs, climbed down and closed the trap door.

'She's not here, Frank. Not in the house.'

'Okay, then, you better get out of there and leave the rest to the techs.'

'In a minute. I want to check the bodies first.'

'Damnit, Maggie . . .'

She broke the connection.

The scene in the living room was as Boucher had described it. Pike lay slumped in his chair. She shone the light on the wound to his head. Blackened GSR – gun shot residue – surrounding the entry hole was plainly visible.

Donelda, shot in the face, lay on her back on the floor. Her left eye blown out. The right one remained open, reflecting the emptiness of death.

Maggie picked up the suicide note, holding it by its edges so as not to disturb the killer's prints, though she doubted they'd find any there. The note was written on plain white paper. Each word spelled out in big block letters like a child had written them. More likely someone trying to disguise his writing.

> I feel so bad about what I done to Tiffany and Teresa. Don't have nobody but me to blame. I feel so bad I don't want to live no more. And neether does Donnie or Tabitha. I hope God finds it in his hart to forgive me for what I am going to do. And Jesus too. Pike Stoddard.

What I done to my daughters? Don't have nobody but me to blame? Maggie tried to remember her conversation with Pike. Had he spoken so ungrammatically? She didn't have McCabe's photographic memory but she didn't think so. She sensed the grammar in the note was constructed by a killer mimicking imagined illiteracy. She put the sheet of paper back where she found it.

Maggie walked out of the house just as Bill Heinrich's Evidence Retrieval Team walked in with their cameras and equipment. Ganzer was talking to a couple of troopers. Frank Boucher stood next to the evidence van.

'What are you doing here, Savage?' Ganzer called to her, 'And what do you think you were doing inside the house?'

Maggie didn't answer. She just yanked off the gloves and stuck them in a pocket of her jeans. She went to where Boucher was standing.

'Oh, I have something for you,' the Chief said, a little too theatrically. 'Your father asked me to make sure I got this to you.'

Positioning his body so Ganzer couldn't see the transaction, Boucher handed Maggie a small vial of blood.

'Thanks, Frank,' she said. After a few seconds she handed it back. 'I'd like you to get this down to the Crime Lab in Augusta for analysis. It occurs to me that I have no official standing in this case. You do. But don't give it to Ganzer.'

Boucher glanced over her shoulder at Ganzer, who was heading their way, then slipped the vial back into his pocket. 'Just so you know I had the EMTs draw two vials. I'll give one to Ganzer and send the second one to the lab myself.'

'Perfect. What are you going to do with the dog?'

Boucher shrugged. 'I don't know. Drop it off at the animal shelter in Calais, I suppose.'

'Okay. Just one more favor,' she said. 'Make sure they don't euthanase and cremate the animal. At least not till we're done with this case. If the tox tests show the dog was tranquilized we may need its body to prove in court it's where this blood came from.'

'No problem.' Boucher smiled.

She offered her thanks and then started back toward her car. Ganzer followed. He caught up with her midway.

'What was going on back there between you and Boucher?'

Maggie smiled. 'He was telling me what a terrific basketball player I used to be.'

'I saw you handing something back and forth. What was it?'

'A blood sample. I asked him to give it to you to send in for a tox report.'

'Whose blood? Stoddard's?'

'No. Stoddard's dog.'

'You know, Savage, I'm getting more than a little tired of your smartass remarks. Now I asked you a question and I'd like a straight answer. Whose blood are we having tested and why?'

'I gave you a straight answer, Emmett.' Maggie studied Ganzer's face. How good an actor was this guy? 'I had the blood drawn from Stoddard's dog.'

'What in hell is dog blood supposed to show us?'

'That Pike Stoddard didn't kill his wife or himself. That a third party, let's call him Conor Riordan, entered the house and tranquilized Stoddard's vicious Rottweiler so it wouldn't attack him while he committed the murders.'

Ganzer looked doubtful. 'Why wouldn't this third party, let's call him Harlan Savage, just shoot the dog as well?'

Maybe Ganzer wasn't a good actor. Maybe he was just stupid. No, she decided, that wasn't it. Emmett Ganzer wasn't stupid. Never had been.

'Because, Emmett, this third party wanted the killings to look like murder-suicide. If the dog is unhurt and there's no evidence it attacked an intruder, that's what it looks like. His only problem is Boucher and I got here a lot faster than the killer was counting on. The dog hadn't recovered yet.'

Maggie started back toward her car. Ganzer followed.

'What were you doing here in the first place? What were you doing in the house? I know Carroll took you off the case.'

Maggie returned Ganzer's tough-guy stare. Almost said, 'None of your business.' Instead, on impulse, she asked a question of her own. 'Where is she, Emmett?'

'Where is who?'

'The child. Tabitha. Tabitha Stoddard. Her body's not in the house with her parents. What have you done with her? Is she dead? Did you kill her as well? Or have you hidden her away somewhere?'

Ganzer looked incredulous. 'Have you lost your mind?'

'Have you been around here the whole time, Emmett? Finding a place to keep her or maybe hide her body while you were supposedly racing up from a motel in Machias to the crime scene?'

'Jesus Christ all fucking mighty. You have lost your mind.'

'Just out of curiosity, exactly where were you between eight and ten P.M. on Friday night? In the state park at Machiasport getting your rocks off ? And where were you at two A.M. this morning? Busy setting up the scene inside? By the way, that suicide note was clumsy. Pike Stoddard was nowhere near that illiterate. Though I am sure you managed to get his prints on it before you shot him. I always said you weren't stupid, Emmett. Just fucked up.'

'What is this? Some weird notion of yours to get your crazy brother off the hook? Well, it's not going to work, Savage. We know he killed Tiff Stoddard and probably killed her parents as well.'

'Goodbye, Emmett.'

Chapter Forty

HARLAN SAVAGE CONTINUED his silent watch from the camouflaged position he and Tabitha and Harold had been hiding in for over an hour now. He heard nothing. Saw nothing. For all that time he'd been lying flat on his gut, with Tabitha forced into a prone position next to and partly under him, his right arm pressing down on her back to hold her in place, his left hand clamped over her mouth to keep her from crying out. The soft flow of air coming from her nostrils assured him she wasn't suffocating. As they lay there he kept whispering a message of reassurance and caution in her ear. 'It's okay, Tabitha. I'm a friend of Tiff's. I'm not going to hurt you. But you have to be quiet. Very, very quiet.'

In the distance Harlan saw the beams of two flashlights moving unsteadily in their direction. Now visible, now disappearing behind a tree, now behind some low brush, now visible again. 'Don't move. Don't breathe,' he told Tabitha and then stopped whispering, put his head down and held her even more tightly. The camouflage he'd used for their position wasn't quite up to Marine Corps standards. He felt terribly exposed.

'Tabitha!' a man's voice called out from behind one of the flashlights. 'Tabitha Stoddard, are you out there?'

'Hey, dumbass,' the second flashlight shouted, 'she ain't gonna answer you if she's dead.'

'We don't know she's dead just 'cause the parents are.'

Harlan felt the muscles in Tabitha's jaw clamp tighter at the words. Felt a tremor course through her body.

'Well, I figure that fucker Pike got what he deserved. Killed himself's what I heard. First Donelda, then himself.'

'It's the kid I feel sorry for.'

A pair of black steel-toed boots stepped within a few feet of where Harlan and Tabitha were hiding. So close Harlan could have reached out and grabbed the man by the ankle. The circle of light swept past them. The man stopped. Harlan held his breath. Hoped Tabbie would as well.

'Tabitha? You out there?' the first flashlight shouted.

'Ssssh. What was that?' The second flashlight said.

'What was what?'

'I thought I heard something.'

The two of them stood and listened.

'Nah. You're just spooking yourself.'

They started walking again. Their voices slowly receded in the distance. Beneath his right arm, Harlan felt Tabitha's body begin to shake with sobs. He felt the wetness of her tears and snot begin to cover the back of his hand.

Harlan didn't ease up on the pressure until the men were long gone and his arm was shaking with fatigue. One good thing about having these searchers tramping around. Make it a hell of a lot tougher for dogs to pick up a scent. Especially if he carried Tabitha at least part of the way.

One thing for sure. They couldn't stay here for ever. He just didn't know where to go.

He leaned in close to Tabitha's ear, hoping she'd recovered enough to be capable of listening, of doing what he asked. He whispered in the gentlest voice he could muster that he was going to loosen his grip on her back and uncover her mouth. But he would only do that if she promised not to make a sound. Not a shout. Not a cry. Not a word.

'Promise?' he asked. 'Nod if you promise.'

He felt her head nod tentatively.

'Listen, Tabitha, Tiff told me when you make a promise you always keep it. Is that true?'

She nodded again. More vigorously this time. Tried to turn her head at the same time to get a look at him.

'Do you promise to be quiet?'

She nodded a third time.

He uncovered her mouth ready to clamp his hand over it again if she cried out. She didn't.

'Who are you?' They were the first words Tabitha had spoken since he grabbed her.

'I told you. I'm a friend of Tiff's.'

'Tiff's dead.'

'I know.'

'What's your name?'

'Harlan.'

'And you're a friend of Tiff's?'

'Yes.'

'Her boyfriend?'

'I guess so. At least I told her I loved her and I think maybe she loved me back so I guess that makes me her boyfriend.'

'Did you really love her?'

'Yes,' Harlan told her, 'I really did.'

'So did I.'

'I know.'

'So you didn't kill her?' asked Tabitha.

'No. A man named Conor Riordan killed her.'

'The December Man.'

'Who?'

'A man Tiff called Conor Riordan came to our house in December. I call him the "December Man".'

'Did you see him?'

'Only for a second. From my bedroom window. When the light went on in Tiff's car when she opened the door.'

'Would you recognize him if you saw him again?'

'I don't know. Maybe. I think so.'

'What did he look like?'

She told him. He nodded, wondering how good a look she'd really gotten in a split second from an upstairs window.

'Does he know you saw him?'

'I think so. He looked at me.'

Harlan wondered if Tabitha had been Riordan's primary target tonight. If Pike and Donelda weren't just collateral damage. Shoot the kid. Take out a witness. Someone who'd seen his face. Seemed reasonable. It meant Riordan would be after her not just for the drugs but also to kill her. He had to take her with him.

He slung the M40 upside down over one shoulder. Picked up Tabitha and her bear to keep any dogs from catching her scent. They started walking.

'Can I talk now?' she asked.

'Whisper in my ear. I can hear you.'

'Those men said my mom was dead. My daddy too.'

'Yes, they did,' said Harlan. 'I'm very sorry about that.'

'Do you suppose they're in a better place?'

He didn't really know what Tabitha was talking about so he just shrugged and shook his head. She started crying again. Softly. To herself. He could feel wet tears rolling down the back of his neck. He rubbed her back in little circles as he walked, trying to comfort her as one would a baby but not really succeeding. He remembered walking this way with an injured infant in Iraq, until he got it to an aid station, where a nurse told him the infant was dead. 'Ssssh, ssssh, ssssh,' he whispered in Tabitha's ear. It didn't do much good. She just kept weeping.

The orange stripe in the sky was wider now. Tinged with red. Harlan knew they had to put more distance between themselves and the searchers before it was fully light. He picked up the pace and tried to figure out how they were going to get off the island. The troopers would be out in force now following the murders of the Stoddards. Most likely the locals as well. They might even try to blame him for the killings. They were probably already blaming him for Tiff's. It seemed like his plan, such as it was, was all shot to hell. He supposed even Maggie would be against him now.

'Where are we going?' Tabitha asked after about ten minutes.

'I don't know,' said Harlan who was still carrying her in his arms. Truth be told his arms were getting tired. She wasn't exactly an infant. She wasn't even light for an eleven-year-old. 'We need someplace we can rest up and talk about what we're going to do next. Where nobody will see us. You have any good ideas?'

She thought about that for a minute. 'We could go to Toby Mahler's grandfather's house.'

'Yeah? How's Toby Mahler's grandfather gonna feel about that?'

'I don't think he'll care. He's in a better place too.'

'That mean he's dead?'

'Since last spring. He died in the fullness of his years.'

'You always say stuff like that? "In the fullness of his years"?'

'That's what the minister said at his funeral. Me and my mom went. My dad said he didn't give a fuck about Toby Mahler's grandfather so he wasn't going to go. The church has a handicapped entrance so he could've gone if he wanted to. But he said he didn't give a fuck.'

Harlan was thinking this kid was more than a little weird. He wondered if Tiff was like her when she was eleven but doubted it.

'The house is just sitting there,' Tabitha said. 'All by itself at the end of Kendall Point Road. Toby's mom says they can't sell it so maybe they just ought to burn the damn thing down. It's kind of a dump anyway. Nobody ever goes there except me and Toby.'

It sounded perfect. 'Anybody know you go there?'

'Just Toby.'

'He going to tell anybody?'

'I don't think so. He goes there to smoke dope and I don't think he'd want anybody to know about that.'

'He your age?'

'He's twelve.'

'And he smokes dope? Where the hell's he get that from?'

'Steals it from his mom. She smokes it all the time.'

'You ever try it?'

'Just once. I didn't like it.'

'How far is it?'

'How far is what?'

'The house.'

'Couple of miles. I usually take my bike.'

She seemed better now thinking about other things and he figured maybe they'd put enough distance between her earlier scent and the dogs. Enough to buy them some time anyway. 'You think maybe you could walk for a little while?'

She told him she could so he put her down and they walked in silence, side by side. She slipped her hand, the one that wasn't holding Harold, into his.

'Did Tiff love you back?' Tabitha asked.

'I think so. We were going to go away together.' Harlan figured that was only a little lie. It *was* something they talked about.

'Get the hell out of Dodge?'

'Something like that.'

They walked hand in hand until it was fully light. Mostly they stayed away from the roads but sometimes were unable to avoid them. Harlan was worried somebody might stop and start asking questions but none of the few people who drove by, including one state police car, gave them a second glance.

Chapter Forty-One

4:51 A.M.*, Monday, August 24, 2009*
Eastport, Maine

AFTER SHE LEFT Perry Road, Maggie drove over to the waterfront, where she hoped to catch Luke Haskell before he headed out for a day's lobstering. The eastern sky was barely painted with the first rosy glow of a summer dawn but the harbor was already bustling with lobstermen clad in orange waterproof overalls. One of the younger captains pointed Maggie to Pike Stoddard's boat tied up at the end of the dock, its stern stacked with green wire-mesh lobster traps. A balding man sat in the wheelhouse, sipping a mug of coffee.

'Luke Haskell?' Maggie called out.

'Not here,' the man responded, dragging out the word *here* into the two-syllable 'he-ah' distinctive to the speech of downeast Maine.

'You're not Luke?'

'Nope.'

'You know where Luke is?'

'Nope.'

'Doesn't he usually sleep on board?'

'Ayah.'

'But he's not here now?'

The man seemed to give the question some thought before responding. 'Don't see him anywhere.'

This was going to be like pulling teeth.

'You Luke's stern man?'

'Ayuh.'

'You have a name?'

She half-expected him to acknowledge that he did have a name without revealing what the name might be. But he fooled her. 'Name's Waltah,' he said. 'Who're you?'

'Well, Walter, I'm a police officer. Detective Margaret Savage.' She pulled back her jacket far enough to reveal the gold shield clipped to her belt. 'I need to ask Luke a few questions. Do you think he'll be here soon?'

'Hope so. Like to get goin'. Be the second day in a row Luke hasn't shown up.'

'Didn't show yesterday?'

'Nope.'

'Any idea why not?'

'Nope.'

'Mind if I wait with you?'

'Suit yourself.'

Maggie climbed on board. Walter held out a large thermos and a chipped mug. 'Care for any coffee?' he asked.

Hoping the offer of coffee represented some sort of communication breakthrough, Maggie smiled her thanks, took the offering and poured some of the steaming black liquid into the mug. It smelled and tasted better than she expected.

'Luke ever been this late before?' she asked.

'Yestahday.'

'I mean aside from yesterday.'

'Nope. Not usually. Fact is, he usually sleeps right down there in the cabin.'

'But he's not there now?'

'Nope.'

'You looked?'

'Didn't look. But I knocked. Twice. He didn't answer.'

Maggie got up and knocked on the hatch herself. Getting no reply, she slid it open, framing her argument, as she did, for probable cause to enter what constituted Haskell's home. *When there was no answer to my knock, I was concerned, Your Honor, that Haskell might be wounded or ill. Might need medical attention.*

As the hatch slid open, a putrid odor of sweat and dirty laundry smacked her in the face. Holding her breath, though not hopeful she could hold it long enough, Maggie went down the two steps into the small cabin and looked around. No Haskell. She knocked on the narrow door of what had to be the head. No answer. She opened the door. No Luke. The cabin itself was a mess. Dirty laundry piled in one corner. Half a dozen porn magazines scattered on the floor. The bunk looked like it had been slept in, but, since it seemed unlikely

Luke ever made his bed, there was no significance to that. She took out her cell phone and punched in Haskell's number. She heard electronic chirps from inside the pile of laundry. Taking the latex gloves from her pocket and putting them on, she sorted through Luke's dirty laundry and finally found the phone under one of his shirts.

It still had some battery life. Holding it by its edges, she checked recent voicemails. Four in the last few days. Two from her, asking Luke to call her back. One from Pike Stoddard: 'Hey, Luke, some female cop's gonna be stopping by asking you questions 'bout last January. Like I told you, you want to work for me again, maybe even keep your skinny ass out of jail, you don't know nothin'. Deaf and dumb. You got it?' One from Dirty Annie's: 'Hey, Luke, it's Annie. You haven't been by tonight, so I thought I'd call and make sure everything's okay. Let me know.' Maggie slipped the phone back into Luke's shirt pocket, buried the shirt in the pile of laundry and climbed back on deck.

She noticed an empty pint bottle of Jack Daniel's lying in the corner of the deck. Its cap about a foot away from it. She picked it up. For the time being, at least, Luke's disappearance could be considered a missing-person case and not a murder. That'd give the Eastport PD legitimate jurisdiction. She'd drop the bottle off at the station and have Frank Boucher's people check it for prints and DNA.

'Luke ever sleep anywhere else?' she asked Walter.

Walter shook his head thoughtfully. 'Sleeps over at Annie's every now and then when she's in the mood.

But not regular. Nothin' regular since Mary Mayo tossed him out on his ear three years ago.'

Maggie nodded, more to herself than to Walter. 'Thanks for the coffee. Here's a card. Luke turns up, tell him to call me right away. It's important.'

Climbing up the gangway to Water Street, Maggie called Frank Boucher. He was still at the Stoddard house.

'What now?' he asked.

'Luke Haskell.'

'What about him?'

'He's missing.'

'Jesus Christ, Savage.' She heard a giant sigh on the other end of the phone. 'How on earth did I ever fill my days before you walked into my life?'

Chapter Forty-Two

6:28 A.M., Monday, August 24, 2009
Machias, Maine

MAGGIE TOOK THE key from under the geranium and let herself in. She double-locked the front door.

She checked to make sure the downstairs windows and the kitchen door were locked as well. She went upstairs. A note from her father was folded over and scotch-taped to her bedroom door. She pulled it off and read the message written in his familiar scrawl:

> Maggie,
>
> Didn't want to wake you. Anya and I left early for Bangor. Going down for my next round of chemo. We'll probably be there overnight but we'll let you know about that. We'll also check in with

Emily. See if she's ready to come home. If so, we'll bring her.

Mostly, I want to apologize for my behavior last night. I was up most of the night feeling bad about it. The notion that my own son might have been involved in that girl's murder was making me crazy, and I suppose my feelings were also mixed up with the anger that's been stewing inside me ever since your mother died.

Regarding the evidence they found at Harlan's place, we'll talk about that when I get back.

I love you. And someplace deep down inside I hope I still have some love left for Harlan. I just have to find that place.

The note was unsigned. Maggie opened the door, hung her jacket and holster belt on the back of the chair, kicked off her shoes and lay down on her bed. A few seconds later she got up, pulled out her Glock and put it by her side on the bed.

She closed her eyes. Things were coming to a head and she figured she ought to at least try to get a few hours' sleep before Detective Emmett J. Ganzer showed up to confront her about her accusations. But sleep wouldn't come. She couldn't erase the image of the plump little girl peeking out at her from the staircase. She couldn't stop thinking about the phrase *like a hog in a slaughterhouse* and how it must have affected Tabitha. She pulled the drawing from her pocket, unfolded it and studied it. And noticed something she'd totally missed before. Too busy feeling guilty about hogs and slaughterhouses to notice what should have been right in front of her eyes. Could it have been an accident? Coincidence? Maybe. Maybe not. She didn't know. It was just a kid's drawing after all. She refolded the sheet of paper and put it back in her pocket and felt a sadness well up inside of her. As she drifted off to sleep, she found herself wondering when, if ever, things would get better.

AT 8:30 SHE was awakened by a call from the State Crime Lab in Augusta.

'Hey, Maggie, Joe Pines.'

'What do you have for me, Joe?'

'The preliminary reads on those saliva samples you sent me. Terri said put 'em on the fast track, so I did.'

'What's the verdict?'

'Neither one's a match for fetal.'

'You're sure.'

'Positive. Whoever spit in those cups wasn't the father of the kid.'

The results wouldn't necessarily clear Harlan of the charges against him. Or, for that matter, Sam. All they proved was someone else, as yet unknown, had sex with Tiff Stoddard. What Maggie had to do was figure out how to get a sample of Ganzer's DNA. If Riordan really was Ganzer, a DNA match would go a long way toward proving it.

'Joe, do me a favor and keep those results to yourself for a couple of days. Don't even tell Terri.'

'Gee, Maggie, I don't know …'

'Joe, trust me on this. It could make a difference whether we get this guy or not.'

'Okay,' he said reluctantly, 'I guess I can stall. But only for a day or so.'

'Thanks, Joe. Meantime, I've got another question for you.'

'Shoot.'

'How long would a tranquilizer drug remain detectable in the blood of a large dog after it's been injected?'

'You sure know how to come up with them, Savage.'

'How long, Joe? This is for real. And it's important.'

'It'd depend on what drug was used. How big a dose the animal took. But, for most drugs, we should be able to find some sign if the blood was pulled in the first twelve hours after injection. Tox report could take some time, though. They always do.'

Maggie thanked Pines. Told him Frank Boucher, the Eastport police chief, would get the blood sample down to him ASAP.

She lay back down on the bed, wondering if she should try to get any more sleep. The decision was made for her. Through the open bedroom window she heard a car pull up in front of the house. An engine turn off. She went to the window, lifted a slat in the blind and saw Emmett Ganzer parked directly across the street. He was looking up at the house.

She'd meant to provoke a reaction with her accusations but hadn't thought it would come this fast. Or here in this house. In broad daylight. She let the slat drop. Ganzer glanced up, perhaps catching the movement in the window. She speed-dialed McCabe, hoping he hadn't checked out of the B&B yet. Hoping he hadn't left for Portland. His phone rang once. Then twice. Then four times.

Ganzer emerged from the car, looked both ways before crossing the street.

McCabe's message kicked in.

Ganzer walked towards the house.

'McCabe,' she said into the phone, 'if you get this message and you're still in Machias, please get your tail over to the house. I may need some backup.'

She clicked off. The doorbell rang. She strapped her gunbelt around her waist. Picked up the Glock from where she'd left it on the bed, chambered a round and slid it back into the holster. Put on her jacket. Took a small digital recording device from her drawer, put it in record mode and slipped it into her breast pocket.

The doorbell rang again. Maggie started down the stairs. The front door came into view. An antique lace curtain covered the door's beveled glass oval. Through the lace she could see Ganzer's face leaning in, hands on either side of his eyes to block out the light. She knew from a lifetime's experience he'd be able to detect motion through the curtain but not be able to tell who was moving.

The bell rang again. And then again. The knob turned. Ganzer testing the lock. Maggie's right hand pushed the flap of her jacket back and rested on the grip of her weapon. If McCabe came, he came. Otherwise she'd handle this herself. She crossed to the side of the door, ready to take care of business.

Chapter Forty-Three

8:30 A.M., Monday, August 24, 2009
Moose Island, Maine

'YOU GONNA SLEEP all day?'

Harlan figured the question, spoken by what sounded like a young female voice, was directed at him. He opened one eye, then the other, and saw Tabitha Stoddard kneeling over him, peering down from only inches away, examining his face as closely as if he were a strange genus of insect she'd never seen before. Magnified by the thick lenses of her glasses, her brown eyes seemed enormous.

It took a couple of seconds for Harlan to remember where he was and why. They were hiding out in Toby Mahler's grandfather's house. Which was, as Tabitha said, pretty much a dump. A four-room cottage not much bigger than his single-wide in Whiting. Both Harlan and Tabitha had slept on the floor, since neither was willing to lie down on the single thin mattress they found rolled up on the iron cot. The mattress was dotted with urine and blood stains and, here and there, a burn hole or two where Toby Mahler's grandfather's cigarette ash must have fallen when he was smoking in bed. The floor where they'd slept wasn't clean but at least it didn't seem like anybody had peed or bled or died on it. Tabitha slept in the sleeping bag. Harlan on his ground cloth using his pack for a pillow.

'What time is it?' Harlan asked.

Tabitha looked down at the phone in her hand. 'According to my iPhone,' she announced in an official voice, 'it's exactly eight-thirty-seven.'

'In the morning?' he asked sleepily.

'Of course in the morning.'

Suddenly Harlan sat bolt upright, awake and alert. He looked at the phone in her hand. 'How long have you had that thing turned on?'

'Just a minute or two.'

'Turn it off.'

'Soon as I check my emails.'

'No. Turn it off now.' He reached up and pulled the phone from her hand. Found the on-off button and pushed it in. Slid the 'Power-Off' bar on the screen.

'Why did you do that?'

'Because people can track you through your cell phone. Home in on your signal and find out where you are.'

'What people?'

'The police.'

'Don't we want the police to know where we are? Then they can help us.'

'No. There's a very important reason we don't want the police to know where we are.'

Tabitha frowned. She didn't approve of what he was saying. 'What is it?'

Harlan decided he'd better let her know what was going on. She was smart enough not to be fooled by a pile of comforting bullshit and he'd get more cooperation if she felt she was part of the decision-making process. A democracy. Well, sort of a democracy. He got two votes. She only got one. He was the squad leader. She was the troop.

He needed a minute to sort out the best way to explain things to her. He also needed to pee. 'Okay,' he said. 'I'll tell you. Soon as I get back from the bathroom. Do we know if the toilet's working?'

'You've got to pour a bucket of water in it to make it flush. There's a bucket right next to it. No toilet paper, though.'

He went to the small bathroom and stood for a long minute, urinating into the rust-stained bowl, planning how he was going to frame the discussion. He zipped up. Figured he'd wait before fetching a bucket of water from the stream out back.

He came back and eased down next to Tabbie, who was sitting cross-legged on the sleeping bag. He leaned against the frame of a sofa. The cushions were almost, but not quite, as dirty as the mattress. At least there didn't seem to be any blood or piss on them.

'Are you hungry?' he asked, playing for time.

'Kinda.'

'Do you know if there's any food in the house?'

'There's some cans of stuff in the pantry but it's got mouse turds all over it.'

'We could wash 'em off.'

'I'm not eating anything with mouse turds on it even if you do wash 'em off. Why don't you just quit stalling and tell me why we don't want the police to know where we are.'

She stared at him through those big glasses of hers. She looked determined. In her own peculiar way, he decided, this kid was tough.

'Okay. I told you last night I was a friend of Tiff's.'

'You didn't say you were a friend. You said you loved her.'

'Yes. I did love her. I do love her. But what's going on is that Tiff was doing some stuff she shouldn't have been doing.'

'Stuff like what?'

'Selling illegal drugs. Your sister got involved in a business deal with a guy named Conor Riordan.'

'The December Man.'

'Yes. The December Man. Tiff arranged for Conor Riordan to use your father's boat. He took it up to Canada and stole a huge pile of a drug called Oxycontin. You ever hear of that?'

Tabitha told him of course she'd heard of Oxycontin. Everybody had heard of it. There were kids at school, especially some of the older kids, who talked about it all the time. She didn't think any of them took it, though she wasn't real sure, because a lot of them didn't talk to her except to tease her about being semi-fat and funny-looking and not having any boobs yet.

'Anyway,' Harlan said, 'Conor Riordan brought the drugs back here to Eastport and he and Tiff and some other people started selling them. But Tiff didn't think Riordan was giving her her fair share of the money they were making. They argued about that a lot. Sometimes when they argued he would hit her. Hurt her.'

Tabitha didn't say anything. Just thought back to the bruises on Tiff's face in the schoolyard when she gave her the package.

'Naturally getting hit as well as cheated made Tiff even angrier. Conor Riordan used to go away on business sometimes so Tiff got this idea that the next time he left town for a few days she would take what she thought was her fair share of the drugs and leave.'

'Get the hell out of Dodge,' said Tabitha.

'That's right. Get the hell out of Dodge. She wanted me to go with her and I would have too, except I didn't want to get involved in selling illegal drugs. Told her to leave the drugs. Forget about them. But she wouldn't listen. Next time Riordan went away, Tiff took some of the drugs. But Riordan came back sooner than he was supposed to. Maybe he was suspicious. I don't know. Anyway, Tiff had to get rid of the drugs fast. She asked me if I would hide them for her. I told her no. Told her just to throw the damn things away. Dump 'em in the ocean, where they couldn't hurt anyone. But she wouldn't listen. Instead she got this nutty idea to drive up here and give them to you to hide. I told her it was nutty but she thought it was brilliant. Thought Riordan would never dream an eleven-year-old kid would have his drugs. But you do, don't you?'

'I guess so.'

'You guess so?'

'Tiff asked me to hide a package for her the same day she was killed.'

The two of them, man and child, sat side by side for more than a few minutes thinking about what they ought to do next. It was Tabitha who broke the silence. 'Anyway, what's all that got to do with not letting the police know where we are?'

'Conor Riordan is the man who killed Tiff. He also killed your parents, though I haven't figured out exactly why he wanted to do that. I also think he may be a policeman. A state cop. One who tried to kill me before I came up here.'

'A *cop* tried to kill you?'

'Yeah. I beat him up before he had a chance to finish the job. But he's looking for me. And, I think, he's looking for you. That's why you can't use your phone. If we let the police know where we are, we'll be letting Riordan know.'

Tabitha remembered the voice calling to her in the woods last night. *Tabitha, leave me Tiff's package and I'll leave you alone. I promise I won't hurt you. I want Tiff's package. Not you.* The December Man was a cop. Jesus Christ.

'So why did *you* come to our house last night?' asked Tabitha.

'To tell your parents you had the drugs. Convince you and them to give them to me. Then somehow let Riordan know I had them. Get him to come after me to get the drugs back.'

'He'd come alone?'

'Yes. He wouldn't bring other cops because then he couldn't keep the drugs for himself.'

'My whole family's dead over a bunch of stupid pills.' Tabitha was crying again.

'Yes. They're worth a lot of money.'

'And then what?' she asked. 'What were you going to do after Conor Riordan found you?'

'I was going to kill him.'

Tabitha stared at Harlan for a minute and seemed to be thinking about what he said. The morning sun pouring in through the window lit her tear-stained face.

'Good,' she said. 'Let's kill him.'

Chapter Forty-Four

8:53 A.M., Monday, August 24, 2009
Machias, Maine

MAGGIE PRESSED HERSELF against the wall next to the front door. Slid an arm across and opened the deadbolt. Called for Ganzer to come in.

The door swung open. Ganzer walked by her before realizing she was behind him. He stopped. 'Now,' said Maggie, 'if you don't mind, please turn around very slowly.'

Ganzer turned. Saw Maggie holding her Glock in a two-handed stance and aiming it at the middle of his body mass.

'Damn,' he said. 'Every time I see one of you Savages, you're pointing a gun at me.'

'What do you want, Emmett?'

'After your outburst up in Eastport, I thought it was time you and I had a little chat. Your old man anywhere around?'

'Yeah,' Maggie lied, figuring it wouldn't hurt if Ganzer thought she had reinforcements. 'He's upstairs taking a nap.'

'Hey, Savage!' Ganzer called out. 'Sheriff John Savage? You in the house?'

Ganzer cocked his head and put a hand to one ear, in a stage pantomime of listening for a response. 'Nah, didn't think so. Only one car in the driveway. Yours.'

'Fine. I was telling a lie. You caught me. Now what do you want, Emmett?'

There was a sound from the kitchen. The dog door opening and closing. Ganzer instantly alert, slid his hand to his own weapon. Polly Four trotted into the hallway and sat, her rear end resting, as usual, on Maggie's foot. Maggie shifted the Glock to one hand and stroked the dog's ear.

'Hey, Harlan,' Ganzer shouted again, even louder this time. 'How about you? You here?' There was still no answer from upstairs. Ganzer smiled. 'Nope. No killers in residence. Guess, it's just you, me and the pooch.'

'One more time. What do you want?'

'Nothing that needs gun pointing. I just want us to sit down and talk. Like civilized grownups.'

She waved him into the living room with the Glock. Pointed it at the couch, where at this hour of the morning the sun would be shining in his eyes. May as well make what use she could of home field advantage. She took one of the wingchairs. 'Okay, Ganzer,' she said, using his name for the sake of the recording device in her pocket. 'You wanted to talk, so talk.'

'First off, why don't you put the artillery away. I promise not to shoot you if you promise not to shoot me.'

Maggie nodded. 'Fair enough.' She slid the gun back into its holster. 'No guns. No shooting. Now what do you want?'

'First thing I want is for you to stop with these wild-ass accusations.'

'I don't think they're so wild-ass.'

'Oh, for Christ's sake, Savage, you don't have even a sliver of evidence I was in any way involved in any of these murders. Or with the drugs. Or with Tabitha Stoddard's disappearance. No physical evidence. No circumstantial evidence. No witnesses. No motive. No nothing.'

'Were you involved?'

'No, I was not involved and you've got nothing that says I was.'

'If you'll spit in a cup for me maybe we could remedy that situation.'

Ganzer snorted. 'Jesus, Savage, you really think I might be the father of Stoddard's kid? Trust me if I could've been screwing someone who looked like Tiff Stoddard, I would have in a heartbeat. The girl was gorgeous. Course, I'm only judging from her pictures. But I never laid eyes on her until after she was dead, much less had sex with her. You can believe me or not believe me, but that's the truth.'

Maggie got up and went to the kitchen and came back with a small Mason jar with a lid. She handed it to Ganzer. 'So spit.'

'Okay.' He spat in the jar, screwed the lid on tight. 'There ain't nothing there, Savage,' he said handing it back to her. 'So go have fun with it.'

Maggie didn't say anything. Just took the jar. She'd have one of Savage's deputies drive it down to Augusta later in the morning.

'Okay,' said Maggie. 'Let's say you're not involved. Let's say I'm wrong. Tell me what really happened when you went out to Harlan's place yesterday. What you said before – that he just walked out of the house and whacked you with a rifle butt – that wasn't true. was it?'

'No. It wasn't. Like you. I was telling a lie.'

'So what really did happen?'

'Okay. Yesterday, in the detectives' meeting, Carroll told us what you told him. That your brother and Stoddard were getting it on. He asked me to go up to Whiting and bring Harlan in and interview him about Stoddard's murder. So after the meeting I drive up there. When I get out of the car he's standing there in his underwear, pointing a rifle at me. I identify myself as a police officer and ask him to put the gun away. He doesn't argue. Goes inside and comes out without the rifle and with some clothes on. Including that Killers t-shirt. He asks me what I want to talk to him about. I tell him it's about Tiff Stoddard.'

'And what did he say to that?'

'Told me he never heard of anyone named Tiff Stoddard. I don't know about you, Savage, but when a suspect lies to me for no obvious reason I get suspicious. I start thinking maybe he's more than a possible suspect who needs to be checked out. I start thinking maybe he really did kill Stoddard. That maybe he's up to his ears in the drug thing and that he killed Sean's wife and Laura Blakemore as well.

'I tell him I think that maybe he's not telling the truth about not knowing Tiff Stoddard. Especially when the t-shirt he's wearing is exactly like the one she had on when the bad guy cut her up and left her lying in the dirt to bleed out and die.'

'What did he say to that?'

'Nothing right off. Just stands there looking at me for a minute like he didn't hear what I said. Then he gets this weird look on his face. A crazy look, if you want to know the truth. Makes me kind of nervous.'

'You were scared?'

'You're damn right I was scared. Here's this tough ex-marine, maybe not as big as me but pretty damn close, and he's got this expression on his face like he wants to do to me what he did to Stoddard.'

'What you *think* he did to Stoddard.'

'All right, what I think he did. But I'll tell you at that point, even before the evidence turned up, I was already pretty sure he was the one. That he'd already killed three people and maybe more. Not even counting those two kids in Canada.'

'So what did you do?'

'I tell him I want him to come to Machias with me. Talk to me about Tiff Stoddard. He snaps out of his trance and tells me to go fuck myself and starts to walk away. So I did exactly what you would've done in the same situation. I drew my piece, told him to lie flat on the ground. He asks me if I'm going to shoot him and I tell him I am if he doesn't do what I'm telling him to do.'

'So then what happened?'

'Next thing I know he's on me. I'll say one thing, sonofabitch is fast. Kicks the gun out of my hand. Puts me on the ground with a judo move. Kicks me in the face and puts me out. I wake up an hour later, with a broken nose and a badly sprained wrist, and your brother's gone. He destroyed my cell phone and the radio in the car and he's slashed my tires. So I get up and walk a mile and a half to the nearest house and call it in.'

'Why are you telling me all this?'

'I don't know. Maybe because he didn't kill me when he could have and I don't know why. You said that yesterday but I was too pissed off to hear you. But I've been thinking about it ever since and I wanted to get it off my chest.'

'That mean you don't think he's guilty?'

'No. It means I think he may have some mental problems so there's no consistency to what he does. But I'm not even sure about that so I need to talk to him about it.'

'You'll have to find him first.'

'That's right. I'll have to find him first.'

'Ahh, now I see why you're here. Well, sorry to break it to you, Emmett, but I have no idea where he is. It's been nearly twenty-four hours. He could be halfway to hell and gone by now.'

'Possible, but unlikely. We found his truck less than a mile from his house. I think he's on foot.'

'Maybe he borrowed a vehicle or stole one.'

'Maybe, but I don't think so. We interviewed every known contact and nobody admits to lending him a car or even seeing him. And nothing's been reported stolen in the last twenty-four hours. I think he's still in the area. I think he's hiding out somewhere with Tabitha Stoddard. Assuming he hasn't killed her yet.'

Maggie looked hard at Ganzer and waited for the explanation.

'This morning, after you left, our ERT people checked the area. A few hundred yards behind the Stoddard house, among all the boot prints from all the searchers who were tramping around, they found a few that are a perfect match for the boot prints we found heading away from the spot where Harlan hid his truck.'

'A lot of guys wear the same kind of boots. Same brand. Same size.'

'Maybe so. Except for one thing.'

Maggie waited to hear what the one thing was.

'One of our troopers reported seeing a man who fits Harlan's description walking hand in hand with a girl who fits Tabitha's.'

'Why didn't the trooper stop them?'

'Good question. Says he knew we were looking for Harlan but hadn't heard about Tabitha yet. He reported the sighting as soon as he did.'

'Could have been any father and daughter he saw.'

'I don't think so. Not from the descriptions. Big, strong-looking guy carrying a backpack and what looked like a hunting rifle. Chubby little girl with light-brown hair and glasses. I think your brother killed the parents and kidnapped the kid.'

'Why?'

'I don't know why. Maybe he likes doing it with little girls.'

'I won't dignify that with a response.'

'Wouldn't be the first guy who likes it with both big and little.'

'If he kidnapped her, why's she holding his hand?'

'Maybe he threatened to hurt her if she didn't. Anyway, I think they're both still somewhere in the area. Somewhere on Moose Island. We've got dogs looking for him but so far no luck. Dogs aren't perfect. But sooner or later he's going to need some help and I think the person he's most likely to contact is you. His loyal and loving big sister.'

'You're an asshole, Ganzer. Harlan did not kill Tiff Stoddard. Or her parents. Or any of the others.'

'You still think I did?'

'Even if the DNA's not a match, I still think it's possible.'

'Your devotion to your brother's innocence is touching. However, if he contacts you, it's your obligation to report it. If you don't, not only will you never work as a police officer again, we'll also issue a warrant for your arrest on charges of Hindering Apprehension. Up to ten years in the state prison. And, frankly, nothing would make me happier than to slap the cuffs on you myself. Think about it, Savage.'

'Get out of here, Ganzer. Get your fat ass out of my house right now and don't come back.'

'Or what? You'll take out your gun again and shoot me?'

'Nah,' said McCabe walking into the living room from the hallway, 'she's not gonna shoot you, Ganzer. On the other hand, if I ever hear you threaten her again, even a tiny bit, I'm not sure I can say the same about myself.'

Ganzer whirled around in surprise. 'Who the hell are you?'

McCabe decided not to tell Ganzer who he was. Decided to let him wonder about it. 'Name's Bond,' he said after a few seconds. 'James Bond. Now, I suggest you do what the lady asked and get your ass out of her house.'

Ganzer left.

'Bond? James Bond?' Maggie said after he was gone.

McCabe shrugged. 'One of the great movie lines of all time. Always wanted to use it. Never had a chance.'

Maggie shook her head. 'You know, sometimes I think you really are twelve years old. Anyway, thanks for stopping by, Mr Bond. I appreciate it.'

'Now will you please tell me what that was all about?'

'How much did you hear?'

'I came in at the part where he was threatening you with jail time if you didn't rat out your brother. Did I miss much?'

'A lot, but I don't want to talk about it here. You bring any running gear?'

'Matter of fact I did.'

'Good. I've got to get some exercise or I'll explode. I'll tell you all about it while we run.'

Chapter Forty-Five

MAGGIE RUMMAGED IN her room upstairs until she found some old Nikes, a pair of shorts with pockets, a t-shirt and a U Maine Black Bears sweatshirt. She hadn't worn any of this stuff since her senior year in Orono and was pleased that, after fourteen years, everything still fit. McCabe waited while she changed, and then they drove in convoy over to the Inn at Schopee Farm, where he was staying. She waited while he changed.

From the Inn, they walked down to the hiking and biking trail that runs behind the place, along the river. They dutifully did a few stretches and set off at a leisurely pace, heading downriver toward the sea.

'You know, McCabe, I love this place,' Maggie said. 'This county. Poor as it is, I've always felt there was something very special about it. I know that's part of the reason Em came back. She felt it was where she belonged.

I sometimes do too. Did you know Washington County is as far east as you can go and still be in the US?'

'Yeah, I've read that.'

'The sun rises here before it comes up anywhere else in America. My father told me that when I was about five and I thought it was about the coolest thing I'd ever heard. I didn't catch on to the flip side till a whole lot later.'

'The flip side?'

'Yeah, you know,' Maggie smiled. 'In Washington County, we get the darkness first as well.'

'Do you ever think you'd like to come back here to live? Like Emily did.'

'I'm occasionally tempted. My father would love it. He's always asking if he can swear me in as a deputy. Hopes I'll succeed him some day as Sheriff. But I don't think so. I like working in the city. For what it's worth, I also like working with you.'

'I like working with you too.'

Maggie glanced over to him. 'I'm glad but I have a question about that.'

'Shoot.'

'What was that kiss about last night?'

'Don't you know?'

'I want to hear it from you.'

'Okay. It was about something I wish could happen but can't. At least not now.'

'Because of Kyra?'

'Yes. Because of Kyra. But also because of me. I'm not very good at cheating. I lived through too much of that, too many lies, too much deception, when I was married to Sandy. And so did Casey. My daughter hated her mother for what she did back then. And in a lot of ways she still hates her. I love Casey far too much to ever risk her feeling that way about me. So, for the time being at least, as you've noted more than once, I'm taken. If that ever stops being the case, I can promise you'll be the first to know. In the meantime, at least part of me hopes you find somebody else, somebody who's right for you.'

'And the other part?'

McCabe smiled. 'The other part would be jealous as hell.'

They jogged on at an easy clip for a couple of miles, watching the morning sun reflect off the river as it widened before emptying into Machias Bay.

'If you look over there,' said Maggie, breaking the silence, 'above the riverbank, there are some ancient petroglyphs carved into the stone thousands of years ago by the Passamaquoddy. Still perfectly visible. A whole lot more of them down in Machiasport at a place called Picture Rocks. If we had time I'd love taking you down there and showing them to you.'

'If we had time I'd like to see them.'

They ran on in silence for another few minutes. 'Okay,' said McCabe, 'we've gone three miles now and you haven't told me word one about what we're supposed to be talking about. Why Ganzer was at your house. Aside from making idle threats, I mean.'

'I'm not sure the threats really matter. I'm beginning to wonder if Ganzer's really our guy.'

'That's not the song you were singing last night.'

'No, it's not. Last night I was at least halfway convinced Ganzer *was* Conor Riordan.'

'So what changed?'

'Couple of things. Starting with a double murder in Eastport last night. Actually early this morning.'

McCabe didn't say anything.

'Tiff Stoddard's parents. Shot to death. Disguised as a murder-suicide.'

McCabe's eyes narrowed but he still didn't say anything.

'Their youngest daughter Tabitha is missing. She could be dead as well. But Ganzer claims Harlan's got her.'

'Keep going.'

Maggie started with the 2:30 A.M. call from Tabitha and the sudden hang-up. Told him the rest of it as well. Pike and Donelda shot to death in the living room. Electra tranquilized on the kitchen floor. The semi-literate suicide note. Her own search for Tabitha and, finally, her subsequent visit to the *Katie Louise* and the discovery of Luke Haskell's disappearance.

'After I realized it was Tabitha on the phone I sent the locals over as quick as I could but they got there too late. The parents were already dead. Tabitha already gone. Basically an entire family wiped out.'

'You still haven't told me what changed your mind on Ganzer.'

'For one thing, unless Emmett's one hell of an actor, he had no idea Stoddard's dog was dangerous. Or why I wanted to draw its blood. Or have it tested. Then later, when I flat out accused him of killing Tiff and her parents to see if I could provoke a reaction, his denials rang true. I believed him this morning when he said he didn't do it.'

'You have anything a little more tangible?'

'Yeah. Emmett had no objection to spitting in a cup for me.' Maggie stopped and took the drawing from her back pocket and handed it to McCabe. 'And also there's this.'

McCabe unfolded the sheet of newsprint.

'I found it in the Stoddards' attic last night. Didn't make anything of it first. Thought it was just a generic kid's drawing.'

'Tabitha's the artist?'

'Yeah.'

'"Like a hog in a slaughterhouse"? What's the significance?'

'Don't worry about that. Take a look at the guy.'

'Anyone we know?'

'Not the features, no. It's basically a cartoon. But take a look at the black curls she put on his head. The light blue circles she stuck in for eyes. Remind you of anyone?'

McCabe had only seen Sean Carroll once. From the rear. But he remembered the curly hair. 'You think it's Carroll?'

'I don't know. Dark curls. Blue eyes. Could be a coincidence. Or not. His wife was one of the first victims. On the other hand, you always tell me how good my radar is, but if this guy is the killer, I missed it big time. I instinctively liked the guy.'

'Your radar may be right. Carlin told me Carroll had a rock-solid alibi for the night his wife was killed.'

'Yeah. That's what you said last night. But I was a little distracted at the time so maybe you could take me through it again.'

They stopped running and sat along the riverbank, watching muddy water flow past.

'After Liz Carroll was murdered,' said McCabe, 'Ganzer told investigators that Sean's original alibi, the one about being on a stakeout with Ganzer, was bullshit. Carroll wasn't there. The investigators confronted Carroll with what Ganzer had said. Carroll responded by saying that yes, in fact, he had been lying. He said he had hoped Ganzer, who worked directly for him, would back him up. But since Ganzer hadn't, Sean was forced to tell investigators the truth – that he had spent the night in the bed of another woman. Naturally they asked who the woman was. He said he felt honor-bound not to reveal her identity.'

'How noble. Were they ever able to confirm his story?'

'Yes. The woman stepped forward and said yes, Sean had been in her bed.'

'And they believed her.'

'Oh, yeah. They believed her. Absolutely.'

'Why?'

'The woman was Susan Marsh.'

'*Our* Susan Marsh?'

'That's right, our Susan Marsh.'

'Jesus. Really?'

'Jesus. Really. Exactly what I said when Tracy told me the name.'

'Think Marsh'll talk to us?'

McCabe shrugged. 'Only one way to find out.'

He pulled his cell phone from a fanny pack, checked to make sure he had a signal and punched in a number he knew by heart. It wasn't that he called Susan Marsh all that often. It was just that he had this weird memory thing going. Remembered every number he'd ever called. Just about everything else too. Useful in his line of work.

'Attorney General's office,' a voice on the other end announced.

'Susan Marsh, please.'

'May I tell her who's calling?'

'Detective Sergeant Michael McCabe.'

'Thank you. I'll see if she's in.'

A few seconds later a familiar female voice said, 'Hello, McCabe. Long time no talk. What can I do for you?'

'Hoped you could spare me and my partner a little time today.'

'What's it about?'

'Some evidence in a murder case I'd like your opinion on.'

'The woman beaten to death in Portland? What was her name? Mary Farrier?'

'No. Another one.'

'Really? Didn't know you had any other murders down there lately.'

McCabe didn't elaborate. 'All we need's a half hour or so.'

'Today's totally jammed. I'm due in court in ten minutes. But if you like, you can stop by the office at the end of the day, say five o'clock?'

'Five's good. But this one's a little sensitive and I'd rather not run into any of your compadres. Why don't we meet down in Capitol Park? Say, on the Union Street side? We could walk and talk at the same time.'

'What's this about, McCabe?' This time she sounded suspicious.

'I'd rather discuss it in person.'

'Very well. But you're making me very curious.'

'See you at five, Susan.' He hit the off button. 'Okay. Done and done.'

'Think she'll mind me being there?'

'Tough shit if she does. In fact, you should do the talking. This is your case.'

Chapter Forty-Six

11:07 A.M., Monday, August 24, 2009
Machias, Maine

AS THEY MADE their way back to the parking lot, Frank Boucher called.

'Haskell's still missing,' Frank told her. 'The last person to lay eyes on him was a woman named Annie O'Malley. She owns a bar here called Dirty Annie's. Kind of Luke's home away from home.'

'Yeah, that's what Stoddard said. Have you questioned her yet?'

'Briefly. She called us and said she was worried 'cause she hadn't heard from Luke in a couple of days. So I had one of my guys stop in at her place and get the basics. But I thought I'd leave the real questioning to you. I told her you're on assignment with the Eastport PD and that you'd be stopping by.'

'You say anything to the staties?'

'Not yet. So far it's a missing-person case and my official position is we're investigating it internally. Far as they're concerned you're working for me. At least until further evidence shows up.'

Maggie drove back to her house, showered and changed, then picked McCabe up at his B&B. They headed north on Route 1 toward Eastport.

THEY FOUND DIRTY Annie's at the south end of Water Street. The place had no windows. Just a green door and a small sign announcing its presence. McCabe pulled the door open and he and Maggie went inside. Even on a bright summer morning it was as dark as a cave. They stood for a minute to let their eyes adjust. When they could finally see, they descended three steps into the main room. About a dozen tables, all empty at this hour except for salt, pepper, ketchup and chrome napkin holders. A few solitary morning drinkers perched on stools at the long bar. Most seemed to be concentrating on their beer and shots and not doing much talking except for one guy who, unless he was wearing a hidden headset, was having a heated conversation with himself. Muttering something about the stupid fucks not knowing what the fuck they were doing. The drinkers glanced at the newcomers then turned their attention back to their drinks. None of them had any interest in talking to cops.

Annie's bar was thinly stocked. Bud, Miller Light and Shipyard on tap. Everything else came from a bottle. Booze consisted of low-end brands of most of the basics: rye, bourbon, scotch, vodka, gin. That was pretty much it. No way in hell was McCabe going to find any of his favorite single malts in Dirty Annie's. A bone-skinny bartender of indeterminate age stood staring up at a muted TV that was tuned to an ESPN talk show. No closed-caption video. No way of knowing what any of the talkers was talking about. Maybe the guy was a lip reader. He was close to six feet tall and couldn't have weighed more than a hundred and twenty pounds. A two-day growth of gray whiskers poked out from his sallow cheeks. Maggie waited a few seconds then called across the bar to him. 'Excuse me? Annie O'Malley around?'

'Who's asking?' A woman's voice directly behind them. A deep, raspy smoker's voice with a hint of a brogue. Maggie and McCabe turned at the same time and faced Dirty Annie. She was a big woman. As tall as Maggie and twice as wide. Some, but not all, of her bulk was fat. The rest looked to be muscle. She could have easily picked up any two of the drinkers at the bar, one under each arm, and tossed them out on their ears.

'I'm Detective Margaret Savage,' said Maggie. 'And this is my partner, Michael McCabe.' McCabe nodded. 'Are you Ms O'Malley?'

'Just call me Annie. Everybody does. Frank told me you were the Sheriff's daughter.'

'I am.'

'How is the old geezer? Always had a soft spot for him.'

'Fit as a fiddle,' Maggie lied. 'Sends his regards.' Another lie. 'Anywhere we can sit and talk?'

'I assume you want to talk about Luke.'

'Yes, we do. By the way, you can call me Maggie.'

'And you?' she said to McCabe. 'What do I call you?'

'McCabe works.'

'Okay. Why don't you take that table in the corner. I'll get us something to drink. What would you like? Beer? Wine? Something stronger?'

'Coffee would be good,' said Maggie.

'Two coffees,' said McCabe.

'Anything to eat? On the house.'

The two Portland cops thanked her but declined the offer. They went to the corner and sat with their backs to the wall facing the front door. Most of the lighting was dim and artificial except for two slanted shafts of sunlight that entered through a pair of rectangular slits just below ceiling height and lit up a million dust motes.

Annie came back, carrying three beige mugs of coffee and three old-fashioned glass thimbles of cream on a round, brown tray. She sat with her back to the door. 'Where do you want to start?'

Maggie took a sip of the coffee. Freshly made and surprisingly good. 'You called Frank Boucher,' she said. 'Told him you were worried about Luke Haskell. What got you worried?'

'Luke didn't show up for dinner last night.'

'Why's that a cause for worry?' asked McCabe.

Annie smiled. 'Luke's one of my lost boys.'

'Lost boys? Like in Peter Pan?'

'Yeah. Like that. Except I'm no Tinkerbell. You find 'em in every fishing community. Guys with no wives, no families, no place to go except a bar they begin to think of as home. In this town, they come to me. Fact of the matter, Luke's my original lost boy. Been coming here since the day I opened nearly twenty years ago. This place is more of a home to him than the *Katie Louise* or anywhere else he's got. Has dinner here most nights but especially on Sunday. He told me he'd be here for sure last night. Bring me a couple of lobsters to grill if the catch was decent. Two of us'd eat 'em upstairs in my apartment.'

'You and Luke have a relationship?' asked Maggie.

'You mean sex?'

'Yeah.'

'Off again, on again over the years. Mostly off again for the last couple. We get together when one of us feels horny. Or when the loneliness of his life starts getting to Luke and he needs a little comfort beyond the booze. I'm willing to offer it. Works for me too. I've been seriously under-fucked for a long time.'

'So he was supposed to come here Sunday but didn't?'

'Nope. Not for dinner. Not for later either. I'm worried something might have happened to him. Especially since I heard about Pike and Donelda Stoddard.'

'When was the last time you saw him?' asked Maggie.

'Saturday night. I poured him out of here around one A.M. while he could still kind of walk. Pointed him in the direction of home.'

'Home being the *Katie Louise*?'

'That's right.'

'Luke a big drinker?'

'They all are.'

'All the lost boys?'

'Yup.'

'How drunk was he when he left?'

'Drunk. But like I said he could walk.'

'If you'd offered him another drink would he have taken it?'

'Oh, yeah. Luke has a hard time turning down alcohol.'

'Anybody you know hold any grudges against Luke? Anybody who might want to see him dead?' asked McCabe.

'Dead? You think Luke's dead?'

'No idea. But it's one reason people go missing.'

'Jesus. Can't imagine why anybody'd want to kill Luke. Nothing to gain from it. The guy's basically a harmless drunk. Got no money, his brains are half-fried and, far as I know, he never took up with anyone's wife. And I can't think of any other reason anybody'd have anything against him.'

'Anybody else you can think of we should talk to?'

'With Pike Stoddard dead, not really. You can try his stern man. Guy named Walter. Don't know his last name.'

ON THE WAY back to the Blazer Maggie told McCabe about the empty bottle of Jack Daniel's she saw lying on the deck of the *Katie Louise*.

'You're saying he went back to the boat, had a few more drinks and tumbled overboard?'

'I might be, except for one thing,' said Maggie.

'Yeah, I know. He goes missing the same night Pike Stoddard is killed. Coincidence, coincidence.'

'Exactly. And you don't believe in that kind of coincidence any more than I do.'

Chapter Forty-Seven

1:00 P.M., Monday, August 24, 2009
Roque Bluffs, Maine

TWO HOURS LATER, at exactly 1 P.M., two tall figures – one male, one female – stood on the stony beach in Roque Bluffs, looking out at the choppy waters of Englishman Bay. Sam Harkness was dressed as he'd been on Saturday night except his blue-and-white-striped shirt had been exchanged for a plain blue Oxford one. Shirt-tails still hung over his khaki shorts. Maggie wore black jeans, a white polo shirt and a beige cotton blazer that concealed her weapon.

'How's Emily?' Sam asked.

'She's going to be fine. Recover completely. My father will be bringing her home. Probably tomorrow.'

'Good. Have you solved the murder yet? Tiff's murder?'

'No. But I think we're making progress.'

'That's good too. I'd appreciate it if you could let me know when you do catch whoever did it.'

'I'm sure it will be in the papers.'

'I don't read the papers. Anyway, what was so important you had to talk to me right away?'

'I need to see your manuscript. *A Slender Thread*. At a bare minimum the pages dealing with Conor Riordan. You didn't bring them in Sunday morning.'

'No. I was still angry at your insinuations.'

'I hope you've had a change of heart. Or at least a change of mind.'

'I have. About quite a few things actually. The manuscript's ready for you. I've marked the relevant pages with Post-It notes. It's in the studio.'

'Good. Thank you.'

'In return I need a small favor,' said Sam.

'Oh?'

'I'm leaving for New York in a couple of days. I won't be back.'

'What's going on, Sam?'

'Margaret, please give me a minute. I'll get there. I've resigned my professorship and I'll be putting the house on the market. But before I do I'd like to give Emily a chance to buy it privately. I'm willing to offer her a price well below market. I'd like you to tell her that. Em is more likely to consider the offer if it comes from you than from me. There's still too much anger there.'

'Why would you sell her the house for less than it's worth?'

'Oh hell, Maggie, I'd give it to her if I didn't need at least some money out of the deal. She loved this place more than I ever did. Almost as much as Julia. And Julia loved her. She would have wanted Em to have it. You can also tell her, if she's interested, I'll leave her most of the paintings. I'll have no room for them in a Manhattan apartment and there were quite a few she liked.'

Maggie didn't react. Just waited for Sam to continue.

'I'd also like you to have some of them. I'm thinking of the ones of you. I've always thought they were some of Julia's best work. There was a youthful energy to you in those days, an exuberance Julia managed to capture. They're really quite beautiful. If, for some reason, you decide you don't want them you can always sell them. These days Julia's work fetches a pretty decent price and those canvases, good as they are, should get well above average.'

'You could sell them yourself.'

'I could. Julia's galleries both in Portland and New York would be eager to have them. But I think you should be the one to decide if you want nude pictures of yourself hanging in public places. Especially in Portland.'

'Thank you, Sam. I doubt anyone would ever know it was me but I appreciate the kindness. Yes, I'd be happy to have them. And not just to save myself embarrassment. You're right, they are good. At least the one you've got hanging in the studio.'

Sam bent down and picked up a golf-ball-sized stone and threw it into the water. Willie dashed in after it and hunted in vain for the missing object, swimming in circles.

'That's a little mean, isn't it?' asked Maggie.

'I think he enjoys it.'

'What triggered this decision?' Maggie asked.

'I've been thinking a lot about my life lately. Really since the divorce. Who I am. What I've become. But it was the events of the last couple of days – Tiff's murder, Em's injury, your visit Saturday night – that really brought things into focus. I've discovered I don't like what I've become. A drunk. A layabout. A third-rate professor in a second-rate college who spends most of his energy trying to screw students barely above the age of consent. It's not a pretty picture. Not what I wanted to be. If I was a character in one of my own novels, I'd have me jump off a bridge.'

'What will you do in New York? Teach?'

'No. I'm a better writer than teacher. I'm going to try to finish the novel. It's the best work I've done in years. Some of the credit for that belongs to Tiff. To the energy and enthusiasm she brought to the book. As well as a number of good plot twists. Not that she'll know it now but I'd always planned to give her credit when the book came out. Certainly the dedication. Maybe some credit in the acknowledgements. I just hope you catch whoever killed her. I think you know by now it wasn't me.'

'I do. Listen. If you really want to do what you're saying, Sam, you have to do something about your drinking. If Saturday night was any indication, it's totally out of control.'

Sam smiled. 'Thank you, Margaret. It's amazing how much you and Emily sound alike.'

'Em was always right about that. The drinking I mean.'

Sam waited a minute before answering. 'Regarding the booze,' he said, 'we'll see. When I get to New York, I'll try to cut down. If that doesn't work maybe I will go into rehab. An old friend from Harvard is on the board of the Caron Institute in Pennsylvania. He's been asking me for years to let him get me a place there.'

'Not a bad idea.'

'Like I said, we'll see.'

They both watched as a beautifully crafted wooden sloop, its sails filled with a strong breeze, tacked just in time to avoid slamming into the rocks.

'The baby wasn't yours, by the way. I thought you'd want to know that.'

'No. I was sure it wasn't.'

Willie emerged from the water and shook himself vigorously, sending a fine spray flying off his long, silky coat a dozen feet in all directions. Sam picked up another stone and tossed it into the water. But Willie, refusing to be fooled a second time, simply flopped down on the warm stones and rolled over on to his back.

They walked back to the studio and Maggie waited while Sam slipped the thick pile of the manuscript, its pages held together with rubber bands, with Post-It notes sticking out here and there, into an oversized yellow envelope.

She looked up at the painting on the far wall. The one she'd posed for. Sam was right. It was good. He was also right that she wouldn't want it hanging in some gallery in

Portland or Manhattan. In her own apartment perhaps. But not on Madison Avenue.

'Here's a copy of the book as it stands right now.' He handed her *A Slender Thread*. 'About 300 pages so far. You can read it all if you like and tell me what you think. I've marked the pages you should focus on.'

'May I read them here now?' She didn't want to wait.

'I'd rather be alone if you don't mind. But you can read them up on the porch.'

'Thank you.' Maggie took the envelope and kissed him on the cheek. 'Goodbye, Sam. And good luck with everything. I'll look for the book when it comes out.'

'Don't forget to tell Emily what I said about the house.'

'I won't.'

Maggie went outside and climbed the steps to the porch. She sat in a wooden Adirondack chair. There were about a dozen pages marked with Post-It notes. She flipped to the first one. Page twenty-six. The opening lines of chapter two. *Conor Riordan was a handsome man. Far handsomer than anyone capable of such evil had any right to be. Tall. Chiseled features. Dark, curly hair. Shockingly bright blue eyes. They met by accident on that last warm day of October.*

Maggie stuffed the pages back into the yellow envelope and drove back to Machias to find McCabe.

Chapter Forty-Eight

Even at ten miles an hour above the speed limit, the drive from Machias to Augusta takes a good two and a half hours. Unless of course you run into traffic or construction holdups. Then it can stretch to three or more. Maggie and McCabe wanted to leave plenty of time, certain that Susan Marsh, if she showed at all, wouldn't waste time hanging around if they arrived late.

Before they left, Maggie handed him the manuscript of *A Slender Thread*. Told him to read the pages marked with Post-It notes. Then she pulled out. They were heading west on route nine by 1:30.

When he'd finished reading he slipped the pages back into the envelope and tossed it on the back seat.

'Is he really that good-looking?'

'Pretty much.'

'So you're sure the bad guy's Carroll?'

'Not a hundred percent. But I'm getting there.'

'I see only one problem.'

'What?'

'Susan Marsh.'

IN MAINE MURDERS are prosecuted not by a DA but by the state Attorney General's office. Though he'd been in court with Marsh only a couple of times, McCabe thought of her as one of the toughest, smartest, most determined assistant AGs he'd ever worked with, not excluding his good buddy Burt Lund. The simple fact that Susan had stepped forward, at considerable risk to her own career, and vouched for Sean Carroll's whereabouts on the night of his wife's murder made it tough to believe Carroll was guilty. He couldn't have picked a better person to provide an alibi. Rock-solid, like Tracy Carlin had said.

'When we get there,' McCabe said, 'you ought to take the lead in asking her about that night.'

'I'm happy to, but why? You know her better than I do.'

'You're a woman. She's a woman. She may be more willing to confide in you than me about a sexual indiscretion. I may even disappear while the two of you talk.'

'She may not want to talk about it no matter who asks.'

McCabe allowed as how that was possible.

If Marsh *had* lied to protect her lover, Maggie asked herself, why on earth *would* she admit it now? To a cop she barely knew? If she had been lying, and the lies came to light, it would finish a promising career already damaged by her initial admission. Hell, if she lied knowing Carroll was a murderer it could even lead to a long prison sentence. No. For Susan Marsh, admitting she'd lied to protect a killer made absolutely no sense. But it didn't mean she hadn't lied. Maggie knew plenty of women who'd done stranger things in the name of love. Supposing, of course, love played any role in the affair.

They drove in silence for another twenty minutes, both lost in their own thoughts.

'What if she wasn't lying?' asked Maggie.

'You mean, what if Carroll's innocent?'

'No. I mean what if Carroll paid someone else to do the dirty work. Meanwhile, knowing that, as the victim's husband, he'd be a prime suspect, he went out and arranged the perfect alibi.'

'One that casts him in the role of adulterer,' said McCabe.

'Better that than a murderer. And, like you said, the noble Sean told his bosses he was reluctant to reveal his paramour's name to avoid besmirching her sterling reputation. Which in turn forced Marsh to step forward on her own to keep her secret lover from being unjustly accused.'

'Okay. So who'd he hire?'

Maggie shrugged. 'Who knows? But if that's the way it happened, I'll bet you a bottle of your favorite whiskey whoever it was is dead.'

'You think?'

'I do think. So far at least, anyone who could possibly threaten Conor Riordan in any way has ended up dead. The males just dead. The females, at least Stoddard, sexually mutilated and then dead.'

'Except, for Susan Marsh.'

'Yeah. Except for her.'

Chapter Forty-Nine

5:03 P.M., Monday, August 24, 2009
Augusta, Maine

AUGUSTA'S CAPITOL PARK is a formal greensward running from the Maine State House, with its elegant green cupola topped by a gold figure of Minerva, the Greek goddess of wisdom, down to the banks of the Kennebec river. The capitol was designed in 1827 by one of the renowned architects of the day, Charles Bulfinch of Boston, who also designed the US capitol building in Washington, DC. Construction was completed in 1832. Nearly a century later the park was laid out by Frederick Law Olmstead's firm. Despite the separation of time, the two elements complemented each other well.

Susan Marsh was waiting for them, behind the wheel of a shiny black Mercedes E550 sedan. The car was parked at the corner of Union and State Streets when Maggie and McCabe pulled in behind her five minutes early.

McCabe got out first and walked up to greet Marsh. She lowered the driver's-side window.

She was a slender woman in her mid-thirties with a trim, athletic frame. Her long, angular features were not unattractive, but McCabe would never have called Susan pretty. Plain, perhaps even severe, was a more apt description. Even dressed expensively, as she almost always was, Susan Marsh managed to look a little dowdy. McCabe sometimes wondered if the dowdiness was a conscious pose, one that worked for her as a prosecutor or if, as the last in a long line of stern New England aristocrats, dowdy was what Susan Marsh truly was. He suspected the latter but either way he could think of only two things likely to have drawn a Hollywood-handsome type like Sean Carroll into an adulterous affair with someone like Marsh. One was that she was rich. The second was that she made a nearly perfect choice to provide an alibi for murder.

Susan glanced in her rearview mirror. 'Is that Maggie Savage back there?'

'It is. This is really her meeting rather than mine.'

'I see. Well, why don't you ask Maggie to join us and get in? We'll drive while we talk. I don't think walking around the park offers any more privacy than sitting in my office.'

McCabe signaled Maggie. Pointed her to the front passenger seat while he slid in back. Susan Marsh pulled out into traffic. McCabe brushed his hand across the butter-soft leather seats. 'Nice car,' he said.

'I like it,' was all she said.

McCabe knew Susan could easily afford the sixty grand plus the Mercedes must have set her back. Assistant AGs in Maine don't make all that much but Susan had been born into money, married more money, and came away with an additional tidy sum when her divorce settlement was finalized three short years later.

Aside from hitting a minor speed bump by providing an obvious suspect with his alibi in the Liz Carroll murder case, Susan Marsh's career trajectory had been otherwise spectacular. A confirmed workaholic, she graduated Law Review from Harvard, clerked for one of the more influential justices on the Maine Supreme Court and then turned down associate positions with all three of the top corporate firms in Portland as well as a couple in Boston. Instead, she surprised everyone by applying for, and accepting, a job as an assistant AG in the state Attorney General's office. She was generally considered, along with McCabe's close friend Burt Lund, as one of the two top prosecutors in the state.

Augusta is a small town, and it wasn't long before they were turning from one narrow country road on to another. 'I'm guessing you want to talk about the murder in Washington County,' she said to Maggie. 'I heard you were getting yourself involved in that.'

Maggie wondered if she'd heard it from Carroll. 'Yes, that's right.'

'Is it because of your brother? Because he's wanted for the murder?'

'Partly. I'm convinced Harlan's innocent. By the way, it's murders plural,' said Maggie. 'There were two more deaths last night. And two more people are missing. They could also be dead.'

Susan gave her a sharp look. Maine wasn't Detroit and body counts usually didn't pile up so quickly.

'Tiff Stoddard's parents were shot to death.'

'I've been holed up in court all day. I hadn't heard. Who's missing?'

'Stoddard's younger sister. Tabitha Stoddard. Just eleven years old. And the guy who captained Pike Stoddard's boat. Name's Luke Haskell.'

'And you want to talk to me because you think your brother didn't do it?'

'I know he didn't do it.'

'I'm sorry, detective. Regardless of whether he did it or not, I can't help you. I won't be prosecuting your brother's case. And even if I was, I wouldn't talk to you about it anyway.'

'We didn't drive down here to talk about my brother.'

'What then?'

'Are you still romantically involved with Sean Carroll?'

'I don't know where you're getting your information but I'm afraid the answer is: it's none of your business.'

Maggie figured the only way to make any progress from here was to plow straight ahead. If Marsh told Carroll about it that's just the way it was. 'I wanted to talk to you,' Maggie said, 'because I think Sean Carroll may have been responsible for Tiff Stoddard's death. And by extension the others.'

'One of the others being Liz Carroll?'

'Yes.'

'Does that mean you came down here to ask me if I was telling the truth when I corroborated Sean's story that he was with me the night his wife died?'

'Yes.'

'What's your involvement, McCabe?'

'Me? It's nothing personal. I just think we may have a cop investigating a murder he committed himself. If that's the case, I sincerely doubt he intends to arrest the right guy.'

'Do you have any evidence that Sean's the killer? Or is this all based on conjecture and a desire to get your brother off the hook?'

'So far, circumstantial evidence only,' said Maggie. She told Marsh about Harlan's run-in with Ganzer. About the too-perfect evidence planted at Harlan's house. About her growing suspicion that Liz Carroll hadn't shared the details of her investigations with any other cops including her own husband, possibly because she thought the bad guy was a cop.

'So far you seem to be implicating Emmett Ganzer and not Sean Carroll.'

'I initially thought it was Ganzer but then I found two descriptions of Stoddard's killer. Conor Riordan he calls himself. One from Stoddard herself. Another from a witness I believe saw him with Tiff.'

Maggie read Marsh the relevant description of Conor Riordan from *A Slender Thread* and told her about Tiff Stoddard's input on the project. Then she took out Tabitha's drawing and showed that to her.

'That's it? An author's description in something clearly labeled a work of fiction and a child's drawing of a figure with blue eyes and curly hair? You've got a good reputation as an investigator, Maggie, but I'm afraid you'd be laughed out of court. If it ever got to court. Which it wouldn't.' Susan paused and softened the harsh tone of her voice. 'But you do believe the child … what's her name?'

'Tabitha.'

'You believe that Tabitha saw whoever killed her sister?'

'And her parents.'

'But you can't ask her because you don't know where she is or if she's even still alive?'

'That's correct.'

'I take it Sean doesn't know you've contacted me. Doesn't know we're talking.'

'No.'

'And you don't plan on informing him?'

'No. We don't. And we'd rather you didn't either.'

'You're taking kind of a risk there aren't you? For all you know Sean and I might still be lovers. You obviously think I lied to cover for him once. If that were true, what would stop me from doing so again?'

'Nothing,' said McCabe. 'But if we're going to prove Carroll's guilty or, for that matter, not guilty, you happen to be a necessary piece of the puzzle. No way to figure it out without talking to you.'

'Well, I may or may not choose to answer your questions. What did you want to know?'

'The alibi you provided for Sean Carroll for the night his wife was murdered?'

'What about it?'

There wasn't any clever way to ease into the question so Maggie decided to just ask it. Marsh would either answer truthfully or she wouldn't. 'Were you telling the truth?'

Marsh pulled to the side of an empty stretch of road, parked and turned to face Maggie. 'Let me ask you a question before I answer yours,' she said. 'Are you serious when you say you believe Sean was responsible for his wife's death as well as Tiff Stoddard's? And the others? Or are you just trying this on for size?'

'Deadly serious.'

'So you expect me to tell you if I was lying.'

'If you were, yes.'

Marsh smiled. An odd smile. Maggie might have described it as ironic. Or perhaps rueful.

'The fact is, I didn't lie. Sean *was* at my apartment that night. And not for the first time. Our affair had been going on for several months. For obvious reasons we didn't like going out together in public. That night, he came over and I made us dinner. Sweetbreads. I've always adored them and Sean's the only man I've ever known who doesn't cringe at the thought. After dinner we sat in front of the fire and had a couple of brandies. We made love and then we fell asleep. He was still in my bed six hours later when the call came from Emmett Ganzer informing Sean of the fire. Of Liz Carroll's death.'

'How long does it take to get from your house to where Sean lived? The house that burned down.'

'Maybe twenty minutes. Less if you're driving fast.'

'Did you wake up at all during the night? To go to the bathroom or anything?'

'No. I assume you're asking because you want to know if Sean might have gotten up during the night, gone home, killed his wife, then come back, undressed and climbed into bed again.'

'Exactly.'

'I think it's a stretch. I don't think he would have risked me waking up and seeing that he was gone. But I suppose it's possible. I slept right through. Like a log.' Susan smiled again. 'On the other hand, I usually do after good sex and a couple of brandies.'

Maggie studied her. 'Who poured the brandies? The ones you had after dinner.'

'Sean did.'

'How did they taste?'

Marsh didn't answer for a second. Just looked at Maggie thoughtfully. 'Fine,' she said after a pause. 'Courvoisier always tastes fine.'

'Not a little more bitter than usual?'

'Absolutely not.'

'Were you in love with Sean?'

'I don't know. I suppose so. Silly in retrospect.'

'Did he love you back?'

'He said he did.' Marsh paused and studied Maggie the way McCabe had often seen her study a witness before deciding on a line of questioning.

'Our relationship was more than sexual, though I must say Sean's very good at sex. He has a beautiful body.' She narrowed her eyes. 'Any chance you've seen it yourself?'

'No. No chance at all,' said Maggie, wondering if Marsh had intuited something in the way Maggie had asked her questions. 'Nor will there be,' she added for emphasis. 'Did you and Sean ever think about marriage?'

'We discussed it. Liz wouldn't agree to a divorce.'

'Not even if he confessed to adultery?'

'No. He said his punishment for wanting to be with me was having to stay with her.'

'Did you ever sleep with him again? After the fire?'

'No. Not since that night.'

'His choice or yours?'

'Mutual. That wouldn't have been a good idea.'

'Any chance he hired someone to set the fire for him?'

'I don't know. Again, I suppose it's possible. You'd be better off talking to Tom Mayhew about that. He's running the investigation, which is still ongoing. I do believe they've explored that possibility but if they've uncovered any evidence, I'm not aware of it. I can tell you Sean seemed genuinely shocked and upset when he got the call that morning. It wasn't like he was expecting it.'

'What time did the call come in?'

'About five A.M.'

'What did he do then?'

'He got dressed and left. Went to the scene.'

'Did you go with him?'

'No. That wouldn't have been a good idea, either.'

Maggie turned away and stared into the woods along the side of the road. There were still a lot of unanswered questions but she was sure they were questions Susan Marsh would never agree to answer.

Chapter Fifty

8:19 P.M., Monday, August 24, 2009
Moose Island, Maine

DARKNESS WAS COMING earlier as August faded into September. You could really notice it now. Summer was nearly over.

Tabitha was growing more restless and cranky by the hour. She was lying on Harlan's sleeping bag, wanting to talk. Harlan lay next to her on his ground cloth, wanting to sleep. He had always subscribed to the military theory that in a combat zone, and he considered this to be one, it was always a good idea to sleep whenever possible, for as long as possible. After all, you never knew when the shit was going to hit the fan and you were going to have to stay awake for a whole hell of a long time.

'I'm hungry,' Tabitha announced.

Harlan sighed, sat up and rooted around in his pack. He found another of his Nature Valley breakfast bars and tossed it to her. She'd already eaten four. After this he only had one left.

'I'm sick of these things,' she said. 'They're disgusting.'

He didn't answer.

'Isn't there anything else we can eat? Can't we go someplace and get some pizza or something?'

'No.'

'I want to go home,' she said.

'You can't,' he told her.

She unwrapped the bar and started munching.

He handed her his canteen. She drank.

Fresh water wouldn't be a problem as long as they stayed here. A clear stream ran behind the house. You never knew these days but it looked unpolluted. Problem was he wasn't sure how long they'd be safe here. The danger wasn't from tainted drinking water but from searchers trying to locate either or both of them. Better, he figured, to get moving sooner rather than later.

What was bothering him was that he'd have to take Tabitha with him. His initial plan had been to get Riordan to come after him alone. One on one. *Mano a mano.* But if Riordan knew the child had seen his face, she wouldn't be safe anywhere. Not until Riordan was dead. It was a chance Harlan couldn't take. Not for himself. Not for Tabitha. If only to honor the feelings he'd once had for her sister, he wasn't going to let this child die.

She watched him watching her. 'Aren't you going to eat anything?'

'The breakfast bars are for you. I can handle the fruit with mouse turds. I'll open one of the cans later.'

'I'm bored,' she said. There were no games in the house. The TV didn't work because the electricity was turned off. There weren't even any books she could look at. Just some yellowed year-old newspapers piled in one corner of the living room and no light to read them by.

He studied her for a minute sitting on the floor munching the breakfast bar. He wondered if she trusted him enough to answer the question. He didn't know. But he couldn't think of any good reason why later would be a better time to ask it than now. 'Tabitha. Where is the package Tiff gave you?'

She finished the last bite and licked her fingers for the crumbs before answering. 'I can't tell you. I promised Tiff I wouldn't tell anyone. No matter what.'

'Tiff is dead.'

'I know Tiff is dead. Still I promised I wouldn't tell.' The little girl picked up the stuffed bear with half its head shot off and hugged it to her body. 'And a promise is a promise.'

'Tabitha, I need you to listen to me carefully. I know a promise is a promise and Tiff would be proud of you for keeping your promise. But I promised Tiff something too. I promised her that, if anything happened to her, I'd do my best to keep you safe.' Okay, Harlan told himself, maybe that was stretching the truth. But Tiff would have wanted him to make a promise like that. At least she would have if she'd thought of it. 'You want us to get the December Man before he gets us, right?'

Tabbie nodded, looking down at the bear in her lap rather than at Harlan's face. 'Yes.'

'The only way I can do that is make the December Man think that I've got Tiff's package. That I've got what she put inside the package.'

'Drugs?'

'That's right, drugs. Drugs that can hurt people. Make them sick. Even kill them. You wouldn't want that, would you?'

'No.'

'All right, then. Where is the package?'

Tabitha sighed deeply. 'Here.'

'Where?'

'Harold has it.'

She passed the bear to Harlan. 'The package is inside.'

Harlan squeezed Harold. Felt an oddly shaped hard object inside. Turned the bear over. Saw the stitches Tabbie had sewn along the back seam. He got up and took Harold into the kitchen. Tabitha followed. He cleared off some space on the counter, lay the bear down and then rooted around till he found a paring knife in Toby Mahler's grandfather's kitchen drawer.

'What are you doing?'

'Okay if we cut him open?'

She looked down at the bear with half its head shot off. 'I guess so. He's ruined anyway.'

'He's your bear,' Harlan said. 'Do you want to do the honors?'

Tabitha nodded.

He gave her the knife. She took a deep breath, slid the tip of the blade under the first stitch and cut. When all the stitches had been pulled out, Tabbie opened the bear and pulled out the package.

She looked up at Harlan. He nodded. 'Go ahead, open it.'

Tabitha felt there ought to be more ceremony to the opening of the package. Maybe they should say a prayer or something. This was the last thing Tiff gave her before she was killed. But Tabbie couldn't think of anything to say. She tore open the wrapping paper.

Inside she found an opaque plastic water bottle, a big one, and also three stacks of money, each held together with a purple rubber band. The bill on top of each stack bore the likeness of President Ulysses S. Grant. Tabitha had never seen a fifty-dollar bill before and she stared at Grant's picture for a minute before putting the money aside. She held up the bottle to the moonlight coming through the kitchen window but couldn't see anything. She shook it. Heard some rattling and then unscrewed the top. The bottle was filled with small greenish oval tablets. Thousands of them. She picked one out. Saw the number 80 stamped on one side. The letters CDN stamped on the other. She handed it to Harlan.

'Oxycontin?' she asked.

'Yes,' he said. 'Canadian, I think.'

Harlan dropped the pill back in the bottle and screwed on the lid.

He picked up one of the stacks of bills. Slipped off the rubber band and started counting. The bills were all fifties. He counted 125 of them: 6,250 dollars. He counted the other two stacks. All the same. A total of 18,750 dollars. That settled one issue. If they were on the run for any length of time they wouldn't have to worry about money.

'Is it real?' Tabitha asked. She'd never seen so much money in her life.

'It's real. And I guess, because you're Tiff's sister, whatever's left after this is over is yours.'

'Mine?'

'Yeah. Except for one thing,' Harlan muttered under his breath. 'The December Man's gonna want it back.'

'He can have it,' Tabbie muttered back. 'The pills too. I don't want any of it.'

'He can't have it back,' said Harlan.

'Why not?'

'Because I say so.'

They went back into the living room. Harlan put the money and the pills into his backpack and went down on to the ground cloth. 'Now try to get some sleep while you can. We may have to leave here tomorrow.'

Chapter Fifty-One

11:07 P.M., Monday, August 24, 2009
Ellsworth, Maine

SEAN CARROLL'S APARTMENT in Ellsworth was on Hobart Avenue, a pleasant residential street in a pleasant residential neighborhood. McCabe circled the block three times without stopping. At eleven o'clock on Monday night the streets were largely empty. After the third circuit, he pulled Emily Kaplan's dark-blue Honda Civic against the curb directly across the street in a spot that would give them the best view of both the front and the parking area at the side of the house. Both Maggie and McCabe agreed the Civic would be less obvious to Carroll than either her Blazer or McCabe's T-Bird.

Carroll's building, number twenty-six, was a three-story colonial with a wide wraparound porch. It had once been a gracious single family home, but at least a couple of decades had passed since the place had been divided into rental apartments.

'Okay, we're here,' said McCabe. 'Up till now you haven't been real talkative. What's your plan?'

'I'm going in,' Maggie told him.

'Even if he's not there?'

''Specially if he's not there.'

'In other words, breaking and entering.'

'In other words.'

'And possible petty larceny.'

'That too.'

'Maybe I should arrest you now before he does.'

'Listen, McCabe, we agreed. We need this guy's DNA and I don't think he's gonna let either of us swab his cheek. And hey, if we really get lucky, maybe I'll even find what's left of the drugs. I'm going in.'

'Without a search warrant none of it, DNA or drugs, will be admissible in court.'

'No, it won't. But no judge is ever going to give us a warrant based on a kid's drawing and some novelist's made-up tale of murder and mayhem. No jury's ever going to convict on that. But even if it's not admissible, if Sean's DNA is a match for fetal, at least we'll have some hard evidence that we're barking up the right tree.'

McCabe stared at her across the darkened car. 'I'd feel better if you let me do this,' he said.

'Please, McCabe, don't go all macho on me,' she told him. 'Carroll doesn't know you. If he happens to be home and you come knocking on his door it will make him suspicious as hell.'

'And you knocking won't?'

'Not so much. I can tell him I'm here to apologize for my bad behavior. For telling him to go fuck himself. I can act all contrite. Maybe even flirt a little.' Maggie's voice took on a lighter, teasing tone. 'Wiggle what Emmett Ganzer called my cute little ass. Based on the time I spent with him Saturday night, I'm pretty sure Sean kind of likes my cute little ass. Gorgeous hunk that you are, I guarantee you Carroll'd find me a whole lot sexier than he'd ever find you.'

McCabe sighed. He clearly wasn't happy about what he was hearing. But there wasn't a whole lot he could do about it. 'Okay. Go on in. Do your thing. But if he is there, please, don't get sucked into anything intimate.'

Maggie smiled. 'I won't. But thanks for caring.' She leaned across and gave him a quick kiss on the cheek.

'Remember, if we're right about Carroll,' said McCabe, 'he's a vicious killer. And trust me, I'd hate to have to break in a new partner.'

'Don't worry. You'll be listening to every word.' Maggie punched McCabe's number into her cell. Once the connection was made, he put his phone on speaker and set it down on the center console. She put hers in her inside breast pocket.

'Your job is to keep your eyes peeled and let me know if Carroll shows up. If he's already in the apartment, listen to our conversation, and if things get ugly, come running. I'll leave downstairs unlocked.'

McCabe nodded in reluctant agreement.

Maggie smiled. 'I'll be fine. Really. I will.'

She turned and grabbed a canvas LL Bean tote bag from the back seat and got out, looked in both directions and crossed the street. Before going up on to the porch, she walked around to the paved parking area at the right of the building. There were six dedicated parking spaces, each with a number painted in white in front of it. At eleven o'clock on a Monday night five of the six were occupied. Only space '4' remained empty. Only Sean Carroll's personal car, according to the Sheriff's Department, a silver 2008 Audi Quattro, was missing. Maybe this would turn out to be easier than she thought.

She went back to the front of the building, climbed the five steps up to the porch. In front of her was a pair of oak-paneled doors with beveled glass ovals, not unlike the one on her father's house. Maggie pushed through into a small entryway. To her left six silver mailboxes were set into the wall. Two rows of three. A white paper strip with the name *S. Carroll* was inserted into the slot for apartment four. She peered through some vertical slits in Carroll's mailbox. It appeared stuffed with circulars and white envelopes. At least a couple of days' worth of mail. She pressed the brass handle on a pair of identical inner doors and to her surprise found them unlocked. She went in and climbed a broad flight of stairs that curved around to the second floor.

There were two apartments. She checked the nameplates. Number three, to her left, was home to someone named Alice Spaulding. Sean Carroll lived in number four, to her right. Before knocking she decided to check out possible escape routes. Dumb not to. Just in case. There was a large double-hung window at the end of the corridor. She pulled up the lower sash. The window slid open. She peered out and looked left, right and then down. No fire escape. No ledge to stand on. No tree limbs within reach. No way at all to the ground except jumping and possibly breaking a leg. Or worse. She closed the window and climbed up the stairs that curved around to the third floor. On the sixth step Carroll's door disappeared from view. At the top of the stairs were two more apartments and one window identical to the one below. The stairs going up offered a reasonable hiding place if Sean returned unexpectedly.

She went back to Carroll's door and knocked. No answer. She waited for a minute then knocked again. Still no answer. It was possible, she supposed, Carroll was inside and not answering because he was otherwise engaged. Taking a shower or a bath. On the phone with a friend. In bed with a woman. There was no way of knowing but that was a chance she'd have to take. She leaned down and checked the lock assembly. More complicated than the one downstairs but definitely pickable. She inspected the door carefully for any telltales Carroll might have left behind. A tiny piece of paper or tape or even a single hair precisely inserted in a particular place in the doorframe. She saw none. She took her brand-new Pro-Lok PKX-20 pick set, purchased just today in Augusta, from the tote, knelt down and gently pushed the tension wrench into the lock opening.

She selected a pick and was about to insert it when she heard the sound of a deadbolt turning. Not from

Carroll's apartment but from behind her. Apartment three. She leaped to her feet and, using her body to block a neighbor's view of the wrench, she raised her arm as if about to knock again. She took a deep breath. The door to apartment three swung open.

She turned and saw an attractive blonde, Alice Spaulding she supposed, emerge holding a set of keys in her right hand and the loop of a leash in her left. A small white ball of fluff pulled at the other end of the leash.

'Oh,' said Alice, sounding surprised. 'You're someone else.'

'Yes, I am,' Maggie agreed.

'I thought I heard knocking,' Alice Spaulding said. 'Looking for Sean?' She double-locked her own door.

Maggie didn't answer immediately. Just looked down and smiled.

'Hi there,' she said. 'Aren't you a cutie?'

The ball of fluff growled.

'I'm afraid he's not very friendly. Are you looking for Sean?' the woman asked again.

'Sorry. Yes. I was passing by and hoped I could catch him.'

'He's not here,' the woman said, pocketing her keys. 'He's out of town.'

'Oh, really? Did he say where he was going?' Maggie asked, hoping to get a sense from the woman's answer how well she knew Carroll, how likely she was to tell him about the tall, slim brunette she saw knocking on his door at eleven o'clock on a Tuesday evening.

'Are you a friend of his?' the blonde asked appraising Maggie coolly.

'Actually I'm a colleague,' Maggie said, deciding lying was pointless. If the blonde told Carroll about his visitor, if she described her appearance, Carroll would know instantly who had come calling. 'Detective Margaret Savage,' she said and held out her hand.

The woman shook it but didn't introduce herself. 'I would have thought,' she said, 'if you worked with Sean you would have known that he was in Machias working a case. Said he'd be gone for several days.' There was a pause. 'It was in all the papers.' The blonde didn't seem eager to leave before Maggie did. 'Anyway, I'll tell him you stopped by. Savage, right? Margaret Savage?'

The ball of fluff barked and tugged even harder at the leash.

'Oh, don't bother,' Maggie said. 'Nothing important. I'll catch him another time.'

'Sorry,' Alice smiled. 'Gotta go.' The dog pulled its mistress toward the stairs. Keeping the tension wrench hidden behind her back, Maggie pulled it out of the lock, slid it into the tote and followed. She and the blonde and the ball of fluff walked out of the front door together. On the sidewalk the dog immediately lifted its leg against the nearest tree. Maggie waited till it had finished and then called out, 'Well, good night then.'

'Good night.' Alice and the dog walked off down the street. Maggie took her cell from her breast pocket and pretended to be making a call.

'Hi, how are you?' she warbled, waiting for Spaulding and the dog to move beyond hearing distance. When they had she lowered her voice. 'A neighbor,' she told McCabe. 'Almost caught me in the act.'

Maggie waited with the phone to her ear until Spaulding turned the corner and walked out of sight. Then she told McCabe she was going back in. She heard him mutter something inaudible. 'Don't argue,' she added.

IT ONLY TOOK a couple of minutes to gain entrance to Carroll's apartment. 'I'm inside,' she said softly.

She relocked the door. Took a mini Maglite from the tote bag and did a quick reconnoiter. The place was indeed empty. A good-size one-bedroom. The furniture and paintings on the wall were what Maggie would have described as late twentieth-century Marriot. Solid but devoid of personality. The place appeared clean and tidy. No books. No mail on the desk in the corner. No photos of either Carroll or his dead wife or, for that matter, anyone else. You could tell almost nothing about the inhabitant of this space except, she supposed, that he was tidy to a degree Maggie felt excessive. She supposed it was possible that, following the fire, Carroll had been left without furniture or anything else and solved the problem by renting a pre-furnished flat. Or maybe he was someone who craved anonymity in everything but his public persona. Maybe this wasn't Sean Carroll's apartment but Conor Riordan's. How had Harlan put it? *The man nobody knows.*

She slipped on a pair of latex gloves and lifted a cordless phone from the desk. She dialed the number for FairPoint Voice Messaging. One new message received at 8:35 this evening from 207-555-9755. The caller said nothing. Simply hung up. Maggie wrote the number on the back of one of her business cards and headed for the bathroom. She wanted to give Joe Pines as many options as possible and the bathroom was always a good place to start.

A single toothbrush stood in a glass at the side of the basin. A tempting target. But way too obvious. Carroll would notice his toothbrush missing immediately. The toilet looked clean. No hairs or other visible stains. A metal wastebasket stood in the corner. She stepped on the pedal and shone the light into the one-third-full plastic bag Carroll used as a liner. She knelt down and started sifting through the trash with a gloved hand. A used condom would have been perfect but she found none. She did, however, find a couple of long strands of dental floss. Not quite as good as a cheek swab but they might do. She slipped the strands into a small ziplock bag and tossed them into the tote. She sifted further and found a throwaway razor. One of the yellow Bic ones she sometimes used herself. Ought to have plenty of hairs and most likely some flakes of skin from which DNA could be drawn if Carroll used it to shave. On the other hand it was useless if some girlfriend had used it on her legs. She rummaged further and hit the jackpot. A band-aid with an uneven circle of blood on the pad. While red blood cells don't carry DNA, white ones do.

As good as it gets, assuming it was Carroll who had cut his finger and not a cleaning lady or Alice from across the hall. Two more ziplock bags made their way into the tote.

'Get out of there,' McCabe's voice startled her. 'A silver Audi's turning into the parking area.'

'You sure it's Carroll?'

'I'm sure. Right car. Right plates. Get out now.'

Maggie looked around to make sure she'd left nothing out of place. That nothing had been moved since she'd entered the apartment. It hadn't. She headed toward the door.

'He's out of the car. Get moving.'

Maggie closed the door behind her. If she didn't relock it he'd know she'd been inside. She inserted the tension wrench and a single pick into the lock. Wiggled it around. Shit. This wasn't going to be a thirty-second job.

'He's on the porch.'

She started rehearsing her lines. What she was going to say if she ran into him. If he was willing to listen. She'd give him a big smile. Maybe even bat her eyelashes a little. *Sean, I'm so glad you're here. I really wanted to see you.* *Apologize for the awful things I said the other day. Can you ever forgive me?* She just hoped it wouldn't all sound like bullshit.

She flipped the first tumbler off the shear line.

'He's going inside. Are you out yet?'

'No.' Tumbler number two joined its mate. Three to go.

'Good.'

'What?'

'The woman with the white dog's right behind him. They've stopped. They're talking to each other.'

'Good,' Maggie agreed. The third tumbler slid off.

'He looks suspicious. I think she told him about you.'

'Has he spotted you?' Maggie asked.

'No.'

'They're inside and heading up the stairs. He's first. She's right behind.'

No time for the other two. Three tumblers would have to do. She tried the door. Locked. Maggie raced toward the stairs to the third floor. Reached the sixth step a microsecond before Sean Carroll stepped out on to the second-floor landing, followed by Alice Spaulding and the ball of fluff. Maggie pressed herself against the wall. Put her phone on mute. Caressed her Glock. Hoped she wouldn't have to use it.

'And she didn't say what she wanted?' Carroll asked Alice.

Maggie held her breath and waited.

'No. Just that she wanted to talk to you. When I told her you weren't here, she left. Same time I did. We went out together.'

'Did you see her drive away?'

'No. She was making a phone call. Still on the phone when Mongo and I turned the corner.'

Jesus. The ball of fluff was *Mongo*?

'Shit,' Carroll muttered, sounding irritated.

'I'm sorry. Did I do something wrong?'

'No. No. I'm sorry. You were fine. Thanks for letting me know. Maggie and I do work together. I just forgot something I really had to get done.'

'Would you like to come in for a drink?' asked the blonde. Her voice, Maggie thought, sounded hopeful.

'No thanks, Ali. I'd love to but not tonight. I'm kind of wiped.'

'Okay.' Hopeful turned disappointed. 'Some other time, then. Good night.'

'Good night.'

Maggie listened as two keys slid into two doors. One door closed. Then the second. She texted McCabe: *I'm ok. Waiting 5 before I leave. Watch his windows. Rt hand side.*

Thirty seconds later, he texted back. *Lights on.*

Maggie waited the five minutes and then slipped silently past Sean Carroll's door, down the stairs and out the door. Hoping Carroll wasn't looking out the window, she crossed the street and climbed into the Honda. McCabe pulled away from the curb.

'Cruise around town for a while,' she said.

'Why?'

'I'm just wondering what brought Carroll home tonight.'

McCabe began a random series of lefts and rights. With his peripheral vision he could see Maggie's right hand nervously caressing the grip of her Glock.

'You okay?'

'Yeah, why?'

''Cause you haven't taken your hand off your gun since you got in the car.'

'Sorry. A little wired I guess.'

For the next ten minutes they turned from one dark and empty street into another. No cars. No lights. No people. Finally, Maggie withdrew a business card from her pocket. 'I have a test for your photographic memory,' she said. '555-9755.'

'Susan Marsh's cell phone number,' said McCabe without a moment's hesitation.

'Did you get it from her today?'

'No. She gave it to me a couple of years ago when she was prosecuting a case I was working on.'

'Careless,' Maggie said, more to herself than to McCabe.

'What?'

'To call from her own phone.' She looked at her watch. 'All right, let's go back to Carroll's place.'

McCabe didn't ask why. Just followed instructions. They turned on to Hobart Avenue about three minutes later. Maggie told him to park the car where they had a good view of number twenty-six.

'What now?' he asked.

'Now, we wait.'

'What are we waiting for?'

'You'll see. I think.'

Forty-five minutes later she shook McCabe awake from his nap. A shiny black Mercedes E550 had pulled up across from Carroll's building.

Maggie scrunched down low in her seat. Susan Marsh looked both ways then crossed the street and climbed the steps to the house.

'Interesting,' said McCabe. 'Ready to go now?'

'No. I want to see how long she plans on staying.'

An hour later the lights went off in Carroll's bedroom and Maggie figured she had her answer. The E550 was still parked across the street.

ON THE WAY out of Ellsworth, McCabe said, 'Okay, I guess we have to assume he knows you think he's the killer,' said McCabe.

'Yeah, he knows.'

'He also knows you were at the apartment.'

'He knows that too.'

'And he knows where you live.'

'What's your point?'

'I don't think you should go home tonight.'

She looked over at McCabe. 'No. I guess I don't either.'

They drove past a large white colonial Maggie had never seen before. 'Wait a minute. Stop.'

He stopped. 'What?'

'Back up,' she said.

He did.

She pointed to a small, elegant oval sign hanging in front of the house: *Connors & Riordan. Funeral Directors.*

Out of Ellsworth they headed north on route 1. About halfway home, McCabe pulled into a no-name motel on the other side of Gouldsboro. McCabe went to the office and then came back to the car.

'Only one vacancy.'

'One's fine. I'll sleep on the couch.'

Maggie stayed in the car while McCabe went back to the office and checked in. He paid cash for the room and parked Emily's Honda around back, where nobody could see it from the road. The room was crummy but clean enough. They argued briefly over who should sleep on the couch. Maggie won. Or maybe lost. It all depended, she supposed, on your point of view.

Chapter Fifty-Two

2:41 A.M., Tuesday, August 25, 2009
Gouldsboro, Maine

THAT NIGHT, ON the couch, Maggie dreamed she was back in Machiasport the night of Tiff Stoddard's murder. In her dream she was walking on a long, empty road, the one that led from Emily's office to the state park. The sky was starless and moonless and, like the road and the trees on either side, as black as pitch. The air even heavier and steamier than it had been in the interview room the day she wrested the confession from Kyle Carnes. As she walked, Maggie felt herself fighting for every breath, gagging with the stench of death and putrification, of sweat and blood and rotting flesh.

She passed the place on the road where Emily was hit. In Maggie's dream, Em was still there, her long, strong athlete's body broken and twisted, one leg turned back and pointing toward her head at an impossible angle. Maggie knelt and took her friend's hand in hers. It felt as cold as death. Em looked up with cold, dead eyes.

Then Em was gone and Maggie was climbing a steep flight of stairs. At the top a boy. Danny Labouisse. Still twelve years old. Still smiling his mean little smile that seemed to say how pleased he was with himself for what he had done to her friend.

Maggie drew closer to the twelve-year-old Danny, who silently beckoned her with one hand. As she climbed toward him she slid her Glock from its holster and chambered a round, determined to finish Labouisse once and for all. She reached the last step and she held the gun outstretched. She aimed at his face. Only it wasn't the face of Danny Labouisse any more.

'Hello, Magpie.'

Harlan stood beside a pool table, smiling his Harlan smile at her. His Killers t-shirt spattered in blood. His right hand holding a slim-bladed knife with a red handle.

On the table the slender naked body of a woman lay spreadeagled across the green felt. Maggie could see cuts on the woman's face and her breasts and between her legs, blood pouring from a gaping wound across her neck. But the woman wasn't Tiff Stoddard. Maggie was looking down at herself, dead and bleeding on to the table but still somehow alive. She looked up, her blood-blinded eyes searching for Harlan. Instead, they found Sean Carroll coming for her, holding the same knife Harlan had held and wanting to kill her yet again. The dead but not dead Maggie sat up, raised her gun and fired. The bullet hit Carroll in the chest but he just smiled and kept coming. She fired again. Again the bullet had no effect. When he reached the table Carroll raised the knife and thrust it down toward her open legs.

Maggie woke, suppressing a scream. Her breath came hard. Her heart beat faster than she had ever remembered it. Her skin felt cold yet damp with sweat. She wrapped her arms around herself. It didn't help. She shivered uncontrollably.

Through the darkness she could hear McCabe breathing from the bed. The sound was steady. Rhythmic. Comforting. Right now, in this room, in this place of death, there was nothing she needed more than comforting. She walked across to where he lay in the double bed. Lifted the sheet and blanket and slid in beside him. McCabe faced away from her, on his side, naked except for a pair of boxers. She rested one hand on the warmth of his back. Then she slipped the other arm around him, part of her hoping that the feel of her body against his wouldn't wake him. Part of her hoping that it would.

McCabe stirred. Then turned. He wrapped his arms around her and pulled her close. He began stroking her hair and then her back and then kissing her gently. He kissed her eyes. Her neck. He felt the wetness on her face as she began to kiss him back.

'Are you okay?' he whispered.

'Yes.' Her lips found his and then began exploring the familiar contours of his face. Not the drop-dead handsomeness of Sean Carroll's face. Something better.

Much better. Because it was real. Suddenly they were kissing hard.

McCabe slid his hand under her t-shirt, began massaging the bare skin of her back. Then his hand came around and began stroking her small breasts.

Before going any further, he pulled away and studied her in the soft light of a crescent moon that spilled like quicksilver through the thin slats of the blinds. 'Are you sure you want to do this?' he asked.

She smiled at the worry she could see etched on his face, knowing this time he worried not for himself but for her.

'Yes,' she whispered, leaning across to kiss him again. 'I'm sure.'

Even if it's only this once, she thought, I'm very sure.

When they were both naked, Maggie turned on to her back and took McCabe inside her. And as they made love, each of them took joy in discovering the only things about each other that they hadn't known before.

Chapter Fifty-Three

2:41 A.M., Tuesday, August 25, 2009
Moose Island, Maine

EIGHTY MILES AWAY, in Toby Mahler's grandfather's house, Conor Riordan's words from the night before played over and over again in Harlan's mind.

Tabitha, Riordan had called out, *leave me Tiff's package and I'll leave you alone. I promise I won't hurt you. I want Tiff's package. Not you.*

I want Tiff's package. Not you.

Lying bastard. He wanted both.

The question Harlan wrestled with now was: how did Riordan know there was a package? How did he know Tabitha had it?

His first thought had been that Riordan had tortured the information out of Tiff before he killed her. But the more he thought about that the less he believed it. Every competent military interrogator he ever talked to in Iraq, and he'd talked to more than a few, always told him the same thing. Torture doesn't work. All it gets you is lies. Inflict enough pain and you can get almost anyone to tell you something. But not the truth. At least not when the truth meant something important to the detainee. Especially not when the detainee was someone as tough and stubborn as Tiff. No. The more he thought about it the surer he was. Tiff would have lied and lied and lied. Lied until hell froze over before she'd give up her little sister. Lied until the bastard Riordan killed her. Lied until she was dead and, finally and safely, beyond his torture.

But if Tiff didn't tell Riordan about the package, who did?

Harlan lay in the dark and pondered the possibilities. He wished he had a cigarette to suck on. One of those little old shorty Camels his father had smoked forever. Harlan remembered sneaking them from the old man, sometimes whole packs at a time, from a carton he kept in his underwear drawer. Harlan liked the smokes. Seemed like they always helped him think. And right now his thinking needed all the help it could get.

Okay, he told himself, only three people knew Tabitha had the package. Tiff. Tabitha. And Harlan himself. He knew he'd never said a word to anybody.

If Tiff hadn't either, that left only Tabbie.

Could the child have been foolish enough to have blurted it out to someone, anyone, who might have passed it on? She'd promised Tiff she wouldn't and, as she had told him over and over, a promise is a promise.

Harlan lifted himself off the ground cloth, leaned over on his elbow and moved his face close to Tabitha's. Her eyes were closed. Her breathing slow and regular. She looked so young and innocent it was almost heartbreaking. He was happy that she'd finally stopped talking and had fallen asleep. But he needed an answer and he needed it now. He shook her awake.

'What is it?' Her voice sounded tired and cranky. She opened her eyes. 'What do you want?'

'Sit up. I need to ask you something.'

'Now?'

'Yes, now.'

Tabitha sat up and rubbed her face. Found her glasses. Put them on. 'What time is it?'

'Three o'clock.'

'In the morning?'

'Yes.'

'What is it?'

'Are you sure you never said anything to anyone about the package Tiff gave you. Except me?'

'Yes. I already told you. I promised Tiff I wouldn't and I didn't. Except to you.'

'How about your mother or your father? Did you say anything to either of them?'

'No. They would've freaked out. Made me give them the package. I didn't tell anyone.'

'All right Tabitha, look at me. I need you to think hard. This is very, very important. Do you remember ever saying anything out loud about the package even when nobody else was around. Even when you didn't think anyone could hear you? Anything at all. Don't answer right away. Think hard.'

Tabitha thought hard. Suddenly she shut her eyes and squeezed her face tightly together like she was in pain. 'Oh shit.'

'Oh shit what?'

She looked up at him. 'I did say something out loud. But only once. And nobody could've heard me.'

'When?'

'I called Tiff's cell phone.'

'Before she was dead?'

'No. After.'

Harlan frowned. 'Why would you call her after she was dead?'

'I called her a bunch of times. I liked hearing her voice on the message. "Hi, this is Tiff. You know the drill. Leave your number and I'll call you back." One time I left her a message.'

'And you mentioned the package?'

Tabitha nodded. 'Yes.'

'Okay. What did you say? Try to remember the exact words if you can.'

'First I said, "Hi, Tiff." Then I told her I was really, really going to miss her and that I was really, really sorry she couldn't get out of town like she wanted. Then I asked her what she wanted me to do with the package she gave me.'

'"What do you want me to do with the package you gave me?" Are those the exact words you used?'

'Pretty much.'

'Did you say anything else?'

'No.'

'And you only left the one message?'

'Yes. Why? Did I do something really bad?'

'No. No, you didn't.'

Harlan smiled. Not only had she not done anything bad, she'd made it blindingly obvious what they had to do next. Right now. Harlan rummaged around in his backpack and found the disposable cell phone at the bottom.

Chapter Fifty-Four

3:14 A.M., Tuesday, August 25, 2009
Gouldsboro, Maine

THE SOUND OF Beethoven woke Maggie with a start. Her first thought was that these middle-of-the-night phone calls were getting really old. Her second thought was it had to be Carroll wanting to know what she'd been doing in his apartment. She disengaged herself from McCabe's body and slipped out of the bed. She found her phone in the pocket of her jeans seconds before the message kicked in. *Unknown caller.* She sat down, still naked, on the couch and clicked Talk.

'Who is this?'

'Hello, Magpie.'

Maggie straightened. 'Harlan? Where are you?'

'Was Tiff Stoddard's cell phone found with her body?'

'What?'

'Was Tiff Stoddard's cell phone found with her body?'

'No,' she said after a few seconds. 'Nobody could find her phone. Not with her body. Not in the apartment. Why?'

'No reason. Don't worry. I'll be in touch.'

'Harlan, where are you?'

She heard only silence.

'Goddamnit, Harlan, you brat, don't you dare hang up on me.'

Too late. He was gone.

'Goddamnit!'

'What is it?' asked McCabe, now sitting up in bed. He flipped on the light.

She ignored the question, clicked 'Recents', found the last number that had called and called it back. It rang four times. No one answered. No message requested. It was only by sheer force of will that Maggie kept herself from throwing her own phone across the room in frustration. 'Goddamn fucking little brat.'

Don't worry. I'll be in touch. What the hell did that mean? When would he be in touch? And about what? And what in hell did he want to know about Tiff Stoddard's phone for? She took a deep breath. What she really wanted to do was get back in bed, snuggle up against McCabe and maybe see if he wanted to make love again. But the cop in her was too strong. She found her clothes and pulled them on and then started pacing around the room.

'What's going on?' McCabe asked, her nervous energy rubbing off on him. 'What did Harlan want?'

She stopped pacing and told him what her brother had asked about.

Chapter Fifty-Five

3:19 A.M., Tuesday, August 25, 2009
Moose Island, Maine

ONCE THE THROWAWAY phone stopped ringing, Harlan turned it off and put it back in the bottom of his backpack. Then he put the pack on the floor to serve once again as his pillow. He lay down on his ground cloth. He told Tabitha to get back in the sleeping bag and go back to sleep. She said she wouldn't be able to sleep. He told her to try.

She wriggled down inside the bag. 'Trying isn't going to help.'

'Okay. Then don't try. Just lie there and look at the ceiling. But don't talk. I need to work something out and I can't think straight when people are talking.'

'Fine,' she said. 'I won't talk.'

Harlan focused on what it was he had to figure out. A foolproof way to offer irresistible bait. He wished the bait could only be the drugs and money. But if Riordan knew Tabitha had seen him and could recognize him, she'd have to be part of the deal. He'd just have to keep her with him. No other way to keep her safe.

As a trained sniper, Harlan saw Toby Mahler's grandfather's house as about the worst place in the world for what he had in mind. If he sat all by himself in an open patch surrounded on all sides by brush and trees, the enemy could approach from any direction and, unless they were incredibly stupid or incredibly careless, he'd never see or hear them coming. He needed to find a better location. He could think of only one that was close enough for Tabitha to make it.

He got up and rummaged around the house until he found a pen and a piece of paper that still had one side blank. He went into the kitchen, where enough moonlight was coming in through the windows.

Tabitha pulled herself out of the sleeping bag and followed. 'What are you doing?'

He lay the paper down on the same counter they'd used to operate on Harold. 'Writing a script,' he said. Then he paused. Looked at Tabitha. 'No. Actually, you ought to be the one writing it. Otherwise it'll sound phony.'

He handed her the pen. She took it.

'Writing what?'

'You're going to call Tiff's number on your phone and leave another message.'

'What am I supposed to say?'

Tabitha put the point of the pen on the paper. Then she lifted it off. 'If it's really supposed to sound like it's coming from me I shouldn't read it off a piece of paper. I should just talk it.'

Harlan thought about that. This kid was smart. Smarter than him in a lot of ways. 'Okay. You're right.'

'So what am I supposed to say?'

'Remember you're talking to Tiff. Like it's just between you and her and you don't think anyone else can hear. Don't tell her where we are now. That's important. Just start by telling her about your parents being dead. Then tell her you've still got the package and you're with me but you haven't told me about it. That it's hidden in your teddy bear.' Harlan grinned. Hearing that really ought to piss Riordan off. If the stupid fuck had only picked the fucking bear up off the ground and felt inside instead of freaking out and shooting it, he'd have his goddamn drugs. And Tiff's money. And the only thing Harlan would have to lure Riordan out would be Tabitha herself.

'What are you laughing about?' Tabitha asked him. She really didn't think this was an appropriate time for anybody to be laughing.

'Nothing. I'm sorry.' Harlan didn't want to tell her he was laughing about Harold getting his head blown half off. 'Next thing to tell Tiff is we're moving fast from place to place so the cops won't find us. Tell her I said tomorrow night we'll be hiding out starting after midnight in the old sardine cannery at Parnell Point …'

Tabitha stared at Harlan like she couldn't believe what he was saying. The old cannery was about the last place in the world she'd ever pick to hide. It was scary and smelly and full of rats and cobwebs. It stunk of fish. And poop. She'd gone in there once with Toby and they'd both run the hell out as soon as they got inside. None of the kids in school, not even the eighth graders and certainly not a sixth grader like her, had enough nerve to set foot in the place more than once.

But then she thought about Tiff being dead and her parents being dead and how she wanted to kill the December Man for killing her family and how Harlan was the only person she knew in the world who could help her do that.

So she didn't say anything about how she felt about the cannery. She just asked him what else he wanted her to say on the message.

He told her. She listened. To make sure she didn't leave out anything important she asked him to tell her again. And then a third time. When she was sure she had it all straight and didn't have any more questions she closed her eyes and thought about Tiff and her mother and how Donelda had given up her own life to save Tabitha's. She even thought about Pike, who, in Tabitha's view, was probably better off dead than alive.

Then Tabitha opened her eyes and told Harlan she was ready. She dug into her pocket and pulled out her iPhone. She speed-dialed Tiff's number. After four rings she heard the familiar voice: 'Hi, this is Tiff. You know the drill. Leave your number and I'll call you back.'

Hearing Tiff's voice again brought tears to Tabbie's eyes. She took a deep breath and started. 'Hi, Tiff. This is Tabitha. I know you're still dead so you can't hear anything I'm saying. But I just wanted you to know how much I miss you and I always, always will. I just hope Mrs St Pierre is right and you and Terri and maybe Mom are all together in the arms of Jesus and maybe if you ask Jesus real nice maybe he'll let you check your messages. I hope he does because there isn't anybody else I'm allowed to talk to about the package you gave me. Yes, I still have it. I put it inside Harold. You remember? Your old teddy bear. That's what I call him. I think you called him Doofus. Anyway, I haven't told anybody about Harold, not even Harlan, who says he was your boyfriend. I hope Harlan is telling the truth about that, 'cause I like him a lot, except when he's telling me to shut up and go to sleep.'

There was a click. Tabitha looked at the phone.

'The message stopped,' she said. She hadn't gotten to any of the important stuff yet.

'That's okay,' Harlan sighed. He didn't want to rush or rattle her. This was good. He thought she sounded exactly like a slightly weird eleven-year-old kid ought to sound and not like some pissed-off sniper with an agenda. 'Just call again and pick up where you left off.'

Tabitha hit the button and called Tiff's phone again.

'Sorry,' she said. 'We kind of got cut off there. Anyway, like I was saying, I still have the package and I haven't said anything to anybody about it. Like I always say, a promise is a promise. Right now it's four in the morning and Harlan's asleep. He keeps dragging me around from place to place 'cause he says the police are looking for us and we've got to keep moving. Tomorrow night ... that's Wednesday I think ... Harlan says we're gonna be at the old cannery at Parnell Point, which I'm a little scared about. Actually, I'm a lot scared about it. Nobody ever goes inside that place except rats and spiders and dead fish. But he says that's a good thing. Nobody'll want to go in there looking for us. Harlan says we'll get there after midnight. Stay for a day. Then he wants to leave again. But I'm not leaving with him. Parnell Point's near home so I've pretty much decided I'm going home. Anyway, I'm going to leave your package inside the cannery, 'cause I'm really, really tired of carrying Harold around with me. If you really are with Jesus maybe he'll let you fly down and get it if you want. That way I can just stop worrying about it and nobody will ever know what you put inside. Including me.'

When she was finished, Tabitha clicked off her phone, then shut it down. 'Okay?' she asked.

'Perfect,' he said and kissed the top of her head. 'You were fabulous. Amazing.'

Harlan's praise was the first thing that made Tabitha feel even a little bit good since she'd heard about Tiff being dead. She put her arms around Harlan and hugged him. 'Thank you,' she said.

'You're welcome. Now go back to sleep.'

She decided not to tell Harlan she didn't feel sleepy. Just slid back into his sleeping bag, thinking how much she really liked her sister's boyfriend. She wondered if maybe, after this was over, Harlan would let her stay with him in his house. Since she was an orphan now he could even adopt her, though she had to admit he was probably a little young to be her father so maybe he could just be a big brother. That'd be nice.

Chapter Fifty-Six

3:31 A.M., Tuesday, August 25, 2009
Machias, Maine

UPSTAIRS, IN THE small bedroom that had once been Harlan's, Emily Kaplan briefly debated whether or not to take a pill to help her sleep and decided not to. She'd never liked taking drugs. Did so only as a last resort. The headaches hadn't gone away and her whole body still hurt, particularly the two cracked ribs. Every time she shifted even slightly in the bed, pain from the ribs made her gasp. She had given in an hour earlier and had taken 800 milligrams of ibuprofen but it wasn't helping much and she didn't want to take anything stronger. Certainly not Oxycontin, though the hospital had offered it.

Finally, Em decided it might hurt less to sit up than lie down. She got out of bed, wearing a pair of pink cotton pajamas a couple of sizes too small that had once belonged to a much younger Maggie. Detritus from a life left behind when Maggie went off to Orono and then Portland. She dragged a straight-back chair from the corner over to the window. She opened the slats in the blinds wide enough to allow her to look out into the night and to enjoy the feel of the cool air on her skin.

Savage had brought her back from Bangor late that afternoon and settled her in a room still filled with mementos of the Savages' youngest son's childhood. Team pictures. Sports trophies. Harlan in a white dinner jacket with a light-blue shirt with a frilly front, his arm around a pretty redhead who must have been his date for the senior prom.

At the hospital, John Savage had told her there was no way he was going to let her go back to her place in Machiasport. Not tonight. Not for several nights. Not with no one to watch out for her. Hell, he said, she'd had a cop guarding her hospital room in Bangor and she'd damn well have a cop guarding her here, even if the cop in question did happen to be a seventy-four-year-old sheriff suffering from lymphoma and feeling the after-effects of chemo. 'No damned arguments,' he told her. 'You're staying with us.' She didn't argue. The idea suited her fine. Through the open window she watched and listened to the swaying of leaves as the wind picked up. She wondered if a change in the weather might be approaching.

Suddenly, a dark figure dashed from behind the big maple to the side of the house. There was something familiar in the way he moved. Yet, try as she might, even though the memory was almost there, like words on the tip of her tongue, she couldn't get it to fall into place. Then, suddenly, it *was* there. Just like that. The fog of amnesia lifted and she *knew*. The man had already disappeared around the side of the house but she *knew*. A tremor of fear passed through her. Emily listened hard through the open window. With the leaves swaying it would have been easy to miss the nearly imperceptible sound of rubber soles squishing on the wooden floor of the porch below. But she didn't. She went to wake up Savage.

Anya and Savage lay side by side in their queen-sized bed. Anya on her back snoring softly. Savage on his side. By the faint glow of a night-light Emily examined his lined face. A man she loved almost as much as her own dead father. Savage had told her about the cancer on the way home from Bangor. Sworn her to secrecy. He needn't have worried. She wouldn't tell anyone. But anyone looking closely enough, certainly any doctor, might well guess. Perhaps not the specifics. But the presence of illness. After a heavy round of chemo the old man would be as weak as a cat. Better, she decided, nervous as she was, if she was the one to confront the intruder. Emily crept silently to the hallway. Closed the bedroom door behind her. She moved to the landing and then down the stairs.

She heard movement on the porch. Through the glass oval she watched a dark shadow raise one hand and run it along the top of the door-frame. Looking for the key she supposed. He'd find it soon enough. She hurried to the kitchen. Went to the cabinet, where she knew Savage kept his gun, hoping against hope it wouldn't be locked.

It wasn't. She pulled out the Peacemaker, made sure it was loaded and cocked. Savage had taught her to use the weapon years before, the same time he taught Maggie, when they were both ten years old. Still, she'd only ever fired at targets, never at a human being. She was hoping she wouldn't have to.

She heard a key turn in the lock and hurried back and positioned herself facing the door in a two-handed firing stance. The door swung open. At first she saw only the dark porch. Then a man appeared moving fast, a black silhouette against a dark sky. She watched the movement of his body as he entered. Watched him peer into the dark room.

'Freeze,' she shouted. 'Or I'll shoot.'

He fired first.

Chapter Fifty-Seven

In a motel room thirty miles south of Machias, Maggie was still trying to figure out why Harlan was so interested in Tiff Stoddard's cell phone. Had he called Tiff and left some kind of threatening message after she had dumped him, which he told her had happened a week before the murder? That was possible. She knew Tiff's phone hadn't been found with the body. Her father had said it wasn't found in the apartment either. So where was it? Did Carroll have it? And if so why did it matter? The state police should already have gotten a record of all her calls and messages both in and out. Pretty standard procedure to get such things for a murder victim.

And that's when another thought popped into her head. *You have reached Tabitha Stoddard's iPhone. If you'd like me to call you back, please leave your number and I will do so as soon as I can.* What was an eleven-year-old kid doing with an expensive cell phone when her parents didn't have two spare dimes to rub together?

You or Donelda have a cell number? She remembered asking Pike. *Yeah, like that's all we need. An extra expense,* he'd answered. So what the hell was Tabitha doing with an iPhone? The only person Maggie could think of who would have had the money to pay for Tabitha's iPhone was Tiff. Maggie wondered if maybe, just maybe, Tiff had had a special reason for doing so.

She picked up her own phone and started punching in numbers.

'What are you doing?' asked McCabe.

'I'm calling Burt Lund.'

'At four in the morning?'

'It's important.'

'I'm sure he'll be pleased to hear that.'

Lund's cell went to message after the first ring, meaning he'd probably switched it off.

'What's Burt's number at home? He's not answering his cell.'

McCabe sighed and sat up. '555-2792. But do me a favor. Don't tell him you got it from me.'

It took five rings before a sleepy Burt Lund answered. 'What do you want, Savage? And it better be good.'

'You're aware of the Tiffany Stoddard murder?'

'I'm aware. I'll probably be heading up the prosecution. I'm also aware, Margaret, that you're no longer working for Carroll. You have no jurisdictional standing.'

'No. But you do and I need a favor. A very urgent favor. One that could substantially aid your case, assuming you are the prosecutor.'

'Go ahead.'

'I need a record of all messages left on Stoddard's iPhone. Particularly to or from her little sister Tabitha both before and since her death.'

'Wouldn't Sean Carroll's people have all that?' Lund sounded suspicious.

'They ought to. I'd like to find out if they do.'

'Ask Carroll.'

'I don't want Carroll knowing about it.'

'Why not?'

Having no idea how Burt Lund would react, Maggie figured this was no time to be beating around the bush. 'I have reason to believe,' she said, 'that Sean Carroll may have been responsible for Tiff Stoddard's death.'

'You can't be serious.'

'I'm absolutely serious.'

There was a long, pregnant pause on the other end of the phone. Lund knew Maggie well enough to know she'd never make an accusation like that unless she had good reason.

'Do you think he killed his own wife as well? And Laura Blakemore?'

'I do.'

Another silence.

'Exactly what are you basing this on?'

'I can't tell you that just yet. Trust me, Burt, this is for real.'

'Have you mentioned your suspicions to anyone else?'

'Yes.'

'Who?'

'McCabe. And Susan Marsh.'

'If I didn't know you as well as I do, Savage, I'd hang up now.'

'Well, you do know me well enough. If I'm asking for the records I have a reason. So please, Burt, can you get me what I need? If I'm wrong you can just say this conversation never happened.'

Maggie heard a sigh on the other end of the line. A deep sigh. 'All right. I'll call you back with whatever I find out in the morning. The real morning.' Lund broke the connection.

Maggie climbed back on the couch. McCabe turned off the lights. They both managed to fall asleep. This time Maggie didn't dream.

Sheriff John Savage's phone call woke them less than an hour later. He told Maggie she better get her butt back to Machias.

Chapter Fifty-Eight

5:50 A.M., Tuesday, August 25, 2009
Downeast Community Hospital, Machias, Maine

IT HAD BEEN a slow night in the ER.

One sixty-eight-year-old woman with a false-alarm heart attack.

One teenager ODed on Oxycontin.

And Dr Emily Kaplan, who had been shot in the chest with a dart containing what Dr Bill Brill hoped was a less than lethal dose of Etorphine, a powerful drug used to tranquilize large animals in the wild.

Maggie and McCabe entered the hospital and found Savage and Anya sitting side by side in the waiting area, looking worried and holding hands.

'How is she?' Maggie asked.

'Alive,' said Savage. 'Just. The guy didn't give her quite enough to kill her. Maybe he didn't realize how big she was.'

At six foot three and more than a hundred and eighty pounds, most of it muscle, Maggie knew Em weighed more than twice as much as the Stoddards' Rottweiler. Nearly forty pounds more than Maggie herself.

'Can we go see her?'

'Not yet. Bill Brill is with her now. Also a veterinarian who works with the Maine Warden Service. Apparently there's a reversal agent that works with this stuff. They're giving her a shot now. The vet says it ought to bring her around.'

'She's being treated by a veterinarian?'

'He's got more experience with this drug than Brill or any of the other docs. Question I've got is, if the guy wanted Em dead,' said Savage, 'why in hell didn't he just shoot her with a bullet instead of with some drug? Or at least give her enough of the drug to do the job?'

Maggie thought about that. 'I guess because he didn't want her dead,' she said. 'At least not right away. Maybe because he wanted something from her first.'

Savaged winced. 'I don't even want to think about that.'

'I'm not talking about anything sexual, though he may have had that in mind as well. He may have wanted to know about the drugs that were found in her pocket. Or maybe he wanted to know if her memory had come back from the night of the murder. Wait a minute,' Maggie paused, frowned and looked hard at Savage. 'Who knew Emily was staying at our place?'

Savage shrugged. 'Nobody.'

'You didn't tell anyone Em was staying there?'

'No. Just the nurse when we were leaving the hospital.'

'And nothing to anyone else?'

'I take your point. How did the bad guy find out?'

'He didn't. It just occurred to me. My car was still in the driveway. Em was wearing my pajamas. Sleeping in my house. It wasn't Em the sonofabitch was after. It was me.'

Maggie heard her name called and turned to see her father's longtime doctor, Bill Brill. 'She's awake and alert,' Brill said. 'She's asking for you.'

'Not me?' asked Savage.

'No. Just Maggie. Follow me and I'll take you to her room.'

Emily was lying in a small single room. Maggie bent down and kissed her friend on the cheek. 'How do you feel?'

'Pretty bad. On top of everything else that was already hurting, now it feels like I've got a doozy of a hangover. Plus a puncture wound in my chest.'

'At least you're alive.'

'So they tell me. Anyway, we need to talk.'

'We certainly do. Is it okay if I make this conversation an official interview?'

Emily nodded and Maggie turned on her recorder. 'This is Detective Margaret Savage of the Portland, Maine, Police Department. The time is 6:15 A.M., August 25th, 2009. I'm interviewing Dr Emily Kaplan in room 214 in Downeast Community Hospital in Machias. Dr Kaplan, can you tell me what happened last night?'

'Well for starters, my memory came back.'

'When did that happen?'

'Around 3:30 this morning. I couldn't sleep because of the pain,' Emily explained. 'So I was sitting in Harlan's bedroom, looking out the window. I thought I saw movement to my right. By the big maple. But I wasn't sure until I saw a man run out and make a dash for the house.'

'Did you get a good look at him?'

'Not his face,' said Em. 'It was too dark and he was looking down. But there was something in the way he moved that clicked. Triggered a latent memory. I'm sure it was the same guy who killed Stoddard. He was running left to right like he ran that night. Same tilt to the body. Same quick, athletic moves,' Em said. 'Like a point guard driving into the paint.'

'But you couldn't see his face?'

'No.'

'Either on the night Tiff Stoddard was killed or last night at the house?'

'No. It was too dark.'

'Both times, both places?'

'Yes.'

'That's too bad. But you're sure it was the same guy?'

'Yes.'

Maggie imagined holding a lineup of five guys running left to right … five point guards driving into the paint … and seeing if Em could pick out the right one. Wondered what a jury would make of that. Wondered what Burt Lund would.

'Do you know how long they're going to be keeping you here?'

'Bill said overnight. Till they're sure I've got all of this crap out of my system.'

Maggie flicked off the recorder and headed for the door.

'Where are you going?' asked Emily.

Maggie looked at her from the door. Just shook her head.

'Never mind,' said Em. 'Just let me know when you catch the bastard.'

Out in the corridor, Maggie asked her father to arrange for a deputy to watch Emily's room. Also asked if he could have somebody run the razor, band-aid and dental floss down to Joe Pines at the Maine State Crime Lab in Augusta. As an afterthought she added the jar containing Emmett Ganzer's saliva. A rush job, she said. She needed to know if any of the DNA samples matched the fetus in Tiff Stoddard's womb as fast as Pines could get even preliminary reads.

MAGGIE WAITED TILL 7:30 before calling Sean Carroll from the house on Center Street.

'Maggie,' he said. 'I was wondering where you'd disappeared to.'

'I had to run down to Portland, Sean, to pick up some personal things. Got back late last night.'

'Anything new to report?' Carroll asked. He sounded cheerful. Glad to hear from her. No mention of last night's visit to Machias. Or her visit to Ellsworth. No mention of Susan Marsh. Or Emily Kaplan.

'Not really. I'm calling because I wanted to tell you how sorry I was about what I said after we got back from Harlan's place the other day. I said some unforgivable things. You didn't deserve it. I shouldn't have shot off my mouth like that.'

'Oh, hey, listen. I understand. You were upset about your brother. I said some pretty unpleasant things myself.'

'Well, Sean, it's been bothering me. Matter of fact I was passing through Ellsworth last night on my way back from Portland and I stopped off at your apartment. Took a chance you might be there so I could apologize in person. In fact, I ran into one of your neighbors who was walking her dog. Alice somebody or other. She told me you weren't home. Guess she didn't mention it.'

'No. I haven't spoken to her. I've been staying in Machias. Thought you knew that. Been here since Saturday. Listen, Mag, there are a couple of things we really do have to talk about.'

'Oh yeah, like what?'

'Like Ganzer told me you were the one to sound the alarm about Pike and Donelda Stoddard.'

'That's right, I did.'

'How did you know what was going on?'

'I didn't,' she said, not wanting to tell him about the aborted call from Tabitha Stoddard. 'I just had a feeling something bad might be happening. So I called Frank Boucher ...'

'Who?'

'You know, the police chief in Eastport. I think I mentioned him the other night at dinner. Anyway, I asked him to go to Stoddard's and check it out.'

'At two in the morning?'

'Yeah. You know. It was just one of those instinctive things I couldn't get out of my head. I'm sure you've had them yourself.' She was sure it sounded like bullshit to Carroll. It certainly did to her.

'So you didn't get a call from Harlan?'

'Harlan? No.'

'And you don't know where he is?'

'No.'

'Would you tell me if you did?'

'Honestly, I don't know.' She figured he was more likely to buy it if she admitted that. 'You know it would be hard for me to do that. I still don't think he's guilty. But the truth of the matter is I haven't seen or heard from Harlan since Saturday night at the Musty Moose. I haven't a clue where he is.'

Carroll didn't respond so Maggie continued. 'Y'know, when I went up to Stoddard's, I also tried calling you but you weren't picking up.'

'Yeah. I saw your number on recents. Emmett tells me when you were there you flat out accused him of being Stoddard's killer. Don't you think that's going a little far?'

Maggie didn't answer immediately. She wondered if it was possible that Susan Marsh hadn't told Carroll about her accusations in Augusta.

'No. I don't think it's going a little far,' she said, finally responding to his question. 'I think Emmett may well be Conor Riordan.'

'Based on what?'

'Mostly opportunity. We all know he was at Harlan's place hours before the evidence was discovered. Nobody had a better opportunity of planting the stuff there. As for the obvious nature of it all, well, nobody ever accused Emmett of being subtle. If he'd managed to kill Harlan at the same time, which I think was his goal, well, that would have sealed the deal. You know the headline. Armed suspect shot and killed resisting arrest. Conclusive evidence of murder found at suspect's home. Yadda, yadda, yadda.'

'Interesting. I suppose that's possible. Listen, Maggie,' Sean said, his voice becoming softer, more intimate, 'maybe you and I could discuss all this over dinner tonight. There's a Mediterranean place I like in Ellsworth. Cleonice.'

She had a hard time sounding interested. But she managed. 'Are you asking me out on a date, Sean?' she asked, making her voice sound more coquettish than she was sure McCabe had ever heard it.

'Of course not,' said Sean, sounding a little flirty himself. 'That wouldn't be appropriate. I'm asking you to meet with me as a confidential informant. To discuss the case.'

And what about after dinner, Maggie wondered. Did he plan to take his confidential informant home for a little spiked brandy, maybe followed by a little non-consensual sex, maybe followed by a little non-consensual murder? You could say one thing about the guy. He sure as hell had a big set of *cojones*.

'Gee, Sean, I'd really love to but I don't see how I can possibly make it tonight. I'm sure you heard about Emily being shot with an animal tranquilizer. I have to be with her.'

'Yes, I did hear about it. I understand.'

'All right. Some other time, then.'

'Yes. I'd love to. Some other time.'

'What's your take?' asked McCabe when she broke the connection.

'More convinced than ever. He's the guy. For starters he lied about going home last night and talking to Alice Spaulding. No mention of Susan Marsh either. Which worries me. The only reason for Carroll to have come home last night is if Marsh told him she needed to discuss something urgent.'

'Our accusations?'

'Yes. If she did, she could be in trouble. Believe it or not, Carroll also asked me to have dinner with him tonight.'

BURT LUND CALLED Maggie twenty minutes later. He'd already obtained Tiff Stoddard's phone records.

'It's interesting,' he said, 'Tiff had not one but two iPhones registered in her name. Both with AT&T. One has a recorded greeting from Tiff herself. The other a greeting from someone who identifies herself as Tabitha Stoddard.'

Maggie told Burt about the call she'd received from Tabitha's phone the night her parents were murdered.

'Yeah. I see your number here on the sheets.'

'What about other activity?'

'Well, Tiff made and received a lot of calls to and from untraceable cell numbers,' said Burt. 'She didn't receive a lot of voicemails, though. Mostly innocuous ones from friends and family. Three were of particular interest because they came in after Tiff was dead.'

'Who from?'

'Her sister. Tabitha Stoddard. All three times Tabitha was aware she was leaving messages for a dead person.'

Christ, Maggie thought, what that kid must be going through. 'Can you play them for me?'

Lund played them. Then he played them again and Maggie recorded them on her digital recorder.

'Any recent messages from my brother Harlan?'

'Not for the last couple of weeks. No text messages either.'

'Did you ask AT&T if there were any other requests for the records?'

'I did. There weren't.'

'Not even from Sean Carroll?'

'Not even.'

Chapter Fifty-Nine

7:12 P.M., Tuesday, August 25, 2009
Moose Island, Maine

HARLAN SHOOK TABITHA awake a little after seven P.M. Told her it was time to get ready.

Tabitha didn't say anything. Just nodded.

While they waited for the last of the summer light to fade, Harlan buried the empty cans of fruit, the wrappers from the breakfast bars and any other visible signs of their brief habitation at Toby Mahler's grandfather's house.

Then he wiped the bottle of pills and the three stacks of fifties clean of fingerprints. Finally, he stuffed both the bottle and the money back inside the teddy bear.

'I won't be able to sew him up,' Tabitha said.

'That's okay. We'll push some newspaper in back. That ought to hold him together well enough.'

Harlan filled his canteen with water from the stream and they left. 'How far do you think you can walk?'

'Pretty far. I sometimes go on hikes with Tiff. *Went* on hikes with Tiff,' she corrected herself. 'We'd go four or five miles.'

'We may have to go farther than that tonight. Do you think you can make it?'

'Yes,' she said, her voice determined.

THEY REACHED THE cannery at Parnell Point a little before ten. The last of more than a dozen canneries that once anchored the economy in and around Eastport, the ruins of Parnell Point remained only because of a protracted legal battle among the heirs of the former owners.

An eight-foot-high chain link fence, now falling into disrepair, surrounded the place. A *No Trespassing* sign hung from the padlocked gate. Harlan, with Tabitha in tow, circled the outer perimeter of the property, checking for possible entry points and stopping every thirty meters or so to scan the area inside for any sign that Conor Riordan had arrived early.

He helped Tabitha slip through a break in the fence near the main gate and then went through himself. Half walking, half jogging, they crossed a broad, open area devoid of cover. Nothing but low brush, rocks and cracked clay all the way to the building.

As they drew closer, the structure rose before them, alone on the edge of the land, like a black dead thing rising from the black dead water behind. The place was falling apart. Much of the roof and interior ceiling had collapsed and the old wooden walls were rotting away. All secondary entrances and exits had been boarded up for decades, leaving only a pair of large barn doors at the front. These were protected by a padlock and another *No Trespassing* sign. Harlan told Tabitha to move behind him. He destroyed the lock with a single shot from the M40 and pulled open one of the doors.

'Are we going inside?' Tabitha asked, her voice quavery.

Harlan didn't like the idea of leaving her outside alone but the kid was obviously terrified.

'Okay. You stand guard out here and try to be invisible. I'll only be a minute.' He handed her a baseball-sized rock. 'Bang on the wall with this if you see or hear anyone coming.'

'Three times?'

'Just once.'

Tabbie nodded. She used her shirt to wipe the mist from her glasses and scooched down next to the building. Harlan took Harold and went inside. Even from out here Tabitha could hear dozens of tiny rat feet skittering across the wooden floor. Fighting an urge to scream, she forced herself to lie still and watch the darkened landscape for intruders. She had to be brave, she told herself. Had to do this one thing. Not just for herself but also for Tiff and for her mother and even for Pike.

I'll only be a minute, Harlan had said. But if it was only a minute it felt like the longest minute of her life. Finally he emerged without Harold.

Minutes later the two of them lay side by side in a shallow culvert 200 meters south of the building. The spot was well camouflaged and provided a perfect field of fire across the entire property. If Riordan was a careful man, and Harlan was sure he was, he'd likely enter from somewhere other than the front. But no matter what direction he came from, the only way to the bear was through the barn doors and Harlan had them covered. For a trained sniper, a 200 or even 300 meter kill is easy. Harlan's longest in Iraq had been over 800, and that wasn't considered exceptional.

Temperatures had been dropping most of the day and a cool breeze from the bay carried the sounds of the ocean and the first hints of autumn and the winter that lay beyond. Tabitha was shivering. Harlan unrolled his sleeping bag and told her to get inside. It would not only keep her warm but would also prevent sudden movements at the wrong time. Two hours passed. Tabitha started getting restless trapped inside the bag. Harlan told her to be still.

A little after midnight, a vehicle, its lights off, pulled to a stop behind a thin stand of shrubs across the road from the front gate. Harlan watched the driver's side window slide down. A face, green through the scope, peered out. A man inside the car raised binoculars to his eyes.

'He's here,' Harlan whispered.

Tabbie scrunched down lower into the culvert.

Five minutes passed before the driver's side door opened. The car's interior remained dark. Through the scope Harlan watched the guy who had come to his house, the guy he had beaten up, step out. Emmett Ganzer's wrist was bandaged, his face still bruised and blackened from the beating he'd taken. Harlan watched him look left and right. Cross the road. Slip through the same break in the fence that he and Tabitha had used. Ganzer drew a hand-gun and walked, in a low crouch, straight down the middle of the property toward the cannery. Careless, Harlan thought as he watched the familiar figure, very, very careless. Even assuming Ganzer was wearing body armor and Harlan had to go for a head-shot, he was making this easy. Harlan studied Ganzer's face and thought about Tabitha's description of the December Man. She'd only seen him for a split second but even so something didn't compute. He unzipped the sleeping bag to free Tabitha's arms and passed her the weapon. 'Look through the eyepiece,' he ordered. 'Is that the guy you saw last December?'

At first Tabitha's glasses got in the way and she couldn't see anything. Harlan told her to take them off. He'd adjust the focus. She just had to tell him when the image appeared sharp.

'Not yet,' she said. 'Not yet. There. Go back a little. That's it.'

She peered at the man slowly crossing the open ground in a crouch. 'No,' she said in a loud whisper.

'No what?'

'That's not him.'

'Are you sure?'

'I'm sure. Face is different. So's the hair. Plus he's way too big.'

'He's probably wearing body armor,' said Harlan. 'That'd make him look bigger.'

'It's not him.' She handed the weapon back to Harlan.

Not him? Shit. Did that mean there were two of them? One going after the bear. One waiting in the car. Or maybe not waiting in the car. Maybe waiting miles away. Or maybe coming around behind them in the dark. The first rule of law enforcement, Harlan's father always told him, was never enter a potentially violent situation without backup.

Harlan whispered to Tabitha to turn and watch their rear. Tap his leg the instant she heard any sounds or spotted any movement coming from behind. The girl nodded.

Harlan studied the car through the scope. At first he saw nothing. But then he sensed movement on the front passenger side. Just the shift of a shoulder. Or maybe an arm. But it meant Conor Riordan, whoever he was, was still there. Waiting, he supposed, for Ganzer to retrieve the bear. Or to get shot, if Riordan suspected the ambush.

That created a problem. If he killed Ganzer first, Riordan would drive away. Escape the trap. Somehow he had to kill the man in the car first. Unfortunately, the odds of hitting Riordan from where he was now were slim to none. His view was obscured by shrubs. His bullet would have to clear the chain link fence, go through the car window and, finally, pass through the headrest on top of the seat, any or all of which would alter its trajectory. No, killing Riordan from here would be like winning the Powerball Lottery: damned near impossible.

To get a clear shot he'd have to leave the compound and go around behind the car without being seen. Worst part was he couldn't bring Tabitha with him. Too dangerous for her. Too likely she'd alert Riordan by making some noise. But leaving the child here by herself with Ganzer on the prowl didn't sit well either.

Harlan was still pondering how best to deal with this when he felt a hand tapping his leg. He spun and looked back where Tabbie was pointing. A dark figure moving toward them in a low crouch, carrying a weapon. Christ, could there be three of them? He peered through the scope. Aimed at the moving shadow. Applied gentle pressure to the trigger. And then eased off.

No way in hell could Harlan Savage ever shoot his own sister.

CROUCHED IN THE darkness on the far side of the ramshackle building, the index finger of his right hand inside the trigger guard of his Glock, Michael McCabe watched Emmett Ganzer rise and run the last hundred yards to the front wall of the old cannery. The running man was definitely Ganzer. No doubt about that. Were the two of them in this together? Ganzer and Carroll? Or had they been wrong about Carroll? McCabe wasn't sure.

EMMETT GANZER, HIS head pounding, his breath short from the effort of running in the heavy body armor, rested his considerable bulk against the outer wall of the cannery. Sweat trickled down his face and he sucked in the cool air of the evening, trying to calm himself. When his heart had finally slowed enough, Ganzer edged toward the door, holding his 9 mm automatic in two hands. It was okay, he thought, for Carroll, who was sitting back there safe in the car. Sonofabitch told him it'd be a piece of cake. Told him no one would be waiting inside the building but rats. But Carroll had always been a lying scumbag and Savage was sneaky. He might just be sitting inside the building pointing his fucking rifle.

Ganzer slipped through the door and dropped instantly to a crouch. He saw no movement. Heard no sound. No flash of a shot. Something soft and furry darted across his ankle. Emmett Ganzer swallowed hard. He hated rats, though not quite as much as he hated the idea that Harlan Savage might be hiding in here, waiting to put a bullet through his head. Emmett pictured himself wounded, his life oozing out in this filthy place, rodents crawling over his body. Lapping his blood. Nibbling at his flesh. Ganzer held his left arm as far from his body as he could, flipped on his Maglite. He saw the bear immediately.

'DROP YOUR RIFLE, Harlan.' Maggie spoke in a soft whisper as she pointed McCabe's Mossberg 590 pump-action riot shotgun at her brother's chest.

'I don't think so, Mag. No way you'd shoot me. Any more than I'd shoot you.'

'I don't have to shoot you, baby brother. All I have to do is fire this cannon into the air and your fox will bolt.'

Harlan stubbornly held on to the M40. 'I came here to kill him, Magpie. Not Ganzer. The one in the car. Both of them if I have to.'

'You're not killing anyone.'

'No way they should live.'

'No way I'm letting you spend the rest of your life behind bars. I'm a cop, Harlan. This is my job, not yours.' Maggie took out a pair of handcuffs. 'Put the rifle down, and put your hands behind your back.'

'You have backup?' Harlan asked.

'I have backup.'

'All right, go do your job,' he sighed. Then he put the rifle down. 'But don't cuff me. Somebody needs to stay with the kid. Keep her safe.'

Maggie thought about that and finally nodded. Harlan was right. Someone did need to protect Tabitha. Besides, it wouldn't hurt to have extra backup. 'All right,' she said. 'But you've got to promise me you won't fire unless it's absolutely necessary.'

Harlan smiled the smile that was uniquely his. 'Cross my heart and hope not to die.'

Maggie asked Tabitha if she was okay. The girl nodded. Maggie disappeared into the darkness the same way she came.

McCabe peered through the split boards on the sidewall of the cannery. Inside, no more than ten feet away, he could see Ganzer's broad back in the faint glow of the Maglite. He was crouching down behind a large block of rusted-out machinery. The narrow beam of his light focused on a large teddy bear propped in the middle of a long table that ran the length of the room. McCabe wondered if Harold still contained the package Tabitha had talked about in the message.

Ganzer flipped off the Maglite. Darkness returned.

'Harlan,' Ganzer called out. 'Harlan Savage. You're under arrest for the murder of Tiffany Stoddard. Let the child go and come out with your hands up. Harlan Savage, can you hear me?'

The only thing that broke the silence was the scurrying of rats.

MAGGIE CREPT TO within twenty yards of the car. Close enough to make out the shape of Sean Carroll's curls in the front passenger seat. Carroll was peering intently through his binoculars, seemingly unaware of her approach.

CARROLL WATCHED EMMETT Ganzer emerge from the building and start back across the open field. Walking normally. Carrying the bear in his arms. This was the moment for Savage to shoot him. But there were no shots. No sound at all except the wind blowing in off the sea. Sean Carroll's sacrificial lamb was still unquestionably alive. Strange. Carroll had been sure Savage was setting up an ambush. But the further Ganzer came toward the fence the more difficult Savage's shot would be. Could he have figured this wrong? Definitely beginning to look that way. When Ganzer was almost all the way across the open ground, Carroll put down the binoculars and stepped out of the car.

Maggie fingered the Mossberg and resisted a strong urge to blow Sean Carroll's too handsome head off his oh so beautiful body and be done with it. Instead, she watched him slip on a pair of white latex gloves and pull a 9 mm from its holster. Why the gloves, she wondered. Why the gun? What was that for? If the two of them were in this thing together, it made no sense. So maybe they weren't. She realized there was no way of knowing. And that was a problem.

Sean Carroll stepped just inside the fence, his gun by his side. 'Hold it, Emmett,' he called out. 'Stop right there.'

Ganzer stopped. 'What? Why? What's going on?'

Carroll studied the bear, its head half shot away. That's when another possibility occurred to him. Harlan Savage had, after all, served two tours in Iraq.

'Move back into the open, Emmett. About ten feet back. I need to check something out.'

'What? Why? What's that?' Ganzer said, looking confused rather than worried. That was good.

'Just do it, Emmett. Everything will be fine.'

Reluctantly, Ganzer moved back.

Carroll withdrew as far away as he could get from Ganzer without leaving the fenced compound. He squatted down. 'Open the back of the bear, Emmett,' he called out. 'Tell me what you see.'

Ganzer shrugged. Yanked at the edges of the fake fur.

Carroll turned away, covered his face with his arms and scrunched down further.

But there were no explosions. There was nothing but silence.

Carroll lowered his arms. 'What's in there?' he called to Ganzer. 'What's inside?'

Ganzer pulled out some newspapers. Let them fall to the ground. 'Plastic bottle,' he said. 'And a bunch of money.'

'Take the bottle out and look inside.'

'I'm not wearing gloves.'

'Don't worry about it. Easy enough to distinguish your prints from Savage's.'

Ganzer opened the bottle and smiled. 'Pills. Canadian Ox. We got it.'

'Nothing else?'

'Just the money. Shouldn't we bag this stuff ?' asked Ganzer. 'It's evidence.'

Carroll rose and moved toward Ganzer. 'That won't be necessary, Emmett. Just put everything back inside the bear.'

Once again, Ganzer did as he was told.

UNDER COVER OF darkness, Maggie moved silently toward the break in the fence.

When she was close enough to hear the words the two men were saying she flipped on her recorder, hoping it was sensitive enough to pick it all up.

'I DO WANT to thank you, Emmett,' Sean Carroll said. 'You've really been a big help.'

Ganzer smiled at the praise.

He stopped smiling when Carroll raised the automatic he was holding and pointed it at Ganzer's face.

'Now put your hands behind your head,' he said.

'The fuck you doing?' asked Ganzer.

Now it was Carroll's turn to smile. It was exactly the same question the boys on the boat had asked. Exactly the same deer-in-the-headlights expression on Emmett's face.

'Hands behind your head, Emmett,' Carroll repeated. 'Or I'll have to blow it off.' This time Ganzer obeyed.

Sean Carroll reached in and removed Ganzer's weapon from its holster. 'I'm sorry I'll have to shoot you in the face, Emmett. But what with the body armor you're wearing … well, I'm sure you understand.'

WHILE HE WAS talking, Maggie slipped through the break in the fence.

'IT WAS YOU?' Ganzer asked, disbelief making his voice quaver. 'You killed Stoddard? And the Blakemore girl? And your own wife?'

'I'm afraid so,' said Carroll. 'But not to worry. I'll be all right. Everyone will think it was Harlan Savage. They'll also think he killed you.' Carroll smiled. 'I'll tell everyone how bravely you died in the line of duty.'

Emmett Ganzer was now only half listening to what his boss was saying. He was more intent on watching Maggie Savage approach silently from behind Carroll, carrying what looked like a shotgun.

From a hundred meters away, all Michael McCabe could see through the night-vision scope of John Savage's bolt-action Remington 700 rifle, the civilian twin to Harlan's M40, was Emmett Ganzer's broad back. 'Move, you oversized fuck,' McCabe muttered to himself.

Maggie waved her hand, silently signaling Emmett Ganzer to move away from Carroll. If he stayed where he was the Mossberg would kill them both. But Ganzer stood as if rooted to the spot. He said nothing. It was his eyes that gave Maggie away.

Carroll whirled. Fired. Ganzer leaped at Carroll's arm, but too late. Maggie went down, clutching her chest. The Mossberg fell to the ground. Carroll spotted McCabe as he turned back to fire at Ganzer. His second bullet struck Emmett dead center between his small eyes. Maggie, shaken by the impact of the bullet against her body armor, struggled to pull her Glock from her holster. Carroll got there before she could.

Through his night-vision scope McCabe saw Sean Carroll lift Maggie from the ground. Pull her up in front of him, his left arm locked around her neck, holding her body against his, his right hand pressing his automatic against her throat.

There was no way McCabe could fire. Not from here. Not without hitting Maggie. He got up and ran across the open yard to his right, hoping to create a possible line of fire. As McCabe moved, Carroll, as if attached by an invisible axle, turned, keeping Maggie between himself and the Portland cop.

Two hundred meters away, Harlan Savage lay flat on the ground, steadying the tripod legs of his M40 on a flat bit of earth. Through the lens of his scope he saw Maggie's black hair brushing against Carroll's face. Their bodies were tight against each other. For the first time in his life Harlan wished his tall, beautiful sister was six inches shorter.

'Drop the rifle, McCabe. Or I'll kill your girlfriend here,' Carroll called out. 'You are McCabe, aren't you?'

'You'll kill her anyway.'

'Oh, you never know. I might let her live. For a little while at least.'

As McCabe moved further to the right, Carroll kept turning, keeping Maggie between himself and McCabe. For Harlan to get any kind of shot, Carroll had to turn five more degrees. And, as McCabe kept moving to the right, he did.

The angle was about as good as it would get. If Carroll pivoted any further Harlan's bullet would go through the back of Carroll's head and then likely go through Maggie's as well. But from this angle Harlan had just enough clearance between the two of them.

As Michael McCabe and Sean Carroll stared each other down, a small red dot danced one inch behind Sean Carroll's ear. Harlan gauged the speed of the wind coming in from the sea. Ten to fifteen knots. Adjusted his aim slightly to the right. The little red dot was now dead center on Maggie. Harlan figured the wind should carry the bullet just far enough to the left to kill Carroll and miss his sister. If he was wrong, well, he didn't want to think about that. It was without question the most difficult shot Harlan Savage had ever attempted in his life. But he couldn't see any other way out of it. He had to try. He put slow pressure on the trigger. *Please God, make him stand still.*

Perhaps God heard Harlan's silent prayer. Perhaps He didn't. Either way for the microsecond it took for the bullet to travel the 200 meters, Sean Carroll and Maggie Savage, their bodies pressed tightly together, stood motionless. The wind held.

SEAN CARROLL NEVER heard the bullet that entered just behind his right ear and came out the left side of his head taking some of Carroll's brains and a few strands of Maggie's hair along with it.

Neither did Conor Riordan. The man who never was was no more.

Chapter Sixty

9:00 A.M., Sunday, August 30, 2009
Augusta, Maine

ON SUNDAY MORNING, August 30th, one week and two days after the death of Tiffany Stoddard, a special meeting was called by Assistant Attorney General Burt Lund. It began on time at nine A.M. in the private conference room of Lund's boss, Maine Attorney General Bradley Freese.

Lund arrived early. Freese, as was his habit, entered five minutes after everyone else and took the seat left open for him at the head of the table. Lund sat at the other end.

In appearance and manner, the two men couldn't have been more different. Lund was a rotund five foot five and 200 pounds. He usually looked like he'd slept in his suit. His shirt-tails stubbornly refused to obey his half-hearted attempts to keep them tucked in. This morning he'd cut himself while shaving and wore a small, round band-aid on the left side of his double chin.

Freese was tall and patrician, his silver hair was immaculately groomed, and his custom-tailored Dunhill suit perfectly outlined his athletic body. A former all-Ivy League quarterback at Princeton, Freese had preceded Susan Marsh by twenty-five years as a member of the Harvard Law Review and, as Attorney General, had hired her to join his team. In spite of his deep disappointment at having Susan provide Sean Carroll's alibi in his wife's death, she remained a particular favorite. Almost a daughter, he liked to say.

The long oval table between Lund and Freese was full. On one side were Sheriff John Savage, Maggie, McCabe, Assistant Medical Examiner Terri Mirabito, and Dr Joe Pines of the Maine State Laboratory in Augusta. Across from them sat Eastport Police Chief Frank Boucher, Portland Police Chief Tom Shockley, Colonel Ed Matthews, commander of the Maine State Police, Sean Carroll's immediate boss, Lieutenant Tom Mayhew, and Anne Marie Lichter, a child welfare supervisor at Maine's Department of Health and Human Services, who was present to represent the interests and welfare of eleven-year-old Tabitha Stoddard. Judy Lombardi, Brad Freese's executive assistant, sat behind her boss and had been tasked with taking detailed notes.

'All right,' said Freese. 'Let's get this show on the road. Now, can anybody please tell me what in hell this monumental screwup was all about.'

'I think I'm the one to do that,' said Lund. He'd spent the previous two days thoroughly debriefing Maggie and McCabe and then following up by interviewing everybody else who had played any role whatsoever in the events of the preceding week.

'Where's Susan Marsh?' asked Freese. 'Shouldn't she be here?'

'Unfortunately,' said Maggie, 'nobody knows where Susan is at the moment. We haven't been able to reach her.'

Freese turned back to Lund, 'Well, then, go ahead, Burt. You'd better get started.'

'I think the best place to start, sir, is about ten months ago, when Sean Carroll's wife, Detective Elizabeth Carroll, and a number of other officers attached to Maine DEA were invited to Saint John, New Brunswick, to review security procedures at the Ecklund Company in Saint John. As you may know, Ecklund is one of eastern Canada's largest distributors of prescription pharmaceuticals. Upon her return, Detective Carroll wrote a lengthy report detailing what she considered shockingly lax security in the Ecklund facility. With the clarity of hindsight, it's obvious now that she shared her report not only with her colleagues at DEA but also with her husband, Sergeant Sean Carroll.'

Lund spent the next hour detailing everything else that was known. Throughout the presentation Freese kept shaking his head in apparent disbelief and disgust. Lund finished up by playing the recording Maggie had made of Sean Carroll's last conversation with Emmett Ganzer. The small recorder had picked up every word.

Lund asked his boss if he had any questions.

'Yes. Quite a few actually.' His gaze found Terri Mirabito. 'Dr Mirabito, your autopsy confirmed that Tiffany Stoddard was in fact pregnant?'

'Yes sir. She was six weeks along,' said Mirabito.

'Do we know who the father was?'

'As of this morning we do. We'd already done an analysis of the fetal DNA and, just an hour ago, DNA samples obtained from Sean Carroll's apartment confirmed that he was the father of her unborn child.'

Freese sighed. 'How about the remainder of the drugs? Have we located them?'

'Yes,' said Ed Matthews. 'We discovered Sean Carroll owned a one-room cabin in the woods about twenty miles west of Skowhegan. We had an ERT team take the place apart. They located the drugs under two false floorboards in the cabin. They also found both Sean Carroll's and Tiff Stoddard's fingerprints all around the cabin, including on the box where the drugs were stored.'

'How many pills were there?'

Matthews let out a long slow breath. 'Out of the original 40,000 stolen from Ecklund in January, 22,562 were in the cabin. There were an additional 5,000 plus found outside the cannery at Parnell Point. They were hidden inside the child's teddy bear which Emmett Ganzer had been carrying just before he was killed by Sean Carroll and Carroll in turn was killed by Sheriff Savage's son,

Harlan. We have to assume the remainder, approximately 13,000 tablets, have already been sold on the streets since the theft in January. We also found a large amount of cash in the same hiding place in the cabin.'

'How much?' asked Freese.

'One million two hundred and sixty thousand dollars.'

'Presumably the proceeds of the drug sales?'

'Presumably.'

'We also have a lot of dead people,' said Freese. 'Do we have any idea what the final body count will turn out to be?'

'I think Detective Savage may be the best person to address that.'

Freese turned toward Maggie and waited.

'As of now,' said Maggie, 'not counting Sean Carroll, we know of seven dead for sure. One more, Luke Haskell, is missing and I suspect may be dead as well.'

'Excuse me,' Chief Boucher interrupted, 'I guess I should have mentioned it earlier. Luke Haskell's body washed up on Campobello Island last Friday. There was no ID on the body, no way to identify him and it took the Canadian police three days to ask us if we knew who he was. We just got word.'

'Cause of death?' asked Freese.

'Luke drowned. We can't prove one way or the other whether Carroll was responsible or if he just tumbled overboard in a drunken stupor but given the timing of events and the fact that Luke probably could possibly have identified Carroll, I think we really do know the answer to that question.'

'What about the child? Tabitha Stoddard?' asked Anne Marie Lichter, the woman from DHHS. 'Where is she now?'

'Tabitha is staying at my house in Machias,' Sheriff Savage said. 'My wife, who is a retired nurse, is looking after her. So is Dr Kaplan.'

'I assume this is a temporary arrangement?'

Savage thought about the question before answering. 'I don't know. We'll see.'

'That work for you?' Freese asked Lichter.

'I'll need to talk with Tabitha, but yes, for the moment, that's fine.'

'How about Susan Marsh?' asked Freese. 'Can somebody explain to me what Susan's involvement in all this was?' It obviously pained him to think of her as somehow involved in a criminal enterprise.

'All we know at this point,' said Maggie, 'is that Susan Marsh went to Sean Carroll's apartment the night after we spoke to her. There's at least some possibility that she went there to question Carroll about whether the brandy he served her the night of Liz Carroll's death might or might not have been spiked with drugs designed to make sure she didn't wake up. In any event, while there, we're reasonably certain she either purposely or inadvertently communicated that McCabe and I suspected that Carroll was, in fact, Conor Riordan. We don't know what Carroll's reaction to that information was other than to come to Machias and try to kill me. We can't ask Susan because at the moment she seems to be missing herself.'

'Well, let's just hope she turns up soon.'

'I don't have a great deal of confidence in that happening, sir,' said Maggie.

'Dear God,' was all Bradley Freese could say as the implication of what Maggie said sunk in. 'What about Emmett Ganzer? What was his role in this?' he asked next.

'In my view,' said Maggie, 'Emmett was guilty of nothing more than excess aggression and mindless ambition. He wanted to be promoted a little too much. As the recording demonstrates, he had nothing to do with the deaths or the drugs.'

'One thing I don't understand, Detective Savage,' said Freese, 'is why Carroll let you work on the case. It's what led ultimately to his downfall.'

'I can only guess,' said Maggie, 'but I think it was because he knew, because of my friendship with Dr Kaplan, I'd investigate the murder on my own anyway. If I was working for him I believe he thought he could control me. That way he'd always know what I knew and be able to keep me from getting too close to the truth.'

'Well, he was obviously wrong about that,' said Freese.

'Yes sir,' said Maggie. 'As he was about so many other things.'

Chapter Sixty-One

THE MEETING BROKE up a little after eleven. Maggie asked McCabe if he wanted to stick around for a while. Spend a little time together. Just relax and shoot the shit for a few days. She could take him up to Bog Pond and teach him the fine art of fly-fishing, which he'd often expressed interest in learning. McCabe said he wished he could but, no, he had to get back. He'd already left his daughter Casey and Kyra, the woman they both lived with, on their own for far too long.

Maggie nodded. 'You're right,' she said, 'I understand.' She leaned over and kissed him on the cheek. 'Thank you for everything. Please give my love to your women. Both of them.'

'Maggie?'

'What?'

'I love you, you know,' said McCabe.

'I know you do,' said Maggie. 'And I know you love Kyra as well. But that's all right. We both love you.'

McCabe climbed in the T-Bird, put the top down and headed out of the parking lot for home. Maggie stood on the sidewalk, watching him go, until the car turned the corner at the end of the block and disappeared from sight.

Then she joined her father, who was waiting for her in the red Blazer. They started back to Machias.

On the way, Tom Shockley called. As predicted, the Chief was basking in the glow of having *a huge case*, as he called it, that had been *totally screwed up* by Ed Matthews and the MSP, cleared by two of his own PPD detectives. In fact, he said, he couldn't wait to hold a press conference and let the whole world know what a great team he had. What incredible talent Maggie and McCabe represented.

Maggie cringed through most of the conversation. She thanked him for his praise but said little else in response except to urge Shockley to hold off on any press conferences till things settled down a little. He said he'd think about it. She doubted he would. He then told her she'd earned some extra time off. 'At least a week,' he said. 'We won't count it as a vacation. Just a reward. Unofficially, of course.'

The time was a gift and she thanked him. She badly wanted to spend some with Savage. Get a real sense of how bad things were with his illness. Tell Harlan about it. Try to get the two of them to reconcile their differences, though she wasn't sure that would ever be possible. Discuss her father's treatment options with Emily.

She also knew there would have to be an official inquiry into Harlan's killing of Sean Carroll. She wanted to assure Harlan that she didn't think, under the circumstances, that any charges against him would be filed.

It'd also be nice to see Trevor and Cathy and her nieces. And, if truth be told, she would enjoy a little fishing. Especially if she could get Savage, or maybe Harlan, or maybe even both of them, to go up to Bog Pond with her.

ANYA, EMILY AND Tabitha were all waiting for them when Maggie and Savage got back to the house around 1:30. Unfortunately, Harlan wasn't. He'd told Emily he wanted to start repairing the damage the police search had done to his house. Maggie believed it was more likely he wanted to avoid seeing his father.

Maggie passed by the living room, where Emily and Tabitha were sitting side by side on the couch, their backs to the door, where she was standing. She stood for a while, silently eavesdropping.

Em asked Tabitha to tell her the story of what had happened. At least the parts she knew about. Tabitha did. By the time she had finished she was sobbing.

Em put her arms around the little girl and hugged her, an action which must have made her cracked ribs scream with pain. But if it did she ignored it. 'It's terrible about your sisters and your parents,' she said. 'I can't tell you how sorry I am.'

'The problem is,' said Tabbie through her tears, 'I don't know where I'm supposed to go now. My whole family's gone. And I don't really believe it's to a better place. I don't think it's to anywhere at all except under the ground. I don't have any uncles or aunts. What am I supposed to do? I'm only eleven years old, you know. I can't get a job or anything. I sort of wanted to stay with Harlan but I don't think he wants me to.'

'I think that would be difficult for Harlan,' said Em. 'But maybe you could stay with me at my place for a while.'

Tabitha looked up at the doctor, who was even taller than the lady cop. She was even taller than Harlan. 'You'd let me do that?'

'Yes, I would. In fact, thinking about it, I'd like very much to have you with me.'

'Are you sure?'

'I'm sure. But, if you like, we could say we're just trying it for a while to see how we get along.'

'You think it would be okay?'

'We'd have to get approval from the Health and Human Services people but I don't think that would be a problem.'

'I don't know,' said Tabitha. 'I'm a little weird. Everybody says so. You might not like me.'

'That's all right,' Emily smiled. 'I'm a little weird myself. And I think I'll like you fine. But I should warn you, right now I only have a small apartment above my office, so we wouldn't have much room to begin with. You'd have to sleep on a pull-out couch. But I'm in the process of buying a wonderful house right on the water in Roque Bluffs and, if it worked out and you decided you wanted to stay, well there'd be plenty of room for both of us.'

'Would that make you my mother?'

'You'll always have your real mother. I wouldn't try to replace her. But I could be kind of a substitute mother. But only if you wanted me to be.'

Tabitha didn't say anything.

'Tell you what,' said Emily. 'Why don't we drive down to Roque Bluffs this afternoon and take a look at the house. If you like it there, then we'll give it a try. Deal?'

Tabitha got up and put her arms around Emily. She was still crying but it looked like things were about to get a whole lot better in her life. 'Deal,' she said.

Maggie turned away before either of them saw her, embarrassed to have been listening in. It was better to let the two of them have this time alone. She went up to her room. Opened her laptop and checked her emails. Nothing of any interest except one from Billy Webb. The road trip would be over in a week and he'd be back in Portland. He hoped she'd have dinner with him.

She still longed to have someone in her life but, whoever it was she longed for, she knew it wasn't Billy.

'Thanks for the offer,' she replied. 'But I think I'm going to have to say no. You're a nice guy, Billy, and I like you, but I just don't think things are going to work out between us.'

She closed the laptop, went downstairs to the fridge and got herself a cold bottle of Geary's. After she popped the top she went out to the porch. As she sat sipping she turned her mind away from her so-called love life to the most pressing problem of the moment. How she was going to spend her week off.

"Would that make you my mother?"

"You'll always have your real mother. I wouldn't try to replace her. But I could be kind of a substitute mother. But only if you wanted me to be."

Tabitha didn't say anything.

"Tell you what," said Emily. "Why don't we drive down to Rogue Bluffs this afternoon and take a look at the house. If you like it there, then we'll give it a try. Deal?"

Tabitha got up and put her arms around Emily. She was still crying but it looked like things were about to get a whole lot better in her life. "Deal," she said.

Maggie turned away before either of them saw her, embarrassed to have been listening in. It was better to let the two of them have this time alone. She went up to her room. Opened her laptop and checked her emails. Nothing of any interest except one from Billy Webb. The road trip would be over in a week and he'd be back in Portland. He hoped she'd have dinner with him.

She still longed to have someone in her life but, whoever it was she longed for, she knew it wasn't Billy.

"Thanks for the offer," she replied. "But I think I'm going to have to say no. You're a nice guy, Billy, and I like you, but I just don't think things are going to work out between us."

She closed the laptop, went downstairs to the fridge and got herself a cold bottle of Geary's. After she popped the top she went out to the porch. As she sat sipping she turned her mind away from her so-called love life to the most pressing problem of the moment. How she was going to spend her week off.

About the Author

JAMES HAYMAN spent more than twenty years as a senior creative director at one of New York's largest advertising agencies. He and his wife now live in Portland, Maine. This is his third novel.

www.jameshaymanthrillers.com

Visit www.AuthorTracker.com for exclusive information on your favorite HarperCollins authors.